The Year of Surprising Acts of Kindness

LAURA KEMP

ORION

An Orion paperback

First published in paperback in Great Britain in 2018
by Orion Books
an imprint of The Orion Publishing Group Ltd
Carmelite House, 50 Victoria Embankment
London EC4Y ODZ

An Hachette UK Company

5 7 9 10 8 6 4

A CIP catalogue record for this book
is available from the British Library.

ISBN 978 1 4091 7483 7

Typeset by Deltatype Ltd, Birkenhead, Merseyside

Printed in Great Britain by Clays Ltd St Ives plc

MIX
Paper from
responsible sources
FSC® C104740

www.orionbooks.co.uk

To Mum and Dad,
whose kindness knows no bounds

Prologue

Tears threatened as Ceri Price caught her sister in the act: packing up Mum's life into shabby cardboard boxes.

It was too soon for that. Ceri was still at the point of coming to the house to check their mother really had gone. As if by some miracle, she'd walk in to find her as she was before she got ill: in a cleaning gilet, humming gently, a cloth in hand, delighted by her daughter's interruption and asking, *did she have time for a quick cuppa?* But, of course, she was never there. Ceri's irrational hope would plummet into fresh, suffocating grief, and she'd have to sit for a minute on the worn sofa, listening to the silence, wondering how on earth there could be any more sadness because surely, in the six weeks since Mum's death, hadn't she used it all up?

Today, though, Ceri had felt an overwhelming gratitude that she wouldn't be alone with her sorrow when she had seen Tash's old banger parked up outside number thirty-three Junction Road. For Ceri to see her own grief reflected in her sister's eyes wouldn't diminish the emptiness inside, but at least they could hang onto each other, as they had done at the funeral, a month ago, when Tash had let down her guard and they'd found mutual comfort in the shared blood pumping through their veins, keeping their mother alive in both their hearts. And as she'd pocketed the mail from the doormat to read later, Ceri had felt the relief only Tash's presence could provide. She would understand that Ceri had nowhere to go to hide from her misery: her ex Dave was long gone and she had no boyfriend to cuddle nor kids to pour her love into. Not even work was an escape as it had once been, because Ceri's business was all wrapped up in Mum. Tash would get that, instinctively, Ceri had thought, turning into the lounge.

But the sight that greeted her had been the deepest and most savage of betrayals. And Ceri could only watch in disbelief as Tash moved purposefully between piles of Mum's belongings, selecting blouses and shoes for one box and throwing tights and bras into a black bin bag.

'What you doing, kid?' Ceri asked shakily, taking in the empty shelves, stripped of every last trace of nearly three decades of what she had called home. This was where they had grown up, sharing the second bedroom from childhood right up until Tash had moved out four and a half years ago, just before Mum's forgetfulness had been diagnosed as dementia. So much more than bricks and mortar, this two-up two-down in Crewe was where they'd learned their table manners; fought over who got to put the angel on top of the Woolworths Christmas tree; argued over who washed up and who wiped after tea when they were old enough to help; dished out advice, most of the time uninvited, on boys and hairstyles as teenagers; laughed and laughed together in front of the TV; and provided unconditional support when the chips were down, the three of them against the world. It was where Mum had taught them to be decent, hardworking and kind human beings, just like her. The birthplace of Ceri's business and where her mother's life ended. But there was nothing left to suggest this house had witnessed their lives, good and bad. Just bare walls, the telly trussed up in a straitjacket of wires and plugs, the glass cabinet robbed of trinkets and four dents in the carpet where the table legs had been.

'Getting it ready, like we said. To sell.' Tash declared inaccurately, not stopping to soften the blow with a smile. Instead she kept busy, avoiding eye contact, emotionless, examining what was next for the cull.

Breathless, Ceri felt faint at the desecration: how could Tash do this? Didn't her sister want to cherish Mum for as long as possible, like she did? It was a bewildering blow to conclude that no, Tash obviously didn't. Particularly when the last will and testament of Angharad Bronwen Price, which had left them her ageing but spotless terrace, her one-careful-owner Ford Fiesta plus £15,000 of hard-earned money from the Rolls-Royce factory, had been filed away less than twenty-four hours ago after the sisters had been granted probate.

'Actually we said we'd do it, you know, when we both felt it was the right time,' Ceri said to Tash's back, hating the nervousness in her voice but this was how it was around her younger sister. *Don't upset Tash, you know how she gets,* she and Mum had always advised one another. But now Mum was gone and Ceri was raw and lost without her – even more so now because Tash was buzzing with focus. How long had she been here, going through Mum's things? And how many times had she been here without telling Ceri? She stepped forward to slow her sister's hands which were wrapping a small crystal dolphin. One of Mum's favourites.

'This is for the charity shop,' Tash said, carrying on, oblivious. 'Over there,' she said, pointing her petite nose at a mound of shiny black bags, 'is for the tip ... I've put your things to one side,' she added, gesturing at a plastic tub by the gas fire, 'but you'd better go through what's going, just to check.'

Her things? These were all her things, their things. Ceri had owned a penthouse flat for a few months now in the nearby leafy town of Alderley Edge, but she'd hardly stayed there. Home was here, where she'd nursed Mum through four years of decline. And until twelve months ago, when she'd finally quit to run her own business, her bar job at the workingmen's club had been just up the road. But even before Mum's health had suffered, Ceri had never wanted to leave because she loved her warm and caring company. It meant that their belongings, Mum's ornaments and Ceri's knick-knacks, sat very happily in the house side by side. So Tash having taken it upon herself to clear Ceri's possessions without asking was hasty, not to mention insensitive. Her smarting eyes wandered over the wreckage – it was a flaming mess.

No longer the 'neat as a pin' nest shining with Mr Muscle in which she and Mum had taken so much satisfaction – instead, it was higgledy-piggledy with clothes draped over the arms of the settee, the rest of which was smothered in Aldi carrier bags of hangers and CDs, and a crate of books and vases marked 'boot sale'. The floor was barely visible in between a mountain of electricals, including her hairdryer, curling tongs, iron and toaster, and battered cardboard boxes which were stacked with breakables wrapped in old copies of the *Crewe Chronicle*. Then she gasped when she saw Mum's pans ready for burial.

'You can't chuck those! They're what started it all. The business. They're special.'

That set of cast-iron pots was everything to Ceri. For the heavy, flat-bottomed saucepans, which she'd used to create homemade make-up when she had been dirt poor, had directly led to what she was now: a self-made entrepreneur with her own cosmetics brand and a faithful following online. And if Tash had ransacked the kitchen … Ceri darted in and saw an empty space where the lovely old single-oven duck-egg blue Aga on which they'd cooked had stood. This wasn't a clearance – this was rape and pillage.

'What have you done with it?'

'Oh come on, Ceri, the Aga was ancient. Kev got fifty quid for it. Your half is in there, on the side.'

As if Ceri was bothered with twenty-five pounds – that cooker was priceless.

'And why's the tea caddy being thrown?' she said, grabbing it from the top of a box that Tash had labelled 'bric-a-brac' which sat on the worktop.

The beautiful full-bellied silver container, with a hinged lockable lid and four intricate feet, had stored their PG Tips for as long as Ceri could remember. But more importantly, it had played a part in her and her Mum's nightly ritual of counting their blessings over a brew at bedtime. Well, it had before Mum had withered away. Ceri had been planning to use it for her remains.

Tash turned to face her, her eyes cold, and shrugged. 'So take whatever you fancy. And feel free to help me. If you're staying?'

Ceri felt the accusing stab that she'd left Tash to do everything and then the injustice of it, for she had been the one to manage the spoon-feeding and hair-combing as Mum's illness worsened. Ceri felt herself reeling inside, shaking. She was already shattered from her bereavement, which had come on top of her mourning as Mum had slipped away, replaced by a stranger. The exhaustion from carrying the guilt of wishing she'd acted sooner, rather than thinking it was scattiness when Mum had turned up in her slippers during one of Ceri's shifts at the club. The uphill struggle of trying to be positive when the prognosis was anything but. Worn out too from caring for her when Ceri's homemade make-up hobby began to take off as a business and she was still working behind the bar. Weary from sleeping on Mum's sofa so she could hear if she wandered lost out of the dining room, which had become her bedroom because the stairs could've killed her. Barely living in her new place, which didn't even feel like hers. It went on and on …

But still she resisted causing a scene. This had to be Tash's way of grieving. Perhaps it was remorse for how absent she'd been this past couple of years. Yet Ceri had never blamed her sister. The official line was that Tash had a young family to raise and a husband who worked all hours to put bread on the table. But Ceri knew that Tash found it hard to cope when Mum had begun to ask who this was coming into her home. The truth was that she and Tash were made of different stuff – different fathers, with one born out of love and the other out of circumstance. Ceri had grown up knowing Mum had adored her dad, Emilio, a handsome fisherman whom she met in Spain on a girls' holiday in 1986. She had gone back over to see him a few times in the following year, to make sure he was The One. And he was. But plans for Mum to emigrate tragically ended when his trawler went down in a Mediterranean storm a month after she'd got back home in 1987, just weeks before she'd found out she was pregnant.

Tash's dad, on the other hand, had been what Mum called 'a mistake' and their marriage, forged on the re-bound, she'd said, hadn't lasted. Neither had Ronnie's role as a father. They had parted when Tash was a baby and Ceri was three. Ceri understood how deeply her sister had felt about only having one parent. It had left her 'strong and silent', as she liked to put it, although Ceri saw it as prickly. Ceri, however, had always felt her father's presence. Mum told her often enough that she had his spirit. She looked like him too, with thick raven hair, olive skin and, she presumed, his chocolate-brown eyes. The only photo there was of him, in a dusted-to-death frame which Ceri had claimed as her own the night Mum had passed away, was a blurry scene of sand, scorching sun and rugged, truffle-coloured rocks. The pair of them were golden: Mum's eyes, as aqua as the twinkling water behind them, dancing with love as he kissed her buttercup hair, which was flying in the warm breeze, obscuring his face. One of Dad's arms was around her back, the other lay across Mum's bronzed tummy – had Ceri been conceived already? – and she was nakedly beautiful, fresh, minus the Eighties sweep of blusher and gooey gloss she wore in every other photo from her youth. Her lime-green bandeau bikini was from when she could fit into Topshop, she'd say, along with how Dad, being from 'the continent', could get away with those tiny white Speedos and a thick silver chain, from which hung a locket containing her picture.

Thinking of the photo reminded Ceri of what was really important and she held up the caddy as she went to Tash in the lounge.

'When we get Mum back, we can take her to Wales, like she wanted. Sprinkle her ashes in the sea in the village where she was born.' Mum had refused to get on a plane again after she lost Emilio. And she'd be damned if she did when she was dead. So Wales it would be, in what Mum said was the most beautiful bay in the world. In her hall-of-mirrors mind during the last few years, she'd say she'd doggy paddle round to the Costa del Sol, find him among the mermaids and sardines.

'We can scatter her ashes and do the reading she left ...' These instructions had been presented to her by the solicitor, Mr Jennings, in a sealed envelope which Ceri carried everywhere with her. 'What you reckon?' Ceri was smiling, hoping this would be enough to remind Tash of their bond as their mother's girls.

Tash swallowed hard and wiped a tear from her cheek. There, the atmosphere was gone and—

'You've got to stop this.' Tash's words were sharp, like her pinched features, which were even more drawn than usual. Ceri's knees went weak and she wished she'd been wearing sensible flats; but heeled boots were part of her image.

'Stop what?' she said, alarmed.

There was silence except for the splash of cars on the rain-slick street outside and the tick of the carriage clock presented to Mum after ten years' factory service, which ... wasn't on the mantelpiece. She scanned the room, straining her ears and located it on some jigsaws destined for a good cause. Ceri didn't think there was any piece of her heart left to shatter. She was wrong.

'Look, Ceri,' Tash said, sighing, dropping her shoulders and tilting her head to show she wasn't after a row. 'Don't take this the wrong way but ... you're living on a different planet to me.'

'What do you mean?' They had the same mum, had gone to the same school, loved sweet and sour chicken balls and had borrowed each other's clothes and eyeliner for as long as they could remember.

'It's just ... Mum was cuckoo by the time she asked to be scattered there. Why don't we just do it in the garden? She loved pottering out the back. Look, it's ... I just don't have the time.'

The swirl of leaves on the beige carpet beneath Ceri's feet began to swim. *What was she on about?*

'The kids, they're exhausting, I hardly see Kev and I know it's only peanuts but we'd go under without my evening job. This house, selling it is our chance for a better life. Or do you want your nieces growing up scallies?' She wasn't being sarky – she sounded desperate.

'If you need money, I'll give you money,' Ceri said, wanting to help, because decency was what Mum had taught them.

'I don't want your money.' Tash didn't say it with spite but resignation. 'This will make all the difference to us.'

'I told you I'd buy your share of the house. What did they say it was worth? A hundred and fifty thousand? I've got seventy-five thousand. I'll give it to you now. The lump sum I got from the contract, it's just sat there doing 'owt in my account.'

9

Surely that would persuade her? Ceri couldn't stand it: wiping out the memories because they had no other option.

But Tash shook her head. She looked just like Mum with her big blue eyes and blonde bob and it caught Ceri in the throat.

'It's not enough. The estate agent says if we do it up, if Kev tarts up the kitchen and the bathroom, you know, in the nights and at the weekend, we'll get another fifty thousand.'

Ceri could get that together too. It gave her a start – to be so loaded she could get the funds no sweat still astonished her. Despite all her hard work and the twenty-hour days, part of her still felt like a barmaid from Crewe. But was this actually about the money? Or Tash's own stab at making it? Just like Ceri had.

'It might not be much to you but to us it's an extra bit of garden, where we could have a swing, or another bedroom so the girls have one each. In the right catchment area for a nice school. Not grotty like round here.'

Her place was two streets away from Mum's. Yes, it might be lacking in the fancy-pants department but Tash would realise not everywhere enjoyed such a community feel, just as Ceri herself had found out, knowing no one in the cut-above stretch of listed townhouses which had been converted into apartments at £350,000 a pop.

'Can't you see? Don't you remember what it's like to be skint?'

Ceri shut her eyes and cast her mind back. Past the personalised numberplate of CER 1 on her nippy sports car, the designer gear and her flat in the area known as the Golden Triangle populated by footballers and their wives, reality stars and actors. Back to the sticky floor of the club where she'd worked for a pittance, calculating meal plans to make her money go further and hunting down the cheapest utilities suppliers. Eking out her nail varnish by adding drops of remover to thin it and adding moisturiser to her foundation to make it go further. Recalling how, four years ago, out of economic necessity, she'd hit upon the idea of creating homemade tinted lip gloss. Once she'd paid the bills and put a bit aside for her wedding to Dave, there was very little left from her minimum wage: she could neither afford to replace the contents of her make-up bag nor buy birthday presents. But if she stirred up her own, using whatever was in the cupboards, she could do both because a little went a long way. It took her back to her childhood when the Avon lady came round and Ceri would imagine her mum getting ready for a ball when really she was only going up the club on a rare Saturday night.

Time had been on her side, too, because she'd stay in when she wasn't working to keep Mum company. And her mother absolutely loved it, especially the cherry lip gloss, made from mashed-up strained fruit added to melted beeswax, cocoa butter and olive oil. Whenever Ceri had touched colour to her lips, Mum would come alive: it was their way of connecting as mother and daughter, even if it was only for a split second. That joy, plus the compliments she received not just for her own made-up face but from those who received her gifts, spurred Ceri on to develop DIY blusher, mascara and eyeshadow. She began to sell some on eBay and came up with the idea of doing online tutorials, loading them onto YouTube, racking up views, likes and shares. Then the cosmetic companies had come calling and the big bucks began to roll in. And yet, still, she saved hard and swore by her own lip gloss. She'd called the business Cheap As Chic, for goodness sake, of course she bloody remembered what it was like to be skint.

'What are you on now? Ten grand a month ...?'

In adverts on her website alone. Never mind the extra when she recommended a product online.

'I'm chuffed to bits for you, I really am. But—'

'But what? I haven't changed.' It came out defensive but Ceri almost believed it, she really did.

Tash's eyebrows lifted ever so slightly. Enough to make the temperature of Ceri's blood rise. 'What are you saying?'

Because she'd worked her butt off for success. She had spent hours and days and weeks and dozens of months making something of herself: cramming in research and ingredient testing while at the same time tending to Mum. A labour of love which had grown and become big enough to earn her a living. More than a living, actually, and more than a way to leave the soggy beer mats behind: a contradiction of her previously held belief that she was no good at anything apart from serving others. She had a business head and could strike a deal.

'You want for nothing,' Tash threw out bitterly.

Yes, this was true. Ceri had so much stuff she didn't know what to do with it. Her apartment was full of handbags, posh frocks and shoes worth what a family would spend on their monthly food shop – and she hadn't even bought most of it. Every day freebie samples would arrive by courier, with invites left, right and centre to events in Manchester, Liverpool and beyond: it was part of the game of 'you scratch my back, I'll scratch yours'. Getting paid ten grand for personal appearances was pretty obscene when all she had to do was turn up wearing a full face of slap.

And it dawned on Ceri, glancing into her mum's little kitchen, where it had all begun, this lifestyle was the opposite of what she had created and what she stood for. Her aim had been to make folk happy and confident, for a fraction of the price you'd pay in the shops. Now she was raking in large sums of money from big corporations. Over the past six weeks, she had started to worry her work was no longer the passion nor the saviour it had been when Mum was alive. Rather, since she'd gone, it had started to feel meaningless and shallow. Ceri had hoped it was just her grief that was making her so unsettled, but it was keeping her awake at night: in the dark she'd question what was next for her in life, and wonder at the state of her integrity. She hadn't known what she wanted to change only that she no longer felt she wanted to go on doing the same. Tash was making out Ceri had lost sight of herself. Was there truth in that?

'Your life, it's all surface,' Tash jabbed again.

Ceri took a shaky breath as she considered the evidence: the hangers-on who'd expected her to pay for the drinks at the best nightspots in Manchester. The men, for once less interested in her bra than her brass. Getting slagged off by so-called friends on Facebook. Her old haunts going quiet when she walked in. Knowing this wasn't all new to her – she'd taken it on the chin when she'd needed her escape. But looking at it now, she was connecting the dots and understanding she was unhappy and had been for a while. This was a reckoning that had been coming for months. And she would've given everything to be back behind the bar when she had been broke but cheery.

'I bet you got a million Valentine's Day cards today but you've not a soul to share it with.'

Tash was right. The office had been filling up with Valentine-related promotional crap all morning – helium love hearts, fancy chocolates, and a teddy bear handed to her by some poor student paid to dress up as Cupid by one company. But there wasn't anyone special. And she wouldn't remind herself by going along to one of a load of 14 February balls or date nights. Dave had been the last man to love her, back when life had been straightforward. When they'd ticked along and it was all laid out for her. The plan to get hitched on the pitch at the Crewe Alexandra ground, a finger buffet at the Gresty pub after, to move in together and have kids. Actually, she was relieved she hadn't been landed with the married name Ceri Berry. And while Dave had been reliable and grounded, he hadn't liked her new lifestyle: he was the traditional type, who wanted a chippy tea on a Friday and his woman beside him. She craved being with someone she could trust. That was why her sister's opinion mattered to her so much, because Tash wasn't afraid of falling out of favour or losing a slot in her schedule: she was one of the few who could still tell her like it was. Ceri was approaching rock bottom now but there was an inch of fight left.

'I've got Jade.' Her best friend with whom she'd worked at the bar, and who made Adele look frumpy. And who'd been the first one to tell her that maybe her make-up could lead somewhere.

'She's your PA,' Tash said sadly. 'She's staff.'

Ceri's stomach dropped and her head whirled: she felt a husk of the person she was, the person she'd been just that morning.

'You think you can fix things with a flash of cash,' Tash said, not unkindly. 'And that's fine for you, you'll not be pulling up the sofa looking for spare change. Never. You're not like the rest of us. You've got everything. But this, now, this is our one shot. Our potential.'

The blunt admission made Ceri's shoulders heave with sobs. Suddenly, drowning in the bleakness, everything she had felt insignificant and pointless. From the expensive clothes on her body to her own Cheap As Chic brand mascara on her lashes. It had always been her goal to give something back, yet she remembered now how she had been too overloaded to answer that charity's call for some donated goodies to use as a prize in their raffle; and the way she had let down the local sixth form college, who'd asked her to talk to the kids about making something of yourself.

Tash's arms enfolded her until Ceri had run out of crying. Her sister pulled back and looked into her eyes.

'Me and Kev, we need to do this. For us. We have to get this house on the market. Please, Ceri. I'm begging you.'

She heard the words rebounding off the naked walls, and as she sniffed, she could still smell Mum's presence. The essence of her had been kindness, that's what she'd stood for, thinking of others. Mum would've wanted Ceri to do this for Tash, to look after her. When it came down to that, how could she refuse?

'Course,' she said, barely a whisper. Not knowing how

she was going to get through this. Because she'd had everything. But really she had nothing. No blessings to count at all. She had to go. To a place where no one knew her. To escape the torment of losing not just her mother but her way.

Eleven days later ...

Ceri blew her cheeks with relief as she turned the hair-pin bend after four and three-quarter hours behind the wheel.

Thank God, she thought as the rain lashed down on the windscreen, *I can't wait to get in a hot bath to warm myself up and – Woah!*

The road plunged suddenly and the sea came at her, smacking her right in the chops. She slammed on the brakes, feeling the wheels skid, wondering if she was hanging off the edge of the land, teetering over water. Her head banking left then right from vertigo, this felt like the end of the world, not how Mum had described it at all.

Her feet were rooted to the pedals but still the car shook from the gusts which came from all around and the wipers, which had been on full since Mid Wales, were screaming in panic.

The terrifying waves were so angry they thrashed against themselves, sending up white spray like furious spittle. *What did you expect, you fool*, she thought. The warnings that she was entering the wilds had been there – down ski-slope dips and up learning-curve climbs, through snaking lanes tunnelled beneath canopies of twisted bare branches and nerve-wracking mountain paths which zig-zagged so perilously close to sheer drops her knuckles had turned white.

The constant 'recalculating' of the sat nav, the asking the way at strange petrol stations and eerie tea rooms. For this was the land M&S and Costa Services had forgotten.

And no wonder, because she was staring at the bleakest excuse for civilisation she'd ever seen.

'You. Have. Got. To. Be. Joking. Mum,' Ceri said to the tea caddy in her bag on the passenger seat.

It was a one-street muddy puddle of a village which hugged a crescent of sea the colour of fag ash and ended in a treacherously steep headland of rock and bracken.

In contrast to what Mum had claimed in her final groggy days full of medication, there was neither sand nor an apple green, sky blue, royal purple, bright white or flamingo pink row of homes to be seen. Instead, the tide threw up on the shore and the handful of dirty death-pallor buildings with harsh black guttering looked like a bad set of teeth. Ceri had the urge to get the Domestos out – no wonder Mum had been obsessed with cleaning if she came from a place like this.

What appeared to be a shop, tongue-twistingly named Caban Cwtch, however you said that, overlooked the so-called beach. It had an empty forecourt save for a prostrate sandwich board which, no doubt, had passed out from boredom. As for the palm trees and ferns and Welsh wildflowers Mum had described, there were dead pots by a broken bench and brambly hedges keeping everything in – or out, it looked that unfriendly.

'I'm sorry to say this, Mum, but what a shithole.'

How differently today had started. Her breezy road

trip in the soft Cheshire sunshine had begun just before midday, when Jade had waved her off from the office in Alderley Edge where Ceri had gone early doors to tie up some loose ends; including recording a video for her YouTube channel to say she was having a little break to get herself ready for the new range. She'd felt upbeat that she'd finally made the decision, for she'd wrestled with taking time off in the days after Tash had asked to sell Mum's house. Ceri had made excuses – the business needed her; she had too many appointments to cancel. But the sadness of life without Mum and the bitter taste when she shook hands with yet another person who'd smelled money didn't subside. It just rose higher. And when a 'for sale' board went up in the tiny square of Mum's front garden, well, she thought she'd drown. Fight or flight had kicked in. A holiday wouldn't kill her, because she felt dead already. So she'd booked a cottage from Friday to Friday, told Jade she was having a week away and messaged her sister to say she was off to Wales; if they received an offer on the house then whatever Tash decided was fine by her.

'Enjoy yourself, cocker!' Jade had said, her immaculate blonde hair swinging around a face so feline it purred. 'I'll look after everything. Don't worry, I won't have my nose in bridal mags all day; only lunchtimes! See you soon!'

Her full tank of excitement had lasted as long as the heater on Mum's car, which conked out an hour in at Oswestry, putting an end to Ceri singing along to the radio into a hot blast of air as if she was Beyoncé. She'd brought the red Fiesta instead of her own racy silver Mazda for the full 'get away from it all' experience.

By lunch, she was in the thick of Wales, so there were no nutty grain and vegetable salads or vitamin-enriched smoothies, and she ended up with a stewed baked-bean pasty from a tray marked '*popty*' in a garage. She had no idea what 'popty' meant but she'd have bet her life on it translating as 'don't leave me here to die alone'. And she'd never seen so many consonants – you'd be banging the desk with frustration if you were on *Countdown*.

Trying to pronounce the name of Mum's village was a nightmare too: Dwynwen wasn't pronounced 'Duh-wuh-yuh-nnn-when', so she was informed at the petrol station, but 'Der-win-when', although you had to say it quickly, like Dwinwhen.

It was quite a shock: she'd only ever been to Rhyl before, where everything was quite normal. There'd been people around and chain shops she recognised.

But the deeper she'd got into Wales, her teeth chattering from the drop in temperature, the more it felt like a foreign land, populated by sheep and cattle grids, squat run-down bungalows in the middle of nowhere and mind-boggling signs for Llanmerewig, Caersws, Llanidloes, Eisteddfa Gurig and Capel Bangor. The blessed A487 from Aberystwyth made her feel briefly that she was re-entering the twenty-first century, until she found herself on the lonely coastal drive south, with trees bent into crones by the wind and glimpses of a sea the colour of nails. The Dwynwen turn-off had become a helter-skelter of potholes, punctuated on either side by derelict barns and farming sheds. There'd been a shabby-looking caravan park on her right, a decrepit rugby club, then on the left a homemade arrow pointing to The Dragon, which she'd hoped – although she doubted it – would have a roaring fire and a cracking seafood risotto. She should've guessed the truth when she saw the battered *Welcome to Dwynwen* sign.

Why the flip had Mum wanted to return here? If only she'd asked to be flown first class to Marbella. Mum's sister, Aunty Delyth, had always said the only thing she could recall about this place was that it made Crewe look like Las Vegas – they'd left when they were teenagers, when Grandad found a job on the railways. Ceri could see what her aunt had meant.

Dumbfounded, she sat there gawping until a horn sounded from behind her. That probably counted as rush hour here. Flustered, she looked around but the road was so narrow she couldn't just pull up anywhere. The only option was to go into the car park of the pub, which was so dilapidated it looked suicidal. In fact it didn't even look like a pub: it was more like a kid's drawing of a house with one door and four square windows. Plastered a wishy-washy grey like fog, the walls were worn and in parts fractured to reveal uneven brickwork the colour of earwax.

Its swinging board was hanging off one hinge and the image of a dragon – with its head seemingly buried up its arse – was more Puff than proud. She navigated herself into a wrecked square of broken tarmac and checked the time. Almost five, it'd be dark within the hour.

Needing to get a move on to get the key to the cottage, she got out her phone to get the details of her booking. A 'charming rustic property in a traditional setting', it'd said. She thought she'd been lucky that it'd been free at such short notice. Now, being here, she feared her bed would be made of straw and her nose would be up a ram's bum. But her mobile had no service. What the heck was she going to do? The van behind her had obviously got lost because it had done a three-point ... no, make that a seven-point turn, and revved off. There were no lights anywhere. She was all alone.

Ceri flopped her head on the steering wheel and considered how long it would take her to get home. If she left now, she'd be back by, what, ten? But would the closest petrol station, about forty miles away, be open? Oh my God, she was doomed and—

A rap on her window brought her to.

'You can't park here, you can't,' blared a foghorn through the streaming glass. 'This is our courtyard. Spaces for guests only, it is.'

A pursed scarlet cat's-bum mouth stood out from a waterproof hood and instantly got Ceri's back up. Opening the door a bit too suddenly so the gob had to leap back, she got out and straightened herself up to her entire five foot five – make that five foot seven if she counted her two-inch Ugg soles – and was almost knocked sideways by an icy blast, which scalped her with spiteful rain.

'Gimme a chance! Who says I'm not a guest?' she said, eyeball to eyeball with this weirdo.

'You can't be, you can't!' the woman cried.

'And why's that?' Ceri said, wishing she'd brought a coat as she cowered under her poxy poncho. At least she was wearing her own range no-run mascara which would've held its own under Niagara Falls.

'Because we haven't had a guest since October, we haven't!'

Ceri wanted to laugh at the woman's emphatic victory cry – it was nothing to brag about. But her humour was dampened by a wind-blown cold shower of salty spray that covered them both.

'High tide, it is. Come in, come in, we'll be drowned rats out here, we will,' the woman said, grabbing Ceri's hand. *Drowned rats? If bloody only* – it was a far more tempting prospect than her invitation.

But before Ceri could resist, the lady tugged her to a quivering stable door which flew open and banged left against a peeling varnished turd-coloured bar decorated with some faded beer towels and one drained empty. The Dragon was deceptively large on the inside, with a thread-bare banquette of seating running along the right, the middle filled with round tables and chairs, the exact same colour and condition of the bar. There was a mounted menu announcing Today's Specials of absolutely bugger all, a swirling red and brown carpet and wood-chip walls. A blackboard declared 'Dolphin Watch' with a tally count of times and dates – from 2007, it seemed. A huge tattered Welsh flag hung at the far end above an open fire beside which was an ancient tiny telly with a wonky aerial. *What was this place? And who was this person who'd been telling her to get lost before dragging her in?* Ceri watched as she took off her coat to reveal a snakeskin leather skirt, immaculate white silk blouse, pearls and black patent heels the height of Blackpool Tower and patted her perfectly styled platinum hairdo.

'Wicked out there, it is! Wicked! I'm Gwen, I am. The landlady. Now, what can I get you?' she said, slipping behind the bar with a dazzling smile, followed by a thunderous shout towards the cobwebbed corridor which must've led to their home: 'GWIL! CUSTOMER, IT IS!'

Stunned but curious, Ceri ordered a latté because she needed a caffeine hit to work out what she was going to do next.

'A what-té?' Gwen said.

Clearly it was instant coffee or nothing down these parts. 'Don't worry. Just a Diet Coke, please.'

'So what brings you here? Because we haven't had any tourists since last year, we haven't. Well, I say tourists but they were a funny bunch, left first thing next day.'

'Oh, I'm not a tourist,' Ceri said, thinking she'd rather go to hell than come here for a holiday.

Gwen narrowed her eyes, folded her arms and unveiled the biggest smile.

'I know who you are!' she sang, wagging a red nail at her and nodding.

Ceri felt the urge to run. How was it possible she'd be recognised here? She took a step back, her heart racing.

'You've come about the job!'

Ceri stared at her.

'You're the first we've had in a month of advertising. You just can't get the staff these days. People are a bit choosy, they are. Any experience?'

She opened her mouth to explain. But was interrupted by Gwen bellowing, 'GWIL! QUICK!' before she raised the hatch and beckoned Ceri round.

'Look, I think there's been some kind of—'

'How do, what's your name?' said a man-mountain who'd bowed his bald head beneath a beam to enter the bar. Gwil, she presumed.

Ceri felt the cage rattling and debated whether or not she should tell the truth. She might be well known to a few people – around two million of them – but this pair

26

weren't in her demographic. And she wasn't a liar.

'Ceri. Ceri Price.' She cringed inwardly, hoping it didn't ring any bells.

Gwen hesitated – and Ceri's heart went like the clappers. Until Gwen shut her eyes and gave a long orgasmic 'oooooh'.

'Ceri! There's a Welsh name, there is!'

She didn't have the heart to tell Gwen she'd actually been christened Cereza, the Spanish word for cherry, even though she'd only ever been known as Ceri.

'I thought there was something Welsh about you. Could tell by your hair and eyes. Like Catherine Zeta-Jones, you are!'

Funny, because the boys at the workingmen's club had said she was a fat version of her, back in the day when she'd had time to eat. But that was her father's genes. *What was this woman talking about?* And anyway never mind! She was being hijacked, blown off course. Why on earth was she even having this conversation?

'The Welsh, they may leave but by God, they always find a way to come back!' Gwil said, handing her a glass and pointing at the tap of Brains.

'Come on, don't be shy!' Gwen said, waiting.

Ceri needed to stop this, make her excuses. But her feet wouldn't move, she was being hypnotised by their large smiles which were as warm as buttered crumpets. She didn't want to disappoint them. And she was worn out. Resistance was clearly futile: they were one short of a six-pack of lager and the only way she was going to find out where she'd get the key from was by playing along.

'The thing is,' she said, as her fingers curled around the cold glass, setting off a memory and an unfurling instinct. 'I'm booked into the Blue House.'

Her hands went to work on autopilot, bringing back the quiet week nights when she'd help old Nobby do his crossword. '... And I need the key ...'

The smell of the ale felt like an old friend, reminding her of the rocking Saturdays of meat raffles and tribute singers they'd had at the workingmen's club back home.

'Do you know who has it?' Ceri asked.

There, the beer was done. She felt a simple satisfaction she hadn't experienced in a long time. 'I need to get it sorted quickly because time's getting on.'

Both Gwen and Gwil were exchanging looks of un- paralleled joy.

'The head is perfect,' Gwil said reverentially.

'Lovely smooth action too,' Gwen echoed. 'And did you see the way she knew when to stop the tap without even breaking eye contact?'

Gwil adjusted the collar of his slightly-too-tight shirt and presented a mammoth hand.

'The job's yours, Ceri. The key's over the road with Mel in Caban Cwtch.' Ah, so that's how you said it: the first word was the same as cabin, the second sounded like cutch except it rhymed with butch. All very baffling. 'The can of pop, it's on us, because you've saved our bacon, young lady.'

The Diet Coke was slightly rusty and covered in dust. Gwil saw her hesitation and gave it a rinse. With a lick of his finger.

'You see, Seren, our barmaid is having to cut her hours,' Gwen said. 'Genius child, she's got, needs to be ferried to chess competitions and so forth. You must have been sent from heaven!'

28

'Up north, actually,' Ceri said with a weak smile.

She was going to have to break it to them. This was deceitful. This wasn't who she was. But Gwen was on a roll now.

'It's Six Nations Saturday tomorrow. All hands on deck for the rugby, we need. Don't worry, you'll be fine. I'll just rustle you up something to eat, love, a nice lamb chop? You look half-starved you do. We'll go through the ropes, get your details. Ceri Rees, did you say it was? A week's trial, will that do you?'

Rees? Where did she get that from? But she couldn't speak up because she'd been flattened by this motor-mouth.

'Gwil will go now to get you the key and light you a fire in the cottage. You must've been confident to book yourself in there! But after seeing you in action, you must've been born in a bar.'

Gobsmacked. Astounded. And completely bloody knackered with not a drop of energy to put up a fight, she let them have their moment. There was no point arguing. Not now. All she wanted was something comforting to eat and to thaw out. This situation was entirely ridiculous. And yet she didn't have the strength to own up. She wasn't sure they'd even care it was a mix-up.

Besides, here she was a nobody who just happened to be able to pull a decent pint. They did seem desperate and their kindness, well, she hadn't been on the receiving end for years. She wouldn't fail them – she'd tell them after the shift tomorrow. It would be one of those things she'd look back on and laugh, just a bit of fun.

Who knows, she thought, you might even enjoy yourself, kid.

2

Melyn Thomas was counting down the days until her hill climb home from work would be in harmony with the sky, sliding from teal and terracotta to fire and love-story red all by the time she'd got her key in the door.

Unable to take her eyes off the sunset, she'd walk backwards up an incline so steep that years ago she'd warned tourists their ears might pop. Arriving breathless at her cottage, it wouldn't be from the effort but from the awe-inspiring, heavenly explosion delivering all the colours of the world to this tiny buried seaside village clinging to the edge of West Wales. Places like St Tropez and Italy, Morocco and ... beyond, places she'd never been and would never go to. Because she would never be able to decide where to visit first. What to pack. Which bag to take. Or if she could ever leave Dwynwen again.

That's why she loved watching the sun going down – it would happen, no matter what: there was no procrastination about it. And as she'd sit on her front wall, the warmth of the stone seeping through to her pear-shaped bottom, when the lilac sky became mulberry then sapphire, she'd promise herself tomorrow she would start anew.

But tonight the fuse blew on her glorious daydream as

she stepped out into the murk of a storm. 'Will you listen to yourself, you great big Glamorgan sausage,' she muttered as she locked the beach cabin, her mitts already solid like uncooked fish fingers. 'Winter isn't done with yet.'

She felt sorry for the new barmaid who was staying in the holiday let next door but one to her. Mel had only had a quick glimpse of her but she didn't seem the type to have brought a waterproof. She'd learn, Mel thought, if she lasted. She'd seen it all before: to stay here you had to have a bit about you and she was sorry to say skinny jeans were no match for the elements.

Beneath a strawberry plastic hood, she peered through the soggy fret to the hug of crooked houses built into the hillside where hers, or rather Dad's, was first on the left, overlooking the secluded bay of Dwynwen. They were all named as if they were in a tube of Love Hearts: the Pink House, where Mel lived, the White House, the Blue House, the Purple House and the Green House, the ramshackle uninhabited one, the only one apart from hers which wasn't a holiday let. Not a trace of colour remained, though. They'd been stripped down to the beige of old bones by the weather, which was doing its worst right now.

Heavy flint clouds squatted on the rooftops like Brillo pads. A raw wind blew in from the churning steely sea and the rain gave everything whiplash. Her lemon meringue hair swirling around her, tasting of salt, Mel set off, nearly knocked forwards by the gale. Hunched over, imagining she was in crampons, her feet crunching into grit, slow and heavy, she headed for the summit where the lane levelled off and doubled back on itself to the Pink House.

At the crest, there was no dilly-dallying to take in the crescent of frosted sand and the ragged rocks which tumbled down to the water. It was a frantic fumble of fingers and keys, blind wet slaps on the wallpaper for the light switch, the abandonment of mac and boots, and scooping up of post. Home sweet home was topsy-turvy – two bedrooms and the bathroom were downstairs while the living area was above, to make the most of the view. When there was one.

It meant she could get into her comfies before going up to start on tea. That's how wild it got for her on a Friday night. Anyway, she had to have her sensible head on for work tomorrow. But first she had to navigate the narrow hallway. Dad always made a fuss about what he called her clutter but it was simple: hold back the overhanging coats and scarves, slide past the dresser so you didn't knock off any of the paperwork waiting to be filed, skirt the 'return to sender' polythene parcels and Bryn's your uncle. She liked it looking lived in – she was a busy woman after all, as the one people turned to for help. The spread of stuff made her feel warm and fuzzy. Cradled and safe. Although when she skidded on a bagged package she did concede a little tidy might be needed. But she'd do it now, in a minute, once she'd got out of her soaking skull leggings, sopping stripy rainbow knee-high socks and damp cerise jumper dress.

Then it was on with her dolphin onesie, a nip to the loo and a guilty glimpse of towering boxes of unsold summer stock in Dad's old room, in hibernation until she could set it outside the cabin without it taking flight all the way to the harbour.

A trek up the stairs, on the left side because the right

half was where she put things such as books and washing to be returned to shelves and cupboards when she was on her way. Not that she had her hands free, because of the mail and two cups of old tea.

Still, she'd sort it later, because she was beyond hungry. But what to eat? Mel sighed at the prospect of her usual dilemma: would it be pasta, jacket potato, noodles, rice or chips? And what to have with it? If only she could make her mind up. She could never decide quickly enough and once she'd snacked on toast and crisps and cheese, she'd lost her appetite and ended up chasing whatever it was she'd made around her plate. At the top of the stairs, she turned up the thermostat and looked across the open-plan lounge-kitchen-diner through the French doors and beyond the balcony. Only the lights from The Dragon gave any hint of life out there in the mist which was silvery grey, in between slate and platinum, shiny almost because of the rainy sheen which gave it a myriad of tones. It was familiar, strangely comforting ... and it struck her right in the heart.

It was the same hue as Alwyn Edwards's eyes. How they'd bickered over the colour: he'd insisted they were grey and that was that, but she had seen a million shades more. Yellows in there, blues too, a pigment of aubergine, even. He was one of the few she could talk to about this extra sensitivity, which the doctors called tetrachromacy. This rare genetic quirk meant Mel saw beyond the normal wavelengths of light and picked up a variety of colours more than one hundred times greater than most people. Al called her superhuman when she spoke of pinks and purples in the rocks. Her art teacher, Mrs Jones, said she was blessed with such vision, which her paintings reflected. Otherwise, though, she'd learned to keep her mouth shut at school because it only stoked the rumours she was a witch. She'd been left alone after Al thumped a couple of her bullies. Because he'd believed in her.

The memory filled Mel's eyes with tears. Al was gone, had been for nine years. They'd had one kiss, which had been the sum of all of her longing. But then everything had changed; as if her happiness had run out.

Almost a decade ago, after she'd lost Al and was weak with grief, she'd come back to the cottage to recover and regroup: Mam had remarried and was miles away, in the next village, and Dad asked her to run the cabin for the summer until she got her head together. At the time, he was a cruise ship engineer, so he came and went and she'd have the Pink House to herself. She'd never spent a night away from Dwynwen again.

The emptiness came to her, sucking the air out of her body, leaving her hollow. She held onto the banister to steady herself and to prove she wasn't a ghost: she was here and whole. She was attached to the past and frightened of the future, that's what this was all about. *The present is where you are*, she told herself, *and breathe and keep breathing and fill the gaping hole inside of you ...* It gave her a quickening and she staggered to her dad's battered sea chest where she had stored her childhood. Onto the wooden floor, flipping the buckles and lid, her hands scrambling for the things which reassured her. Collections of treasures, worthless to anyone else, but pieces of hers and Al's history which slowly restored her soul. The smooth stones they'd collected from the shore, safe in a velvet drawstring bag, the colour of Eden. Faded notes they'd passed between their desks, trading juvenile insults in Welsh: he was a *drewgi* – a smelly dog – and she was a *twmffat*, an idiot. And, as she felt herself steadying, the stubs of her favourite Crayola crayons in a scratched Tupperware box. Scented with banana, jellybean, coconut and lime, there were teeth marks where she'd taken a nibble. Another with its torn label, called Soap, had lost its tip in a dare. Her prized one – pristine, unused, it was lemon yellow, over which Al had scrawled '*melyn*'... The gap was closing now and she was able to reset herself. Carefully placing everything back, she exhaled long and slow and got up to face the night.

The post would divert her. There were a couple of bills which she placed on the pile on the worktop. A flyer from a mobile phone company boasting 'even more coverage' – but not here, where the mountains kept the village out of range. Even so, she kept it, just in case. And a letter for Mr L. Thomas, her dad, who used this address because when he'd taken early retirement due to his dodgy hip, he'd decided to live on a houseboat down at the harbour. Windowed and white, it looked official so she opened it in case it was urgent and scanned the words. 'Thank you for your enquiry ... please contact us for a valuation appointment ... be aware it's a difficult market, particularly given the location of the property ...'

My God, he was thinking of selling the cabin. It was like an earthquake going off. It couldn't be. She reread it, hoping she'd got the wrong end of the leek, but there it was in black and white. And a bit of lily pad and peach. Caban Cwtch was just as its English translation, a cuddly cabin where the villagers came for their papers and milk, bread and cheese. For a chat and a cup of tea, a ham bap

35

or chips. Mel prided herself on having whatever anyone wanted, be it a sewing kit or some batteries, a laugh or a shoulder to cry on. It was their lifeline and hers. It made her feel useful, it filled six days a week from 8 a.m. to 6 p.m., and it didn't point out that her one chance of love had gone.

Yet deep down she understood why Dad wanted to sell. Ten years ago, it had been a goldmine of wetsuits and bodyboards, buckets and spades: the holidaymakers had come in herds from April to September, generations of families who'd stay in the static caravans on the hill or in the lets dotted around the village. But over time, they'd drifted away, up and down the coast to the towns which had piers and boat trips, trendy restaurants and boutiques, even wifi. People here poo-poohed their rivals at first because here was a traditional slice of life, away from the nonsense of the internet and Starbucks. Here in Dwynwen, things were simple. Sit and stare out to sea, perhaps go out on a surfboard, read a book, hike the coastal path and wash it down with food and drink while watching the dolphins from The Dragon.

But when takings nosedived and the dolphins inexplicably went with them, the villagers had gone into a kind of shock, stupefied by the rapid fall in its standing. Mel included. She'd had plans to update Caban Cwtch, turn it into a craft shop too, add a gallery, improve the menu. But how could she do that when there was so much unsold and so little income? Okay, the winter was always hard, but this year it had been the worst.

Why hadn't Dad spoken to her about this? Or, to be fair, why, when he had spoken to her about this, hadn't he made it clearer that it was getting serious? The '*we might have to shut up shop'* was approaching fast and no longer distant on the horizon.

Mel squeezed her eyes shut and rubbed her face. Where the hell did this leave her? If Caban Cwtch closed, she would have nothing but a gaping chasm leading to … she couldn't bear thinking where. Because she was feeling giddy as it was. If a sinkhole opened up, she would topple in and they'd hear her screams as far away as … and she racked her brain to find somewhere exotic she'd been and could only come up with Cardiff. She was hopeless and—

The phone went and she was so glad of the distraction she hurled herself at it like a rugby prop in a scrum.

'Melyn, it's me, love, Gwen.' The sing-song Valleys voice of The Dragon's landlady was music to her ears. 'I'm after a favour, I am.' It was just as Mel had wanted because it meant she mattered. And how she needed to hear that.

'Hiya, Gwen, of course.' *Anything*, she could've added, *anything to take my mind off things.*

'What it is, see, we're out of crisps. You haven't got any at the cabin, have you?'

'Loads!' The relief she could be useful came flooding out of her. 'Any flavour in particular?'

'Oh, marvellous. Ready salted, salt and vinegar, Caerphilly cheese and onion, whatever you've got!'

Mel set off down the stairs with intent.

'You'll have to excuse my onesie,' she said, tugging on her wellies and mac, not caring she was going to get a second soaking. It was a better offer than losing her mind in here.

'Disturbing a hot date, am I, love? I'm awful sorry.'

'As if, Gwen.'

'I'll warn the boys to keep their hands to themselves.'

'No need, I'm probably related to half of them,' she said, knowing the crowd well. They were faithful, the regulars, coming from the village and hamlets and farms from all around. And what did it matter if she was in a giant Babygro when they were mostly over fifty and stank of sheep or fish? Al wouldn't be there, so she cared for nothing more. 'I'll be there now.'

'Fablas! What would we do without you? And if you haven't eaten,' *oh, lord, she knew her so well,* 'there's chicken curry half-rice half-chips. I owe you, love.'

Hardly, thought Mel as she opened the door and got a face of hail. It was the other way round: she owed Gwen for giving her a distraction from her troubles.

3

Usually when Rhodri Cadwalader took off his cardboard cycling helmet, he would spend a moment admiring its eco credentials.

The innovative honeycomb structure of wood-cellulose fibre board didn't just meet the highest safety standards, it was an environmental triumph. He'd tilt it this way and that, beneath an imaginary spotlight (an energy-saving one, obviously), appreciating its aerodynamic curve and fully recyclable central core as he hummed a tune worthy of such majesty. Which could only be the Welsh national anthem.

But his only need now was to hide it in Mum's utility room away from smirking eyes. If his brothers saw his headgear, they'd only make 'helmet' jokes. From anyone else, it was water off a sheep's back. But Dai, short for Dafydd, and Iolo – aptly pronounced Yolo, as in You Only Live Once – were like a pack of wolves with Rhodri. Maybe, he wondered hopefully, he had beaten them to it? He hadn't seen Dai's gas guzzler outside their parents' huge converted barn because he'd come the back way, via a winding lane which passed the rear of the remote property four miles from Dwynwen, and he'd have to have X-ray vision to see his brother's car on the driveway.

Rhodri might be Waste Management and Recycling Officer of the Year but he wasn't a superhero! But, as it was half six and he'd cycled the forty gusty minutes from work, he suspected with a sinking heart he was the last to get here for Mum's birthday.

With care, he took out his present from his backpack and placed it on the island in the kitchen. It was a sustainably sourced bracelet made by his friend Seren, who crafted jewellery from silver spoons, knives and forks she found in charity shops and antique markets. He peered into the atrium hallway and even though he was expecting it, his balls still contracted at the sight of two pairs of shoes lined up by the front door.

Dai's brown brogues looked down their polished toes at him, and Iolo's abandoned high-tops stuck out their tongues. Mum insisted they walked around in their socks – she didn't want her rugs dirtied or in Rhodri's case her parquet scratched by his clipless pedal trainers. By taking away their footwear, she reduced them to kids again and guess who was always the butt of the joke?

He sighed and made his way towards them, their deep voices bouncing on vast glass walls and up and down double-height ceilings and off the chandeliers all the way to his ears. Which were apparently the size of jugs, according to them, and why he kept his shaggy mop at lobe length.

Hearing their guffaws at something Iolo had said, Rhodri braced himself for their mirth. He was in no doubt that in their day-to-day lives, they were perfectly decent men. It was just when they were back under the same roof for the first hour or so they reverted to type.

Although what they'd find to poke fun at was beyond

him, because he'd removed all traces of any potential source of amusement …

'Is that a padded arse, Rhod?'

… apart from his supportive cycling shorts.

'Nice of you to come, Kim Kardashian.'

Oh, dear God, he'd completely overlooked he was head to toe in Lycra. Trust Dai, the competitive eldest, to go for the first blood, setting off Iolo's hoots. Even the creases round the pockets of his chinos looked like they were having a laugh at his expense.

'What bloody time do you call this?' Dai added, standing at the fireplace, checking his expensive watch. He was master of ceremonies, following in Dad's footsteps, set up for life as future MD of CadCon, Cadwalader Construction.

'All right, Yoda?' The standard ears gag, lobbed his way by baby bro Iolo, who was slouching on a chaise longue which made him look as if he was about to get his nappy changed.

Rhodri was about to tell them to 'bollock off' when Mum came at him, her arms outspread.

He'd missed his cue. As ever.

But that was his place. The mysterious middle child, he was what was called 'the sensitive one', delivered in a whispered innuendo — there was something different about him. The way he'd saved ladybirds rather than squirting their yellow innards across thumbs and shorts, for example. His love of going off alone into the woods with his penknife to whittle some sticks. Preferring a book to a punch-up. In other words, he was boring.

'Happy birthday, Mum,' he said, letting her squeeze him tight because today was about her and he wasn't going to spoil it. Tomorrow, he'd have his revenge when they watched the rugby together. Well, he probably wouldn't because he just didn't have the appetite for savagery but by then they'd all have relaxed and stopped showing off. This was what they did, every year, their annual get together without other halves or kids – a family tradition which, once the cock-waving had stopped, was one of the highlights of Rhodri's year.

He just had to get past the initial ridicule.

'Just ignore them,' she said into his chest, making him feel eight years old rather than thirty-one. She held him at arm's length to take in his frame.

'Look how big you are!' she said, her blue eyes bright because she had her boys to herself.

This was where he trumped them. He was the tallest, broadest one – six foot three and strapping was what they called it. Dai had the contented thirty-five-year-old mid-riff that came with fatherhood, marriage and a big house in St Davids. And twenty-nine-year-old Iolo remained lanky, living off the adrenaline of a young, free and single life as a graphic designer in London.

Facially, though, they were very similar: what people described as 'a handsome bunch', with Dad's dark eyes, confident nose and strong jawline. And their hair was thick and brown, although Iolo's was in a man bun and Dai's was greying from executive stress. Rhodri's was between outdoorsy and windswept – although once, at uni, a girl, Pippa, said he had come-to-bed hair. So he did. But by the time they'd woken up the next morning, his stubble had emerged, as ginger as a biscuit and apparently hilarious. And that had been the sum of his career as an international playboy.

'Where's Dad?' he said.

'In the study. Just finishing something off.'

Dai flexed on his heels and Rhodri had a feeling something was afoot.

'Then he's going to pop out for the takeaway.' Just Eat hadn't arrived here yet – mainly because the internet was still patchy.

'He's going to get caught in the rain if he's not careful. I was lucky there was a break in it. It should pass overnight, though. My weather station is ever so ...'

He shut his eyes as Iolo curled his fingers into the palm of his right hand and rocked it in accordance with the universal sign for wanker. An act the brothers had all referred to in adolescence as 'dusting your daffodil'.

'It'll be nice to have a meal, just us, here,' Mum said. 'We can have a really good catch-up. Not that I don't want to see my daughter-in-law or the grandchildren, of course.'

'Lydia's gone to her sister's with the kids,' Dai said. 'Good timing really ... a lot on.'

There it was again. Something was brewing.

'Got to leave crack of dawn so I can get a few things done.'

'Can I have a lift? My train's early,' Iolo said. 'Party tomorrow in the smoke. Can't miss it.'

Rhodri's jaw fell open. 'But the game? Wales–England. Two p.m. kick-off. Six Nations. Aren't you staying for it? The rugby club is unveiling its big screen, we won't be crowding round the telly anymore, and—' *That's what we do.*

What they always did on Mum's birthday weekend. Starting with a full Welsh breakfast, cooked by Rhodri at his place, consisting of organic dry-cured back bacon from the farm shop, eggs fresh from Mum and Dad's smallholding and his very own *bara lawr*, or laverbread, made from seaweed he'd foraged himself, slow-cooked for hours, ground into a paste and mixed with oatmeal which he'd fry with local cockles. The rich smell of it, the scent of the sea and the fat of the land combined: it was Wales on a plate.

A walk on the beach, minus coats to show off their red shirts, a couple of pints in The Dragon, up the hill to Dwynwen Rugby Club where they would sing their hearts out to 'Land of Our Fathers' and roar the boys over the try line before one of Mum's casseroles back at theirs. But clearly, by the looks on their shifty faces, they didn't treasure it as he did.

'Dai?' he said desperately, deferring to the one who held sway.

'Entertaining clients in the box at the Millennium Stadium with Mum and Dad.' The box he'd only ever once been to because he couldn't do small talk or in fact any talk without incurring the embarrassed 'he's into the environment' explanation from Dad.

Rhodri heard a lid falling on their family tradition. The fat lady wasn't just singing, she was doing a duet with Tom Jones. Gutted, he was. Absolutely gutted. Didn't it mean anything to them?

'What's changed? Why didn't anyone tell me?'

They all traded looks – even Mum. 'It's just, Dai's so busy and it's a long way for Iolo to come, isn't it?'

He checked out their faces and they were nodding. They'd clearly been talking about this behind his back.

'I'm busy too but I make sure it's first in the diary every year.'

'It's home to us, Rhodri, love, but ...'

'What? To them it isn't anymore?'

His question was greeted with silence. So that was it – this ritual was no longer their priority.

What Mum had really meant was his brothers were making a life for themselves and it was about time he did too. Find a woman, settle down. As if he hadn't tried. He felt foolish, like a child who'd discovered there was no tooth fairy or Father Christmas. And then something took him over – he wanted to show that he wasn't a loser.

'I'll have you know I've been offered a post in Sweden.'

That grabbed their attention and he felt a rising pride. Despite all evidence to the contrary, he did have the capacity to leave and make it somewhere else. He chose to stay in his beloved homeland. There was no way he'd be part of the brain drain – he was too loyal to commit such treason.

'Yes,' he said boldly. 'A four-month sabbatical on a fact-finding mission to find out ways in which we can follow Sweden's zero waste policy.'

Oh, now their eyes were on stalks.

'You're going, right?' Iolo said. 'The chicks are hot there.'

'Did you know they recycle ninety-nine per cent of their household waste compared to, on average, sixty per cent in Wales?'

'It's a great opportunity,' Dai said, artificially bright. 'You have to take it.'

Rhodri stopped – Dai was never that happy. He'd been about to tell them he was in two minds because he didn't want to leave God's country. On paper it sounded great – gathering ideas to bring home to make Wales greener. But everyone knew that when you left, it was hard to come back. He was the only one of his school friends who'd returned as soon as he'd graduated. He'd got a 2:1 in environmental science at the University of East Anglia and could've gone anywhere, but he was homesick and had vowed never to go away again. Yet he wasn't going to tell Dai he would never betray Wales because something about his positive reaction made Rhodri wonder.

'You reckon?' he said, holding Dai's gaze.

'Absolutely,' he said. 'It's about time you left home.'

Again, he felt the judgement and it seared through him, as if he was weak to remain here, when couldn't they see it was harder to stick to your guns?

Before Rhodri could respond, Dad appeared, extending a palm to his sons.

'Boys! Good to see you back at Cas-Blaidd!' he said, name-checking the house that translated as Wolf's Castle, which Rhodri had fled as often as he could as a kid to get away from his bloodthirsty brothers. Dad left Rhodri's hand until last. It had only been last night he'd seen him when Rhodri had come up to get some eggs.

'You told them yet?' he said, beaming, to Dai, whose restless shifting had stopped now he had back-up.

'I thought you should. Sum of your life's work, Dad.'

'You completed the purchase of the land, son,' Dad said, slapping Dai on the back. 'Credit where credit's due.'

Rhodri felt queasy. Something told him this wasn't going to be good – Dad's firm was pretty ruthless and had carved through some of the nicest countryside in Wales.

'Just submitted a planning application for forty homes, bringing jobs and new life to our community.'

'Whereabouts?' Rhodri asked, in a small voice.

Dad walked past him to the hallway to locate his wax jacket. 'I'll get the Indian Banquet, shall I? The one with all the different types of curry.'

'Dad,' Rhodri, said, louder. 'Where are you going to build this time?'

His father picked up his keys and swirled them around his finger.

'There's a patch of scrubland, long neglected, with a sea view. Rural enough for country living but close enough to the amenities if we stick in an access road. Great for families.'

Oh no. It began to dawn on Rhodri where his dad was talking about. Dwynwen's Wood, where St Dwynwen, the Welsh patron saint of love, had passed through in the fifth century on her way to Anglesey in the north. A beautiful spot where you could hide from the elements, wander alone or with a special person ... It was breathtakingly lovely, an ancient place of gnarled trunks, moss beds and carpets of bluebells, sustaining wildlife and clean air. A tumbling waterfall and bubbling stream, so bewitching it could clear the foggiest of heads. Rhodri's escape when he needed answers.

It was irreplaceable. But that didn't matter when there was such pressure for housing. This was why they were encouraging him to leave: so he wouldn't interfere.

'That's not scrubland!' Rhodri said. 'That's sacred ground!'

'Sacred? Come off it, Rhod!' Dad said, putting on a brown herringboned tweed flat cap which gave him the air of a country squire. Which he basically was.

'Don't forget some naan. And mango chutney,' Iolo said.

'I'll come with you, actually,' Dai said, legging it as he saw steam coming from Rhodri's ears.

'You can't do this, Dad … Dai,' he said, following them to the door. 'It's our heritage.'

'Look, son, we'll talk about this later,' Dad said, in his best we've-agreed-to-disagree voice. 'All I'll say is this place is done for. I'm doing it for the next generation. For the likes of you. When was the last time you saw a tourist here? People don't bother anymore. And the young leave in droves. Times are changing.'

Mum began to flap at the stand-off. 'Alun, please …'

'Well, he has to face it, Sian.'

'Not today, he hasn't,' she said, all but confirming that she was on Dad's side. 'Rhodri, come and help me a minute. There's plenty to do … we'll get the plates ready.'

He felt his hands clenching at his father's vision of the future: one he fundamentally disagreed with. Because his was to raze every tree to the ground, to bulldoze anything in his way. Nothing he'd ever built was in keeping with the local area – it wasn't good enough, just giving streets on these faceless poky boxed estates tokenistic Welshified names.

Still, he backed off, and did as his mother asked.

Because even while he hated his dad's version of progress, Rhodri knew he was right about Dwynwen.

It was dying a slow death. And he was going to have to do something about it. But what?

Ceri counts her blessings

Hi, Mum, it's me, Ceri.

I'm here, in Dwynwen, like you asked. In a cottage for the week. You're sat beside me on the bedside table: well, your ashes are. In the tea caddy next to the photo of you and my dad. It's twelve minutes past eleven, I don't know if it's the same time zone where you are, wherever that is, but it's around about when you and me would sit down with a cuppa in our dressing gowns. I'd have got in from the club and we'd go over the day and gloss over the bad bits and count our blessings. Maybe it'd been sunny, say, or we'd had a good laugh over something that happened at work. We still did it when you were ill. It was one of the few constants in the before and after of dementia. Although sometimes it would be midnight when you'd taken ages in the bathroom, forgetting why you were in there. The times you'd come out with your nightie on inside out. Hugging a hot brew, we'd thank heavens for small mercies, as you'd say. Although as you got worse, you'd just stare at the wall, but I'd keep doing it, night after night, picking five good things that'd happened because it was my way of giving you a routine. And I always hoped you were taking it in.

I stopped when you died, I couldn't find joy anywhere.

The shock and the numbness; the bargaining with God to bring you back; the bottomless sadness; the endless wishing you'd walk in. Being angry, with you for leaving me, with me for being angry with you. The guilt that I should've found a way to slow down your decline. Those feelings would come at me all at once. They still do. I can't accept you're gone. It's a madness of sorts. That's why I'm talking like this in my head, like the idiot I am.

Perhaps it's loneliness too. I've been by myself now for five hours, almost in complete silence because the wind is howling and the waves are crashing, and it's the longest I've gone like that in what ... forever. Even if I'm alone I've still got my phone, which never stops ringing. But here, it's dead. Like a slab of rock. I keep picking it up just to check but there's not a spit of service. All those calls and emails and alerts and pings I'm used to not getting through makes me feel panicky. I needed some space, to try to move on, and guess what, now I've got it I'm freaking out. It's this place; it's a boil on the backside of beyond. You couldn't get any more isolated. Why did you want to come here? I don't get it. Even when you were lost in one of your hazes, you had more to you than this lot. They speak weird, they're nosy parkers and they're off their heads. I was only here five minutes and the landlady and landlord offered me a job as a barmaid. They thought I'd come for an interview! *As if.* The daft old bat Gwen misheard me when I introduced myself – they only think I'm Ceri Rees – and roped me into a shift tomorrow! I didn't have the heart to refuse. I've brought a rolling pin to bed with me. Just in case they're actually zombies. Although I reckon zombies wouldn't be seen dead here. It crossed my mind to just sack off the week, scatter you at sea in the morning then get the heck out. Perhaps this is why you always looked on the bright side – coming from here, anywhere's better. Listen to me, I'm so harsh and cynical these days.

I keep thinking what you'd say to me. And the conclusion I keep coming to is that you'd tell me to count my blessings. You'd say it'd help me see that life wasn't so bad. So here goes ... wish me luck.

First, I suppose it'd have to be the cottage. It's cosy. Clean, comfy settee, telly, ooh and an Aga, would you believe, like yours, like the one flaming Kev ripped out. It made my fingers itch when I saw it, like I wanted to stir up something scented and sweet. Like I used to. What else? There's a real fire, not like our pretend one with glowing plastic coals. I'm nice and warm too – I got into bed all snooty because it's sheets and blankets. But I must say I'm pleasantly surprised.

So, my second ... let me think ... well, I have been treated with kindness. They fed me at the pub, some lovely chops, although when I said so it got a bit grating being told it was because it was Welsh lamb and Pembrokeshire spuds. Seriously, they seem to think Wales is the greatest nation on earth, but what's so great about sheep and singing? The girl at the cabin gave me a box of provisions: milk and bread, biscuits and beans, spaghetti, sauce and tea bags. No questions asked, no asides, nothing expected in return. Not like in Crewe, eh? Like if I ever go to the chippy at home, that Bob always asks, 'How's the caviar, chuck?' and people are forever after freebies from me. Cheeky beggars.

Third, well, at least I can be a nobody here. Away from all the crap of being Ceri Price. Work pressure and ... I don't want to drag you into it, I know how much you hated me and Tash arguing, but she insisted on putting the house on the market straight away. I don't see why we need to rush; I offered to buy her out but she wouldn't have it. Then it all came out, how superficial my life is, how out of touch I am with reality, how the money's changed me. But she's all right, she's settled, ready for life to go on. I'm still raging inside, wanting the world to stop, to recognise what its lost. I want to get off and hold on to you. Keep you alive. Like your gentleman friend, the one from the factory, who sent you a Valentine's every year just in case you ever changed your mind. He'd have known you'd gone but he still hand-delivered one of his usual soppy Forever Friends teddy bear cards. I found it among a pile of post and just as it had every year, it had three kisses inside it, without any other words. I cried my eyes out at this man doing it even though you'd passed. It was the loveliest gesture. But I didn't tell Tash because she would've made me feel like I should be over you. So, being here, I can escape from all of that shit.

The shift behind the bar tomorrow will distract me too, so that'd be my fourth. It sounds desperate ... that's because I am. Tash and Jade would think I'd lost my marbles if they knew. I may as well because there's jeff all else to do. I've never been any good at doing nothing, have I? Besides, I'm not setting foot on that beach while the weather's bad. It's not exactly the beautiful bay you said it was. I didn't see a speck of sand and the sea, oh my God, I feel sick just thinking about it. The tide was in, and I mean right in, thrashing against the lane almost, in huge angry waves. Further out it was this vast lurching and rolling mass which made me feel off-balance, as if the ground was swaying. So I'm sorry but you'll have to wait to see my dad. A few days more and I promise, you'll be with him.

Right, I think that's me done. Four out of five the first time back counting my blessings when I'm in Nowheresville isn't bad. I do feel a bit better, Mum, so night, night, love you and sleep tight.

4

Mel knocked once on the door of the Blue House
and went to turn the handle and let herself in. But
she got a forehead of wood when it refused to budge. A
definite bruise, that'd be, probably the colour of a Dairy
Milk wrapper with a tinge of spinach green.

Funny to find it all locked up. So she banged with
her fist and flapped the letterbox, calling, 'Hello?' After a
minute or so of battering, there was a rattle of bolts and
the lady from yesterday opened up a crack. She was looking cross and creased. In midnight-blue silky pyjamas,
like the ones you saw actresses wearing when they were
doing sophisticated.

'Everything all right?' Mel said, pushing through.
'Because you had it locked. And the curtains were still
drawn and it's quarter to nine. The storm's gone! We've
sky as blue as bliss. You got to make the most of it, you
do. And you might've been dead! Thought you would
need some milk. So I've brought you some.'

She smiled, expecting a string of thanks. Because this
was what she loved about being useful.

But the lady, Ceri Rees, was still frowning. Which was
a bit off. And she was supposed to be a barmaid! Being

in the service trade herself, Mel knew the importance of first impressions.

Perhaps she'd forgotten who she was.

'I'm Mel, remember? From the cabin?' The soon-to-be-shut cabin, she found herself remembering, but she elbowed it right out of her mind because today it was all about positive thinking. She hadn't told anyone about it – and she wouldn't until she'd spoken to Dad. 'I look after the cottages for their owners. For holiday lets.'

'Yes, I know who you are,' Ceri said, in a tone which suggested she was cross with Mel, which was weird because she hadn't done anything wrong. 'The door was locked,' she continued slowly, 'and the curtains were drawn. Because I was asleep.'

Blimey, there was no need to talk to her like she was an idiot when this Ceri was the stupid one!

'But it's Six Nations day! The rugby!' Mel laughed, because who didn't know this was David's chance to beat Goliath? A country of three million taking on another seventeen times its size? When centuries of English oppression could be righted by a victory within eighty minutes? 'Aren't you supposed to be Welsh?!'

She didn't sound local, possibly from a border town. Mel waited for the penny to drop but Ceri didn't look at all impressed. Maybe she was one of those football fans she'd heard about. She had sceptical eyes which were shady with suspicion. Burned wood or a steak of Welsh Black beef. And still lacking any recognition today was the greatest day ever! Bringing everyone out like before, when Dwynwen would be bustling by 9 a.m. with people ordering tea and Welshcakes and buying papers and taking their drinks down onto the beach. She'd try being informative instead, see if Ceri came out of herself.

'I didn't want you to miss your first shift. It starts at eleven a.m., Gwen asked me to remind you. Here, I've made you a breakfast bap. Egg with a yolk so yellow you'll think you're eating sunshine; crispy bacon, salsa red tomato and local sausage. Lovely, they are. And take the milk too.'

Ceri looked as puzzled as a newborn. Her arms were clamped protectively over her chest and she was sizing her up. It was as if no one had ever offered her a thing in her life. And then she relaxed, dropped her arms to take the provisions and gave her a smile. Talk about the clouds parting: she was gorgeous!

Like a rainbow.

'I'm not being funny but you look much better when you smile,' Mel gasped. 'And no make-up suits you. I got a peek of you yesterday, I did. When your make-up was trowelled on. I mean, I love make-up but you don't need to wear as much as you do.'

Oh, crikey Moses, Ceri was curling up again. Some people just couldn't take a compliment.

'I'm not being rude, I just mean you're as fresh as a daisy you are, although your skin isn't white like mine! All pasty pale! I have to put on foundation and blusher and things to not look ill. But you, your complexion, it's beautiful, like caramel. Lucky you are, having that West Wales look. They say the swarthy ones descend from the Spanish Armada, from sailors washed up on our shores when the English blocked the Channel and they came this way.'

'Really?' Ceri said, looking engaged for the first time since Mel had come in.

'Probably poppycock but it's a nice story.'

A flash of something flickered across her face. Mel didn't know what it was. She pulled back the thick Cuban-cigar brown velvet curtains to see if she could catch it. But when the light flooded into the room, Ceri's expression was back to blank and Mel looked around for something to say.

It was all driftwood and bronze in here, a nice sofa by the fire and a shaggy forest floor rug. The upstairs was pretty much the same, truffle throws and clove furnishings. All right for a visit, she supposed, but a bit empty.

'Sleep well?'

Ceri groaned. 'Like a flaming baby. The bed is something else. And it's so dark here.'

'But what darkness, eh? Atlantic ocean and violet and peacock ...' She'd lost her now, she could tell by the gawp. 'Anyway ... you'll be rested for later when it gets heaving at the pub. You won't know what's hit you! They come from miles around for the atmosphere. Well, they used to. Still get a fair few for the game but most will go up to the rugby club for the new big screen. I can't go up there because of the cabin. Anyone who wants anything can just go in and help themselves and bring the money over to me. We watch it on Gwil's telly. It's a bit small but we turn the sound up and it's magic.'

She was giving her that weird look again. It must be her chattering away. Some people didn't like that.

'Sorry, I know I talk a lot of *lol*.'

'Lol?' Ceri said.

'Nonsense. That's what "lol" is in Welsh.'

'I thought you meant "laugh out loud", you know ...'

'Oh, no point in text speak for us here, no bloody signal!'

The pair of them laughed and Mel felt much better and she waited for an invite for tea. Because it was only polite.

'Right, er, thanks for the milk and breakfast, I expect you're busy. So ...'

Perhaps she was shy? Mel would bring her out of herself, that was only helpful.

'Rhodri won't mind if I have a quick cuppa. He's holding the fort for me.'

Ceri said nothing and walked off into the kitchen. Mel followed, curious about this guarded lady.

'Lovely this place, isn't it? Belonged to Mrs Lewis, now to her son who lives abroad. Newcastle. Says he's waiting until things pick up and he can sell it, although I'm not sure when or if it's ever going to happen ...'

'Yes, it is a bit ... sad here,' she said, picking up the kettle. 'A bit grey.'

'Grey? I don't think so! It's more colourful here than in the city where lights turn everything a horrible orange.'

'Well ... now you come to mention it, you might be right, Mel. Or is it Melanie?' Ceri asked.

'Melyn. It's the colour yellow in Welsh.'

'Nice,' Ceri said, looking for the mugs.

'On the hooks, by there. On the dresser.'

'Right ... thanks.'

'You say "*diolch*", here,' Mel said. She liked to educate people about the Welsh language.

'What?'

'Thank you. We say *diolch*. D-I-O-L-C-H. Have a go!'

'Um ... dee-yock. That sound right?'

'Awesome.' She beamed. 'You'll hear it lots now, you'll see.'

While Ceri found the tea bags and so on, Mel took the chance to have a quick looksy around her. Funny, there didn't seem to be anything Ceri had brought with her, like books or bags or food or anything. The surfaces were bare, and apart from a big open vanity case on the table full of beauty stuff, there was no real sign she was here at all.

'So, I live next door but one. Not as fancy as this. But at least I have it cosy. It's a bit naked, here.'

At this, Ceri stopped at the tap.

'Do you know what? That's why I like it. It makes a change from stuff everywhere. You know, all that baggage ...'

Now this was interesting. But how anyone could live like it was beyond Mel. All that openness and space. She felt all breathy.

'Are you one of those minimalists?'

Ceri shook her head. 'Christ, no. My place is the opposite of this. It's ... busy like my life ... um, sorry, which tap is cold? It says P-O-E-T-H on this one and O-E-R on that one.'

'*Oer*. You say it "oy-er". The hot is "poyth".'

She had a go at saying them and didn't do too badly. But if you grew up where no one spoke Welsh, it'd be hard to get to grips with the language. It wasn't like here where you picked it up from the cradle and went to Welsh school and used it in your dreams.

'The baggage. Is that why you came for the job here?' She couldn't help but ask.

At this, Ceri paused. 'Kind of. Gwen asked me to do a shift. I've done bar work before ... so ...'

Hmm, intriguing. Like she hadn't been a barmaid lately. This one had so many layers she could be an onion.

'... why not? And I'm not here for long. It's just a break really. But nice to help out. Odd but nice.'

That Mel understood. 'Oh, I know. I like to be helpful.'

'I'd never have guessed,' Ceri said, her eyes glinting playfully.

Mel giggled. 'That's what Dad says. Too bloody helpful.'

They fell into silence, listening to the rumble of the water as it began to bubble and pop. It was like the build-up to the match, the minutes leading up to the explosion when it started and your heart swelled with *hwyl*, a passion, a stirring from within making you thank God you were Welsh. She felt awful sorry for people who weren't.

'Hello?'

Ceri's head swung round like she'd heard Anthony Hopkins do his *Silence of the Lambs* tongue slither. Very jumpy, she was. On edge.

'It's only Rhodri!' Mel explained, 'He'll be after me.' It settled Ceri and they both went into the lounge. 'He lives up by the woods. He's one of the village people, he is.'

'Which one?' Ceri asked as Rhodri hovered at the threshold, which his shoulders easily filled. Oddly, there was a subtle shift in Ceri's voice. It was lighter and friendlier. And in her body language – she was less closed. As if Mel had warmed her up a bit. Although, *no, hang on*, she was tilting her hips towards him – was she admiring him? Probably, she thought with an inner eye roll: some people were so shallow. Mel was so used to Rhodri she forgot he was so striking in a Roman statue kind of way, with deeply carved tousled dark hair, noble features and handsome angles. Not that he realised or capitalised on it. That was why Mel loved him. 'The cowboy or the cop?'

Rhodri snorted through his nose and Ceri's laugh tinkled. Mel didn't get the joke and she looked from her to him for a clue. Then he did a YMCA move and it clicked.

'Oh! I see!' she said, clapping her hands together. 'Actually, if he was in the Village People he'd be the one in the hi-vis vest because he's a recycling officer for the council.'

Rhodri blushed with self-consciousness, his cheeks turning bordeaux, matching his rugby shirt. He'd gone from manly to boyish in seconds – this was his charm and she could see Ceri had almost defrosted. *So this one was a man's woman, obviously.*

'In fact, Rhod, you could tell Ceri here, the new barmaid, about what to put in which boxes and what day to put them out.'

His favourite subject. His blush became a flush of excitement. Mel caught herself in the grip of the green monster, thinking Ceri shouldn't take it as a show of interest from Rhodri – he treated everyone with the same manner: in his eyes, everyone was equal. Well, apart from one person.

'My absolute pleasure! We have a little saying, don't we, Mel, I like to talk ... rubbish!'

Mel grinned, seeing beyond his dad gag. He'd said once that an ex had dumped him for being a bit dull: okay, recycling wasn't the most fascinating subject but it showed he had huge passion and that was the important thing, not what he enthused about. It showed he had depth.

'So, collection day is Tuesday,' he said, with his happy-to-assist cheer. 'Orange bags take plastic, cans, aluminium foil, newspapers, magazines and cardboard. Glass goes in the green box and food waste in the green caddies. Black bags and garden cuttings alternate every week. Black bags this Tuesday. Your waste needs to go out by 8 a.m. at the latest. Any queries, don't hesitate to ask.'

'Cool,' Ceri said, looking bemused now. She was probably from one of those curious one-box-for-all areas Rhodri had told Mel about. 'Right, so ... I need to get ready really.'

'Of course, of course!' Rhodri slammed his hand on his brow. 'I'm so sorry to disturb you. I'm after Mel. I've got to go, a few things to do before the game.'

'Of course! I'll come with you now.'

Mel turned to Ceri, wished her good luck for her debut at The Dragon, and apologised profusely for having to run.

'The cup of tea. I'm so sorry to let you down. We'll have it another time, okay?'

'I'm sure we will,' Ceri said, inching towards them as if she was a dog rounding them out.

So Mel grabbed Rhodri by the arm and left, whispering to him the visitor was a true enigma. Looking back as she closed the little gate, Mel gave a big wave. But Ceri had already shut the door and was bolting it all back up again.

Christ, Mel pitied her, what planet was she from if she didn't know how to handle a friendly welcome?

5

I t was as if Ceri had never stopped being a barmaid.

Behind the bar, she was dancing, moving from one side to the other, starting a pint, switching to the vodka, spraying tonic while calculating the price, before setting the drinks down with a 'Six pounds seventy, please!'

In a place so alien to her, it was uncanny the way she felt so at home. Because from the second she'd taken up her position at The Dragon, she'd been treated as a long lost relative who'd returned to the fatherland – or, motherland in her case. Okay, some of them ordered in Welsh, but Gwen was on hand to excuse her ignorance. Very loudly. Ceri learned people who were thirsty were willing to make an exception. *Besides*, they all said, *you'll learn.*

That was the thing she couldn't get over: it was assumed she would stay because why would anyone want to leave? She wasn't so impolite as to point out the reasons, such as the lack of mobile reception, broadband, proper coffee, skimmed milk and avocados.

And she did want to get out of here alive.

They had a crazed look about them. Had done since they'd arrived en masse. Only because the rugby club's fêted big screen had broken down in the build-up. So one minute she was cleaning glasses and listening to Gwen's life story, told in shoes, from the stilettos of her youth in Merthyr Tydfil discos and police officer's boots when she met Gwil in the force, so dreamy he was with his thick black hair, to the flip-flops of summers with their two kids in West Wales and finally here, now, back in heels because landladies needed to have something about them. The next, an army of men, women and children waving blow-up leeks and wearing daffodil hats had poured in. Such was the rush to the bar, Ceri had been afraid the pub would go bum over tit. Luckily, there were enough still coming in to take position around the tiny telly to even things out.

Just in time too, Gwen had said, yelling at whoever was closest to turn up the commentary because apparently, judging by the reaction, the teams were walking out onto the pitch.

The laughter and shouting and booming had suddenly stopped: a perfect silence fell and Gwil gave her a nod to stop what she was doing mid-pint.

The punters had taken a collective in-breath and burst into a most incredible chorus. Like a flash-mob choir.

But why were they singing 'my hen laid a haddock on top of a tree'? What did that have to do with Wales? Although, admittedly they were all bloody bonkers as far as she could tell.

Ah, it was in Welsh. And every single one of them was word perfect, eyes shut, chest heaving with emotion, the men as wide as Hagrid was tall dabbing their wet faces.

Luckily, what with all the eye-shutting, no one had seen her failing to join in. She didn't think she'd have been able to if she'd known the words anyway – it was the most beautiful and stirring thing she'd heard. When it was over, she'd turned to grab some crisps and by the time she'd swivelled back round, Gwil had raised a finger as the notes began for 'God Save The Queen'.

A lone man had begun to sing along – up the front in a white shirt. She'd waited for everyone to start laughing because he was flaming awful. But no! Everyone had stayed respectfully quiet.

'English, he is,' Gwen had said, to clarify. 'English Dick. Runs the caravan site, he does, been here twenty years. He won't give in, he won't!'

What was it with these weirdos? Where she came from, no one bothered to sing let alone stand for their country. Here, though, it was all about hearts on sleeves. Why did they care so much? She hadn't the time to consider it anymore because it had all gone wild. Cheering, singing – something about bread and heaven – and their running commentary of *numbers! knock-on! rolling maul!*. In English now but still meaningless to Ceri. Women shouting as well as men. Everyone knew the rules. In her world, rugby was played by posh boys and there'd never been any of them in Crewe. Chucking a ball backwards seemed, well, backwards, to Ceri. One local, a pot-bellied scarecrow-haired farmer who'd divulged he was Barri 'with an i' and had athlete's foot, had taken it upon himself to keep her up to date with the score, thoroughly confusing her with his description of a try involving five Joneses. She'd felt under siege but in a nice cosy buffered way, busying her mind away from why she was here, her business and the cold turkey withdrawal from checking her phone every five seconds. Her only worry was keeping up with demand. And what demand – this lot were drinking the workingmen's club not just under the table but the cocking chairs too. Mad for it, they were. Just then, a roar went up, which made Ceri jump out of her boots. She saw hands fly into the air and a slow-motion fountain of beer shot up and cascaded onto her face.

'We've beaten England!' she heard Gwen say as Ceri groped along the bar for a mat to wipe herself with. 'No Grand Slam for us this year but this is much better, it is!' She opened her eyes and thanked God no one important was here to see her looking so rough – it'd be a deal-breaker, that's for sure. There before her were Gwen's zebra-print wedges.

She was only stood on top of the bar! And she began to conduct a tune from on high. People were hugging each other and crying and belting out a song which if she was correct was about bloody saucepans. There was no menace, like she had been used to in Crewe when sport plus ten pints usually led to a brawl. Just pure joy. Apart from English Dick, who was shaking his head but taking the consolatory pats on the back with good grace.

Clearly, they were absolutely stark raving. Talk about going over the top. It's only a flaming game!

'You what?' said an aggressive fiver being waved in her face.

Oh, heck. She'd only said it out loud – Ceri was in for it now ...

The note dropped to reveal quite possibly the fittest bloke she'd ever seen in her life. Who still managed to look gorgeous with a face like a slapped arse. Which immediately relaxed into a smile, making him, quite impossibly, even more handsome.

She placed a hand on her soggy beery top and noticed

her pulse was racing like a horse in the Grand National.

'You had me there!' she said, flushing with relief. And there was no foundation to hide it.

'Not from round here, are you?' the man said. *Man*? Actually he was a sex god. Chiselled, as if he'd come from Screwfix, via heaven. Blond David Beckham hair, wide green eyes, Cupid's bow lips and the complexion of a baby's bum. Lovely hands, too: probably late thirties and no wedding ring – just, you know, an observation.

'I'm Logan. Postman by morning, surf instructor by afternoon,' he said, in one of those southern accents you couldn't locate beyond laid-back Dermot O'Leary. 'Not from round here either but you get used to it.'

What? He lived here? But he was too … spectacular. How could a village this pifflingly small have not just Rhodri but also Logan? They were both sexy, in different ways. Rhodri was tall, dark and hulking if you forgot the bin man bit and Logan looked like a model from the Next catalogue.

She opened her mouth to speak but Barri was ahead of her with the introductions.

'Unlike you, butt, she's Welsh, got it in her blood, haven't you, Ceri?' Gwen had obviously been filling him in, which reminded her to keep her mouth shut because apparently she was hot gossip. 'You need to watch this one, you do.'

Watch him? She'd binge on him like a box set if she could.

'Guinness, Ceri,' Logan said, rolling his eyes at her, then to Barri, 'You're as English as I am, Baz. You were born there.'

As Barri choked on his ale, a loud series of thumps

sent a hush around the room. It was a good job Gwil and Gwen were ex-coppers, seeing as the local constabulary would have a job getting to the middle of nowhere. It was so remote and 1950s backward, they'd probably have to come by Tardis.

Peering over the throng, Ceri couldn't see any trouble, though – just Rhodri banging a table.

'Sorry to interrupt, I promise I'll be brief,' he said hoarsely.

'That'll be the day!' Logan said, which got everyone laughing. Her first thought was what a double act they could be, these two lookers. But then Rhodri didn't seem amused. More as if he was trying to contain himself.

'All right, all right, I know, I'm a windbag. But I've news and it seems appropriate on this day of all days, when we have retained a scrap of dignity by beating the old enemy, when this very pub is jumping like it did before … before we got left behind.'

A murmur went up.

'You see, there's a plan to build forty homes on the hallowed earth of Dwynwen's Wood.'

A gasp went round the pub. Then cries of 'No!' and 'Never!'

He nodded solemnly. But it sounded like a good idea to Ceri – people equalled traffic and money. She knew all about that.

'Yes, yes, I know. Worse, I'm ashamed to say the application has been submitted by …' he took a deep breath '… CadCon. My father's company.'

The revellers booed as shock swept the floor.

'It's a disgrace. And we must take action,' he said to cheers.

'But I don't mean getting angry or being negative, as easy as it would be. Because, believe me, I've spent the last twenty-four hours doing exactly that and it's done me no good. No good at all. My father believes Dwynwen is dying.'

Ha! It was dead, more like. A tombstone would be more suitable as a *Welcome to Dwynwen* sign.

Jeers went up but Rhodri shook his head.

'And, it hurts me to say this, you know how much this will hurt me, but he's right. I'm sorry, he is. Remember the days when we'd be booked out all summer? When we'd have lines of people queuing for baps at Caban Cwtch, Mel?'

Ceri saw her royal highness of nuttiness, now sporting a big angry bump on her forehead, agreeing vigorously. She was one devoted girlfriend – she seemed to hang off his every word. She had no idea how old Mel was, she was one of those ageless people; she could be as young as her early twenties but Rhodri was talking of past times so she had to be older.

'When you'd wait an hour for food here, Gwen? Gwil?' They nodded too.

'When the beach would be jam-packed with people and kids and happiness? Logan, your surf school would be busy all day? Yes?'

Logan acknowledged his point. And Ceri acknowledged a vision of him in a skin-tight wetsuit.

'Sunshine Caravan Park would be full, Dick ...' English Dick, who was squat and bald, put a finger under his nostrils to stem his sadness.

'Barri, your chickens couldn't lay eggs quick enough for the farm shop.' Barri swallowed at the memory. So did Ceri – it sounded like a daydream. How could this backwater have ever been a popular resort?

'We need to get it back.'

Ceri bit her cheek to stop herself spluttering, 'Good luck with that.'

Louder now, he said: 'To breathe new life into Dwynwen – make it desirable again. And quickly, so we can make a case to the planners that our village doesn't need this development. We are vibrant enough as a destination – our roads and services couldn't cope with an extra, what, forty families?'

'Hear, hear!' someone said.

'We need to prove to the world, or perhaps the rest of Wales to start with, we haven't rolled over – we still have a welcome inside of us so warm visitors will take their coats off even if it's blowing a gale.'

He was good with words and he spoke in a lovely melody, she'd give him that, but he was deluded. And it wasn't exactly friendly to say 'you can visit, we just don't want you to live here'.

As if he'd read her mind, he said: 'This is not about keeping incomers out – this is about bringing people in to enjoy the riches bestowed upon us. Doubling the size of the village with a featureless estate will kill what we are, our history. It would be irresponsible of us to not preserve what makes us unique.'

Okay, now she understood. But still, what a romantic. Not a very practical approach to resuscitation at all. It was wishy-washy claptrap.

'Our breathtaking views of sea so blue, our clear air which revives the soul, the wild garlic in the wood, the

70

fish so fresh they're still flapping on our plates, our un-spoiled natural beauty.'

He'd reached a crescendo and it did sound nice but she wondered if he'd been sniffing glue. He was as off his head as the rest of them.

'What's the plan, Rhod?' Logan said.

'Ah, now this is the bit I'm not sure about ...'

A groan went up and Ceri caught Logan wincing. People started to look away from Rhodri. Ceri too. But only because Logan had got up and was walking to the gents in keks so tight it was as if his rear end was winking at her.

'Hang on! I have an idea but it would need everyone on board.' He waited until a hush fell.

'Dwynwen, the clue is in our name! Saint Dwynwen is our patron saint of love! We could use it to make us stand out.' His eyes had gone big and he was grabbing the air with splayed fingers.

'Right. But how?' Mel asked.

'We could call ourselves the Village of Love!' His cheeks had gone red again, and he looked very pleased with himself.

'Brilliant!' Mel said, clearly cheerleader in chief. 'I love it! What do we need to do?'

'Put our heads together and work it out!' he said, pointing at everyone. Rhodri was clearly one excitable puppy. The trouble was, a collective disappointed drop of the shoulders was going round: it seemed no one wanted to play.

'Love?' Barri said, wistfully. 'I'm not sure I remember what that is.'

'Ay,' English Dick added. 'We're old dogs, Rhod, I'm

71

not sure you can teach us new tricks. I still don't know how to set the video recorder.'

Oh dear. Ceri had thought it was quite a good concept. But if this was who Rhodri had to rely on, he was going to be as successful as a vegetarian butcher. And this place, with its scraggy buildings and basic menu, was hardly the city of eternal love, was it?

'But if we just try, then ...'

He was starting to lose them.

A few conversations broke out.

'Anything, any ideas at all ...'

No one was listening anymore.

'Anyone? And don't forget it's black bags on Tuesday ...'

His voice trailed off as he dropped his chin and stared into his pint. Mel appeared at his side and Ceri could see she was trying to cheer him up. It was pitiful how two people who were both about her own age could think this was the centre of the earth. If she was them, she'd have got out of here a long time ago. Mum should've thanked her lucky stars she left – and not wasted time nostalgically chasing the past. Maybe they were trapped – it did feel a bit cultish here. They had to be because you wouldn't stay here out of choice. Christ, Ceri was going to nail this shift then tell Gwen the truth. She'd be free to relax a bit, scatter the ashes and go – misery back home was preferable to watching the inmates revolting here inside the asylum. Her life didn't seem so bad, after all. The fact was she couldn't understand their infatuation with Dwynwen: Mel was evangelical and Rhodri hadn't spoken like he was being held hostage. She felt sorry for them, especially him. Mel was fruity enough to fit in.

72

But Rhodri? He seemed less of a freak. Yet hadn't he put his faith in a bunch of oddballs? He was sweet but it was steel that was needed. No wonder it had all gone to shit here. For despite the buzz she'd felt today, it was obviously a one-off. There was no hope for Dwynwen whatsoever.

6

Usually, on a Sunday morning, Mel would have a pot of Welsh Brew ready and waiting for Dad, plus an extra mug set out for his dog, who was just as partial to a cup of tea.

The waggy, shaggy leather-jacket-brown mongrel's sweet rosy tongue would lap it up then hang lopsided and steaming in a wonky grin of thanks. He was as loyal as his namesake Gelert, a hound of Welsh legend killed by his master Llewelyn the Great, who believed the dog had savaged his baby son. It turned out – too late – that Gelert had been protecting the boy from a wolf. Not to be dramatic, but Mel was feeling a sense of betrayal herself.

That's why she'd parted with tradition today and was sat on the wall outside her cottage, kicking the bricks in anticipation of her father's visit. Inside the Pink House was where she felt warm and safe: any upset over Caban Cwtch would only contaminate it.

Also, she didn't want Dad in the house. He'd give her ears a battering about what he saw as a jumble sale of a mess rather than the treasures and little collections of things they were. Really, she was just a bit untidy. He was the opposite – he had to be, on his poky boat. He'd only go on at her about filling some boxes so he could take them to the tip. And she couldn't face it. Probably because she had a sore head, from yesterday's celebrations after the rugby. And from the bump on her forehead which had turned the same colour as the sea. A sharp emerald green, probably the shade of viridian in her Winsor and Newton watercolours which were stored in a bamboo box. In the spare room. Out of sight. A decade ago, she'd packed away her paints. Yet she could still feel the cold tube collapse between her fingers as she squeezed a blob onto an old plate.

'Get a grip, woman,' she mumbled, seeing her breath steam in the air and fade into the overcast gloom. Raking over the blackest of coals of her foundation year in Cardiff, supposedly to prepare her for a degree in Fine Art, wasn't going to help anyone solve this problem.

She heard the crush of stone beneath tyres and saw a van approaching. Mel stood up to snap herself out of the trance and waved gingerly.

'My gorgeous girl,' Dad said smiling, his head popping up like a piece of toast, as he slammed the door after Gelert, who was bounding up, knocking into her, up on his back feet scratching at her flamingo leggings. He was one of those big dogs who thought he was small. And human. It was impossible to get him off the bed if she was looking after him for Dad. It's what he did with him and habits were hard to break. Fussing him, she was unable to meet Dad's mahogany eyes. She was cross and hurt and confused but she didn't want him to see it so soon and for things to get off on the wrong foot.

'No cuppa?' he said, seeing her wrapped up in her damson duffel coat and tiger-with-ears hat, all ready to go, before he put his arms around her and bent to kiss her on the cheek.

'I've a flask, if that's okay?' she said softly, looking up. 'Forecast says we're in for rain later. A dumping for twenty-fours, apparently. So we could have a walk on the beach now, get some air. You'd like that, Gelert, wouldn't you?'

'All right,' Dad said, his hair glinting silver like a thimble. 'Nice to have a change, eh?'

Well, no, not really. That was what this was all about.

'See the game yesterday, Mel? My word, what a nail-biter!'

'Yes!' The memory hurled her back to the excitement. 'The pub was banging! It was awesome!'

'Didn't pass out, did you?' he asked, his eyes laughing, as he nodded to her bump.

'No! Although Barri did. He missed out on the curry Gwen had made for the night. No,' she said, tapping her bonce with a Christmas-red mitten, 'this was from ...' she jerked her head towards the Blue House '... walking into the door, there. She's the new barmaid. Although I have no idea what she's doing here. She's a bit snooty, she is. Won't last the week. She had her door locked, would you believe!'

'Maybe she heard about the crime wave from three months ago when a rat broke into Mrs Williams's shed fifty miles from here!' Dad said, dead serious.

Ah, he was a good man, was Dad. He'd never let her down. Even when Mam had left him for Huw when Mel was fourteen and he could've let distance grow between father and daughter like other men, either because it was too painful or it caused too much anger. No, he'd kept the promise she'd made him give her, to have her half the week when he wasn't away on a cruise ship. He could easily have moved on and found himself a new family. Especially as her parents had alluded to their marriage as an arrangement of sorts. They had loved each other once but had never been *in love*. He could've disappeared from Mel's life forever.

She had to remember that when they got down to talking. He hooked his arm through hers and led her down the steep hill in pursuit of Gelert, who was already a dot in the distance.

'So ... what will it be today at the pub? Beef? Chicken? Pork?'

'Lamb, I think.' She sniffed the air as they passed The Dragon and there was a definite smell of roast. Lovely.

'Lamb. Again. Always lamb,' Dad said. 'Maybe we should try somewhere else?'

She didn't reply. This was one of his jokes which he said every week. Passing the cabin, she felt her stomach contract and she waited for Dad to say something. But there was nothing. He was still on about lunch.

'We could go to the harbour.'

'Don't be daft!' she said, as the hard ground beneath her clover Doc Martens gave way to sand. Gelert was already gambolling in the waves. It was contagious, his enthusiasm. She broke free, as she always did when she got to the bay. Like a child, the urge to run and get lost in the space and stamp your footprints across the blank canvas of beach. Spinning round and round, she saw a blur of land and sea and Dad and land, sea, Dad ... she pulled a dizzy face as she came to a stop.

'There's a nice new place opened up, a what-you-call-it

bistro thing. The boys at the boat club, they say they do a cracking bit of crackling.'

Her feet might have come to a halt but her tummy was now churning. He was serious. The wind whipped her eyes and she felt them watering.

'Oh, there's no need to cry if you don't want pork.' He said it without a smile, full of sadness. 'What is it, love?'

'A new place? You want to go to a new place? What if everyone did it and forgot all the old places?' It was insensitive of him, considering that's exactly what had happened to the cabin and the village.

'I'm sorry, love, you're going to have to explain this to your old man, I'm not with you.'

This wasn't how she'd wanted it to go. But the feeling of loss took over.

'The cabin,' she said, her tears tinting her vision with a blurry sheen of granite. 'I opened a letter, addressed to you, like you said I should, in case it was anything urgent, and ...'

Saying it out loud, she'd dreaded it, because it would make it real. But she couldn't sit on it any longer. 'You're going to sell it. I didn't think you meant it.'

His bristly eyebrows, as big as badgers, arched with melancholy.

'Oh, Melyn. We've spoken about this, you know we need to shut up shop. Not for me, my time is gone, but for you. That money from the sale, it'll be yours, I told you, to put towards a dream or a trip or a vocation or whatever it is you're going to do, because ... you can't stay here forever.'

'Why not?' she snapped.

'Because it's no good for you. Your mother agrees.'

'Oh, so you've been talking about me behind my back.'

'We're your parents, of course we talk about you. When are you seeing her next?'

As if she'd listen to Mam, who'd interrupted Mel's happy childhood by running off with Huw – and leaving Mel feeling like a spare part in her new family.

'Don't start,' she said, 'I'm going round for an early tea tomorrow. All right?'

It would be just her and Mam, who'd invited her only because she probably didn't want to be alone. Thursday was Huw's skittles night and her half-sister Ffion would have something on. Fi came along shortly after Mam re-married and it had coincided with Mel's stroppy teenage phase. She'd felt pushed out; it had been hard to feel included when the baby had needed so much attention. When Fi was toddling, Mel had left for Cardiff. The age gap of nearly fifteen years, Fi's age now, had been huge. Mel had never tried to close it and it remained a gaping sore.

Dad nodded with approval. But it made her exasperation peak. What could Mam say that would make her agree that yes, she should up sticks?

'I know it'd suit you all if I left, I wouldn't be the big fat fly of disappointment in your soup anymore. But my life is here. The cabin. If it goes ...'

'It'll be the best thing that ever happens to you. Because nothing is ever going to change for you here.'

Her desperation kicked in. 'What if I do it up a bit? Because it's a bit tatty and I could give it a lick of something ... say, a blue, like the domes of churches in Greece.' She'd always wanted to go there, to try the

79

fairest of feta and olives so black you could use them for a snowman's eyes. She'd seen them on a travel programme.

He blinked slowly. She took it as a rejection.

'The accounts, you've seen them, love.'

'I can turn it around.' She needed to fight because the alternative was too horrifying.

'We've had ten years to turn it around. It's dragging you down. It's a mess, that shop too.'

'No! I'm going to tidy it up, the summer delivery is coming any day so I'll pack away the winter stock and get it ready.'

'How long have you been saying you'll give it a tidy?'

'I know, but it's hard fitting it in when people need me.'

Dad was staring out to sea now, waiting until she blew herself out. It just made her even more determined in her denial.

'We're going to do something. Me and Rhodri. Bring back the tourists and the long summers. His father wants to build on the woodland, forty homes. We're going to stop him.'

'Wouldn't it be better for everyone if they were built?'

'Dad!' *How could he say that? He was Dwynwen born and bred.*

'You'd at least get a footfall of customers. What do you get now? A few locals and some ramblers on the odd occasion.'

'But if the development goes up, we would lose what makes Dwynwen, well, Dwynwen. It'd be new roads up the top of the village where there'd be a Spar and a bookies. Our unique selling points – our peace and quiet and natural wonders and individuality – they would be gone forever. And we down here by the bay would be forgotten. Cut off.'

'Like we are now. No, Melyn. Look at you, you're full of ideas and passion and I wish you'd put this into yourself. You're a young woman. Thirty years old. You're not dead yet.'

'So why do I feel like it?'

'Because you're frightened. But you don't have to be.'

She spun round and howled a cry up to the dirty sky.

His hand was on her shoulder. 'You don't have to go far. You don't have to leave Wales if you don't want to. What about Cardiff? It's changed since you were there.'

'You know I can't go there,' she said, whirling back round to face him.

'How do you know if you don't try? You might want to try that new place in the harbour, to see if you could. I know you go to see your mam in the next village but that's something you have to do. This is different – this is about choice. Melyn, please, I'm worried, love.'

She hated his look of disappointment. It gutted her like a bloody fish. And it made her angry.

'Well, you're the one who wants to rid me of a job and a home and a living and a life.'

As soon as she'd said it, she knew she was being unfair. And Dad, being Dad, only responded with love.

'I want you to have a future, Melyn.'

So did she. But it was impossible.

'It's too late for a future. I stopped having one … when Alwyn died.' She covered her face and wanted it all to go as black as death.

'You've got to let it go. You've got to move on now.'

'How can I, Dad, when it was my fault?' She wept,

81

turning around and walking away and walking and walking, shooing Gelert to return to her father, until she could reach the firm wet sand and she wouldn't be able to hear Dad anymore. But she hadn't got there yet.

'It wasn't your fault, Melyn, it was an accident.' His words flew up into the wind and circled her head like a lasso rope, trying to catch her and bring her to her knees. Because when she fell, as she always did eventually, she would be pinned down by the lie. For the truth was that if she hadn't been with Al that night, he would still be alive now. So onwards she went, until her feet smacked the rocks at the end of the bay, onwards to the waterfall where the flush and the fury would drown the sound of her father and her own sorrow.

7

What the flip had happened to her, Ceri wondered as she left the pub in a state of shock.

She was supposed to be a businesswoman, with an online empire where her subscribers hung on her every word, but in the forty-eight hours or so she'd been here, she'd turned into a wimp of a walkover. Three times she'd meant to tell Gwen there'd been a cock-up, she hadn't come for the job and she had been happy to help but enough was enough. Trouble was, Ceri had got dead drunk Saturday night when Gwen and Gwil hosted a lock-in. She could barely talk, let alone talk sense. Yesterday, she'd intended to pop over to speak to them but a head like a bag of spanners had put a stop to that. Midday it was when she'd got up – *midday*! It had been yonks since she'd done that – and she took her time soaking in a long, hot bath before she made a pasta thing from the welcome pack in the fridge. Cooking on the Aga, well, she'd felt her mother at her side and she'd had a little cry. After that, it was the rest of the day in front of the box, flicking between the Welsh channel S4C, which was oddly hypnotic, an Irish station and the Beeb and ITV. Yet more rugby, then *Countryfile* – a gushing special on the rare and threatened Barbastelle bat, which as far as

Ceri could see were ugly, pug-nosed little blighters. In the end, she hadn't left the house. Or put on her standard lip gloss and got dressed. The thrill of not having to bother looking good 'just in case' she was seen hadn't left her all day. And anyway, it had started hammering it down. Tomorrow, she'd kept thinking, tomorrow she'd come clean and go to the beach on a recce to find a spot where she'd scatter Mum's ashes before she left for home at the end of the week.

But Monday had come and she'd braved the remains of the rain to see Gwen, whom she'd found in a sheer zebra-print dressing gown and lacy nightie, complaining of a headache. Over a cup of tea, Ceri had said, 'Listen, I don't quite know how I ended up working here, but the job, I didn't actually come for it. I'm just visiting and—'

Gwil had interrupted, stooping as he came into the snug. He was away now for the day on brewery business, and was Gwen sure she could cope? Yes, she'd said, putting on her best face until he'd gone – and then breaking down in tears.

'There's a meeting in Cardiff, there is. Lack of long-term viability, they say. Seeking alternative uses for the pub. Curtains, it'll be, if we don't turn it around. We're the heart of the community – if we go, it'll be the end here.'

Ceri should've extended her sympathies and gone. This was nowt to do with her.

But a light bulb went on inside of her and a casino wheel spun in her head. It was that feeling she got when she saw potential – just the same as the early days when she'd come up with a new product, just the same as the later days when she'd had a whole range to launch. The racing pulse of possibilities and the *oomph* of adrenaline that she could make her mark in the world. She couldn't help it: in fact she tried to stop them by digging her nails into her palm, but a defiant barrel-load of questions came to her: how long did they have? What had they tried so far to bring people in? Maybe they could have a go at *x*, *y* and *z*? And, why oh why did her brain ignore the note to self she was on holiday? Gwen saw the flicker of life in Ceri's eyes and she wasted no time.

'Ideas, that's what we need,' Gwen had said. 'Bring some in tonight. You can't cover for me, can you? I can't face the customers like this, can I? Seren's on too, you'll love her, you will. Bit like you, sparky.'

What else could Ceri do but agree? Standing here now, on the cracked step of The Dragon, Ceri considered why she'd felt a spark of fire in her belly. She didn't understand it because she had no proper connection here: was this what Mum had meant about her drive? That she took after her father, who'd started off as a boy flogging sardines and ended up running his own boat and supplying half the restaurants in his Spanish town with fish. *Entrepreneurial* is how she'd put it, and while Ceri had scoffed – wasn't it that she'd got lucky and had been in the right place at the right time? – it was curious how instinctive it was to fix things. Supposed to be on holiday, my arse! And, even after being bamboozled into another shift tonight, with the roar of the waves in her ears and the wind pushing her in the opposite direction, Ceri still couldn't shake off the way she was looking at the grotty cabin opposite, with eyes working out ways to tart it up. It meant she could avoid the beach, too: the sand had shown itself, looking damp and boggy, pocked with raindrops as if it had cellulite, and the petrol sea was whipped with freezing foam. Ceri was going nowhere near it: not yet anyway, and certainly not to enjoy herself. It would be like abandoning her mum if she did.

There was no sign – just that clapped-out wobbly sandwich board with *Caban Cwtch* written on it in a black and white font more suited to a newsagent. Why wasn't the name painted on the bare wall in a cosy and inviting swirly design? No suggestion either what was for sale – apparently it was a café too: a simple chalkboard menu with an image of a steaming hot chocolate with whipped cream would work wonders on a cold day like this. Maybe it was just tired-looking on the outside, she thought as she crossed the lane for a 'quick look', maybe inside it was an Aladdin's cave, a 'best kept secret' which only needed a bit of promotion and placement ...

Or maybe not. Because as she pushed the creaky wooden door, an electric bell buzzed above her head, making her cower, and she peered round it to see total and utter chaos. Trying to get in was a task in itself – something was jamming it on the right-hand side so she had to squeeze through.

Breathing in, she found a wall of cardboard boxes stacked to the ceiling. Beyond, it was hard to see because of the gloom. Half of the shop was on that side and yet you wouldn't wander there for fear of what you might find. Straight ahead was a large wide window which should've been a postcard, framing the priceless sea view. But, criminally, it was obscured by a moth-eaten net curtain and a set of basic metal shelves bursting with a riot of junk.

To put it kindly, it was the seaside version of what you'd

find on a Saturday afternoon in Primark. A shambolic mishmash of stuff with no order, sequence or method. Spades and towels and buckets and windmills and tat – all shrieking in garish colours – were fighting for air among loaves of bread and packets of biscuits and sweets which might well have been there since the turn of the century. To her left lay the café area. And this was the saddest sight of all. Steel diner stools with bits of cardboard lodged beneath uneven feet here and there had the edge over metal circular tables – you'd have been better off parking your bum on one of them and using the seats to set down your cup. And there were no menus, no decorations, not even a coffee machine. Just a kettle, a ripped box of tea bags on the counter beside a stack of newspapers and an old spike with a handful of customer receipts. It was tragic.

What this place could be with a bit of love and a giant buttered teacake and a good old sort-out. Because there was definitely some character lurking, with its charming exposed-brick walls, shiny multi-coloured spotted tablecloths, cool stone slabs on the floor, the radio playing some sort of folk music and a cheery wood burner in the corner. A rustling and banging sounded and Mel emerged from behind the cardboard tower with a tray piled high with something delicious-smelling.

'Hiya, Ceri!' Mel sang, looking very pleased to see her. 'Just in time for my Welshcakes! Homemade, they are.' This was not in doubt, seeing as she had a dusting of flour on both her nose and her red pinny which was emblazoned with the cringeworthy words: 'Every day when I wake up I thank the Lord I'm Welsh'. 'My own recipe, well, my mam's it is, made on her mother's mother's bakestone ...'

She said it as if she was an old maid and yet she was dressed like a teenager with those bunches.

'... back there in the kitchen.'

Ah, so that's what lay behind the boxes. Another feature to add to the list of pros – which Ceri wasn't going to consider. How she wished her stupid noggin would switch off. Like her hands, which had given up checking her phone. They'd accepted that in the dark ages, mobile masts hadn't been invented yet.

'Three flavours today,' Mel said. 'I couldn't decide which ones to make so I did all of them! Traditional with mixed spice and currants, coconut and lime and last but not least my heart-shaped ones with chocolate drops, I call these ones love cakes. You know, after Saint Dwynwen.'

Love cakes? And that saint again? It was further evidence of Mel's eccentricity.

'Still warm, they are. One of each? With a cuppa?'

'Go on.' Why not, she wanted to delay the moment her feet first touched the sand.

'Take a pew and I'll bring them over.'

Ceri perched herself on one of the rickety stools and watched as Mel bustled around the counter, humming to herself, blind to the real work needing doing here.

'Fresh from the *popty*, they are,' Mel said, plonking a plate and mug below her.

That word again – the one Ceri had seen at the garage on her drive here. '*Popty?*'

'The oven, of course,' Mel said, looking at her as if she should know better. 'And I don't mean popty ping either,' she said scathingly.

'Popty ping?' Ceri asked. 'Is it some kind of table tennis spin-off?'

'Popty ping is what non-Welsh speakers think we call the microwave,' she said with irritation. 'It's lies. My cakes have never been near a microwave in their lives.'

'Right, good,' Ceri said, eyeing up a plastic windmill should she need to defend herself if Mel went doolally.

She examined the circle of slate before her, immediately soothed because it was the same colour as Mum's pots and pans. The contents were small and round, about the diameter of the rim of a champagne glass, a sort of bastard child of a scone and a biscuit. But squatter and denser-looking. They didn't look as pretty as they smelled. Put it this way, even if she had any connection, she still wouldn't be posting a photo of them on Instagram.

'I've no idea where I'll store all the stuff. There's no room in here and the cottage is heaving. I'm going to have to do a sale.' Mel looked momentarily glum. No wonder, it would be a hell of a job.

Ceri gave her a look of sympathy as she took a mouthful, preparing herself for it to be dry, grateful there was a brew to wash it down. But she ended up moaning in appreciation at the way it crumbled and melted in her mouth. It was as if it'd been made by Willy Wonka, such was the swing from delicate coconut to sharp lime and back again.

'Bloody gorgeous!' she said, to Mel's delight. The other was a tongue-tingling beauty of cinnamon and juicy raisins and the heart-shaped one, well, it turned her to goo, just like the runny chocolate inside.

'Woman cannot live on Welshcakes alone, though,' Mel said, sighing, holding her arms out in despair at the bundles of stock.

'You just need to get the word out, advertise, go on Facebook and Twitter. Update your website.'

Mel picked at a nail. Ceri understood she would do none of the above because she didn't do any of the above. She had no frigging clue. How did she operate without social media – how had she managed to give the modern world such a swerve?

'Anyway,' she said quietly, 'why would I want to tell the world it's an everything-must-go clearance? Dad is selling up.'

'What?' Ceri said, holding her hand under her chin to stop crumbs spraying everywhere. Jesus, was there nothing here not on the endangered list?

But the klaxon went off again and Mel was all smiles as a woman in her mid-thirties walked through the door, with bum-length wavy light blue hair, in a pair of dungarees which revealed a naked midriff covered in tattoos. Punk had clearly only just reached Wales. Ceri zoned out, knowing they'd start gabbling away in Welsh and she'd just eat up, pay and go back to the cottage and try to read the book she'd started six months ago.

But they were talking in English – and, oh shite, this person was only asking about the new barmaid! Where she could find her ...

Ceri froze and stared into her cup. What if it was someone who knew she wasn't Ceri Rees – how would she explain it? She was supposed to be a brand ambassador for Cheap As Chic – it'd look like she was having a breakdown. What had she got herself into through her own stupid fault? *Calm down, Ceri, you daft a'porth, because no one knows you're here apart from Jade and Tash.* Mel, though, was doing the opposite, looking about to burst as she flapped like a chicken.

'Who wants to know?' Ceri said suspiciously.

'It's Seren, it is!' Mel crowed. 'The other barmaid, the one you're job-sharing with. Seren, this is Ceri. Ceri, this is Seren. At last, you meet!'

Seren clasped her hands to her chest and said, 'My saviour!'

Brilliant. Another crackpot. Just what Ceri needed. It was time to shoot. She got up and put a fiver on the table, which Mel waved away.

'Have it on me,' she said. No wonder this place was in trouble. Ceri left the money there, though.

'I won't take it,' Mel said, reaching over and handing it back with determination. Ceri didn't want a scene so she accepted the note with a thank you.

'Lovely to meet you, Seren. Got to go, a lot on.'

'Yeah, because there's so much to do here, right?' Seren said, poker-faced.

Ceri stopped, unsure of Seren's tone. Was she having a go? Or, holy God damn, she might be the only person in this place who could see Dwynwen needed not just a revamp but bloody electric shock treatment. If so, she was going to snog her.

'Why do you think I dye my hair like this? Cabin fever. Hey, why not change the name to that?'

'Oh, Seren!' Mel tutted. 'You love it really, you do!'

'Er, I'm here because I have to be, Mel.' To Ceri, she explained: 'Stuck here by virtue of a husband and son.'

'But you live in the city!' Mel said.

'She means St Davids, down the road. The world's smallest city. Population of two thousand. Not exactly London. Take my advice, Ceri' – Seren winked with twinkling crystal-blue eyes – 'don't fall for a man here. You'll never leave.'

Ceri gave a big belly laugh because she immediately loved this Seren. Not even because she'd been starved of sane company but because Gwen was right – there was something about her, something a bit magical and creative, as if her head was filled with ideas and inventions.

'There's no fear of that.' No way would she get involved with a man from here – every morning would start off with a weep over the national anthem.

'Not if Saint Dwynwen has her way!' Mel wagged her finger.

That saint was beginning to get right on her nerves. Ceri would have to find out more, if only to prove to herself she wasn't making a rash judgement that Mel was off her rocker.

'Or Logan!' Seren laughed. 'Has he tried it on yet?'

'No!' Ceri said. She'd only spoken to him twice – at the pub and then this morning when he'd knocked with a signed-for delivery from Jade detailing the new 'OMG' Cheap As Chic range which she'd glanced at then chucked on the side for another day. 'Really. I won't be here long. I'm not looking for love, thanks.'

'Oh, we all say that.'

'Well, I like it here,' Mel said defensively and Seren put an arm round her.

'I know. And what would we do without you? Anyway, I've got something for you, Ceri,' she said, rustling around in her chest pocket. 'Because if you hadn't showed up, I would be even more stuck here. But you've halved my hours. Been wanting to do it for ages – my son's highly gifted, they say; nothing to do with me, his father's genes. And he needs ferrying to extra tuition and things, so I can do it now. All I want is for him to see there's life beyond the green, green grass of home. Fulfil his potential, see the big world. And the rest of the time, I can get on with this ...'

She produced a beautiful silver ring, which curled once, twice and signed off with a cluster of ornate flowers.

'My little bit on the side. My jewellery business, called Fork Off. I make things out of old cutlery. Nice for things to be reused and remembered. This piece is from the handle of a teaspoon from the 1940s.'

'Oh, it's gorgeous,' Ceri said, feeling unexpectedly touched by the blend of old and new.

Seren's hand moved towards her. 'Take it, it's yours.'

Ceri stared at her. She didn't get it.

'Oh, no, I couldn't. Thank you, though, it's ... perfect. You made it? Wow. But ... I can't.' She shook her head decisively. This was making Ceri feel awkward and embarrassed.

Seren looked at Mel, confused, and back at Ceri. 'Why not?'

Such a simple question Ceri was battling to answer. *Because it had to mean she wanted a trade-off – a favour. And she'd come here to get away from that.*

'Well, it's just ... it's very nice of you but what can I do for you in return? You know, I won't be around long. I just got sucked in here. This is just a pit stop.'

'You've already done something for me, I told you!'

Ceri was astounded. She hadn't intended to do a good turn or to help someone out. She hadn't been able to say no, that was all.

'I'll pay you for it,' Ceri said. 'I love it. That's what I'll do. Because you can't just give me, a stranger, this when you don't know me or ...'

She winced as she said it – it made her look like some kind of suspicious freak who wasn't familiar with the concept of a no-strings gift. Which was true, actually – people gave her presents for a favour down the line. A crushed look crossed Seren's face: where her eyes had been a blue lagoon on a sunny day, they misted over with hurt.

'Oh, God, listen, I didn't mean to offend you.'

'No, no,' Seren said, covering it up, pulling her hand away.

Ceri felt it then – the moment when she had to either remain closed off or open herself up. Stay as she was, as she had become, protective and cautious. Afraid. Full of grief and self-pity, an orphan now, with a business which was so far from what she'd first created. Or take a chance and trust in a simple act of kindness that could define her future ... It was time to choose. *Kindness, the world needs more of it,* Ceri could hear her mother say. Slowly she reached out and Seren's fingers unfurled. Ceri took the ring, slid it onto the middle finger of her right hand. Instantly, she felt lighter and happier as a glow spread around her body. And as she thanked Seren from the bottom of her heart, she vowed to herself that somehow she was going to repay this gesture a thousandfold.

8

Oh, God. Oh God, oh God, oh God. Rhodri's mouth froze mid-chew on his sandwich as he saw someone that looked very much like her. Squinting from his promotional stand in St Davids city centre, he sized up the person heading his way in a tugged-down cream bobble hat and huge dark sunglasses. Slightly unnecessary, seeing as it was a dismally dull day. But … *Shit*! It was Ceri Rees. He was in no doubt – he recognised the mathematical perfection of her nose with its one-hundred-and-six-degree nasal tip rotation. He'd been taken with its economic no-waste beauty from the morning she'd cracked the YMCA joke.

Two immediate concerns presented themselves: first, he was eating a dirty BLT on *#meatfreelunch* day because it was the only cure known to man for a home-brew hangover. He had to get rid of it before he had a word with her. Because when he was informing those like her who were unfamiliar with recycling parameters, they would look for anything to discredit him as a weirdy beardy eco-warrior. And second, he needed to hold it together because his body and mind had ignored instructions not to take a liking to anyone who was not around permanently. He'd tried a long-distance relationship before and Ruth, *oh Ruth*, the one he'd thought was The One, had ended it because she didn't want to relocate from London to Wales.

But not even the memory of that could stop his cheeks reddening. Attending to the first matter, he threw his bap into the bin – apologising under his breath for not saving it for his compost caddy – and ran his tongue around his mouth in case of lettuce in his front teeth. As for the second, he unzipped his council fleece and took off his beanie hat so he would cool down. Relax, he told himself, because Ceri is a) not your type, too polished, b) out of your league and c) as likely to remain in Dwynwen for as long as an ice cube in a soup bowl of Welsh cawl. He braced himself because she'd spotted him and she was walking over, smiling, carrying a bag. A plastic one. He'd give her one of the council's branded hemp bags for life to soften the blow. If only he was off-duty, then he wouldn't have been compelled to give her his helpful advice. Oh, who was he kidding? Of course he would've done. The environment was for life, not just for forty-three-point-six hours of his working week.

'Ceri!' he said, rocking on his heels like a bloody estate agent. Close up, he could see what Mel meant about her looking Spanish: gorgeous, she was, with that dusky complexion and long black hair. *I bet she smells of lemons.*

'Hi! Rhodri, isn't it?' she said, clearly not sure, which made him feel utterly foolish for having gone to the trouble of 'casually' finding out about her.

'Yes! Yes, it is …' *Sounded a bit desperate there, butty.* 'So … how are you enjoying life in Dwynwen and the surrounding area?' And now he was a sad dad. *Kill me now and bury me in a biodegradable cardboard coffin.*

'Yeah ... good,' she said cautiously, then bolder, 'Dead good actually.'

He was usually quite decent at spotting if someone genuinely meant something – that was because more often than not they didn't. And fair dos, she came across naturally enough.

'A nice change from ... the usual,' she said vaguely. 'You working?'

He was tempted to make a joke that no, he liked to spend his free time in reflective waterproof trousers, getting laughed at by the public. But actually, he *did* spend his free time in reflective waterproof trousers getting laughed at by the public.

'Yes. It's one of my outreach days, when I come out into the community to inform them about recycling. As the sign says there.' He indicated, pointing to the sign saying exactly what he'd said. Oh fuck this, he was just going to be sarky. 'And as you can see, I'm snowed under with altruistic citizens who are desperate to preserve the blessings bestowed on this most glorious of nations.'

Pleasingly, he'd made her laugh. A throaty one. That, *for God's sake*, *man*, made him excited. Fortunately, the stirring was brief thanks to an elderly lady shuffling up to ask if he was giving away anything for free. He saw her off with a pencil made from local timber.

'See? They're recycling crazy,' he said once she'd gone. 'Can I interest you in a bag, too?'

'Sorry, hands full and, to be honest, I'm not one of those "save the whales" types.'

How immensely disappointing. But all for the better for quashing his romantic aspirations, he supposed.

'Can I ask you something,' she said suddenly. 'Why

are people wearing leeks on their coats? And I just saw a load of kids in the most ridiculous outfits. Boys dressed as chimneysweeps and girls in shawls and big, tall bonnets.'

Dear oh dear, she might have a Welsh mother – according to Mel and Gwen – but she was as ignorant as … well, the English.

'Today is March the first,' he said wearily. 'It's St David's Day, when children wear national dress, and you're in St Davids, which is the final resting place of Saint David. And over there,' he said, pointing at the cathedral in the distance, 'is one of Christendom's most sacred shrines. A popular place of pilgrimage ever since the Middle Ages. Because of St David.'

'Right. Got you.' She looked as if she was holding back a smirk.

'And the boys aren't doing Dick Van Dyke in *Mary Poppins*. They're miners. We're quite famous for coal. Or at least we were.'

'Quite the educator, aren't you?' she said, releasing the smirk. You could really go off someone. 'While you're at it, you may as well fill me in about this other saint everyone bangs on about.'

'This other saint,' he said pithily, 'is Saint Dwynwen, Wales's patron saint of lovers. She was the prettiest of King Brychan's twenty-four daughters—'

'Twenty-four? What a goer he was!'

'The legend goes,' he said, ignoring her comment, 'she fell in love with a man her father wouldn't let her marry. She prayed to God to ask for help to forget him and an angel gave her a potion to erase her memory. Afterwards, she devoted her life to God in thanks. She set up a convent off the coast of Anglesey. The remains are still there. Beautiful, isn't it?' he sighed.

It was clear, though, she wasn't as affected as him.

'But Anglesey's up north! What's the connection with the village?' She sounded exasperated, as if it wasn't neat and tidy enough for her.

'She passed through on her way, she was from South Wales.'

'Hmm. It all sounds a bit ... tenuous to me. Like calling, I dunno, Crewe, for example, *Bruce* because Mr Springsteen once got a train there.'

He bit his tongue. She clearly had no soul. Rhodri felt the final spark of interest in her go out. It meant his nerves disappeared and he was able to seize the moment.

'I'm glad I saw you, actually, because in accordance with the local authority waste management and recycling initiative 2016, which targets individuals who do not adhere to recycling objectives, such as yourself, I am inviting you to attend an awareness course next week. The very first of its kind in the United Kingdom.'

'Mel said you were funny.' She spoke with an edge, which irked him.

'I'm serious.'

'You flaming what?'

She took off her sunglasses and his heart skipped a beat when he saw her eyes – they were the same colour as his favourite Fair Trade chocolate. Burnt Toffee by Green and Black's. But he wasn't going to be thrown by appearances, no way. What counted was underneath. Values. Environmental ones.

'I checked your orange bag this morning and you'd put a glass Dolmio container inside it rather than in the appropriate green box. And you hadn't flattened your loo rolls for space-saving.'

Ceri gasped. 'You've been snooping in my rubbish?' There was no need to make it sound like that.

'Not snooping, no!' he said, horrified at the suggestion, 'Supervising your waste management.'

'Are you taking the piss? Because it sounds like you are. You're flipping off the scale.'

Abuse. Just as he'd expected. In his experience it was best to let them vent until they'd run out of steam.

She obliged, furious. 'You're lucky I even remembered to do it! I trust you're aware the international market for recyclable commodities has taken a nosedive? And what's so "green" about sending our cans and plastic abroad, millions of miles away, on a belching ship?'

So this one thought she knew better.

'Do ye the little things in life,' he said, feeling riled. 'Saint David, those were his last words. We can't all do great things but we can do small things well. Look, I'm just trying to do my bit for our little corner of the planet. Harmful chemicals and greenhouse gases are released from rubbish in landfill sites. If we recycle, we protect the rainforests because we don't need so many raw materials. And we don't use as much energy.'

'Thanks for the lecture,' she smarted.

'I just care. A lot. And ... these courses, they're my initiative. If I can make them work they could be rolled out across the country.'

'Oh, self-interest is it?' Ceri said, lifting an eyebrow.

'No! No! Well, kind of. But not for my own gain. For the environment's.' He really meant it. He wasn't after recognition. Although how nice would it be to be the first back-to-back Waste Management and Recycling Officer of the Year?

Ceri let out a groan. Was this the moment she would agree, and become the fourth offender on his course who would see the error of their ways?

'Do I have to come? Or can I pay a fine instead?'

Money. He hated the stuff. It created arrogance and excuses. Why did people think they could throw it at their problems?

'We don't issue fines. We don't have the legislation in place and I think—'

'They'd backfire?'

She got it! He was delighted. On a professional basis. Not on an emotional one. He was definitely not thinking they were on the same mental wavelength.

'Yes, absolutely. We'd rather encourage people to re-cycle through education than criminalise them. And by the way, even if we did do fixed penalties, I wouldn't take your wages off you. You've only just started at the pub! So ... will you come?'

She was silent now. And shaking her head, biting her lip and her eyes were moistening. *Oh no*, he'd only gone and upset her.

'You okay, Ceri? I'm sorry, I didn't mean to ...'

She looked at her feet and back up at him.

'It's nothing. I'm fine.'

Then she burst into proper tears. 'I wanted to do good here too.'

She said it to herself, not him and he wondered what she meant. He couldn't ask so he searched for something else to say – a bit of empathy usually helped.

'I know what you mean. You were there on Saturday,

when no one bothered with my Village of Love idea. They think I'm an interfering arsehole who has nothing better to do than irritate them from my soapbox.'

'They're right,' she said cheekily. 'But I don't want to make any trouble. So ...'

'You'll come?'

'If I have to.'

'Brilliant! Oh, I'm chuffed to bits. Honestly, it's not an awful all-day thing. Just two hours of your time. Refreshments included. It'll be fun. There's a quiz too!'

She didn't look convinced. In fact, if anything she looked even worse. He started fussing round her, apologising but promising her it would be worth it.

'I'm not crying over this,' she sniffed. 'It's something else. It comes in waves. My mum, she's only recently passed.'

Now he felt a thundertwat and presented her with a hankie, which she refused.

'It's the grief. And the confusion. How I've found myself here. She was from the area. I'm just overwhelmed. Like, I brought my phone with me to catch up on anything I might've missed.'

'No reception in Dwynwen,' they both said at the same time. Which he ignored, or tried to, because he didn't want to read anything into their great minds thinking alike. It would feel like he was taking advantage of this poor damsel.

'And I knew there'd be a few things. But I had four hundred emails, seventy-seven missed calls, twenty-four Facebook and WhatsApp messages and a thousand texts.'

'What? I don't even get that many in a year.'

'Stuff at home and ... a few things I'm working on.'

She seemed reticent now. Like she wished she hadn't said anything. But she gave him a defeated look as if she might as well just explain herself.

'I'm so confused. Home, it feels so far away.'

'Where is home, if you don't mind me asking? Mel mentioned a Welsh border town.'

'No. Near Manchester,' she said.

'In a town called Bruce?' he asked, guessing that's why she'd brought up Crewe as an example.

'Yes.' She gave a wry smile.

So she was English, he should've guessed. He felt the familiar disappointment of being let down.

Her despondency returned. 'But it hasn't felt like home for a while, either. I came here, thinking, maybe it'd be a way of getting closer to my mum. But she never did the Welsh thing, like you all do.' Ceri gave him an apologetic glance. 'She didn't speak the language or even have an accent. It feels so strange here. Like, how can I explain? My dad, he was Spanish, and I've been a few times, mostly Ibiza and Fuerteventura, and I understood the paella and sunshine and castanets. Yet Wales, it's got hardly any vowels and your religion is rugby and where the hell are the department stores?'

'Precisely why I love it.'

'It's just so ... foreign.'

'But we've made you welcome?' he said, thinking that was the main thing.

'Oh, yes, absolutely. Too much, actually! Look, Seren gave me this ring just for helping her out.'

He shrugged. 'It's what we do.'

'I know and it's lovely. But it's quite ... overpowering.' She looked teary again and he felt very sad for her.

He couldn't imagine not belonging somewhere or feeling confused by a helping hand. He didn't know what came over him but he hugged her. Quite incomprehensibly. He never did things like that. It felt very nice to have her tucked in under his chin.

Once she'd pulled away – probably after two seconds but it had felt like hours, so long it had been since he'd touched a woman – she gave him a brave expression. 'Thanks, Rhodri, I really needed a cuddle. Or a *cwtch*, as Mel taught me.'

He was impressed she'd tried some Welsh.

'Absolutely my pleasure. Anytime,' he said, then realising he might've sounded like a pervert: 'Not anytime, obviously. But you know, if you're lonely. I get lonely too. *Oh God ...*'

He covered his face with both hands but when he peeked through his fingers he saw she hadn't run a mile. Extraordinarily.

'Don't worry,' she laughed. 'You've helped me. Made my mind up about something.'

'Oh, great. I think?'

She didn't expand, even though he was all ears. *Shit, his ears.* They were sticking out. He could feel spots of rain on them at the same time as he heard the jeers of his brothers. He should've kept his hat on.

'Right, well, I'd better get on. I've a load of shopping to do.'

'I'll let you know about the course,' he said, adjusting his hair to cover up his jugs as she turned to go.

'You do that,' she said, her shades back on, the barrier back up. 'And don't give up on the Village of Love, eh, if it matters to you.'

Mel was right – she was an enigma. He watched her bobble hat until she was swallowed up by the crowd. And Rhodri cursed himself. Because how could he be fascinated by an English ignoramus who didn't even know about St David's Day, let alone who pooh-poohed recycling?

9

'Gwil ... I think I heard something ... Gwil! Wake up!'
'Oh dear God, Gwen, can't a man sleep?'
'Outside! There's rustling. There ... did you hear that?'
'No.'
'What if we're murdered in our own beds?'
'Then a man might get a night's rest.'
'Suit yourself, it's your fault if we're robbed blind.'
'Robbed? We're not in Merthyr any more. And what would they take? A box of smoky bacon and your Royal Wedding tea towel?'

🌿

This morning was all about her feet. Taking off her pink iced-doughnut bedsocks with her big toes. Pointing her size fours into a pair of smoky tattoo tights adorned with Hello Sailor girls and anchors. Stepping into her polar-bear-paw slippers until she was ready to leave for work in her tan-and-turquoise cowboy boots. Looking down, not wanting to look anything in the eye.

This was how it went when Melyn could see the anniversary of Al's death on the horizon. That day, nine years ago, when he'd come to see her in Cardiff where she was at art college and they'd gone for cheesy chips in the arcade and he'd told her he had a surprise. He'd held up some keys and said he was joining her in the big city: he'd got a job here at last and ... and ... he'd wanted to tell her something else. The firework display of happiness, in all the brightest colours, should've been the start of it. Her adult life. But it had all gone monochrome.

The counsellor said that grief was a long process and while you never got over it, you learned to accept it; get used to it, adapt. And she had, kind of, getting on with things here. But not all the time. Like now, when she was in full stare-at-the-floor mode. Lifting her head to see her surroundings only reminded her of the mess she was in. Better to keep her eyes down and the curtains closed and wait for it to pass.

Her feet were shuffling reluctantly now as they approached the front door. How tempting it was to go back to bed. But she wouldn't be so selfish as to deny the villagers their papers and milk and bread. So her hand felt for the latch and she saw her right boot step forward ... as a honeyed light seeped in through the crack and spread up her legs and body. It was a pure and unadulterated brightness, like Al's kiss had been, blinding in that moment. And despite herself, she let it all in, shutting her eyes as she lifted her face, seeing white spots on her inner eyelids, feeling the warmth of almost spring. The promise of the season starting, the bustle of customers in the shop ... that feeling from times past, it was there in the sky now as she finally allowed herself to look up. And, oh! What a sky it was!

Blue, blue, through and through. Not quite blueberry, which was too concentrated. Not as light as the colour of water in a swimming pool, though, either. Sapphire, it was, and not a cloud up there to dilute its wonder. Why was it people said they 'felt blue' when they were sad? It was such an uplifting shade! She tried to work out what colour she'd call her sadness. Brown? Because there were plenty of horrible things which were brown, it was scatological and dated, Seventies and ... but she couldn't see brown as sad when it was also chocolate and leather and rich, warm earthy soil. No, more appropriately, people should maybe say they felt grey. Never blue, though. Blue always made her feel closer to happiness. And at half past seven, there would be nobody at Caban Cwtch yet so she could dawdle down the hill and pretend this vista was all hers to enjoy. The stillness too, hardly any wind. Cold but only just. It was almost as if life was good again ...

Which only reminded her of the uncertainty of her future. It weighed heavily on her once more – what would happen to the shop, to the woods, to Dwynwen? – and her vision was dragged down again. Stones scattering and scratching as she walked, her ears filled with sound, serrated and filthy. Like a saw in her head, it felt, as she approached the left turn which took her to the beach. The quicker she got to the shop, the sooner she could put on the radio, switch on the kettle, slam the papers on the counter and clatter the frying pan for bacon. *That's it, busy your mind*, Mel told herself as she swung into the lane, but hang on ... what the fudge was this?

She stopped dead. There were hundreds of love hearts suspended in the air! As red as phone boxes and strawberries, peppers and roses! Hanging in swags of cheery bunting, fluttering in the breeze, between the posts and railings on both sides of the lane, as far as she could see. Past the pub – *and on the pub!* – and yes, even on

Caban Cwtch! It was the most charming thing and look! the love hearts and red trim of tape were made of shiny cotton-coated PVC, like her wipe-clean tablecloths in the café. She was tickled to realise whoever had done this had made sure the bunting was waterproof. It was such good thinking!

Whoever *had* done it? And when? Because it hadn't been there yesterday – it must have been put up in the dead of night. Mel felt her breath catch because it was such a jaunty sight. Gay was the word; smart, too, and she picked up the pace to see how The Dragon and Caban Cwtch looked close up. Circling round, her head up and whirling as she took in the continuous line of decoration, she felt as if she was on a film set, like it wasn't real. Swooping swathes of hearts were draped on the empty hooks for hanging baskets around the pub door. On the car park gates as well! What would Gwen and Gwil make of it? She'd love it, for sure; so would he, eventually, because first he'd have to inspect how it had been attached, mumbling about damage to their facade, but it had been cleverly looped so he couldn't possibly complain.

As for the shop, well, it was so merry, it reminded Mel of Christmas – and she loved Christmas. So strange how a bit of bunting zig-zagging from old rusting brackets which Dad had put up many moons ago for buckets and spades made it look so inviting. This place was posh enough for the Prince of Wales, she thought, suddenly aware now of her aching, smiling cheeks. She wanted to run around until she was dizzy. But the shop wouldn't open itself, girl!

A few minutes later, the locals started flying in. Mrs Morris from the top cottages glowed with surprise on her daily stop-off after her morning dog walk on the beach for a pint of milk and a *Daily Express*. Cheers Drive, whose real name was Carl but who had been rechristened because he worked for the local bus company, was even more scarlet in the face than normal when he came in for a takeaway fry-up bap and his *Daily Mirror*. And Carys the Chop, who was collecting her chat mags, well, she was beside herself because she'd be first with the gossip on her hairdressing rounds. They'd all asked the same thing: who was behind it? Was it because of Rhodri's speech in the pub after the game on Saturday? In fact, was it him?

She'd ask; but *hang on*, he'd said he wouldn't be in for his usual flapjack this morning because he was starting work very early – there was a conference in Cardiff he was going to with his team and they had a train to catch. Could he have done all of this before he'd gone? It was a big call. But yes, he was a romantic bugger: he spoke like a poet and saw beauty in dandelions.

Here came Gwen, practically doing the cha-cha-cha through the shop; she might know something.

'Was it you?' Gwen panted, reaching Mel at the counter. 'Was it you?'

'Me?' Mel said, all high-pitched, 'Hardly! I was fasto all night. What about you? Are you the queen of hearts?'

But even as she asked, Mel knew she was way off target. Gwen didn't go up ladders – that was Gwil's job and if it had been him, then surely Gwen would have known.

'No! I heard something in the night, though, Gwil said I was hearing things! To think if he'd gone out to look we'd know who it was,' she said, patting her rollers. 'It has to be Rhodri. Even if he didn't do it.'

'What?'

'He *inspired* it is what I mean. It'll have been someone who was in the pub on Saturday, someone who heard him and had a vision. To prove us wrong, because I won't lie, I thought he was talking out of his derrière myself.'

She spread her arms wide and took a breath. *Stick a gold sequin dress on her and she'd be Shirley Bassey*, Mel thought.

'Because those hearts look smashing! Absolutely smashing! Who cares if he did or didn't do it – what he did was plant a seed. And look at the impact it's had already, put smiles on all our faces. I bet you've been busy.'

'Yes, I have. Had lots of people coming for a nose.'

'It's so simple, but effective. It's a bloody marvel. And this . . .' she said, waving an envelope that was in her hand '. . . was waiting for me on the mat this morning.'

As Gwen picked up the pince-nez glasses which hung on a chain round her neck, popped them on the end of her nose and took out a card, Mel saw a crimson heart on the front.

'It says: *Welcome to the Village of Love.*'

'Any signature?'

Gwen gave the card to Mel who saw the words had been inked by individual letter stamps so there was no handwriting to analyse. It made her feel all warm that somebody had taken the time to do this without wanting any credit for it.

'Well, well, well,' Mel said, handing it back.

'Isn't it just!' Gwen echoed. 'It's a sign, it is. That we can fight the development and we can bring back the tourists.'

'To get ourselves back on the map as the Village of Love!'

Then Mel had a thought which sent her into a spin of

excitement. 'We'll be famous, we will! We might even make it on the BBC Wales news! This is like the kiss of life!'

She felt ecstatic and full of hope. It had been a long time since she'd known that feeling. This had come at the right time for her: just when she'd been at her lowest ebb, a rush of love had picked her up. If they could build on this, maybe they could prevent the housing development and it might save her shop too.

'I'd better go and take my rollers out, then!' Gwen cackled. 'See you later. We'll grab Rhodri when he's back and see what he knows.'

'Okay, deffo,' Mel said, drifting off, staring into the steam of the kettle, floating in the cleavage of a love heart. She would make a start on sorting through her stock, clear a bit of space, speak to her suppliers and see if they had any love-heart bits and pieces like key rings and mugs. And what fun she could have if she got some themed napkins and a couple of moulds for the kitchen – she could serve heart-shaped fried eggs, poached ones too. How beautiful this place would be with some red fairy lights! Even a mural ... if only she had the courage to pick up a paintbrush. As thrilling as the idea was, Mel didn't know if she had it in her to do it.

But there was one thing she was certain of, and she could feel it bursting within her: if her heart couldn't beat for any man ever again, it could beat for Dwynwen.

10

'**B**ut you can't go, Ceri, you can't!' Gwen said, stabbing the bar with a finger. 'All those ideas you had. A new menu. Fresh fish Friday, quiz night ... you can't just come up with some fabulous ideas then not do them.'

'You don't need me to do it,' Ceri sighed, adding lemonade to make a lager top. 'I told you, I never meant to get the job. It happened by mistake. I was only here for a holiday.'

'But Seren's off next week.' Gwen was eyeballing her now, looking desperate. Surely they could cope, she and Gwil? Three farmers and a dog didn't need that much looking after.

'You could go behind the bar yourself ...' Ceri tried. You know, what with her being a landlady.

'Don't be rid-ick-a-lus. There's the bookkeeping ...' *How long can it take to add up six pints and a can of Fanta?*

'... I've got a food hygiene course ...' *What? In Preparing Anything That Isn't Lamb or Chicken Curry?*

'I've responsibilities at home,' Ceri added firmly.

'But you're a breath of fresh air, you are. Don't leave us. Tell her, Rhodri, tell her not to go.'

'Go where?' he said, pulling up a stool. 'Pint of Reverend James, please.'

113

'She's only handed in her notice.'

A look of something crossed Rhodri's face. Ceri had seen it in folk before. She had a think – it was the look of a dog who'd been told his walk had been cancelled: disappointed but powerless to do anything about it.

'And you're surprised, Gwen? That's what people do. They come and they go.' He shrugged.

'Seren!' Gwen yelled her name as she came in to take over from Ceri. 'Stop her going!'

'I'll do nothing of the sort. Run, Ceri, run for the hills and don't stop until you find a twenty-four-hour supermarket, a hairdresser who can do more than a perm and a non-instant coffee.'

Ceri high-fived Seren as they swapped places.

'Have a drink,' Seren said. 'It can be your leaving do. And look, Rhodri's even out of his leave-nothing-to-the-imagination Lycra for the occasion.'

'Sometimes I do wear normal clothes, you know. If only to stop you ladies treating me like a piece of meat.'

Ceri couldn't help but laugh, especially as he delivered the comment with a moustache of foamy booze. He seemed to be easy company, able to take the piss out of himself, melting into the circle here without need for a fanfare but holding his own, comfortable in his own skin. He was, admittedly, easy on the eye, too. A red checked shirt done up to the top accentuated his broad shoulders, which weren't shoulders now she came to think of it but man shelves. And he was even in tight jeans – *blimey*, geek chic had made it to Wales, then. Big strong thighs tapered down to cyclist's calves and blue Converse.

'Glass of wine then, please, white, dry,' Ceri said, sitting beside him, getting a whiff of the old Brut. Maybe he was on his way to a date? She'd seen it enough in her days as a barmaid, fellas coming in for a bit of Dutch courage beforehand. Seren clocked it too.

'Meeting anyone, Rhod?' she said, wiping the wood down, not letting him see what would definitely be playful eyes.

'Obviously! Mel, of course.'

Ceri was surprised to feel something – not jealousy or envy or anything bad. It was a warmth from knowing he was good boyfriend material. If you were into that sort of wholesome thing. It didn't surprise her that they were a couple – they seemed very close, as if they'd been together for years.

'I know I always say this but I've never worked out why you two aren't together,' Seren said.

Oh! They weren't! Her heart skipped a fraction – there was no harm in window shopping.

'Yeah. But we're just friends. Like brother and sister.'

He took another drink, completely unperturbed. *All credit to him for not doing a shifty squirm there*; most blokes under pressure would've found something offensive to say about the woman in question to bail themselves out. He could've easily pointed out she was cuckoo, for starters.

'I'd drive her up the wall with the way I reuse everything! And I'd bore her to tears.'

Bless him, he was self-deprecating and self-aware too. Seriously, Dwynwen could make poster boys out of him and Logan: two eligible bachelors within a spit of each other would have the hordes here in a minute.

'We're meeting to talk about the Village of Love. What we can do next. You're all very welcome to chip in.'

'You sure it's not you, Rhodri? Behind the bunting?' Gwen asked, with narrowed eyes.

He'd been suspect number one since the village had woken up to the love hearts, which had really perked the place up: Dwynwen was understandably fixated on the whodunnit. During her shifts, Ceri had had to stop herself guffawing at Gwen and Gwil's good-cop, bad-cop cross-examination routine on anyone who'd stepped over the threshold. One poor fella, who used a walking stick, had even been asked if he had an alibi!

'I've told you a thousand times. No!' he said, with good-natured exasperation.

'I don't believe you,' Gwen said, as if she was cranking up the heat on her interrogation.

'I wish it had been, because it's genius! Don't you worry, someone will come forward – it's human nature to want to claim the glory, eh? Anyway,' he said, turning to Ceri, 'what's this about you going?'

Their company felt so natural, she had the urge to let it all out – to tell them who she actually was. But she didn't know these people really: she was in a false lull, that was all.

'I've got a business back home. I need to get back. I was only here for a break.'

'Ooh, what kind of business?' Seren said, leaning in.

'It's in the beauty industry,' she said.

'Like a beauty therapist?' Seren asked.

'Kind of.' She felt bad glossing over the details, but she was enjoying the freedom these last few days had given her: no being stopped for selfies and no #makeup updates on her social media accounts. 'I came here to scatter my mum's ashes. She was from this area, it's what she wanted.'

'And I thought it was man trouble! You know, woman turns up alone for some space ...'

'No. No man to blame.'

Ceri hadn't considered relationships in a long time. She and Dave had parted ways after seven years together because they'd wanted different things. It hadn't started out like that. They'd met at the club when she was twenty-two, same age as him; he was one of the regulars, and he wasn't laddish like the others. Quieter, considerate, nice manners. She'd fallen comfortably in love with a man who wanted nothing more than what they already had. *Great expectations*, he'd say, *caused bother*. They'd never moved in together like couples they knew: both of them shared the desire to do it properly. Tash had flown the nest when she was twenty-one, seven months after meeting Kev. Ceri suspected she wanted to play house to erase the memory of having a disappointment for a father. Prove to herself not every man was feckless – luckily Kev was up to the task. Ceri, though, didn't think the same way. She'd been born out of love, and she didn't feel the need to rush. But then Mum fell ill.

Dave was great about that – he understood Mum needed her. And he didn't see why they had to go out if Ceri wasn't working. He knew she'd wanted to stop in to look after her mum. So he'd bring some of his mother's shepherd's pie for the three of them, or sometimes he'd turn up with a box set of Mum's favourite TV shows, like *Dallas* and *Dynasty*, and they'd be happy as Larry. He liked her idea of relaxation, too – her hobby meant he knew where she'd be: in the kitchen rather than out at the gym, eyeing up blokes. But things changed when she started vlogging DIY make-up tutorials under the name Cheap As Chic. *Talking to yourself again, are you?* he'd say, not realising her audience was growing all the time. Dave viewed it with suspicion: it wasn't the real world. But that was why Ceri loved it: talking shades of this and spoonfuls of that, unimportant stuff that made her and her followers happy.

He'd get the hump when she was busy editing her videos – because it took an age to get the technicals right. *She was obsessed*, he'd fume. She put it down to him wanting attention – so she suggested she did a men's range and he could be her guinea pig: how about beeswax for a more matte finish on his perma-gelled blond spikes? Or a gentler moisturiser rather than his tears-to-the-eyes astringent after-shave? With blue eyes bulging, he'd told her in the frankest terms he was all man, ta very much. And that's when he'd floated the idea she was beginning to act above her station. By then she'd started making a bit from advertising on her site and she'd offer to get the chips on a Friday. He'd almost conked out at the suggestion. Their differences were beginning to show: they might have had the same values, but they didn't have the same ambition, which was a dirty word where she grew up.

Maybe she should've reined it in but by then it had become both her passion and her escape from caring for Mum. And why did she have to choose between Dave and her hobby? Which was fast becoming a little source of income, thanks to her chirpy videos, makeovers of Jade and trialling samples which company PRs had started to send her. Not enough of an income to jack in the job.

That would come. Followed by Dave having had enough and walking away. The night when he'd said it was over, she'd told him she could see a time coming when she could support them both and he could cut his hours. She might as well have cut off his balls. He was the one who did the providing.

She poured her heartache into Cheap As Chic and she found herself quite a following on YouTube, which led to sponsorship and endorsements and all the trappings a girl from Crewe would die for. She'd be a fool to turn anything down, Jade would say, and it felt sweet that her BTEC in business had actually come in handy. No one before then had ever assumed she'd be up to much. She didn't blame them – she hadn't had any faith in herself either. That was what years of being a barmaid did to you. Making money had been a thrill – she wasn't going to complain about those noughts in the bank – but she found it was the achievement that mattered more. Self-belief, she treasured most of all. And it got her through the downside of her good fortune: the loneliness and the piss-takers who never picked up the bill, particularly if they were her date for the night. Love wasn't for her, not at the moment.

'There is no man,' she repeated firmly.

'What about your mam then?' Gwen said. 'We might know her!'

She'd love to find out more but Mum had left years ago, way before any of this lot were either alive or living here.

'I doubt it. She left in the Seventies.'

'So what's taking you back?' Seren asked. 'Why do you have to go?'

It was a good question. What did she have to go back for? No man, no kids, not even family, really. She didn't want to go back to Crewe to see Tash celebrating a viewing or an offer on her childhood home. Nor to Alderley Edge, where it was all about what you looked like and what you were wearing. She had got used to her wellies now, and there was no point trying to flatten out the curls in her hair with all the salt in the air and the rain. And her skin, well, it felt much better without all the make-up she usually wore. Which was basically a betrayal of her own business. How about friends? Only Jade to speak of. But they'd known each other since the workingmen's club and their bond wouldn't be broken by an extra week away.

It would only be for the business. Trouble was, there were meetings lined up and new products to sign off; she needed to see her accountant, too, and how long did she have before her absence made people ask questions? But Jade had said it was all going swimmingly. She had her laptop with her if anything urgent came up – there had to be a café with wifi somewhere around here. The bottom line was that Ceri didn't feel prepared to return to the world she lived in – she still felt worn out emotionally. She'd sort of enjoyed herself in Dwynwen and she was feeling the benefits. As if her creases of stress were being smoothed by the waves, the slower less complicated pace of living and the benevolence of the villagers. As if her mother's hand was on her brow, her cooling palm soothing her forehead, as she did when Ceri was small. Her shoulders were no longer knotted and her frown had melted away. Yet the rational voice inside her head told her it was entirely loony to stay in the back of beyond. Perhaps that's why she liked it here ...

'It's hard, there's stuff at home ...' she said, a bit dashed her heart had surrendered so readily to her head. 'You know, life.'

But Gwen had sensed her hesitation and went for it.

'Can it wait another week? Stay here, help us out, can you? Weather is supposed to be lifting, it is.'

A ceremony for Mum without waterproofs – it was an enticing prospect and not just climate-related. Because she wanted to hold on to Mum for as long as she could – the beach wasn't going anywhere and Ceri was no way near going on the beach. Rhodri jumped in.

'And I know you could easily leg it and my course isn't compulsory but—'

Shit! The course! She'd forgotten it.

'... if you stay you could come along.' He was begging with his big baby browns which did make her swoon a bit.

'I can't stay just because of that!' she laughed.

'You would if you knew the others who were due to attend have wised up to the fact they can get out of it. They've postponed with various flimsy excuses. You're the only one coming. I'm going to look a right Billy No Recycling Offender Mates to my boss if she asks ... This can't fail before it's even begun.'

It was the silliest reason but somehow he won her over. Or, more likely, it proved she hadn't the strength to say no, which meant she hadn't the strength to go back to work. And hadn't she said she'd do good while she was here? Immediately, she got up and put on her coat.

'Right, well I'd better speak to Mel to see if the cottage is free.'

'Marvellous news!' Gwen crowed as Rhodri held up his pint to her.

'Mel should be back by now,' he said. 'She's been at her mam's. Tell her we're waiting for her if she's not in her onesie already. And you, of course.'

It was nice of him to include her.

She nodded. Seren, though, was tutting.

'Watch out, you'll become one of us,' Ceri heard her say as she left the pub and it made her chuckle all the way to Mel's door. So much for handing in her bloody notice.

Ceri knocked and waited, still full of smiles, hoping now she could stick around for a bit. It might be a good night down the pub and she was intrigued to know what Rhodri and Mel would come up with for the Village of Love. She stamped her feet: these wellies weren't half as warm as Uggs. She should've listened to the shopkeeper, who had recommended ones made from wetsuit material. But she hadn't known she'd be getting further use out of them – if there wasn't another booking to evict her. *Blimey, Mel was taking her time*. She rapped again and looked up to the balcony to see if there were any lights on. There weren't. Maybe she wasn't home yet. But just then Ceri heard Mel call out 'coming'.

A bit more of a wait. *Come on, lady, it's cold out here.* The door opened a crack and Ceri stepped forward – bumping her forehead, just as Mel had done when she came along to hers on Saturday. *Jesus, maybe Seren was right*, maybe she was turning into one of them … Mel must've had her foot by the door or there was something preventing entry. So Ceri tried again, pushing hard, announcing, 'It's only me.' But she felt the wood resisting. *How odd.*

'Mel?'

Her face popped out, but only her face.

'Did I catch you in the bath?'

But she saw her red eyes and a raw nose showing the signs of having been blown after a cry.

'Oh, Mel, are you all right?'

'Yep.' It was a clipped squeak. Not like her at all.

'You sure you're okay?'

'Yep.' The same noise. And she was in complete darkness. What was going on?

'Everyone's waiting in the pub to see you.'

'I'm a bit tired.' Her voice wobbled.

'Oh, no. Shall I tell them?'

Mel shrugged limply. Ceri needed to keep her talking to see if she could get it out of her.

'Hey, guess what, I'm going to stay another week. If the cottage is free?' That should do it.

'Yep.' Mel's hand remained on the doorframe, resolutely barring Ceri's entry.

'I'll pay tomorrow. Okay?'

'Fine.'

'Rhodri wants to talk about the Village of Love, what you can do next.' She said it softly, trying to coax her out, she didn't want to scare her off.

But Mel put her hand over her eyes, as if she was a child. She was supposed to be ... how old? Ceri didn't know.

'I'm not in the mood. All right?' she lashed out. But it barely registered with Ceri.

'If that's supposed to put me off, let me tell you I've had a lot worse from my sister! I'm not leaving you like this.'

Ceri waited, and slowly Mel stepped back. Ceri gently touched the door until it began to creak open. And, oh, Mel was staring at her, looking broken.

'You poor thing, what's happened? Let's turn the light on,' she said, groping for the switch, 'and have a cup of—'

Ceri swallowed the words. Gagged on them because the place was an absolute wreck. *What the hell had happened?* Had there been a break-in? But taking it in, things seemed to be ordered in a crazy kind of way. There was barely a sight of wall or floor, just stuff in piles, stacked high, in some parts almost reaching the ceiling. A dresser, hardly visible behind flyers and envelopes and notebooks. By their feet, bags, bulging bags, full of who knew what, layered with jackets and scarves and no wonder because there was no room left on the coat hooks, if that's what was behind the hodgepodge hanging off them. Beyond, past Mel, there should've been a corridor but it was a narrow tunnel to the stairs and well over half of each step was littered too, leaving only just enough room to climb up. There was a smell, too. She felt awful for noticing it; a musty scent, where the air had gone stale.

Ceri struggled to take it all in: it was as if her brain was incapable of understanding how someone so merry on the outside could be so tortured within. The cabin had been bad enough. She'd taken Mel at her word the shambles there was down to the delivery and space issues. Now, she could see they had nothing to do with it. It was an extension of whatever was going on in her home and in her head. This ... Ceri didn't want to admit it, but ... it was like something off one of those TV shows about hoarders.

Dear God, had no one been here recently to see what a state she was in? Maybe they were used to it, used to her being 'messy Mel'. Or she didn't let anyone in. It couldn't be she'd been let down by her friends – they seemed a solid bunch. It had to be she tried to hide it. Folk couldn't be helped if they didn't want to help themselves. And Mel, well, right now she was a shadow of her normal self. Dressed in black all over, no sign of any colour in her clothes. As if the light had gone out inside of her.

'Mel, love, come here,' she said, pulling her in for a hug. Resistant, lifeless, she felt like a sack of spuds.

'Whatever it is,' Ceri said, squeezing her tight, 'we'll fix it, all right?'

She wasn't one to make empty promises. And so she was surprised she had. But her gut was adamant.

'I've tried. You can't,' Mel said, strangled, 'I'm trapped. I'm never going to get out.'

'Has something happened at your mum's?'

She gave a nod which as tiny as it was looked like it caused her enormous pain.

Ceri's heart shrank at the size of Mel's anguish before swelling with concern. Because she knew why this was touching her: it was how she had once felt when Mum had been so helpless and dependent. She'd had the same feeling of the walls closing in on her. But she'd been able to get herself out. Mel needed to know you could turn things around, whatever it was troubling her. Ceri's own problems seemed smaller now – at least she'd had the strength to accept she had reached crisis point. But Mel, she was almost paralysed.

'Trust me, kid,' she said to this little scrap in her arms, 'we're going to sort this.' Inside a voice was wondering if an extra week was enough. This might be a longer stay than she thought.

Ceri stroked her hair and began to rock her from side to side, vowing in a whisper, 'I'm only leaving when you can too.'

11

'No lights,' Mel croaked, as Ceri sat her on the sofa and wrapped a heavy blanket around her shaking body. The weight of the woollen throw, shorn from a local flock and hand-woven on a loom, subdued the tremors: it was as if she'd had a reassuring hug from the generations on her father's side who'd sought its comfort. And its black and grey geometric design was muted enough to let her swollen eyes rest.

Ceri nodded at her request: the spread across the lounge was illuminated enough by the moon. A trove of treasures, it was to Mel; others, though, they always saw it as a crime scene. Leaving the bulbs cold would prevent a second explicit shock – Ceri had witnessed the wreckage of the hallway, why would she want to see more? The lacklustre matt of the shadowy room would lessen Mel's trauma at catching Ceri's reaction in technicolour too.

For even though the storm had passed and her tears had gone, even in this barely beating stillness, where she was exposed, drained of emotion, spent and flat, Mel could still taste the bile from registering her visitor's shock and disgust downstairs. And now, as Ceri backed away, looking down at the floor, careful not to disturb anything, frightened of being tainted by touch, Mel knew what was coming next. She'd seen it all before. On Mam's face when her teenage bedroom had been a state. The slurs from her youth – she was lazy, she was irresponsible – had become pleas for her to seek help because how could she live like this, inflicting so much pain not just on herself but on her parents? They loved her deeply and she mirrored their every heartbeat – but they just didn't understand. Mel had no reason to think that Ceri would not condemn her as they did. Yet she couldn't rustle up the energy to prepare for the blows. She couldn't even rustle up the energy to watch Ceri as she heard her slow manoeuvre back towards her.

A steaming mug appeared by her hand. There was no empty space or surface to put it nearby. Mel felt the reflex of relief because her precious possessions hadn't been treated as a glorified coaster to soak up wet rings and spillages. Then a bud of realisation: Ceri hadn't returned with black bin bags and ordered Mel to start clearing up this mess. That was how Mam had dealt with it: her collections were dismissed as 'stuff', as if they were useless. But to Mel, they were the stuff of dreams: a magical elixir which granted the eternal youth of her yesterdays. She took the tea and flinched at the heat, not having expected to feel anymore. They sat in silence for a while, the waves sounding tinny and distant.

'What set this off?' Ceri said eventually, quietly.

Mel was taken aback by the question. Usually she was asked *Why?* and *How?*, questions which made her feel judged. But Ceri's *What?* was different, open and carefully neutral. It made Mel look up, and to her surprise there was no condemnation in Ceri's eyes, only concern. Disarmed, she pushed back stuffed toys, including Roo the frayed elephant from when she was a baby, and old jumpers which smelled of safety, making way for Ceri to join her on the sofa. Why was she seemingly so unperturbed now? Was it because she had had time to collect herself, put on her poker face? Or was this person, a relative stranger, simply blessed with compassion? Wanting to trust that Ceri would listen, Mel began to speak.

'What set this off? You mean tonight, do you? Or ...' *Beyond.*

'Wherever you want to begin,' Ceri said evenly.

A rush of memories flickered in random sequence through her mind. Where was the beginning? Losing Alwyn? Before? Now? She was disoriented – it was all a muddle. But she took a breath and plumped for now because if she got that straight perhaps she could, if she dared, follow her stream of consciousness.

'I was at Mam's, for my tea ...' she said, hesitant, used to concealing her sorrow, knowing it was too much of a burden for her loved ones. But, she reasoned, if she started with the details maybe the rest would unfold. 'My sister, my half-sister, she wasn't there. It was all fine, it was ... Mam had made my favourite, Carmarthen Bay mussels and *crempog*, pancakes, for afters. We were talking and she said she was worried, she was, because Ffion's turned into a chopsy teenager, hiding in her room, slamming doors. Like we all were.'

Ceri gave a little nod in agreement that hormonal schoolgirls were the same the world, or Wales, over.

'Mam asked if I'd talk to her ... see if there was anything going on. Thing is, we might look alike, we both take after Mam with our blonde hair, but we're not close. She wouldn't open up to me. She's a lot younger, stuck

to her phone, she is. I tried to say but Mam kept on ...
and ...' The whip cracked as Mel felt the shame of letting
rip at her mother. '... I snapped. Said she hadn't shown
me the same concern when I was her age ... said she was
scared Ffion would turn out like me.'

'Like you?'

Mel felt herself blooming under Ceri's gaze because
she wasn't presuming anything.

'She'd end up a fuck-up, like me.' Saying it out loud,
hearing what she thought of herself, it was brutal, deliberately so to lash herself. But it was also liberating, getting
it out there. And the words were beginning to flow. 'But
it won't happen, I said. Ffion is a lovely thing actually.
It's just hormones. She hasn't been through what I have
... because I've been such a nuisance. I have been ever
since they split up, her and Dad. Who's not my dad, by
the way. He's as good as, though, but not my biological
father. I've known forever my real one legged it as soon
as Mam was up the duff. Lyn has brought me up.'

Ceri swallowed.

'But that's fine,' Mel said to clarify this wasn't the
issue. 'No, it goes back to when they sold the house. We
lived just outside of Dwynwen, we did ... a chocolate
box cottage with the lushest of grass in the garden, where
I had a swing and Rhodri would come over. Okay, he
was a boy but he was down the road, around here you
couldn't be fussy for playmates.'

Mel smiled but instantly the happy times faded.

'So I went with Mam, no sense going with Dad because
he was away with work fixing the cruise ships. Partly
why their marriage didn't work. Mam needed someone
twenty-four-seven. We went to the next village.' She

pulled a grimace. 'To her new fella Huw's house; he's all right, nice enough, but his place, it was pebble-dashed, like vomit. It hurt my eyes, all that mustard and brown and orange like puked-up carrots. I'd had to go through all my things, sort them into keep or rubbish. Instead I refused to chuck anything. It drove them mad, it was to be a new start. And Mam and Dad, they got on much better. Their sadness had gone. But I held onto my things, wouldn't be parted from them. If I had my lovelies I'd be okay. I'd feel better, I would, and when I did I'd go through them. Chuck them. But ...'

She stretched out an arm and pointed at all of her valuables around her. 'I never got rid of anything. It's all here.'

Ceri ran her eyes over Mel's security blanket of bits and pieces scattered across the surfaces and the shelves and on the floor and on the table. Not gasping, she wasn't. Just observing. 'What is there? It's hard to make out.'

'My smelly rubbers collection from the age of nine ... the superhero comics I made, I was Dolphin Girl, able to breathe underwater, used to see dolphins every day, I did ... special shells and sea glass, loads of that ... flavoured lip glosses ... badges ... candles ... earrings ... posters of works of art ... tickets from bus trips and the cinema ... cuddly bears ... nail polishes ... sweetie wrappers ... bookmarks ... books ...' It was a tapestry of joy. And pain.

'Is it like this all the time or ...?'

She shook her head.

'Most of it was all packed away until this week. I allowed myself a few special things in the trunk, by there. The rest had been in boxes from when I'd been okay.

When I'd left for Cardiff to do art. Mam and me, we'd moved it here to Dad's, into his spare room. I thought it was over.' Ceri handed her a tissue just in case. But the well had run dry inside of Mel. The hollow feeling was there instead.

'But?'

'I've unravelled. It's coming up to ten years since my Alwyn died.' Echoes inside of her now, like a dull thump. 'He was my best friend, who stuck with me through everything, the divorce, when I got bullied ... about my eyes.' *Another problem to add to the list. Why had she brought it up?* She kept it to herself mostly, this bit, because it made her look even more of a freak.

'Your eyes? You don't wear glasses ...'

'No. I've twenty-twenty vision. It's about ... what I can see. Not dead people or ghosts or anything, don't worry.' But she'd started now, she wasn't going to reverse – she already looked deranged, what did she have to lose?

Ceri moved forward slightly, like a mouse moving towards a piece of cheese.

'Lots of colours, millions of them, a whole lot more than other people. Animals have it too – like some fish and birds, they can see ultra-violet light.'

A frown of incomprehension furrowed Ceri's forehead.

'Like, if I go to the shops and see a top and skirt apparently matching, I see they're not the same, they're clashing. Same with make-up, lips and nails.'

Now Ceri got it.

'We didn't know it had a name when I was at school. They said I was a witch. Silly stuff but hurtful when you're fourteen. We know now it's called tetrachromacy. Very rare. A variation in a gene controlling the development of the retina, the doctors have been all over me. I can see hues and shades invisible to most. Things ordinary to you, well, to me they shine like jewels.'

'Wow. I've never heard of it. What a ... gift.'

Mel felt the thrill of having been right to trust Ceri.

'That's what Al said. He was so great and alive and ...' *She was floating up.* 'He wanted to be a musician. He was brilliant, an ear for it, could play anything and everything.' *Higher.* 'So one time he came to visit me in Cardiff and he'd got a job in a record shop and he had some gigs lined up. We'd save up and afterwards when I'd graduated, we'd travel, see the places I see in the sunsets here. We got drunk to celebrate and ... I told him I loved him.' *Soaring.* 'All brave from the drink, knowing I could take it back, couldn't I, but he said it too.' The moment in the city centre bar replayed in her head, fuzzy from the number of times she'd watched it over and over and over. 'Now that was perfect.' *His lips met hers.* 'We only kissed once. I'd waited years. Just one kiss.' *Colours popped like camera flashes.* 'He had to get some money ... I should've insisted I'd pay, I tried to but he wouldn't hear of it.' *The searing.* 'He didn't see the car.' *His body flying, smashing, blood, too many shades, overwhelming her.* 'The life support machine was turned off three weeks later. I came home.' *Down, down, down.* 'And I've never left. Not for a single night.'

The telling of the story never got easier.

Ceri rubbed her face. It was a lot to take in. But her mind was working, Mel could tell. *Please*, she begged inside, *please understand, I'm putting my faith in you.*

'So the things from your childhood ... they were when you were happy, yes?'

Mel gave a minute nod, hoping ...

'They calm you. And it gets worse when you're troubled.' *Oh, glory be*, it was the first time anyone had got it. Everyone else prescribed a deep, savage, no-quibbling cleanse.

'Yes!' Mel said, coming back to life. 'That's why I've been going through them, losing myself in the memories, letting myself drown in them, *wishing* I could drown in them. This, what they call stuff, is loaded with love.'

'But do you feel soothed by this?' Ceri gestured to the room.

When she put it like that, Mel couldn't say she did. It was like seeing her scrambled brain on a piece of toast dropped from a great height. Her chin went down in surrender. 'No. The opposite. I've tried to move on,' she said, pulling at a thread on her lap. 'To love again. Two there've been, but they knew my heart wasn't in it. They weren't Al. I cut myself off from his family too, his sister Betsi who'd become like my own. I always mean to get back in touch but I'm in a prison. Rhodri and Seren, they think I'm over it, or at least not as bad as I am. I don't want to worry them. It's ridiculous, it is. At my age.'

'What is your age, because, you seem so young ...'

'I'm ... thirty.' Embarrassment made her insides simmer.

And this time Ceri did do big eyes. 'Crikey ... I'd have put you at early twenties. You lucky mare.'

'What about you?' Because Ceri seemed so much older but didn't she look it. In the way she carried herself.

'Thirty, next month.'

'Pathetic, I am. But ... I feel stuck at twenty when I lost Al.' She shrugged. 'So ... time to lock me up or what?'

Ceri studied her nails. 'You're not the only one attached to the past.'

'What?' This woman who was so together and confident? But then Mel knew all about a suit of armour.

'It's not just you,' Ceri said, now daring to trust. 'I can't let go either. My mother was from here, you see. This village.'

Mel nodded, Rhodri had told her.

'I was meant to come here for a week. Scatter her ashes on the beach, you know fulfil her dying wish, then bugger off back home,' she said, straightforward. 'But it's been so much harder ...'

Ceri sniffed and covered her mouth for a few seconds to compose herself.

Oh, Mel knew how the waves came without warning.

'She passed away at the beginning of January. She managed a spoon of mashed potato and turkey on Christmas Day and a mouthful of pudding and custard. Dementia. That's what she had. Four years of seeing her fade away. It was heartbreaking. Tash wasn't much cop when it came to caring for her. See, I've got sister trouble too, same thing as you, different fathers. Mine, lovely. Hers, not so much.'

Her confession and their similarities were forming a bond between them, Mel could feel it.

'I don't blame Tash for not doing hands-on caring. I never said a word to her about it. She preferred to get prescriptions and shopping. But Mum left us the house and Tash asked me to agree to sell it. I couldn't say no. It's complicated. But I wanted to hold on to it for a bit. I'd lived there all my life nearly. Tash, though, she's devoted hers to making sure history doesn't repeat itself

– her own family unit was all she wanted. She's got no ties with it. But for me, it was a safety net. Because life has changed for me a bit ...'

'Is that what you meant when you talked about baggage, the day I ... barged in on you?' Mel was seeing how this village, how she, must've looked when Ceri got here. It was easy to forget when you buried your head in the sand.

'Exactly. It was where I learned I could cope. I couldn't leave Mum in the nights to go out, I was skint anyway, so, well, this is silly, but I once had a google at homemade make-up, she loved getting dolled up did Mum, and we had a lot of the ingredients in the cupboards. So, I'd make our own, pretend it was a department store, put her face on for her and it brought her alive – she'd talk about when she was a lass, her friends and all sorts. It got me through it.'

Ceri was back there in her mind, Mel could tell.

'Never mentioned Dwynwen, though, it only came when she was on her last legs. The house, well, it was my coping mechanism. And with it going, if I throw her into the sea, I'll have nothing left.'

Her defences had lowered.

'I don't want to say goodbye.' Ceri swallowed. 'Can you believe I've only made it as far as the gritty sand, you know, the bit at the top which is mixed with stones from the lane. My feet won't move any further. I'm the pathetic one, not you.'

Mel's chest rose with empathy. 'No, you're grieving, nothing makes sense in the early days. But the funny thing is, the beach is where I go to think. Round the rocks to the waterfall. I try to remember it has been here before I came along and will remain after I pop off. It doesn't always work, as you can see ... but there's something about the place ...' It was no good trying to explain, Ceri had to see it. 'Look, let me take you there ... you need to get to know it before you take your mam ... it's not a dead end, it's the start of the rest of the world out there ...'

'The future,' Ceri said, twisting the ring Seren had given her with thought, as if she'd had a revelation. Just as Mel realised it too.

'Yes, the future! We both need one.' Suddenly, everything seemed brighter.

'We can help each other. I've got another week, I can join you, tidy the shop ... and here if you like? Nothing major, small steps.'

'Ceri, I'd love that, I would. Because the Village of Love is something for Dwynwen. The bunting, well, it's the start, you know.'

'Listen, do you want to go to the pub or shall I nip home and get a bottle? Unless you want to turn in?'

'A nightcap would be great,' Mel said, reaching out to touch Ceri's hand. She felt warm and true and as Ceri clutched hers back, Mel understood they were shaking on their pledges to support one another. She'd been wrong to think she was a man's woman – underneath, she was a people person and a beautiful one at that.

'I'll be two minutes.'

And as Ceri disappeared next door but one, Mel felt a long, long way from being left behind.

12

'And so,' Rhodri said, his voice booming as he reached the crescendo of his Powerpoint presentation, 'as you will remember from pie chart seventeen-c, while we are recycling sixty per cent of household waste here in Pembrokeshire, still too much of the rest ends up, unnecessarily, in landfill, creating a blight on our landscape, polluting our air, earth and sea ...'

Just as he'd practised over and over to make sure he would nail it, he paused for maximum effect to let the tragedy sink in. Then, boom, he would let them have it. Or in this instance, let *her* have it because Ceri Rees was the only other person with him, but what did it matter if it was one or one hundred when it came to missionary work?

'... And once our natural wonders are gone, they're gone. For. Ever.'

He dipped his head theatrically: the council's Daffodil Suite – room four, second level – was in semi-darkness for his slideshow which, he believed, only served to add drama to his silhouette. A few seconds of silence to hammer it home and he would soften – for his audience needed not intimidation but warmth if they, she, were to absorb his message.

'So the next time you prepare to throw out that can of pop, that tea bag, that roll of toilet paper, know it has a home: in the correct waste receptacle, as detailed in the hand-out. For that can save enough energy to power a TV for around four hours. Six tea bags produce enough energy to make a cup of tea. And if every household in Wales recycled two toilet-roll tubes it would recoup enough energy to power your local hospital for two weeks. If we all do our bit, we can save the environment.'

He finished with his favourite image, of a Dwynwen sunrise looking out from the rocks onto a pod of frolicking dolphins. He walked to the switch and slowly turned up the dimmer: he was particularly pleased with this bit because it was like a new dawn for his disciples. *Er ... disciple.* With satisfaction surging in his chest, he prepared to bask in the glow of her awakening – because this session had gone well, very well, in fact. Judging by her near-silence throughout, Ceri had clearly been enraptured: she'd even declined a comfort break because she didn't want to stop him mid-flow. Yes, he must have really got her to reconsider her old ways. As his eyes adjusted to the light, he saw she was blinking heavily. Was she emotional, too? Never in his wildest dreams had he imagined he would convert her so quickly ... But, oh, her pulling-herself-together act wasn't from the wake-up call he'd anticipated: it was more of a general waking up and – no! – her jaw was stretched and her cheeks were hollow as she stifled a yawn. Quickly, Ceri opened her eyes wide and plastered on a smile, and, with awkwardness, she gave him a clap. Which, to his ears, was a tad not fast enough to differentiate itself from a slow mocking applause. His face was burning and her hands stopped, hesitating self-consciously before reaching back to adjust her ponytail.

'Was it that bad?' he said, crestfallen.

'No! No! Not at all, it was dead interesting and inform-ative and I liked your diagrams.' Too eager, she was, and she bit her lip.

His shoulders collapsed, then came a mental avalanche of doubt and embarrassment. To think he'd accepted his mother's praise when he'd run through this in front of her last night.

But unexpectedly, Ceri added, 'It was definitely worth staying the extra week for. It was a re-education. And I had your undivided attention. It's made me think.'

Shuffling his papers, he looked up and saw her eyes weren't laughing but sincere, and his dimples began to hurt.

'Really?'

She nodded. Possibly because she'd snort if she made a sound – but he was past caring and he could've *cwtch*ed her. This was becoming quite a regular thought. Rhodri decided he was going to take her word for it because he believed in seeing the good in people. Or more truthfully, he was seeing a lot of good in her.

'Would you be able to fill in the feedback form?' He'd squeaked it, he was that desperate. 'My boss ... she in-sisted this was part of the deal.'

'Yes, course.' Reaching for her bag, which, glory be, was the hemp one he'd given her, Ceri sought his permis-sion to pack up. 'Do you need it now or ...?'

'Not at all. Any time you like. No rush whatsoever. By tomorrow, Wednesday, if possible. The form is in the pack I've got for you to take away,' he said, flustered by her kindness, hunting for the stapled sheets of gold dust among his documents and leaflets. 'If I can find it … here, there you go. It underlines the main themes of the talk, plus a very handy list of ways you can further reduce your waste, such as donating to clothes banks, buying unpackaged fruit and veg, taking your own reusable cup to coffee shops, stopping junk mail and so on. There's even a bit in there you might like, what with you being in the beauty industry: you can even make your own deodorant and make-up. No toxic chemical nonsense!'

At this, she raised her brows momentarily. He had her hooked! He'd chat to her about this again, he resolved, invigorated at being able to broaden her horizons. Most women found him a bit on the dull side. 'Any questions before we shoot?' Because she was bound to have a wealth of them. She just smiled as she pushed away the notes.

'Dolphins, by the way? Since when were there any dolphins here?'

Rhodri spluttered in disbelief. 'I'll have you know our stretch of coast has Britain's largest population – between three and four hundred.'

'So how come I haven't seen any?'

'It's not Florida, where they come out tap-dancing every day for lunch! They're wild. Sightings are most common between April and November.' Yet she had a point. 'Scientists believe pollution may affect their fertility,' he admitted. 'And they fear numbers could decline. It certainly feels it. The photo of mine, I took it years ago, I haven't seen a display so close to the shore for a while.'

'Maybe they've had a better offer somewhere else,' Ceri said, with what she'd presumably call wit, getting up. 'Better pay, better sardines elsewhere.'

He wouldn't even dignify that with a remark. He'd allowed himself to drop his guard. Outsiders just didn't understand: what he would give to see them back, he thought, staring into space, imagining the grey flash of sleek and shiny bottlenoses jumping like rainbows up and over the waves.

The tinny sound of keys brought him to. Ceri was dangling hers at him.

'Can we go now?' Her attention span had clearly reached its limit.

He swung his rucksack heavily onto his shoulder with frustration and opened the door for her: a Cadwalader 'warrior' he might be, but even environmental soldiers had to accept there were some who resisted more strongly than others. She just needed more persuading.

Through the labyrinth of the office corridors, she matched his every step despite their height difference, they walked out into the late afternoon sunshine. Spring was coming and the days of Rhodri's synthetic insulated jacket which combined plenty of circulated heat with freedom of movement were pleasantly limited.

'Aaah,' he sighed, relaxing into the passenger seat of her Fiesta. He opened his mouth to mention the benefits of green cars, such as less tax and better fuel efficiency, but the alternative prospect was waiting for a bus which took an hour to weave its way to the outskirts of Dwynwen. And he was ravenous.

As Ceri started the engine, he rubbed his thighs, savouring the thought of his tea of slow-cooked saffron chicken which he'd add to risotto rice and prawns, and how he'd wear his moisture-wicking activity utility shorts tomorrow. But when the car didn't move, he felt her combative stare on his right cheek. He turned his head to see she was doing one of her smirks and it made him nervous.

'This is just an observation, Rhodri,' she said, her eyes dancing with mischief, 'but maybe it would've been more eco-friendly to email the talk to me?'

A hotness spread through him: this was a dig and he was learning she never went anywhere without a spade. It was maddening – and, God damn it, incredibly exciting. Usually when he was the victim of a piss-take, he'd shrug it off as he'd learned to do, thanks to his brothers. But when she did it, he found it stirred him in areas long dormant. Not physically. *Okay*, slightly physically, but principally in a thrilling mental way because it meant she wasn't just giving him attention but she'd noticed how he did things. And her banter wasn't scornful, like he was used to from climate change deniers; it was playful, irresistibly so. He couldn't help but return the bounce back at her.

'So predictable,' he said, looking straight ahead, depriving her of a rise in spite of how much he wanted to lap it up. 'Ask me why I don't shit in a pit, eat berries and wear clothes made of leaves and bark.'

Ceri let rip a cackle and reversed.

'This is the trouble,' he said, pretending to be absorbed by the window winder on his door as she navigated them out of the one-way car park. 'You put your head above the parapet and people attack you, looking for anything to show you're not doing everything on the planet to save the planet. But, forgive me if I'm wrong, we did car-share, didn't we? It wasn't a gratuitous journey, was it? You got to have a lovely morning in St Davids,' he said, thumbing at her shopping bags on the back seat.

'You got me there, cocker,' she said, making him throb with victory. They'd reached a T-junction and he stole the opportunity to study her as he pretended to check both ways for traffic. Lovely, she was. Not straightforward, there was something about her, something different and intriguing and ... *sexy*. Even though she was from England. Which he hadn't mentioned to anyone else, because it would look as if he cared. But he preferred to think of her as half-Welsh half-Spanish ... Oh, how he'd love to share his supper with her.

'Prawns,' he heard himself mutter breathily, to his absolute shame.

'Prawns? What prawns?' she laughed.

You unbelievable pen coc of a dickhead. Scrabbling for a reason why he'd said it, he wondered if he was brave enough to invite her in for tea? More of this mental ping-pong over the table, with a bottle of red between them, not knowing if it would lead to flirtation. The image cracked, replaced by Ruth on their last night together, her plate of wild Penclawdd mussels untouched as she tucked her soft, thick auburn hair behind her ears and told him that while she loved him, he was more in love with Wales than he was with her. London was where she wanted to be. The irony that she, an air quality consultant he'd met at a conference, preferred the smog to God's own heavenly breath. Two blissful years they had spent together, alternate weekends at each other's homes, side-stepping the reality that one day it would come down to a compromise neither could make. He had been so in love with her – the hikes, the science lectures, the surfing, their lovemaking and the deep conversations late into the night were proof they were soulmates. But when he thought about her now, gone for two years, he wasn't sure they'd ever really known each other: forty-eight hours, once a week kept them in an artificial honeymoon period. When the first challenge had presented itself, that they should take it to the next level and move in, they'd buckled. He still felt cheated by the tangible turning out to be nothing but the empty sensation of a palmful of dry sand disappearing through his fingers. So no, he wasn't brave enough to let another flighty English lady eat in his home.

Instead, Rhodri moved the topic on to Welsh cuisine. 'Do you like laverbread? Have you tried it yet?'

'Lava, as in volcanoes?'

Was she playing stupid? 'No. As in seaweed.'

'Like the stuff you get at the Chinese?'

'Like the stuff you pluck from the rocks. Free of charge. Gathered from water so pure it only needs a few rinses – and you don't want to get rid of all trace of the sea. Simmer it for a few hours, use it in a fish stew or fry it up with cockles. But I like it with lemon juice, oil and seasoning. Very healthy too, full of iodine and iron. Rich in glutamates, laver is one of the ingredients of umami, a savoury flavour which is one of the five basic tastes.'

Pulling up at the last traffic lights before the lane on the left wound its way to Dwynwen, Ceri hovered the car at biting point and faced him.

'See, no offence, Rhodri, but the local interest thing makes me care far more about the environment than statistics.'

'Oh.' He didn't know how to feel. 'Go on.'

'Well, your course was … it's your knowledge of

what's around which gets me. And if you could weave it in, it might make it seem more relevant?'

He mulled it over as they headed west, following the sun which hung low and orange in the sky. She read his mind wrong, though.

'Oh, listen to me. Flaming hell, I should just keep my gob shut. What do I know?'

He jerked his body round and spoke to her profile.

'Actually ... I like it ...' he said. 'Let me see, the national park here, well, the ages of the rocks range from late Precambrian to late Carboniferous, circa six hundred and fifty to two hundred and ninety million years old. The coastal path covers one hundred and eighty miles of stunning views of bays and-'

'Nice detail, Rhodri, but it's a bit dry.'

'Right.' She could be quite cutting.

'No, wait ... what about ...' She chewed her cheek in concentration. 'Would Saint Dwynwen have travelled that path?' Ceri used her forefingers to 'walk' the steering wheel.

'I have no idea but—'

'She could have!' *They'd said it in unison!* And if he could make people care about the rich heritage of this place they might be more inclined to want to preserve it. How had she done it? It was as if she was his muse: leading him along with questions and curiosities, taking him here and there in the search for inspiration, which was coming fast now.

'Love ... this land has been built on love,' he began, imagining he was the great Welsh actor Richard Burton on the stage. 'The patron saint of love, Saint Dwynwen, laid the foundations when she trod this ground on her way to Ynys Môn, you'd know it as Anglesey, helping those in pain through passion. Her footsteps may be long gone but her spirit remains in our very soil and it is our duty as citizens of the world to keep her message alive: to love, whether one another or this blessed country ... blah blah blah ... reuse, recycle, reduce.'

'Yes!' Ceri said, slamming her palm on the dashboard. She might be on to something: if he tweaked his presentation, or massacred it.

'She was one hell of a broad, this saint.'

Wasn't she just.

'It's hard to believe now but in the Middle Ages, pilgrims would walk the length and breadth of Wales to visit the church of Saint Dwynwen on Llanddwyn, the island of love. They went to see if their union was blessed. There was a well and lovers thought it was home to sacred fish that could predict if a relationship would flourish: if they saw fish swimming around it was a sign of a faithful husband.'

'What? Ridiculous!'

'It is in a way and yet ...' How could he explain it? 'Barely an island really but at high tide, it's cut off from the mainland in an area of outstanding natural beauty. Little coves, glorious blue sea, rolling sand dunes, all in the shadow of Snowdonia, the mountains some know in Welsh as Eryri from the word for eagles, which translates as the land of eagles. There's magic there, do you see?'

She went to talk and he clenched his jaw in advance. But out came a sigh which was sweet and long.

Maybe she did have a soul after all.

'Wow,' she said. 'It sounds beautiful.'

'It is. Apparently. Although I haven't been ...' He had

a lump in his throat. It was the ideal place to propose. Not that he'd ever had the chance. 'The remains are still there,' he said, hugging the facts in comfort. 'People go, even today. Especially on January the twenty-fifth.'

'Why then?'

'It's St Dwynwen's Day. The equivalent of February fourteenth, your Valentine's Day.'

'Yeah?'

'Yes. We celebrate it with cards and lovespoons.'

'Love-whats?'

'Ornate spoons carved out of wood. They're decorative and given as gifts to your true love.'

'Again, weird. But kind of sweet. Does everyone have one? Have you?'

He gulped. The question left him floundering: was she asking as a way of knowing if he had anyone on the go? To know his relationship history? Of course not. It was just out of conversation. Still, it felt personal and she picked up on his hesitation.

'Sorry, I didn't mean to pry.'

'No, it's fine.' Why be shy when she was leaving in a few days? 'Yes ... I did have one. Seren made it for me.'

'You and Seren?' she blurted out.

'No! My ex got her to do it. It was the finest of craftsman ... womanship. Ruth gave her a thick piece of branch we'd found on our first ever walk through Dwynwen Woods, it'd sat in my fireplace, a proof of our falling in love ...' Now it was sat in the loft: had it been downstairs, he'd have been tempted to burn it and he'd have felt as if he'd let down Seren.

'Oh, Rhodri.' Ceri spoke softly, with empathy. As if she knew what it was like to be broken by another person. But she'd never understand it, not completely. She was too worldly and wise and attractive and canny to have ever been left wanting.

'Seren carved some of the traditional symbols, Ruth had chosen them: a heart for the obvious reason and a chain for the wish to be together forever. The writing was on the wall, though, when I took her for a surprise weekend away and she expected Paris but I'd booked us into a nature reserve on the Welsh island of Skomer to watch puffins. So basically, we weren't on the same wavelength. On the surface, we should've been. Both into the environment and the great outdoors but I think we had different values.'

'Same with me and Dave,' Ceri said. 'Like, we were from the same place, had the same upbringing, you know, family, *Daily Mirror*, Findus Crispy Pancakes, Peter Kay DVDs. But he didn't like it when I … well, he said I put work first, there was something else important to me that wasn't him. Like he'd moan when I'd go out dressed up with my face on for a business meeting. He just didn't get what it was about, the image I had to project.'

The man was a complete bell-end! 'I can't imagine you like that,' he said, because she didn't need make-up. He understood why women wore it, though – didn't he have his hair this way to cover his ears? Talking of which, she had the nicest pair going. They were flush against her scalp as if she had been created aerodynamically for cycling.

'Yeah, I kind of can't imagine it myself anymore.'

The drive went quiet for a while and the road began to narrow as they got closer to home.

After a while, Ceri spoke. 'Any news on the planning application? For the new estate?'

149

Jesus, he was only just getting up to standing after pouring his heart out. She knew how to kick a man back down.

'There's a site visit coming up. I don't know exactly when. The planning committee head honcho is going up to inspect it. I'm hoping someone in the department will tip me off. I just don't know how we're going to stop it. Councils these days are poor, there are so few jobs and potholes everywhere ... if a developer says it will employ locals and create new roads, it's obvious what the local authority will do. But it's so short term. I think our best bet is to ramp up the Village of Love. Get a buzz going, invite the local paper down, get onto social media.'

'Oh, definitely, you have to have a social media presence these days. It's all about the branding.'

'Plus leg work. The villagers are very enthusiastic, well, now they are, after the bunting. Not when I first brought it up, though. Not that I'm bitter! They're all offering to help. I still haven't a clue who's behind it.'

Ceri said nothing. It didn't surprise him – it was probably going right over her head. She hadn't even known what St David's Day was!

Her phone began to ring as they reached the top of a hill. She apologised, she had to pick up – this was the last hope of any reception before the village – and he reached for her bag as she nipped into a lay-by.

'Jade, love!' Ceri shouted as Rhodri heard a detached voice reply 'hiyaaaa!'. It was obviously a good friend, judging by the way they were gabbling and laughing. 'Have you turned into bridezilla yet?' Ceri got out of the car, mouthing 'five minutes' and he waved her off, happy to spend a while reflecting on the prospect of fighting his father not with placards and vitriol but with something far more positive. Dwynwen would need a website, a Facebook page and a Twitter account ... a hashtag ... all things he could do from the office at lunch ... Mel could bake some of her love-heart Welshcakes, Seren could do some lovespoons ... he'd ring his contact at the paper ... they could sell Village of Love merchandise and print T-shirts and postcards and ... the possibilities were huge. He could see it now: couples coming for romantic weekends and families feeling the love for a fortnight. The pub would be busy again, the shop might not need to be sold and he could even do guided tours of the woods and the waterfall. If he could get some money from the department, he might be able to get some recycling bins in the pub car park.

The car door opened slowly and he couldn't wait to share his vision with Ceri but *oh dear*, the way she moved slowly into her seat indicated her fizz had gone flat. She was quiet except for the odd sniff, and motionless, her head bowed.

'Okay?' he said, feeling his own excitement fade as concern took over.

'Yes ... no,' she whispered. 'News from home. Nothing major.'

'From a town called Bruce?'

She turned to him, her eyes heavy with hurt, and nodded. 'It's fine, though.'

'Right.'

But she didn't turn the ignition.

'No pressure at all. But if you like, I'll sit here all night if you want to talk,' he said. 'Sometimes it helps if you tell someone uninvolved.'

She looked beyond him towards the hedgerow, her face glazed as she considered his offer.

'That was Jade, we work together,' she announced. 'She wanted to know when I was coming back. People are asking after me, where I am.' Ceri raised both hands in desperation. 'Flamin' hell, am I not allowed a holiday?'

'Course you are.'

'There's a new line that she wants feedback on. But I'm not sure about it. It doesn't feel me anymore. Things have changed ...'

This meant nothing to him in detail yet he got the impression she was questioning things on a deeper level.

'I don't feel the same as I did. And yes it may be foolish to say this because I'm away from it but I haven't woken up once wanting to go back to the business. Not once. I used to live and breathe it.'

He understood about having a passion: the natural world was his and it would take something momentous to make him fall out of love with it.

'It must be hard, your mum gone.'

'It is, it's horrible.' She squeezed her eyes shut and clenched her fists to show how horrible. 'I miss her so much. Maybe you're right, maybe it is the grief,' she said, focusing on him now, 'but I'm wondering if it's made me see what little else there is in my life.'

'Oh, I can't imagine that's true. You must have lots of people around you, you seem the type.'

'You reckon? Jade's my only friend. The others stuck by my ex when we split up. I don't trust anyone any-more. My work is ... *was* my support network, it never let me down. It was everything to me, helped me when my mum was dying of dementia. But now, I don't want to be there anymore …'

'What about family? I mean, I know about your mum and dad, but is there …?'

'Only my sister now.'

She burst into tears and once again she was cuddling up to him. This time, though, there was no swift recovery. Bawling, she was, big dollops of it: his handkerchief was a write-off.

What he gathered when she'd managed to speak was Jade had seen the 'sold' on the 'for sale' sign outside Ceri's mother's house, but Ceri's sister hadn't told her. He tried to suggest that perhaps she'd missed a call; but it turned out Ceri had tried to ring three times this week to explain she was staying on. The upshot was Ceri believed her last remaining flesh and blood didn't care about her: unlike the people here, who'd welcomed her without question, who, in ten days, had made her feel more treasured than anyone had in a long time. She wasn't going to rush back: she felt closer to her mum here. And despite thinking at first Dwynwen had been a frontier village on the edge of civilisation, she'd started to love it and it was beginning to feel more like home than home. Therefore, she would be staying another week. She also mentioned keeping a promise to Mel but he didn't probe – he was now ready to eat not a horse but an entire stable.

It wasn't what he would've done – he believed in negotiation and reconciliation, he'd had to because falling out and fisticuffs with his father would have killed his mother. But he didn't know what pressures Ceri was under: not really, beneath what she'd told him. And he was glad she would be around. Ceri brightened his days.

He loved cuddles too, even when a handbrake was sticking into his right thigh. These feelings for her were only a crush: nothing would come of it. She floated in and she would float off again when her journey took her away.

'I'm sorry, I seem to be making a habit out of crying over you.' Finally, she pulled away and wiped her eyes with her sleeves.

'I didn't like to say anything but now you mention it, I am thinking of charging you for the use of my hankies.'

'You're a lovely person, Rhodri, do you know that?'

'Yes. The loveliest. My mother tells me all the time. Go on, out you get, I'll drive us home. You'll never find the way with those puffy eyes.'

She was so drained she didn't even bother to put up a fight.

'Thanks,' she said, as they passed each other by the bonnet. As much as he wished he could be more to Ceri than a shoulder to cry on, he accepted that was how it would be: he'd been with an English woman once and it'd done him no favours. He wasn't going to do it again.

'Don't worry,' Rhodri said, belting up, the clunk and click underlining his resolve. 'Just don't tell anyone I've been driving a vehicle with such low fuel economy.'

13

Mel pressed her fingertips onto her eyelids, seeking the blackest black in the universe.

It was a hard ask because she was in the Pink House and not a black hole light years away in the Milky Way. She wanted to disappear, to not exist. But no such luck. Even with the pressure on her eyeballs, she could still see dots the colour of dandelion seeds and parma violets jiggling around, reminding her she had no escape.

She was on her knees, having fallen at the first hurdle of her clear-up. The recommended books and printouts she'd kept from counselling years ago when this problem had first reared its head were beside her, dug out from a box at the very bottom of Dad's wardrobe, highlighted in neon, instructing her to focus on small, achievable goals, such as sorting through an area of a room in short bursts. *Make decisions on an object's worth within twenty seconds, thereby reducing your physical attachment*: a straightforward instruction of either keep or let go. *Keep if it is regularly used or needed, let go if not. Set it free – either by throwing it away or donating it to somebody for them to enjoy – and set yourself free.* But all she'd managed to do was move things between piles: churning, it was called, summing up the feeling in her tummy, and the classic symptom of avoidance, sabotaging her attempt to move forward.

A creak from the second-to-top stair set off an adrenaline rush of panic which tumbled like a messy wave down, down into shame. She should've locked the front door, but she'd assumed everyone else would be enjoying their Sunday morning coffee. Who had come in? Who was catching her red-handed, guilty of inaction and self-hate?

'I'm not one of those stinking hoarders, I'm not,' Mel said, defensively, her breath quick on her palms, 'the ones who've got fifty-five cats and have relationships with their possessions.'

'I know.'

Ceri's voice was low and kind, absent of any criticism. *Thank God it was her.* Dear Ceri, who was on her side. Mel exhaled slowly, removing her hands, seeing gold rushing towards her from her new friend. It was like the sun coming up on fast-forward, a vision of faith itself.

'Been up long?' Ceri unwound her eucalyptus-leaf scarf and hung it on the bannister, a sign that she was intending to stay for some time.

'A while. I wanted to do this … I haven't got very far.'

Ceri's eyes drifted across the mounds of memories of happier days and people and places. Mel winced instinctively, afraid that Ceri wouldn't be able to keep up her show of support, that underneath it all, she was repulsed by what she would see as the mess both in the room and in Mel's head. But she remained neutral, coming to kneel beside Mel on the floor.

'I've been reading up on it and they say to tackle it in fifteen-minute periods,' she said. 'So I can go through it with you, if you like?'

Mel nodded, still frightened of letting her in. Whenever

Mam had arrived with rubber gloves and bin bags, it was as if she was performing a caesarean section, raking around inside of her, disposing of her babies.

'Then we could go for a walk. To the woods? I'm not ready to go on the beach yet.'

Bringing her own sadness into it touched Mel deeply: Ceri was telling her she was on Mel's level, they shared a bond and they would find their way through their troubles together.

'You take the lead, Mel. I'm right here.'

The shoot of trust within Mel's heart began to bud and she found the strength to begin.

'Right, okay, so I'm working on this shelf. I know it looks small but—'

'You have to start somewhere, right?'

'*Exactly.*'

'I won't touch anything unless you want me to. It's your call. All of it.'

Growing in the warmth of Ceri's patience, Mel explained, 'I'm doing keep, chuck and donate. I'll pass them to you as we go. And ... you could take away the things if you don't mind because it ... it hurts, it does.'

'Course, leave it to me.'

Ceri folded her hands on her lap. She was waiting for Mel to walk the walk, to cross the bridge from one side to the other. To accept that not everything here was part of a precious collection; that some of it was a drain on her wellbeing, dragging her back to the past and denying her a future. Mel felt a pain in her head and in her heart at the prospect of making a decision. The time had come and she had to fight to get to the front of herself, to resist the pull of putting it off yet again.

Slowly she reached out for the first item. Trembling, she picked up the burned-down stub of a candle, inhaling sharply because the touch of the smooth wax reminded her of Alwyn's skin. The crisp wick, she imagined, still smoked from his pinch at the beach party when they'd been sixteen and rolling down sand dunes, drunk on cans of cider. He'd held her hand when he'd walked her home but her dad had come out of the darkness on his way back from the pub and they'd dropped the contact. She felt the absence of him anew and it came out in a sob. *How could she regard this as rubbish? This was impossible, she wasn't able to do this, no way*, and her hand squeezed the gem protectively. Mel became aware of Ceri's hand rubbing her back, soothing her, reminding her of what she needed to do.

Somehow, she found herself thinking 'this candle is not him' over and over in a trance which unfurled her fingers. She had to let this go. She had to give herself a chance. Mel couldn't watch herself do it but her arm stretched towards Ceri as she offered up her sacrifice. As it left her palm, she felt the trace of its weight lingering and a sickness rising in her throat. The agony seized her and she throbbed all over but she knew too well she would feel this way anyway if she didn't act: it was self-inflicted torture whether she hoarded or shed her skin. This process was going to hurt but ultimately decluttering would hurt less. Clenching every muscle, she waited for herself to splinter.

But incredibly she wasn't falling apart – she could still hold on to Al's memory whether she had that candle stub or not. And so it would be with the things representing her childhood before her parents divorced. The flicker carried her through a stack of ancient menus from restaurants long closed which she had saved from special occasions, including the very first Chinese she'd had with Mum and Dad, still tasting the strange lemony chicken and the spicy ribs and the crunch of prawn crackers. How grown-up she'd felt holding chopsticks! She hadn't known her childhood would end too soon. What she'd considered to be 'exotic' food wrappers from the French supermarket when they'd gone camping – a scratched Milka bar, a long ghostly string of empty plastic cases which had contained fizzy strawberry sweets and the flattened rectangle of yellow Carambar caramel sticks which still hung onto the twists at either end.

Postcards from ports across the world where Dad had worked on the cruise ships, sent without fail from wherever he was; Miami, Barcelona, Casablanca, Los Angeles, Lisbon ... they had once ignited a wanderlust, a desire which she had later packed away, to punish herself. But then she felt joy as she came across her favourite postcard from Colombo. The edge of the frilly stamp had arrived dog-eared and, just as she did now, she would touch it to feel where his fingers had been: to connect with him if she'd had a silly row with Mum or Huw. The image too mattered: a vivid spectrally pure Sri Lankan sunset of cinnamon and cumin, saffron and ginger, which Dad had said could almost be Dwynwen's, give or take a few palm trees and thirty degrees. It had comforted her that they were both under the same sky which sported the same shades even though they were thousands of miles apart. What she would do to be able to mix these colours, she thought, as the word 'recovery' hovered on her horizon ...

'Keep,' she said, holding it to her chest, feeling lighter as she handed the rest of the pile to Ceri. Surprise, relief and wonder swarmed inside of her and she took a breath to let it sink in: she'd done it! She'd actually managed to do it!

'I make that fifteen minutes,' Ceri said, getting up, wasting no time to give Mel the chance to claw back her possessions. The itch was there, definitely, but it felt enough to have picked one thing to hold on to.

'I don't know if I'd have been able to do this without you,' Mel said. 'Sometimes I wonder, I do, if I feel more things than most people. Not like I'm special or anything, but if I can see a myriad of colours what if I feel a myriad of emotions too? It might make me more vulnerable, less resilient.'

'It might be true, it might not. But if it is, your super senses might mean you could be happier than most, don't you think? Because you've had your fair share of sadness, love. Right, I'll put these in the car. You get yourself ready and I'll meet you outside. You won't need a coat, it's glorious out there. For once!'

'Ceri, would you mind if I didn't come?' Mel said, staying put on the floor, as a rush of something hit her. 'Not to be rude, and I know I'm letting you down. If it was the beach I wouldn't ... and I'm so pleased you're staying around for a while longer, I meant it when I said you can stay as long as you like. There's no bookings for ... ever ... but I'm going to ring my dad.'

It was an extraordinary sensation, like a boldness of heart. 'There's something I need to ask him. If that's okay?'

Ceri balanced the bin bag on her knee to pick up her scarf and gave her a big smile. 'Of course!'

'We'll do the beach soon, yes?'

'Great.'

'Oh, thank you! It just feels like I have to seize the day.'

'You so do,' Ceri said, as she went down the stairs. Then she added from below, 'Mums are worth calling too, you know. You're lucky to have one.'

Mel understood what she was getting at: that she should try to move on with her mam. That would be for another day, though. For now, she only wanted to speak to one person, she thought, reaching for the phone.

'Dad,' she said when he picked up, 'don't keel over but how do you fancy trying that new place in the harbour for lunch?'

14

With a sweaty forehead, damp squelching wellies and screaming thighs, Ceri was hardly Snow White.

But as she finally reached the peak of the long and narrow steep hill climb up to Dwynwen Woods, it was as if she'd just walked into a fairytale. Panting heavily, she was fighting for breath but not just because she was more unfit than she realised – apparently marching to meetings and out for a sandwich hadn't counted for much. It was also because she'd emerged from the claustrophobic scratchy brambly path into a huge umbrella of trees which floated on a sea of bluebells. Diagonal strips of sunshine hazy with midges and birds lit up the indigo flowers and a slight breeze made their heads nod which, for a second, made them look as though they were gossiping at her arrival. '*Not from round these parts*,' they would be saying. Spot on – where she came from, a walk meant popping out to the shop, not a flaming hike.

But she wasn't there – she was here, in the most magical place. Not wanting to break the spell, she stood still, taking it all in. There was a bank of trees in front of her and to her left. On the right was a small clearing where the thick woodland fell away like stage curtains, the earth carved in two by a busy fast-flowing stream. The effect was like looking through a vast porthole, framed by the tips of touching branches, their trunks leaning outwards as if to admire the view. She could see for miles – the edge of the sandy beach, dazzling today, lapped by a calm green sea where a figure was paddle-boarding gracefully without a splash. It was the picture of tranquillity. Nature hadn't meant much to her – she lived in a world of arranged bouquets which looked as though they'd just stepped out of a salon. A yucca in her flat was half-dead and cobwebbed, and as for wildlife, Mum would never have tolerated animal hairs on the sofa. Yet now she was among the flora and fauna, she found it stirring. The tweeting birds which she imagined were whistling while they worked, the scurry of squirrel paws, the rustle of leaves and crack of twigs underfoot. *Hang on*, a crack of twigs underfoot meant she had company ... a spurt of adrenaline made her look for a hiding place and she crouched down behind a tree stump, fearing an armed psychopath, or at the very least Grumpy and Dopey, as voices drifted towards her. A child, it sounded like, and adults. She relaxed, cursing her urban ways, and drew the mossy air up into her nostrils to clear the dusty tickle from Mel's house. There was a flash of a boy in red and further away a man ... no, two.

'Henry! Don't run with your penknife!' a voice called from the depths.

Henry? You can't have got many of them to the pound in deepest, darkest Wales. Perhaps, she thought with amazement, she was about to witness a lesser spotted bunch of tourists? Or not, her senses recovering, because Rhodri's head, and only his head, appeared, as the rest of his body was camouflaged in khaki shorts and T-shirt. The boy froze as he caught sight of Ceri appearing out of the bushes and he took a startled step back.

'All right, kid?' she said. 'You with Rhodri? He's a friend of mine.'

'Yes,' he said, relaxing. 'And Owen. On our way to see Seren.'

'Oh, right. I'm Ceri, I job-share with her at the pub.'

The threat passing, he nodded then picked up a thick piece of fallen branch and whittled it with fierce concentration. Ceri examined him, fascinated. He was every inch the little boy with sticky-up hair and dirty knees. But instead of awkward clumsy hands, he expertly pared and shaved and carved the wood, his tongue poking out as he worked, and by the time the others had reached him, he had created a mushroom complete with gills.

'For you, Ceri,' he said. 'Can you tell me, where you'd find fungi?'

Shit! She had no idea, not really, not the scientific explanation – she was about to be humiliated by a child in front of Rhodri, who'd just emerged, and his mate, another one of the crazy bunch judging by his biker beard, shaved head and inked Welsh dragon breathing fire down his left forearm.

'Um ... well ...' She played for time by turning the smooth mushroom in her hands.

'You'd find fungi at a party,' he said, straight-faced.

'Sorry?'

It sank in. Fungi as in 'fun guy'. And she began to laugh, feeling ridiculous for having expected a nine-year-old to—

'Mushrooms can be used in a process called

mycoremediation, which is the process of using fungi to degrade contaminants in the environment.'

Silly her. He was way ahead, this one. It was like listening to a mini-Rhodri – in fact, were they related? She compared their faces but he was the opposite, fair and neat to Rhodri's generous features.

'You've met Henry,' Rhodri said, ruffling the boy's blond hair, before doing the introductions. 'Ceri, this is Seren's son and her husband, Owen.'

So he was the child genius! She should've known seeing as he'd referred to his parents by their Christian names. She'd seen some do that on a TV show and had found them endearing, their mums and dads not so much.

'Heard a lot about you,' Owen said, his voice as musical as a male voice choir. 'You're the woman who gave Seren back her life, so she says.'

'Yeah, not sure how it happened but I'll take the credit.'

Then he looked at his watch and did a dramatic leap back. 'We're going to have to go, Rhod. Table's booked for lunch and we're late. Seren won't be happy if we haven't finished by the time her shift ends.'

'I'll walk you down,' Rhodri offered.

'No, no. No need.' Owen extended a hand. 'Hope I helped with a few things.'

'You did.'

'Sorry it wasn't better news. Right … maybe we'll catch you at the circus next week?'

'Cool.'

As they waved goodbye, Ceri waited until they were out of earshot before she opened her mouth. But Rhodri got in first.

'He's a professor, teaches rural enterprise management at St Davids University,' he said wearily.

'I thought so,' she said, trying to coax a smile which usually he handed out for free. 'Could tell by the tattoo. But the circus? Don't tell me, is he a strong man or a juggler?'

'The circus is a craft fair.' His tone was edged with irritation as if he was fed up with explaining things to her. 'Seren does one every month. They're a bit hard up. Henry's got an international chess competition coming up in New York in the new year. He was the world number one for under-tens last year so ... anyway, what do you think?'

He held his arms out wide but where he was usually ramrod with pride he seemed to have wilted.

'It's beautiful.'

He picked up a dead branch and snapped it with force. She wasn't one for macho acts but she couldn't help admiring his bulging biceps. 'The perfect spot for forty houses, eh?'

So that's what was up.

'I was talking to Owen about it. This is ancient woodland, supposedly protected by law. Planning authorities are meant to refuse developments which would lead to the loss of irreplaceable habitats. But that flies out of the window if the need for and benefits of the development outweigh the loss. The government wants a million new homes in the UK within a few years. Guess which way it's going to go.' His frown cut his forehead in two. God, even when he was cross, he was still adorable.

'Not necessarily. It's remote here, not everyone's cup of tea.'

'It's not about what's here now,' he said, obviously agitated by this ignorant townie before him. 'It's what comes after new housing. Hard to imagine now but in a decade there'll be a Starbucks and a supermarket up the road. Super-fast broadband.'

'Count me in,' she said drily.

But if looks could kill, she'd have been throttled by a pair of angry eyebrows. There was something different about him today: he didn't want to play. It made Ceri want the normal Rhodri back.

'There'll be litter, pollution, no trees, no wildlife ...'

'But what about the Village of Love? You said the other day it could be the answer! Why've you changed your tune?'

'Because after hearing from Owen, I don't think a few hearts and an ageing fucking saint is going to stop it, do you?'

Ceri flinched. He was the equivalent of Professor Stephen Hawking here; the rest of Dwynwen were on the way to barking. If he gave up it was game over.

'Don't lose faith,' she heard herself say needily. 'Come on, I'll get you a pint at the pub. I'm taking over from Seren at two p.m. so I've got time.'

'Nah. Thanks, though.'

He turned and walked away and she felt a keen sense of rejection. This was a side of him she hadn't seen before. And it unsettled her: he was the one the village was depending on to survive. Why did she care? A fortnight ago she'd been blissfully ignorant of this place. But now it mattered to her, she realised, because Dwynwen was the way it had been when her mother lived here. It needed to be preserved. Otherwise it would be like losing another piece of her mother.

'Rhodri!' she called to his broad back which right now looked like a slammed door.

'What?' he said gruffly, pausing at the pathway.

She had to convince him that until the plans had been rubber-stamped, there was still a chance. And she could only do that if she could spend some time with him. What would happen when she left on Friday? Maybe she had better think about stopping on. In the meantime, she had to do something about it right now.

'I need some advice,' she said, making it up on the spot as she trotted to him.

'Right,' he said, setting off again. 'Make it quick because I've got stuff to do.'

He walked faster and she was breathless keeping up but it did give her a moment to think of something to ask him. He stopped when they reached a break in the hedgerow just before the pub, which she hadn't noticed on her way up.

'So this is me. What is it then?' His amber eyes weren't enquiring and helpful as usual but guarded by his lowered brow which spelled out that she only had a small window. He'd crossed his arms to make it clear there was no invitation to join him for a brew. Quite disproportionately, it was like a punch in the stomach. It set off a moment of insecurity and self-doubt. She was going to make a fool of herself. Scarier, what if this was the real him? Perhaps she'd been sucked in by his nicey-nice act. In her previous life, it would've been something she'd expected but here, it mattered to her. And she knew why now as she looked up at him, willing him to be the person she'd thought he was: he had become part of her rehabilitation from a miserable mourning moneybags into an ever-so-slightly happier and contented soul. His openness, his glow, it had been infectious. He'd made her laugh and he had listened to her problems. He was good and true, she still believed it, and she needed him to prove it. So she began to speak before her brain was in gear.

'The best environmentally friendly cleaning products to use in the house,' she said, feeling as lame as a three-legged donkey. 'What do you recommend?'

His eyes examined her with scepticism. He'd seen right through her flimsy desperation, she could tell by his unimpressed stare. But she wouldn't, she couldn't stop.

'Because my mum, she was one of those "if it doesn't move, bleach it" types and I was brought up on Domestos.'

'Were you now?' He tutted.

'Yes,' she whispered, thinking he was about to rumble her. 'Look, it's just, I'm ...'

'Bursting, I get it,' he said, sighing as he dropped his arms, 'I wish you'd just asked to use the loo rather than take the Mick about cleaning products.'

Ceri could've cried at his innocence: there was the proof she'd needed he had no side. How could she have doubted him? Her heart swelling with elation that he hadn't let her down, she promised herself she'd do less of the teasing from now on.

'Oh, thanks, Rhodri,' she gushed with too much grati-tude, hopping for effect. 'I wasn't taking the pee. I just need one.'

'Come on then,' he said, mock reluctantly, and motioned for her to follow him through the overgrown ferns which brushed her as if they were frisking her for non-recyclables. She wouldn't stay long, just enough time to convince him he was Dwynwen's guardian angel. Not a biggie or anything. Besides, she wasn't sure his place would be very homely anyway. It was bound to be a yurt powered by a bicycle-run generator with a rotting compost heap out the back. The peeling wooden gate engraved with the words Murmur Y Coed suggested as much.

'One of the jobs I need to do,' he said, holding it open for her. 'Varnishing.'

Varnish, her head screamed, *wasn't that a bit poisonous?* But she held her tongue because she'd made a vow not to rib him.

'I make my own. All natural. From beeswax and olive oil. See, I bet you didn't know you could use household things for everyday purposes? There you are, tip one.'

The urge to shout 'of course I bloody know!' was a strong one. She went for the safer option of having a go at pronouncing the name of his house.

'*Murmur why co-ed?*' she tried hopefully.

'*Murmur eeeeee coyd.* It means Whisper of the Woods.'

'That's just too romantic, that ...' *For a hovel*, she didn't say, as she looked up a winding pathway to see something so unexpected she grabbed Rhodri's arm to steady herself.

'All right? Did you lose your footing? It is a bit muddy up here,' he said, unaware she was dying of shame for assuming he lived like Stig of the dump. That and the coolest thing she'd ever seen conspired to leave her speechless.

Contemporary yet in keeping with the surroundings, his house was a long single-storey log cabin, its front made entirely of glass, along which ran a veranda the length of the building, nestled in a garden of wildflowers and palms. It was like something out of Scandinavia: to brand it 'Ikea' did it no justice. Instead it was the type of place you'd see surrounded by snow in winter which transformed into a summer house when the warmer weather allowed. Drawn to it, she went closer, seeing now the floor-to-ceiling windows were slide-back doors, imagining herself star-gazing on the wicker lie-back loungers or cuddled up toasting marshmallows in a sunken seated fire pit. *Rhodri beside her with his arm around her.* Candles everywhere, communions of them, on the decking, two low-slung hammocks and a healthy wood store, which threw up a picture of Rhodri axing logs. Topless.

'What? This ... it's yours?'

'Built it myself, it's been a labour of love, I can tell you,' he said, hands on hips. 'Not quite there yet, lots still to do, such as the outdoor shower; you know, for when I've caught a few waves, with saloon half-doors so I can feel as if I'm among nature.'

She needed a cold one never mind an outdoor shower at the thought of him soaping himself down, his chin lifted to the sky as rivers of water ran down his back ... Maybe there were perks to eco extremism.

'No outdoor loo, though.' He winked before leading her up wide wooden steps to the veranda and in through the front door where she kicked off her wellies.

Again she was lost for words. The living space was white and open plan, starting with a high-gloss kitchen then a cloud-shaped dining table. The last third ended with a metallic wood burner and a deep L-shaped sofa facing the view which, because they were much higher than the path, looked over an infinity pool of sea. Somehow the inside merged seamlessly with the outside: tasteful shades of grey, blue and green mimicked the natural world. Behind her four doors ran along the back wall, leading presumably to bedrooms and the bathroom. She could see herself waking up here of a morning, thank you very much.

'It's flaming gorgeous,' she finally said as he pointed her in the direction of the loo. 'And cosy.' Not like her flat, which was still in boxes. She wanted a place of her own to cuddle her up like this: only Mum's had ever done that.

'Thanks,' he said bashfully. 'It's greener than the Eden Project. Most people are surprised it doesn't smell of farts.'

Ceri let out a honk of laughter, thrilled he was himself again.

'The thing is, Ceri, what floats my boat is what's beneath.'

Of course, she nodded, chastising herself for being so taken with the shiny surfaces.

'It's as eco as you can get. There are no man-made carbon-footprint-heavy materials. It's all locally sourced timber – renewable and non-toxic. There's a green roof, the plants provide insulation. The loo's flushed by rainwater. The table and chairs are made from recycled plastic such as yogurt pots and bottles. All NASA-approved air-filtering houseplants. Organic veggie garden out the back. And every cleaning product,' he said, waggling his eyebrows as he opened a cupboard stacked with brands she'd never seen, 'is free from ammonia, chlorofluorocarbons, chlorine and parabens.'

He gave her a big grin. That was more like the Rhodri she'd come to know.

Then she spied something miraculous. A modem on the worktop and she jabbered, 'Wifi! Have you got wifi?'

All of a sudden Rhodri spied his laptop and slammed it shut.

'Oh, Rhodri,' she said, laying on her disapproval with a butter knife, 'you haven't been looking at mucky sites have you?'

'No! No. Nothing ... like that.' He shook his head until it almost fell off.

'I believe you, thousands wouldn't,' she said. 'Who cares! I thought there was no wifi around here!'

'There isn't. Not the kind you're thinking of. The quick kind. This version is slower than dial-up. You can't download anything. It takes an age for a website to come up. I just try it every now and again.'

'Can't have it all, I suppose,' she said, letting him off the hook. 'Did it cost much to build?'

'Less than buying a house actually.' He was merrier now his browsing history wasn't under scrutiny. 'It was a shack to start with, I could afford it as it was. But I needed a loan off Dad to get it habitable and he never stops reminding me. He thinks I'm a hypocrite. Living off the spoils of his unethical success and criticising him for it.' Rhodri's shoulders dropped. 'He's right.'

'Hey,' she said, 'that's what parents are supposed to do. Help you out.'

Glum wasn't the word. And she was meant to be inspiring him.

'Look, you're lucky to have a dad around. Mine died even before I was born.' Rhodri did the '*I'm sorry for your loss'* nose wrinkle she had seen so many times in her life before. She waved it away. 'My mum made up for it. But sometimes I do wonder what would've happened if he'd been around. If we'd have moved to Spain … early morning blue sky, siestas, a swim in the Med, tapas for tea …'

'Well, you might not be as far away from your dad as you think.'

'You what?' Just when she had him down as the sane one in Dwynwen, he turned bonkers.

'Seriously. The Welsh are apparently descended from a tribe of Iberian fishermen who crossed the Bay of Biscay.'

'Excuse me?'

'DNA analysis by a geneticist at Oxford University shows we have an almost identical genetic fingerprint to coastal dwellers in Spain. Might explain in very crude terms why you get so many dark-haired and dark-skinned people in West Wales. Like us.' He smiled and his chest heaved with emotion.

'Hang on. Was that what Mel was going on about when she said some of the Armada washed up here?'

'Christ, no. That's a load of rot. I'm talking six thousand years ago, there's real scientific evidence to say we are all Spanish fishermen. Dwynwen, this village, it's a part of you. I hope you feel more at home now?'

'Um … sort of,' she said, not wanting to prick his bubble with the revelation her mum had been a blonde. 'It's a lovely thought. Poetic and dreamy. Not quite how I was brought up to see life, though. In Crewe it was never about *what ifs*. It was always about graft and making the most of what you have. Going for it, you know, with your whole heart.'

Rhodri tilted his head, wondering, so she seized the moment.

'Like you've done here with your house and like you could do with the Village of Love ...'

She let it hang in the air, stopping short of exclaiming 'hint! hint!' so he could consider it for himself.

'Yeah,' he said wistfully, 'I suppose it is possible the council might vote in our favour if it sees what we're building here. We've just got to get a move on with it.'

'That's the spirit!' she said, full of relief he'd taken the bait. With that, it was time to go. Gwen would've plated one up for her before she started work so she put on her wellies and skipped down the steps just as Rhodri remembered the reason for her visit.

'You haven't been to the loo!' he shouted to her from the decking.

'It was a false alarm,' she called back. Probably just like the feelings she was having for Rhodri, she realised as she ambled down the last section of the pathway to the pub. She loved his company and every time she saw him, she'd think he was a little bit more gorgeous than the time before. It was a good job she did have to get behind the bar because she could've spent the rest of the afternoon up there with him, if he'd have had her. That was the thing, she didn't get any vibes from him that he liked her more than a friend. And anyway, what was she even thinking going down this path? She was here for only a few more days and holidays weren't real life. Crushes burned themselves out, as this one would do. She was just coming out of loneliness and he was there. They were opposites too – completely. They couldn't be more different; him with his country ways and her an urban socialite. The trouble was, though, she wasn't seeing herself quite like that anymore. Rhodri's house was a revelation, making her see more possibilities here. Even though they were just friends, her feet were beginning to take root beside his. This bond made her see what she was lacking at home. Ceri wasn't sure what lesson it was she was learning here but she had the sense that the direction of her life was turning. And being here was something to do with it. Rhodri needed her to keep him from losing confidence in the village. Mel needed her to help her break her cycle of self-destruction. The business could manage for one more week under Jade's expert eye. That was all there was to it, there were no counter-arguments: after her shift she'd go and see Mel and extend her booking.

15

'Did ye know, Cap'n Henry,' Rhodri said in his best pirate voice, 'in them there coves of West Wales, smugglers did hide their loot. But a terrible end did come to some o' those swashbucklin' scallywag scurvy dogs o'the sea before they could reclaim it, and people say there still be treasure waitin' for landlubbers to find.'

Crouching low on the sand, he waited to see if Henry was going to bite: he was so intelligent he sometimes gave him a look which clearly stated he was not going to demean himself with silly games. To be fair to the boy, Rhodri did look an absolute buffoon with his trousers tucked into his socks and his belt tied diagonally around his head so it covered one eye. But other times, he would be the nine-year-old he was.

'Aarrrrr!' Henry shouted, slicing the air with a stick. 'Out o'me way, Gingerbeard, ya stinkin' pox-faced swine!'

It was excellent role-play but he could've done without being poked in the ribs while being reminded of his ostentatious facial hair which he'd grown once and no one had let him forget it.

'There be the spirit! Now,' Rhodri said, putting on a scowl, 'shall we go alookin' for the booty?'

'Aye!' Henry bawled, picking up some seaweed and draping it over his head like it was a Jack Sparrow wig of dreads.

This was the bit Rhodri loved the most – he distracted Henry by asking him to look out for a Jolly Roger at sea, took a handful of coins out of his thigh pocket on the left side of his trousers and threw them onto the sand, which he covered up with a scuff of his performance-meshed aqua-lined eco-lite boot. It always descended into a scrap when he did it for Dai's kids, his three nephews reminding him of his own childhood when Dad had performed the same trick. Eldest brother Dai had dropped to the floor like a commando, covering as much surface area as he could to prevent usurpers from stealing the money. Rhodri would jump on him only to be tickled under the armpits by Iolo so he'd roll over, at which point Dai would punch him, kick sand into his eyes, dangle spit-strings over his face and fart on his head until he surrendered. The spoils were Iolo's, who would calmly walk up to Rhodri and whisper in his ear everyone hated him and he was secretly adopted. And would casually pocket the lot.

Happy days, they were, if you didn't mind getting called a chicken when you ran to Mum in tears and the others stuck their fingers up behind her back and you ended up getting sent to the side because you'd gone mad and shouted 'shitheads' at everyone. While Dad was cited as the ultimate threat, he never got involved in the discipline. Rhodri had once overheard him tell Mum it was good for the boys to engage in fisticuffs because it prepared them for life. But it had just reinforced their birth order. Dai remained the leader, Iolo developed his own tactics and Rhodri was the wet one. If he ever had the fortune to be a father, he'd do it all differently, he swore. Be more involved rather than playing them off against each another.

'Cap'n Henry!' Rhodri said, curling his fingers up and placing them to his seeing eye like a telescope. 'I spy some pieces of eight!'

With a yelp, Henry jigged about and fell on his knees, scrabbling for the shiny swag. Now he could get to the educational bit. About time too because he could see brooding black clouds in the distance. After this, they'd go back and do the secret stuff Henry was sworn not to divulge to anyone.

'West Wales really does have a history of smuggling, Henry,' Rhodri said, settling down cross-legged next to the now empty picnic basket. 'Three hundred years ago, whole villages would be involved, storing goods such as wine, salt and soap, providing lookouts and lighting warning beacons so the smugglers didn't have to pay taxes at the ports. People were so poor they helped out because crime paid.'

'Found one! It's a pound! I've found a pound!' Henry's little face was alight before it became fierce with focus as he returned to digging like a dog.

'It still happens today. Modern-day pirates are at large,' Rhodri went on, not wanting to go into drugs, tobacco and people-trafficking. Even though that included the story of Welshman Howard Marks, an international cannabis smuggler who became the FBI's most wanted after foiling them with up to forty-three different aliases, including Mr Nice, which became his nickname. Rhodri felt himself curdling at the memory of Logan calling him the same term. Except he hadn't been referring to his cunning or guile. No, Logan had gone for his boring, dismal, dull jugular.

'And another! Oh. It's only 2p, this one,' Henry said, pulling Rhodri back from the brink of self-flagellation.

'But it's nothing to worry about. Customs ships patrol the waves. We're all perfectly safe.'

'Fifty pence this time!'

'Afternoon!' a voice said. It was Ceri's, full of bounce, which gave him so much pleasure.

He got up and brushed the sand off his legs and asked what she was up to.

'Me? Shouldn't you be explaining why you're wearing a tea towel bandana on a Monday afternoon? You do make me laugh.'

Shit. He'd forgotten.

'Oh, yes,' he said, his hands reaching to the edges of his impromptu headgear to pull them down so they covered his ears. 'Well, Henry's on an inset day. I offered to look after him so Seren could get on with preparing for her craft fair. I'm his godfather. And I was owed time so I took it. Spontaneously. Like the mad devil I am. We're being pirates.'

'So sweet!'

Sweet? He wished he wasn't. Exciting! Daring! Irresistible! That would've been better to hear.

Henry piped up. 'Is it you?'

'Is it me what?' Ceri answered, getting down to his level.

'Who did the bunting?'

Befuddled, Rhodri looked from Henry to Ceri and back to Henry, wondering how on earth he'd come up with that idea.

'Me?' Ceri said with a screech. 'Why on earth would you say that?'

Henry put his hands behind his back as if he was presenting the case for the prosecution. 'Because it happened since you got here.'

'Henry!' Rhodri said, taken aback by his forthrightness although Henry was right about things having happened since she'd arrived, namely in his heart. 'Just because there's a causal link doesn't make it a correlation! Besides, Ceri's a barmaid, sorry, bar person, and they don't earn much money, apologies, Ceri.'

'It's okay, Rhodri. It's a good theory. Henry is obviously a big thinker, aren't you?'

Henry nodded. Then he frowned. 'So who would it have been?'

'I just think of it like Father Christmas. Does he visit you?'

Rhodri caught himself turning gooey at the way she related to him.

'Santa? Really?' Henry said in a mocking tone. Rhodri and Ceri swapped sad eyes over his lost innocence. 'I've looked into it and he'd never get round to deliver all those presents in one night. No, it's the elves who do it, they're the ones who come down the chimneys because there's millions of elves. Santa just directs it from the North Pole. So perhaps it's elves? What they do when Christmas is over.'

Satisfied with his conclusion, he returned to his quest for pennies.

Ceri mouthed '*aw*' at Rhodri and he felt his tummy flip like a Welsh pancake. She jumped as she remembered why she was there.

'Shit, I haven't told you. I was driving back from St Davids and on the way, I saw two vans parked at the top of the woodland where the road passes by. Can you get access to the woods from there?'

'There's an old stile. What about the vans?' His chest was thumping.

'There was a council one ...' Ceri paused and her eyes dropped. 'Plus a CadCon one.'

'Damn it,' Rhodri said, stamping his foot. 'Right, let's go. Henry, come on, we need to get up there.'

The three of them raced off the beach and up the lane, past Rhodri's house and into the trees where several yellow hardhats were visible right at the peak of the woods. He saw his father, and Dai, and felt a surge of rage.

'Dad!' Rhodri yelled. 'Dai!'

He saw their heads turn, there was a discussion and an age passed as the pair of them navigated the path down to him.

'What's going on?' he demanded.

'Site visit, son,' his dad said importantly. 'What does it look like?'

'Why didn't you tell me?'

'The information is in the public arena,' Dai said. 'You should know that.'

He was struggling to keep calm in the face of Dai's pomposity. So he aimed his anger at their father.

'Dad, this is wrong and you know it. Look at it, look at this place, why would you want to chop it all down?'

'Rhodri, this is what the village needs. It'll bring work to the people, I'll be using local tradesmen and so on, and it will, in time, improve the provision of services. A new health centre, better schools. Otherwise the youngsters born here will leave, like they do now.'

'But tourism, if we can bring it back, that's a trade in itself, something we can manage as a community. Your development will be out of keeping with our traditional way of life. Dad, you're just coming across as heartless.'

'Everything I've ever done has been done with heart!' his dad cried. 'For my family, for you boys.'

'See, this is what you do. Make me out to be ungrateful. But I'm the one who's stayed in this village, not the others.'

Dad's silence confirmed what Rhodri knew: his father thought he wasn't fulfilling his potential. Talk about double standards.

'We're going to have to get on.' Dai turned and left without any farewell.

'This isn't the last of it,' Rhodri raged.

'You can't fight this, Rhodri,' his father said. 'And your mother is worried sick we're going to fall out.'

The gall of him, trying to emotionally blackmail him into backing down.

He stood his ground. 'I can't watch this happen and do nothing.'

'You'd best lodge your objections to the planning committee then,' his father said, sounding like a true suit. 'I'll see you later, son.'

Rhodri wanted to cry with frustration. His fists were balled and he had to turn away from the sight of his father's departing back to regain control. Deep breaths in through the nose, hold for six, out through the mouth. He rooted his heels into the soft mossy bed to bring himself back to earth, seeing Ceri at work with Henry building a den. When she saw he was watching, she told

Henry to keep going and came over to Rhodri's side.

'Did it go as badly as it looked?'

'Worse,' he said, as the reality began to sink in. 'Dad'll be smooth-talking his way now to a decision in his favour. An appeal would take forever. We're running out of time.'

'Oh, no. Do you really think so?'

'Yes. I do. We're going to have to get a petition going and fix a date for a demo. Write to the papers, the MP, all of that.'

'Great. I'll do as much as I can. If that's any good. Although I'm not sure how much help I can be in a few days. I'm off on Friday.'

'That's fantastic, Ceri.' But something occurred to him. 'Why do you care so much?'

She wrung her hands and took a breath.

'It's going to sound silly but ... I kind of feel like I'm having a holiday romance.'

He gulped. He knew how she felt and his voice broke because how could he not ask. 'With whom?'

'Dwynwen!' she cried. 'Don't look so flaming shocked! You were the one who got me hooked.'

At least he'd managed that.

'But I thought you found us a bit ... foreign.'

'Not so much anymore.' She smiled. 'I suppose I'm getting used to your funny ways. It is different here but everything has its place and everyone has the right to be what they are. Like, Dwynwen, it doesn't need to be brought up to date or gentrified or anything. That's not to say it doesn't need a helping hand. But it's perfect, most of the time, as it is.'

How could it be they always ended up having these

sorts of deep conversations when they barely knew each other? This was the problem: inexplicably, she made him feel things deeper than anyone else ever had. And he couldn't stop his own outpouring.

'It's about finding happiness in what is there, in the ordinary, isn't it? Rather than thinking, *if it was just like that, it'd be perfect*. A bit like relationships.'

'Seconded,' Ceri said.

'The thing is,' he said, 'we have to get cracking. We haven't got the luxury of time. And it won't be easy fighting my father and brother, let alone my employer.'

He looked up into the branches and saw change was coming. The breeze was stiff now, Ceri's hair was whipping her lovely face, and out west, at sea, its blue beauty was covered with a sheet of corrugated iron. It all pointed one way.

'Things are going to get rough, Ceri,' he said. 'And I don't just mean the weather.'

16

The wind had blown Ceri in and today it was going to blow her out again. This time, though, it had a name, Storm Elsie. And she was giving it her all with ninety five mile per hour gusts which Ceri battled to stay upright on her way to the car. The bags full of goodbyes bought for her friends in Dwynwen flapped and flew in her hands as she found her keys and it took a gut-busting effort to pull open the door before she could throw herself in. It slammed on her just in the nick too as Elsie chucked a deluge of rain on St Davids which made the Friday morning shoppers scatter like dropped marbles for refuge. Some farewell this was from Wales as the downpour turned to deafening hail, pelting the roof, and an inch of ice quickly buried the wipers. If there wasn't a break in this weather bomb, Mum's ashes would be blasted all the way to Spain. Not how Ceri had planned it but maybe it was for the best: Mum would be with Emilio in the click of a castanet and Ceri's dreaded drawn-out ta-ta would be cut short by the elements. There'd be no lingering walk in the woods and no chance to touch the bunting or wave out of the car until everyone was out of sight. And her sorrow would be eclipsed by the urge to outrun the battering. All there was to do was to wheel her stand-up suitcase from the hallway and pick up Mum and her letter and set her free.

She took out her phone to see if Tash had answered the text she'd sent as soon as she'd got to town to tell her she was coming home and would she mind if she crashed Mother's Day tomorrow because it was going to be difficult. She hadn't bothered to mention finding out about the house being sold from Jade because Tash would only get narky. It needed to be done face to face. And really, Ceri wanted to hold on to the warmth of her holiday for as long as she could. The sadness she felt at leaving was in her core but she'd be back one day. Her worry now was work – how she was going to get back into the groove of selling herself again, when she'd loved her anonymity so much. But she'd file it away for Monday.

Yes, Tash had replied – 'Sorry, we've gone to Kev's sister's, back in the week' – and there were five missed FaceTime calls from Jade. It was the last thing Ceri wanted to do but she had been away for three weeks now – she owed it to her mate. And she might as well reacquaint herself with technology.

Seeing her own face as the call connected, Ceri looked rested, albeit windswept. Jade's sunny smile lit up the screen and Ceri grinned, so pleased to see her after so long.

'Hiya!' she said just as Jade's image froze. Even though she was caught mid-blink, she still looked glamorous with her styled blonde bob framing her big blue eyes and gorgeous bee-sting lips. Ceri knew instantly she was wearing the Cheap As Chic range aimed at the office girl in her twenties – Dawn 2 Dusky Cream foundation, In the Spotlight contouring highlighter, Sassy Black liquid liner and mascara, Cheeky Pink blush and Classy Bird barely there lip gloss. It felt a world away – and Jade was shouting now as if she was.

'Pricey? Is that you?' For a beat, she didn't recognise herself as Price, she was so used to being Rees.

'Yes! Can you hear me? I can hear you. The 4G here is crap!'

'Oh my God, Ceri ... what's going on? You're all fuzzy!'

'I'm in the car in a storm.'

'Shit! Are you all right? You look terrible.'

'Don't panic, I'm fine!'

Jade's mouth began to move again and there was no mistaking her grimace. 'But your face ... and your hair, you look awful.' She was never one to mince her words. 'You're supposed to be doing a photoshoot in an hour. You are on your way home, aren't you?'

'Eh?' What photoshoot?

'Oh, Ceri, I've been taking it as read that even if you haven't been able to reply you'll be reading your emails.' Jade's eyes were bulging. 'I had to sign off the OMG range. I hadn't heard from you so I assumed it'd be okay. The photographer is coming to do promo shots. Jesus ... what are we going to do?'

'Shit. I'm so sorry, kid.'

'Why are you looking like that anyway? What if you get spotted? The company will go bananas. You're supposed to be an ambassador!' Manicured nails in Ceri Price cherry covered her mouth. It was a far cry from Ceri's own plain fingers which hadn't seen varnish for days.

'What do you mean? I thought I looked quite nice. Natural.'

'You look a flamin' state! Haven't you got any make-up on?'

'No,' she said, offended. She didn't look such a wreck surely?

'But it was your rule! Neither of us to go out without a face on! Have you gone raving? Look, the phone's ringing … I've got to pick up. What the frig am I going to say?'

Ceri's mind went frantic for an excuse for her no-show. 'Tell them I'm ill.' Because apparently she looked it to Jade.

'Ceri, I can't be making up these excuses any more. This has gone on too long now. I've had to stick up a post on Twitter and Facebook saying you're just having some time out. But three weeks is a long time on social media. They're asking why you've done no videos of late. A couple of the advertisers are getting a bit heavy.'

This was like a telling-off from the boss – and rightly so. Ceri did feel bad she'd let the tables turn and left it all to Jade to cover. But going back to vlogging and tweeting and Facebooking would do her head in. The answer was staring her in her naked face.

'You're going to have to do it.'

'Me?' Jade yelped.

Thinking on her feet, Ceri made a decision. 'Think of it as a practice run for your wedding make-up. Tell them the new range needs a new campaign, a new face. You.'

Jade went silent and rested her chin on her hand. 'Ceri, this will change things. It's not just something you throw out willy-nilly. What about our strategy?'

Ceri couldn't even remember the strategy, only their brain-storming meetings at an Alderley Edge wine bar where they cackled and snorted from too much prosecco.

She saw a crossroads looming and before she knew it, she had chosen a new direction.

'Look, the way I see it, you're younger than me. You're twenty-five. I'm banging on the door of thirty and I'm getting too old to spend my life online. And you're exactly what Cheap As Chic needs. You're the market.'

And just like that, she was walking away from herself. Resigning from the position of Ceri Price. Jade was staring at her open-mouthed. Ceri nodded slowly because even though she hadn't consciously sat down to work it out, it made sense because it was true.

'If you do this now,' Jade said, 'there's no going back.'

Her finger-wagging went blank and was replaced by the word *reconnecting*.

There's no going back echoed in Ceri's ears. It had all moved on. The range wasn't hers anymore – in her heart of hearts, she knew she couldn't sell it when she couldn't relate to her old life. It wasn't who she was now. Jade would manage and she'd do it bloody well. What's more, Tash hadn't made a 'welcome home' sign for her. Why should she? There was no one else to blame. This was Ceri's doing. She started the engine and felt ... what? Upset, excluded, lost, frightened, aimless? Not a bit. Just sheer relief the load was off her shoulders. Up north wasn't home anymore. But what did that make Dwynwen?

She crawled back to the village, with all these thoughts whirling around her head like the leaves and branches careering across the treacherous waterlogged roads. It was a dangerous, blustery drive under squalling cats-and-dogs and twice she had to swerve to avoid debris. She was operating on adrenaline, both from the journey and from the sinking enormity of what she'd just done, and so when she reached the final bend to Dwynwen she screamed out loud at the sight of a fallen tree across the road. Her body jolted forward and the seatbelt propelled her back and for a while, she sat catching her breath as the wipers whirred over and over on their fastest setting, which was useless in the rain. The effect made the tree look as if it was melting then rearing, on repeat, and it was scary to think how close she'd been to smashing into it. Was this a sign she should go to Cheshire instead and she'd made a mistake returning here? A physical barrier warning her in no uncertain terms not to do this? Her heart raced at the question. But it was like flipping a coin on a dilemma: it wasn't either heads or tails telling you what to do, it was what your gut called out for when it was revolving. Now she understood what she wanted: to stay in Dwynwen permanently. But now she'd admitted it, irrational panic set in – what if she couldn't get back there?

She flicked on her hazard lights and got out to see if there was a way she could clamber over or around the tree, but it was taller than she was and it completely blocked the lane. She gave it a futile push and kicked the bark in frustration, as the heavens opened once more and drenched her in seconds. She was about to get back in the car to work out what to do next when she heard shouting and the whine of a chainsaw.

'Hello!' she yelled, cupping her hands around her mouth, jumping to try to be seen.

'We're coming! Stay where you are!' somebody ordered and where there was a slight taper in the trunk, she saw flying sawdust. *Thank God!* Ceri kept up a commentary of 'nearly there' and 'keep going' until a jagged slash ran from top to bottom at the left end and the tree inched towards her, beginning to come apart. Within a few minutes, she saw the heave of men with soaked dropped heads driving it forward like a rugby scrum. She spotted Rhodri first and her spirits leapt, then Gwil, Rhodri's father, Barri, another few she didn't recognise and English Dick. Mel nipped through the gap in her mac and threw her arms around Ceri.

'Ceri! We've been so worried! Rhodri saw you go, we thought you'd left without saying goodbye!'

'As if, kid! I've still got the keys to the cottage!'

'Oh, yes! Of course, the storm's making me think bent.'

'And ... I'm not leaving,' Ceri said.

'Not again! You're like an actress who wants another bloody encore!' Mel laughed.

'It's the last time, I promise,' Ceri vowed. 'I'm staying here ... for good.' Saying the words out loud gave her a thrill – those same words would've choked her in February.

'Never!' Mel said, dancing, calling to Rhodri, 'She's staying! Forever!'

His bulk turned around and Ceri saw a kind of drunk disbelief on his face. She waved madly and he raised a confused hand at her before he was pulled back into the effort of clearing the road.

'Oh, Ceri, you'll have to tell me all about it. In the pub because there's no power anywhere. Usually lasts twelve hours at least. Gwen's got a gas oven so we'll be fed and we can light a fire and some candles. We'll get the radio on so we can listen to the last Six Nations games too – Wales can't win the whole thing but if Ireland beat

France then England come second and that's as good as a win for us! I'll start the petition against the development as well, everyone will walk down later, you'll see, to compare storm damage. Oh, and I almost forgot, my dad has said he'll put off selling the cabin till the end of summer, I've had a reprieve! Coming?'

Sodden, out of a job and in bits at the thought of her first Mothering Sunday without her mum, Ceri couldn't think of a better way to spend her day.

'You bloody bet I am,' she said, feeling finally she belonged somewhere.

Ceri counts her blessings

I've made it, Mum, onto the beach. It only took me three weeks. How I managed to avoid it when there's chuff-all to do here just shows what you can achieve if you put your mind to it. But I'd run out of excuses. And it means I don't have to see any Mother's Day lunches or bouquets; that'd hurt too much. I can just sit here and cry and no one will know. I remember your last Mother's Day. Tash had popped in to see you first thing with a card and choccies but Kev and the kids were taking her out so I went with you to the dementia group afternoon tea. You sang in the choir and it was incredible seeing you and all the other lost souls who could barely talk knowing the words off by heart to the songs of your pasts, as if the music had flicked a switch in your brains. Your face changed too, you looked alive again, especially during 'Save A Prayer' by Duran Duran, which was one of your favourites. Perhaps you were reliving the rubbish dance routines Tash and me did to your records, when we'd fight over who was best, and you'd tell us we were both equally 'triffic' and give us a standing ovation! And here come more tears ... I'll be glad when today is over. Just when I think I'm adjusting to you being gone, the emptiness comes back. *Glass half full, girl*, you'd say, so deep breath, I'll stop my moping and count some blessings.

Number one, it's getting myself on the beach. Which is all thanks to my lovely friend Mel, who would have to be number two – she held my hand for ages on the stony edge where the lane ends and the sand begins. I kept looking for rain clouds to give me a get-out but yesterday's storm blew them away. And shock, horror, the sun was threatening to come out. Mel stuck by me, she told me about her trip to the harbour last week with her dad. It was the first time in yonks she'd left the village out of choice rather than duty. It's only round the next bay, five miles or thereabouts, but it could've been Timbuktu. Her dad said he'd turn around if she wanted but she did it. Mel knew she had to make a change; to stop her past ruling her present. I realised she had crossed a line and I needed to as well: she said I didn't have to see the beach as where I'd lose you when I eventually built up the courage to scatter you. I could see it as the place where you'd been and where I'd always find you.

I took a step and felt the soft slip of sand. My stomach went with it. But Mel was there, her arm linked through mine, holding me up. The squeak of my wellies took me back to Blackpool, when I was about six, and you'd taken us for our first holiday you could afford in the five years after Tash's dad had gone. We were so hard up, weren't we, we went in February rather than the summer and we stayed in one double bed in that tired old B&B, you in the middle, playing hell with us for bringing back half the beach in our boots and making the sheets sandy. That memory made me smile and I began to feel okay. Mel let me go and I kept walking back and forth, imagining I was in your footsteps; and it's the strangest thing but suddenly it felt familiar as if I knew the place, which is impossible because you never brought us here. And I found myself wondering why you didn't ... when Dwynwen obviously mattered enough to you to be your final resting place. But I can't ask. I can only presume you were confused. I found a rock to perch on, where I am now, and I watched the waves and their softness made it seem all right, like your hand would do on my forehead and through my hair if I was poorly on the sofa. It's not quite me mending, but it's the closest I've got to peace.

That brings to me my third blessing. And your head will spin when I tell you ... because this is the first day of the rest of my life. Yep, I've decided to stay here for a while. Maybe you'll think I'm mad, and maybe I am, because I was all ready to leave twenty-four-hours ago. But Jade's call was the final straw – the business isn't 'me' anymore. At least, that's what made me decide it. I'd been thinking it for a while. I can do the behind the scenes stuff, sure, but I can't be the public face of it when I don't feel it. How can I when I haven't used heated rollers since February and my make-up bag is untouched? Jade is more than capable of that. You see, I love being Ceri Rees. There's none of the shit of being Ceri Price. Like that party I put on when I hit one million subscribers in that posh bar in Manchester and I put on a minibus for the workingmen's club thinking they'd be made up to be included, but afterwards nobody said a word of thanks. There was even an anonymous letter saying I was up myself. Or that bloke who wined and dined me, whatsisname Gary something, who ran a sports car garage, who said he was setting up a charity to pay for his four-year-old niece's flight to Florida for pioneering treatment. Only it turned out he was a panel beater and there was no sick child. The people here are kind and helpful, modest and unpretentious without a pinch of arrogance or boastfulness. They've come up with calling Dwynwen the Village of Love to woo back the tourists. At first I thought there was more charm in a cat-litter tray, but there's a kind of magic here. The way they've taken to the bunting which turned up overnight, it's glorious. No one knows who's behind it but they've accepted it as if it was some divine intervention from the saint! It disappeared yesterday and I assumed it'd been vandalised, like it would be anywhere else, but it was Mel, who'd taken it down to keep it out of harm's way until the storm passed. If the Village of Love was going to work anywhere, it'll be here.

Tash will think I'm cuckoo for staying – she'll say it's typical of me, going from the sublime to the ridiculous, but she'll be glad to be rid of me. My emotions are too messy for her. I either catch her at a bad moment, say it's Lola's ballet class or she's at soft play with Gracie, or it's the answerphone. She hardly returns my calls. She's done her usual – dusted herself off and got on with things. You know, I only ever saw her upset twice after you'd died. The first time, at your bedside when you'd passed. She'd missed you by three minutes and ran over in her dressing gown just after midnight and howled. Then at the funeral. Other than that, she's not leaned on me at all. She didn't even let me know the house was sold. God, I'm still upset about that – I heard that from Jade. That's why the villagers' warmth matters so much. Like

197

last night; it should've been a disaster. We had no power and it was so windy we wouldn't have been surprised if chunks of Ireland had crash-landed on The Dragon. But we had a great time drying off like wet dogs in front of a blazing fire, scoffing bowls of stew, having lots to drink and plenty of singing. Technically that was yesterday but I didn't get in until two a.m., so I'll count that as my fourth blessing.

My last ... hmm ... well, I suppose I can trust you not to say anything to anyone. It's Rhodri. Don't get excited, I haven't found The One. For him to be that he'd have to like me back, because I do like him, a lot. But there's no chance of it going anywhere – it's a little window shop, that's all. Same with Logan, he's another hottie, although I've not seen much of him – there must be something in the water here! We're too different, poles apart – his idea of a dirty weekend is perving over puffins on a windy Welsh island, for goodness sakes. But Rhodri's a nice person, that's all, he's funny and serious all at once, unlike anyone I've ever met. Almost like one of those fairytale heroes, good and true, proper and principled. He's taking on his father, who's planning to build forty homes on the woods. Most people would shrug and think of the inheritance. But not him. He cares so much for Dwynwen and it's catching. And I've caught it – I mean, how else could you explain a woman like me, who would never leave the house without heels or eyelash extensions, being outside in flats minus slap in a water-repellent fleece?

17

'Delivery. Sign here, please. And make it quick, it's taken us all day to find you.'

'Delivery? We're not expecting anything.'

'Says here The Dragon, Dwynwen. No returns.'

'Well, I never ... hang on, I bet it's my husband. He's done this before, got a hot tub, thinking it'd bring in punters; but I made him send it back because I couldn't bear the thought of Barri in his budgies. What's he ordered this time?'

'Furniture.'

'Furniture? But we've only just had a new lazyboy recliner.'

'Loveseats, the invoice says.'

'Loveseats, is it? Oh my days ... I knew I shouldn't have let Gwil read Fifty Shades of Grey.*'*

❧

'Right, so if everyone agrees, I'll ring the *Cambrian News* and let them know we're ready for a photographer to come in the morning. Okay?'

A loud cheer went up from Barri and English Dick, who'd been sinking pints since lunch at a guess, but Rhodri didn't doubt their support or the others who murmured theirs. It was everywhere, it seemed. The petition calling on the council to protect the woods had amassed an incredible one thousand signatures, thanks to volunteers dropping them off at village shops, libraries and petrol stations. He himself had collected a few hundred in his lunch hour. Mel had handed in fifty signatures from the cabin; it wasn't much but she was stuck there day and night with the same old faces so she had tried her best. Ceri had been the biggest hitter, though, with a door-knock up and down the estates around the area. It had been a terrific effort and proved he'd been right to wait till they had enough names before they went public with the Village of Love. It gave the news piece two jabs: it showed they weren't only complaining, they were doing something about it. Plus, the start of April meant more people were thinking about the summer, which felt as if it was just around the corner. The story would be live by lunchtime tomorrow; then he would email it personally to every councillor on the planning committee. Victory would be theirs!

Satisfied with the meeting, he thanked everyone and went about finishing his pint. He had a nice Monday night tea planned – a locally caught bit of pollock which he'd turn into Thai fishcakes – and then he was going to dig a trench for his runner beans: he'd saved all of his tea bags, peelings and egg shells for weeks to give the soil the best start. But most exciting of all he was almost done building his own outdoor wood-fired pizza oven. He'd created the base, laid firebricks, made the dome out of clay and sand and cut the entrance at the weekend – all that was left was the final insulation layer. He wanted to do a grand pizza evening: his dream scenario would be sharing a margarita and roasted artichokes in the glow of the fire with Ceri, licking olive-oiled fingers and toasting each other with posh Italian lager. The reality would be a scrum of locals and the stink of singed eyebrows. Because he'd never get away with inviting her alone. It would look as if he had designs on her. Which he had, but he didn't want everyone to know in case she felt uncomfortable. But then how would he ever be able to make a move if he didn't make a move? This was one of the drawbacks of living in such a small place. The inevitable knock-back would make things awkward and he'd be a laughing stock. Perhaps if he got her on her own and dropped it into the conversation: *you, me, pizza*, then he might summon the courage.

He drained his glass and took it back to the bar, where Ceri was lit up like an angel by the evening sun which streamed through the windows. She was so lovely, he thought, watching her flip a tap just at the right moment before the beer spilled over the top. He could just ask her now, casually …

The heavenly vision shattered when Gwen raced in at fever pitch through the front door.

'ALL HANDS ON DECK!' she yelled, going bananas. 'SANTA'S BEEN AGAIN!'

A chorus of 'What?' and 'Talk sense, woman!' went up and she was forced to take a breath.

'It's another surprise! Quick! Come see!'

A collective gasp went up and the pub emptied out onto the courtyard. Rhodri couldn't believe his eyes. An assortment of beautiful hand-carved dark wooden chairs and tables, heavy sacks and towering palms in huge pots were on the tarmac and a van was halfway up the hill. Gwil was looking stunned, holding a slip which Rhodri bent closer to read. It was addressed to the Village of Love and specified no returns under any circumstances!

'It's a beer garden,' Gwil said. 'For us. For free. Five pairs of loveseats, six sets of tables and chairs, gravel for the floor and plants and flowers. And some solar lights ... love heart ones.'

'Bloody hell!' Rhodri said. 'Saint Dwynwen has struck again! What's the flat-packed stuff?'

'Some planters, it says here,' Gwil said, quite over-come. Rhodri had only seen him this emotional when Wales were playing rugby.

'We'd better get some spades and rakes and screw-drivers and things!' Ceri said, whooping next to him, as the locals crawled over the goodies like ants. On closer inspection, each loveseat, which was joined by a table in the middle, had slightly different designs but all had intricate hearts chiselled into their backs. *Who could be behind it?* Immediately he thought of Seren, who wasn't here and had said she'd been working very long hours on some new designs. She'd sold nothing at her craft fair – the storm had stopped people coming out. It certainly was craftsmanship of the highest standard – it reminded him of the lovespoon she'd made for him. But would she be capable of producing all of this in a matter of weeks? He just didn't know. And right now, he didn't care because all that mattered was that it gave the Village of Love another boost. Once word got out – and it would tomorrow – people would come to watch the sunset in this most charming of beer gardens. It was another step towards Dwynwen's revival, he thought happily.

He turned to mention it to Ceri but Logan had slinked up beside her. And, oh God, his wetsuit was peeled to his belly button, revealing a muscular chest that was fresh from the cover of *Men's Health*. The utter wanker. Not only that but he was holding a screwdriver in her face like some kind of exhibitionist.

'I'm well equipped if nothing else,' he heard him say.

Rhodri's toes curled at the innuendo and he waited to see how Ceri would react, praying she wouldn't stoop so low to make some naff retort. She hesitated, though, before she took it. Rhodri wanted to scream at her, 'Don't touch his screwdriver, you don't know where it's been! I'll get mine instead, I regularly clean them.' But he kept his mouth clamped shut because if he mentioned his well-oiled tools, he knew he'd be the one who came off worst.

'I've another in the van,' Logan said, persuading her, referring to his sleek black VW parked oh-so-handily next to him with its boot indecently wide open, flaunting an oar.

'Ooh, you paddle board, then?' she said. Rhodri contained the urge to yell, 'Yes, but I taught him! I'm much better than him!'

'Yes, perfect day for it,' Logan said. 'No waves. You get a different perspective on things out there. It's so quiet.'

'Oh, wow. It must be like having the sea to yourself.' She was smiling her dazzling smile and *hang on*, there wasn't one of her trademark smirks to be seen. Clearly, she reserved those for idiots like himself.

'Almost,' Logan said, pulling on a long-sleeved T-shirt. *Phew, he was getting dressed.* 'A couple of seals joined me.' *Not this line*, Rhodri groaned, he'd heard this one before.

'Wow, did they come up close?' *And Ceri was falling for it.*

'Quite close. But they didn't stay for a chat or anything.

They're shy.' *Unlike you,* he hissed inside. 'The sea will warm up now April's coming, you should try it if you haven't already?'

No! No! He knew where this was going.

'I'm more of a lay-by-the-pool person. And before today, before I decided to stay on even, it always looked too cold and rough.'

'I've got some kayaks, much more stable. Come out with me,' Logan said, finally acknowledging Rhodri with a nod which had a distant whiff of smug about it. As if he hadn't known Rhodri was eavesdropping. This was brinkmanship. In the language spoken by Neanderthals, Logan had gone and cocked his leg on him. All he cared about now was her. He didn't have a chance with her – she was way out of his league – he just didn't think Logan was worthy. He hoped Ceri would see what Logan was like before she got hurt. He just didn't get it: she was one of the most switched-on people he'd ever come across. She must've met Logan's type before.

'I've got life jackets if you're nervous.'

Rhodri clenched his backside as he waited for her to agree – *because she would, women always did with Logan –* and when the inevitable happened, he decided he'd heard enough. He marched off to get his tools, grumbling all the way back to his shed. How the hell could Logan just walk in and ask her out like that without even making it sound like he was asking her out? Because that's what it came down to, since Logan didn't do anything without an ulterior motive. Yet had Rhodri dared to do the same, it would've come out in a very unnatural stumble and a stammer. It just wasn't fair. Then he ran back down the lane as fast as he could to make sure Logan didn't have

Ceri to himself, stopping to walk just before he popped out by the pub so he didn't look desperate. He had to remember to adjust the sour milk expression on his face, too or Ceri would wonder what had got his goat.

When he got to her, she was watching Logan rip open plastic sacks of gravel with his teeth and deposit them onto the ground in great dusty clouds with a flick of his wrists. It was quite sickening. Still, he managed to give her a smile. She returned it and gave his arm a friendly squeeze. Her attention made him fluster and he fussed about with his beige utility belt. At least it made him look manly, he thought.

But Ceri just laughed. 'Come on, Batman,' she said, pointing at his pouch which made him die of embarrassment, 'let's go and build this pub a beer garden.'

18

There were people in the cabin Mel had never seen before. Complete strangers. Ordering food and drinks and perusing her shelves. It was fabulous – and all thanks to the news story which had broken online on Tuesday and then made the front page today, Thursday, in the print version. She'd pinned it up on the community noticeboard in Caban Cwtch and smiled every time she saw the headline *Village Makes Love Not War*. The piece featured a photo of Gwen and Gwil in a loveseat beneath the bunting, each waving a thick wad of petition signatures against the housing development. Rhodri's dad, who'd been asked to comment, had spoken like a politician, trusting the council to do what was best for the declining local economy. Poor Rhodri. But it had made him even more determined to press ahead with the demo next week. She'd read the article so many times she knew it word for word, yet still she felt a thrill each time it caught her eye on her way back and forth from the kitchen.

Over pints in the beer garden, Dwynwen had concluded now it wasn't Rhodri behind the bunting and the furniture – he was a council worker on council wages and the hand-crafted tables and chairs would've cost a fortune, a few grand at least. Seren was now prime suspect because of the quality of the carving but she'd pointed out the delivery driver had come from Mid Wales. So Gwil wondered if it was someone who had ties with the place: perhaps they'd moved away or used to spend their summers here but had heard it was down on its luck? But no, Gwen imagined somebody had bequeathed the bunting and the beer garden with strict instructions to keep it anonymous. All that was left was for Rhodri to ring the number on the invoice, which belonged to a co-operative of carpenters who'd quoted data protection at him. As for Mel, she had come to the conclusion that maybe they should be focusing not on who was behind it but on appreciating it – if they were meant to find out, they would. And the important thing was to use it to fight the housing plan. That was her answer to those asking what she thought. Including a few curious customers who'd read the story. People hadn't quite flooded into The Dragon and the cabin: it was more of a slow trickle but it was a start. Thank goodness she'd worked her butt off the last few days, and nights, tidying it up. It hadn't been easy – she'd found it painful to throw broken buckets and curling postcards, ripped sandcastle flags and fraying beach towels because they felt like comrades who'd been with her through thick and mostly thin. But it hadn't compared to the blitz at home, which was proving much harder. The fifteen-minute bursts seemed eternal, milking her memories afresh, and as soon as she'd cleared one shelf, it would become home to another pile she was supposed to be sorting. Dad had come across it for himself when he'd popped into the Pink House for the mail this morning. By the gulp in his voice, she'd known he'd seen the mess when he'd come here to replace the buzzer over the door with a little brass bell. But he hadn't added to her shame: he'd spoken around it, praising her efforts here for making it lighter and lovelier than ever before. Something Ceri was seeing for herself now, her eyes on stalks as the tinkle of the new bell announced her arrival.

'Look at this! It's like Cupid's love-nest in here! You've done an amazing job!'

'I've even got love-heart tights on too!' Mel said, showing a leg from behind the café counter.

Ceri clapped and twirled around, then mimed a scream when she realised there were actual customers not villagers having elevenses at a table.

'The window! The nets have gone!' she said, pointing, 'You can see the sea! And wow ... that is beautiful ...'

She was gazing at a hanging heart welded from gleaming metal forks which dangled in front of the glass in a declaration of love for the view.

'Seren made it for me. Isn't she clever?'

'Totally. It's all neat in here, there's no boxes to fall over,' she laughed, 'And, oh! Love-heart tablecloths and love-heart fairy lights!'

'Got them off Amazon, cheap as chips! I've done some photos too, I managed to nail some driftwood together for frames,' Mel said, nodding at the pictures overlooking the seating area. There was a close-up of two fern buds which had curled into a heart, her own hands making a heart over sunrise, a huge heart she'd drawn in the sand and a heart-shaped notch in a tree which she'd found in the woods.

'You're an absolute star. You could sell those prints!

Flippin' 'eck, Mel, it's such a turnaround,' Ceri said, pulling out a chair and ordering a brew.

'Couldn't have done it without you,' Mel said, switching on the kettle and taking a pew with Ceri. 'Which is strange because when I first met you I thought you would never last here. No offence!'

'Charming!' Ceri said.

Mel laughed, it was so easy to talk like this to her. 'I can't imagine you not being here now.' She squeezed her hand to show she meant it. 'Any regrets packing it all in to stay here?'

'None. No regrets at all.' She beamed. 'Apart from the coffee situation.'

'What do you mean? What's wrong with my instant?'

'Tastes like piss. No offence,' she said with an arch of her eyebrow. 'But don't you crave a proper one? Ground beans, hot steam, frothy milk – the gleaming stainless-steel theatre of it all?'

'I did look into it once. Posh coffees were just coming onto the high street when I was in Cardiff,' she said, drifting away for a moment, remembering her first bitter taste of an Americano. 'But those machines, they cost a few thousand pounds at least.'

'The mark-up on a cup is massive, though. And there's no competition when you come to the beach. We've got the start of a brand here, you've got a niche market, there's so many handy types around who could mend the machine if it went wrong, you could get a loyalty card and a heart-shaped stamp!'

Mel expected to see a day-dream bubble over Ceri's head. Instead she had eyes like flint.

'I'm not sure ... how do you know this stuff?' She

didn't like to add 'when you're just a barmaid-stroke-beauty-therapist' but come on, Ceri was hardly one of the *Dragons' Den* lot. Ceri opened her mouth to speak, probably to admit as much. Then she clamped it shut, scratched her nose and began again.

'Right, this is a mad idea, and feel free to bum me off because maybe I'm talking out of my rear end. But I'm looking for an investment opportunity. I've got money from my mum's estate. How would you feel if I came in with you on the cabin?'

How *would* she feel?

'You're proper screwy,' Mel spluttered. 'Why would you want to risk it?'

'Potential, Melyn, potential.'

She'd never seen Ceri look so ... well, determined.

'How much is this place worth? Thirty-five, forty grand?'

'I'd guess so.'

'We'd get it valued properly. You keep running the place, I'll share the shifts, no problem, but I'll handle the marketing. Get the word out. We can get a coffee machine, do up the menu, buy new furniture, revamp the kitchen ...'

'Wow!' It was quite a vision.

'We could even get wifi.'

'No way!'

'I've had a look and there are ways to get broadband in remote places. We can get someone in. Every business needs high-speed internet access.'

'But isn't being cut off part of our charm?'

'Definitely, but there doesn't have to be a mast on top of the cabin! I just think it's one of those essentials, whether we like it or not. Whatever, just think of what we could do here. We could sell Seren's stuff. And if we get really busy we could always hire a Saturday girl ... like Ffion.'

It was too much. Mel looked at her scarlet nails – she felt under siege all of a sudden, as if Ceri was talking about more than the cabin. Mel was trying her best but it was as if it wasn't enough.

'Maybe,' she muttered, getting up to make tea and hide behind the counter.

'Oh, I'm sorry,' Ceri said at Mel's withdrawal. 'I get over-excited.'

'It's okay. I know you mean well ...'

'But I'm the incomer, I get it.'

'No ... it's just we move slower here than where you're from. You've got to make people think it's their idea. You can't rush us.'

Ceri held up her hands. 'Absolutely. My mum always said I took after my dad, he was a dynamo when it came to work.'

'Better that than the other. Mine, the biological one, was a dynamo at shirking,' Mel said, matter-of-factly. 'Oh, don't give me those eyes. I'm not sad about it. I've the best dad in the world.'

'What do you think he'd say, if I went halves?'

'I could ask him, I suppose,' Mel said, handing over Ceri's cuppa. 'I'm not sure if he'll take you up on it because he's stubborn, he is, but ... he did do something sort of unexpected when he took me on.'

'How do you mean?'

'My mam, she got pregnant with me with this other bloke. Thirty years ago, it was a big deal. When she told him, he didn't want to know. So she was there by herself and she hooked up with Lyn, my dad. They'd known each other since school, very close because they'd grown up together. He was a good listener, they talked a lot; her father wanted to kick her out. Dad married her just before I was born, so Mam wouldn't be on her own.'

'Incredible,' Ceri said.

'Yes, very. He gave up his own hopes and dreams for me. But over the years, duty sort of suffocated them. It kept them together too long. I don't blame Mam for leaving him, although I used to. I think it's why I fell so deeply for Al. I grew up seeing my parents not in love but in a kind of arrangement, like it was normal. So when I met Al and all of the fireworks went off, it was as if I was the first person in the world to fall in love.' Her hand trembled so she shoved it in her skirt pocket.

'How lovely. For me, I always knew this great love of your life existed because my mum had it with my dad. But I've never had it myself. Work's been my other half. Family, too. Although it feels now I haven't got any at all anymore. My sister, she's gone distant on me since Mum died. I haven't even bothered to tell her I'm staying on here.'

It was funny how they had things in common, when they were from different galaxies. Ceri's eyes, though, they felt familiar.

'Why don't you invite her to see it for herself? You've got the cottage for as long as you want it.'

'Tash doesn't understand why I came here in the first place. She'd be crying because there's no twenty-four-hour Tesco up the road. And if I told her I was thinking about buying somewhere here ...'

'Really?'

'Yeah. I'm serious about staying here. My mum, it'd be like she wasn't gone.' Ceri's chin quivered, which made Mel ache.

'It's okay, it is. I was the same with my first guinea pig, Eluned. Couldn't mention her for years without bawling. I do understand.'

Ceri smiled. 'Well, if you can cope with that,' she said, taking a deep breath. 'Her name ... it was ... Angharad. Although everyone called her Ange. Being in Crewe, we only lived, what, a stone's throw from Wales, but it was a different world to us. She never spoke about Dwynwen. I s'pose she'd left it behind. I wish I knew where she'd lived, which house.'

'Maybe ask Barri? He's Dwynwen through and through.'

'Yeah, I could, I suppose. But it was forty-plus years ago. I wouldn't expect him to know.'

It was a polite way of putting it that Barri's brain cells had been shot to smithereens by the booze.

'At least you found us,' Mel said, patting her heart.

'That's very true, kid,' Ceri said. 'It does feel right here. For the first time in ... well, forever ... I'm content. I haven't stopped for years, it's always been nose to the grindstone, but it's like I've raised my head to actually appreciate what's around me. And Dwynwen, it's made me richer than any bank account could. I don't need anything over and above the necessities here – apart from a proper coffee – and I feel so at home, because I feel so myself. And it's been a surprise because I never knew this was who I was. I just have such a good feeling about staying here. Like I'll get to share in happiness.'

This new friend of hers was so often upbeat and funny,

Mel forgot that underneath it all she was an orphan. Adrift in the world, she was, no wonder she wanted to put down her anchor. It convinced her to approach her father to see if she could find some meaning for Ceri.

'No promises,' Mel said, reaching out and taking Ceri's hand. 'But let me talk to Dad about the investment idea.'

19

B obbing around on the serene sea, Ceri could almost forget Logan had been subjected to a face-full of her arse as she'd clambered into her kayak.

It wouldn't have been so bad had she not been taken out seconds before by a shocking, freezing wave which had left her choking on salt water, putting paid to what little confidence she'd had. And so she'd half-heartedly launched herself into the slippery wobbly length of plastic, knowing the moment she'd thrown herself on she was going to slide off. Logan had grabbed at whatever he could of her body to heave her in – which happened to be her backside. In an unforgivingly tight wetsuit, which she'd borrowed from Logan's surf school collection in his lock-up on the beach. Probably in size Huge Camel Toe.

'Just like a seal,' he'd teased, expertly mounting his kayak without a splash. Squinting into the sunshine, she'd checked him for gills, he was so effortless.

'It'd be easier to stand up on a bouncy castle after a skinful,' she'd muttered, mortified at having shown herself up. Her soaking corkscrewed hair deposited stinging sodium onto her face, her feet had gone blue and one of her ears was blocked. It wasn't quite how she'd imagined this lazy Sunday to go. 'You said it was like bathwater today.'

'It is!'

'Since when did anyone have a wash in water this cold?' She shivered in spite of the full-watt sun. March had become April, but though it was bright and spring-like it was still too early for real warmth.

'Let's get moving.'

A series of instructions followed as she fought to keep herself straight with an oar which had a mind of its own. 'Strong arms!' and 'left, left!' then 'right! Go right to stop yourself going in circles.'

Eventually, when she'd got used to the bulk of her life jacket and past the rise and dip of the water as she moved away from the shore, she got into a rhythm of one-two, one-two.

When he'd shouted, 'You've got it!' she began to trust she wouldn't capsize. She'd looked up around her and a new sense of panic kicked in – they were what felt like miles out. The cabin and pub were dots in the distance and they were in very deep water. What the hell lurked beneath? She shot a nervous glance over the side and switched her gaze back to her sodden lap. What had she been thinking, coming out here? She wouldn't be happy until she was back on land.

'Jesus Christ! I'm not going any further out, Logan, I'll tell you that for free!' she'd said, past caring she was freaking out in the company of the prince of hotness.

'Relax. We'll head parallel to the coast now, to the waterfall. It's worth it. Trust me.'

'Oh, great. There's only rocks and shit to crash into.'

'We won't go near them, don't worry.' He'd reached out a hand and brought her kayak to his so they bumped.

Like kissing lips. 'And I used to be a lifeguard, so if anything happens I'll save you, all right?'

Ceri felt the surge of gratitude that came when you felt helpless. She hadn't experienced that in a long time. She'd been trained to fix things herself, to be the saviour of her own soul, learned from Mum who'd had two kids on her tod. Dave the ex had helped out if things needed doing around the house but she'd never relied on him. Self-sufficiency was king. *No, it was queen.* So she was appalled at herself when she felt her chest swell against the compression of her wettie as if it was heaving within a straining bodice. It had taken just a blip of vulnerability to turn her into a simpering maiden. Yet how could she be anything else when she felt so incapable and the man alongside her remained bone dry in the middle of the sea? 'If you want to go back at any point, just say, okay?' he said, his hand brushing hers, 'You're doing really well but I don't want you to be scared.'

Oh God, he had empathy and insight too. Emotional intelligence. Something she'd never discovered in Dave, who'd had the sensitivity of a dustbin. If she had to be rescued by anyone Logan would do very nicely.

So on they went, the repetitive action of the paddle settling her down, and she started to breathe more easily as they crossed the bay until she looked up and saw the majesty of the waterfall.

This was where she was now, stunned by its awesome power: the spill of the stream she'd seen in the woods, at the crest between the trees, hurtling down over the cliff edge, splashing against the sheer rock face and spraying out white as it hit the sand. And it went on and on for eternity. It would have been here when Mum was a girl and it would be here forever ... like love.

'Can you get to that bit of the beach by the waterfall? On foot?' she asked.

'At low tide, yes. But not many know you can. It's an insider's secret.'

She nodded, knowing she'd found the spot to scatter Mum. She didn't want to do it but she was beginning to understand that life went on. Just like the waterfall.

Mum's request to be laid to rest here hadn't made sense to Ceri. How could it when it was made in a meandering mumble three days before she'd died? Yet Ceri had wanted to honour it no matter what. Tash suggesting the garden as her final resting place had hurt her very much: it was as if her sister had wanted to do it out of convenience. And where was the meaning in it when the house was going to be sold?

No, it had to be done here. Even though Ceri now understood there wasn't some deeper reason hidden behind the request. She'd wondered if it had surfaced when Mum would think she was in the past as plain as day, telling Ceri to get ready for school and not to forget her lunchbox. Those conversations, though, had been fleeting: the reality was that Mum spoke rubbish more than sense. Perhaps she had remembered this place because it was jumbled up in her mind with the memory of Ceri's father who'd died at sea. In her grief, Ceri had searched for meaning. Yet watching the torrent of water seemingly on endless repeat, she didn't feel as wretched. *What did people say? It is what it is.* Don't analyse, just accept. The kayak seemed to agree with her in its gentle sway.

It was a breakthrough: she couldn't ask her mother what it had all been about, if it had been about anything. What she would do instead was reunite her parents in the sea. At the least it was a lovely notion and could be a step towards closure. Take what she could from this experience. Checking out of her old life had given her wealth of a different kind: genuine people pulling together who shared a passion for their surroundings. In other words, things she couldn't have bought for money. The realisation gave her a sudden sense of purpose: she had to make the most of it here ... starting right now this very second.

'So how are you feeling?' Logan asked. 'Glad you came along?'

'Very,' she said, swishing the clear water with her fingers, feeling the contented ache in her arms. 'It's so peaceful.'

'You've got to watch out for the sharks, though, Ceri,' Logan said, straight-faced.

'That's right, poke fun at the townie.'

'I'm serious!'

Ceri snatched her hand out of the sea and sized him up. He was very convincingly wide-eyed but she wasn't going to fall for it. 'No, you're not.'

'Honest to God, Ceri. A nineteen-stone nine-footer was caught off the coast recently, attracted by the mackerel.'

'Oh my God, shouldn't we go back in?' She looked around frantically, as *duh-duh duh-duh* music played in her head. Her kayak began to rock with her movement and she felt fear creeping up on her.

'They very rarely come in,' he said, steadying her with a touch on the kayak's nose. 'Summertime usually, so we're safe for another few weeks at least.'

Ceri clutched her chest as the threat passed. 'Bloody hell, you gave me a right fright.'

He made a fin out of his right palm and stuck it on top of his head, making her laugh out loud. God, she felt an idiot! *Ha*, and now she'd get some revenge!

'I've heard there are sharks on land too.' She folded her arms and gave him an over-the-top panto stare.

His eyebrows shot up – and the edges of his lips curled. She felt an electricity go through her: he'd not just understood she was talking about his reputation, but also he was amused by her daring to bring it up. His smile was like a reward which made her want to shimmy.

'I see,' he said, his eyes dancing. 'You know, Ceri, I wouldn't listen to what people say about other people.'

He was absolutely right, of course, and absolutely flaming gorgeous.

'I mean, I haven't, when they've been gossiping about you ...'

Oh, touché! He had turned it onto her with *anything you can do I can do better* and now she had an itch she was desperate to scratch but couldn't. *What had they been saying about her?* She knew they'd talk about her, it was human nature, but his tone suggested there was something more. Was it about her identity? It couldn't be – someone would've said. Whatever, she wasn't going to ask, no way, she wouldn't give him the rise.

'Very good,' she said, appreciating the banter because it'd been so long since someone had played with her like this. It was almost flirtatious, if she wanted to see it. Which she didn't, not at all.

But sadness shadowed his eyes.

'I know what they think of me here,' he began, now

softly, 'I'm single, not married like them. I don't spend every night down the pub, like them. I have a busy life, unlike them, other things to do. I have the surf school, which they think is a jolly but I've busted my balls to keep going. *How can he afford to live on a postman's wages, he must have more*' . . .' he said, in a light Welsh mimic, 'but they don't know about loss and I don't air stuff like they do. I'm English too, it's enough for some.' He sniffed the air and shook his head. 'Don't get me wrong, this is home, it has been for fifteen years, and I love it here, for all of this.' He spread his arms and looked around him. 'It's just people make assumptions about you when they don't know you. Based on something they think you are . . . or you've done.'

Blimey, it rang so many bells he could've been morris dancing. Just like him, she was on her own, hard-working and English, despite what they said about her mum making her Welsh. His words reflected her experience – it was as if she'd found someone on her wavelength.

'I get it.'

'Yeah?' he said nervously, fiddling with the toggle on his life jacket as if he was a little kid.

'Yep.' Ceri didn't want to say any more because she had to be sensible. And the way he was looking at her with a very unplatonic mix of tenderness and gratitude, she was feeling anything but.

'Right,' she said, picking up her paddle.

'Course,' he answered, clearing his throat. 'I don't think we're going to see any seals today. If we were going to, they'd be on the rocks. So, do you want to head in?'

'Yeah. I'm starving, actually.'

He pulled alongside her as they turned themselves

towards the shore and made for home.

'Me too. Fancy lunch somewhere?'

'Yeah,' Ceri said, 'I've had my fill of baps from the cabin if I'm being honest.'

'Cool. It's on me, no arguments, to say thanks for listening. Or to buy your silence! It's a beachside restaurant. Called La Casa.'

'Wait ... is it a Spanish place?'

'Yes. Do you know it?'

'No. But ... well, my dad was Spanish.'

'Really?' Logan looked impressed, which people often did, although she never really understood why because she had nowt to do with it.

'Yeah,' she said, feeling happy and relaxed. The happiest and most relaxed she'd been in yonks.

'Funny ...' he said '... because they told me you were from the exotic town of Crewe!'

She let out a huge guffaw, drunk on his company as if she'd been necking bubbles of fun.

'Ha bloody ha!' she said, brimming over with hilarity. 'But you're in for it now ...'

And with a cheeky swipe of her paddle, she covered him in water and headed for the sand, digging deep and defying the coming blisters on her hand because the pain, the joy, the everything right now was making her feel so very alive.

On the shore, she changed in Logan's van, only sneaking one look at his snake-hipped body which gleamed with salt water.

Once he was done, he jumped in and shook his dripping dirty blond hair before fixing her with his green eyes, framed by thick wet lashes.

'Ready?' he said, switching on the ignition. He was a handsome hot mess of a cliché – and it was impossible he didn't know it. Yet he wasn't anything like the gossip made him out to be. She'd developed a bullshit radar and good-looking men made it beep like a flatlining heart monitor but honestly, right now, she couldn't see anything nasty about Logan. Yes, he had a reputation here but could it be he'd been pigeonholed as a single man – hadn't she been labelled the career bitch by Dave's mates when they'd split up? She bit her lip and decided to take him as she found him.

She nodded and they set off, climbing out of Dwynwen, rising up and up to the A-road and then back down to the left where they dropped again to the coast to a village called Glan-y-mor, which translated as sea shore. From the moment they drove in, passing busy shops and white cottages, Ceri saw why Dwynwen had fallen by the wayside. The beach was studded with stylish little eateries and cool bars which opened out onto decking on the sand as if it was something out of the Med. Deckchairs for hire were all the same sunny yellow and white design. And a small stylish pier at the furthest end offered boat trips to watch dolphins. As Ceri strolled with Logan on the neat prom, which proved irresistible to couples and families, scootering children and panting dogs, she noted the free wifi signs, outdoor heaters and posh facades of the village, no bigger than Dwynwen but busy and alive. If there was a beauty contest then Glan-y-mor would come second for it wasn't blessed with its rival's natural assets, nor did it have much Welsh character. But it was smart and upmarket – and it knew it.

'So this is why Dwynwen's gone down the dumper,'

Ceri said, as Logan showed her to her seat in the bijou bistro he'd mentioned.

He laughed and called to the waiter, checking she was okay with a beer and a platter of whatever was on the menu.

'Nice place,' she said, sniffing the air rich with garlic and seafood and taking in the vintage bull-fighting posters, lobster pots and guitars on La Casa's walls.

'Glan-y-mor is great, isn't it?' Logan sighed as two bottles landed on their table.

'I meant the restaurant.'

'You don't think Glan-y-mor is great?' he said, confused.

'Well, it looks good but … this is just my opinion … it just seems a bit soulless, if you know what I mean? It could be anywhere, it doesn't feel Welsh like Dwynwen does.'

'You say that like it's a bad thing!' Then he rubbed his fingers and thumb together. 'It attracts money, though. You should see its surf school. Open every day and busy from April to October.'

She couldn't argue with that and over succulent prawns and juicy chorizo they chatted easily, him full of interest in her life. Whereas once she'd been guarded, she felt freer than ever before, confident in his company – apart from when he'd put a hand on her and she turned to jelly. He asked her questions about her family, what she liked to do in her spare time and her opinions on anything and everything. He actually listened, too, which Ceri wasn't used to with the men she'd dated. And there was no work chat either, which was a relief. By the time the bill came, she felt awful she'd been the one doing all the talking. He went to his back pocket but Ceri beat him to it, snatching the card machine just in time.

'No! It's my treat. I invited you!' Logan protested, still fiddling for his wallet.

'You took me kayaking. This is on me,' she insisted, pushing in her Visa.

Then his shoulders sank and he shook his head. 'It's a good job actually ... I left my wallet in the van.'

'Classic!' Ceri laughed.

'Embarrassing,' he muttered. 'I'll pay you back.'

'Nope.'

'I'll just have to take you out again then,' he said, his eyes full of challenge.

'Maybe,' Ceri said, shrugging non-committally.

But inside she was privately praying she remembered her PIN because right now, her head was not paying attention to anything other than her cartwheeling heart.

Ceri counts her blessings

It's my birthday, Mum, the seventeenth of April, and I won't lie, I woke up feeling miserable.

Hitting thirty is a milestone and I suppose I have been wondering if I'll always be alone. But that wasn't why — it's because it's another first without you. I miss you so much. If only I could have you back for one day to hear your laugh or watch you pottering about ... sometimes I think I see you out of the corner of my eye and my heart beats so fast and then when I realise I feel so sick and angry and sad.

Last year, remember, I had a huge birthday, a big party in a five-star hotel paid for by the cosmetics people with an ice sculpture of a lipstick, a cake in the shape of a perfect pout and vodka on tap, surrounded by fake mates. It was all right but my favourite bit had been the day before when you and me had a spa afternoon at home. I had all my treatments done, new eyelashes, spray tan, all that, and you had a hand massage. It calmed you right down and you seemed to know who I was for a while.

I went into St Davids this morning to do some shopping and Tash texted me happy birthday. It read like it was an effort for her. There was no 'card and pressie to follow', just a 'so busy with the kids and house-hunting'

226

finishing with a 'see you soon', which is unlikely. We spoke the other week, she said she hoped my break might make me see sense and I'd go back up north. Running away didn't solve anything, she said, but I can't win with her – my life there was all surface back in February and yet now, when it feels more meaningful, she thinks I'm in la-la-land. The bond we have is unravelling, as if you were the only thing connecting us ... Good old Jade saved the day with a big bunch of flowers but they're flashy exotic ones and they look so out of place here. As for Dwynwen, no one knows and I prefer it that way, I don't feel like celebrating.

Those blessings were impossible to find this morning. But I decided if you couldn't come to me, I'd come to you, so number one, I'm at the Aga and the tea caddy is beside me. You're keeping an eye on things, as you used to, suggesting a bit of this and a bit of that to add to the pot. And little by little, as I'm stirring away, it feels like the fog is lifting. We did this, didn't we, every now and again, go back to how it all started by making a lip gloss from scratch. Two tablespoons of coconut oil, one of beeswax and cocoa butter, melting in a glass bowl in simmering water. While I'd mix it up, you'd tell me you were off out later, going to a disco with your friends or getting ready to see Emilio. And then we'd put in the essential oils and I'd add strained cherries and once we'd poured it into tubs to set, you'd ask for a makeover. Eighties-style, that was your era, so it'd be pinks and blues and lots of blush. I'd put on the Human League, maybe, and you'd wonder whether you should wear your spaghetti-strapped yellow dress or the puffball skirt and shoulder pads.

This one I'm making now, I'm using one of your saucepans that I rescued from Junction Road. I think you'd like it – it's Welshcake flavour with orange, clove and cinnamon oils I bought in an organics shop in town. Then it'll be into some nice little heart-shaped pots to set – I'm not sure what I'll do with them. But it's lovely to know the knack is still there. Even after all this time ...

Can you believe it'll be May in a couple of weeks? The days are getting longer, that's worth a blessing alone. I'm in a routine of sorts now: breakfast of Welsh butter and local honey on toast on the decking, which sits above the rooftops because the cottage is cut into the hillside, where I follow the comings and goings in the village, plus look out to sea at birds and boats. In the evenings, I sit and watch the sunset, which is like those holiday cocktails starting with orange then sinking into red.

Third, the weather's improving, getting warmer and clearer. The sky is incredible – whether it's big and blue when I'm on my way to work or twinkling with stars when I finish; I've never seen the Milky Way before, you've no chance with the M6. Now I understand why Brian Cox makes such a fuss. That sea too, it's actually emerald green when the sun's out. And so clear! How would I know, you'll be asking, well ... that Logan, the postman-surfer guy, took me out on a kayak and it was brilliant. I've never done anything like that in my life before and it was scary, being out of my depth, but I saw the waterfall and now I understand why you loved that beach. From the sea, you could see how tiny the village is, sat at the bottom of a basin with the hills beyond. No wonder you can hear the waves from the cottage, it's like being in an amphitheatre.

Listen to me, I'm turning into one of the locals! Yes, the locals who I suspected at first were the victims of a secret experimental psychotic drug trial by the government. But I just wasn't used to kindness. And now I feel as if I belong, that's a blessing, especially when Dwynwen is going through this transformation into the Village of Love. A delivery of beer garden furniture was received like the crown jewels and from my spot on the decking, I've seen Gwen and Gwil cuddling up with a cuppa on one of the loveseats. It's very sweet to see they're still so in love, bar the odd frank exchange when Gwil sits on Gwen's side. It means I've still got the chance to find someone who feels the same way about me as I do them. That brings me to you again. I haven't forgotten the ashes, I'm working up to it.

As much as I feel settled, I still can't face letting you go yet. But I'm beginning to see that it'll come. There's a bit of hope inside of me and that feels like the best of all today's blessings.

20

Where was everybody? Rhodri looked up and down the road for his allies but he saw only strangers' eyes which dropped quickly, uncomfortably, to the pavement.

It was no wonder: he was wearing a cardboard sandwich board declaring *Save Our Woods* in black Sharpie and at first sight, he probably did look like one of those religious nutters declaring the end was nigh. He'd certainly felt a bit of a melon chanting his slogan on his own as his alternately amused and bemused co-workers popped in and out of the council building for lunch.

Rhodri checked his trusty Casio, model F-91W, which was still accurate despite its worn condition. Yup. He'd been making a fool of himself for fifteen minutes. *Make that my whole life*, he thought. Last night at the pub he'd made sure everyone knew the demo was starting at one o'clock – he'd said he could be flexible with the time, it didn't have to be then, but no, everyone supported a Wednesday lunch hour protest. Lots of people would be around for maximum impact and, as Rhodri had explained, planning councillors who would be making a decision on the housing development in a couple of months' time would be arriving for the April committee meeting, which would start at 2 p.m. It was a golden opportunity to remind them of the one thousand signatures against the housing development. Seren would dive between the pub and the cabin so nobody had to shut up shop. They'd bring their banners, although Rhodri hoped Barri would forget his because *Mouses Not Houses* didn't even make sense. And Mel would be dressed head to toe in love hearts while she distributed the Village of Love postcards he'd ordered online. He'd tried handing them out himself and had managed a few but most people swerved his advances. Desperate wasn't a good look. *Oh how he knew that* – he'd seen it on his face for days now, ever since Logan had asked Ceri out. Shame was written across him too. Because when she'd been invited to go kayaking, he'd felt disgustingly jealous – he'd actually thought, *she's mine, not yours*. And he didn't believe people, or women, were property. It had ignited a basic, foreign emotion of wanting to protect her, which had shaken him – women were equals not trinkets. If only he'd got in there first with the offer of pizza. For this woman was special. She inspired him to fight for good. Except he'd missed the boat and she'd caught a kayak instead.

'Rhodri!'

Ceri was here all rosy-cheeked and glowing and he was so pleased not to be alone he went to hug her, which was a huge mistake because all she got was a face of cardboard.

'Sorry I'm late,' she said, breathing hard, hoisting her placard into the air. Hers was very clever, reading *Woods Not Hoods* and she'd taken his advice to draw a house next to the last word because he wasn't sure the average resident was up on gangster slang.

'Where are the rest?' he asked, looking behind her to check for the other villagers.

'Aren't they here yet? I left after them as well. They were coming in a convoy behind Barri.'

It all made sense now. Barri only ever went anywhere in his bloody tractor. 'Right,' Rhodri said, deflated. 'Well, we'll have to do this by ourselves then.'

'Didn't you put it out on Twitter and Facebook and stuff?' Ceri asked, grabbing the postcards and switching on a smile. 'You know, to get the message out?'

She heard his silence and turned to him, shaking her head.

'It's on my to-do list,' he said meekly, 'I haven't got round to setting up accounts yet.'

'It'll help,' she said gently. 'Instagram too. Visuals are so important. Our unique selling point is Dwynwen's natural wonders.'

'Yes, thank you,' he said. 'I am aware of that.'

'I know. Sorry. Look, I went to Glan-y-mor and saw what they had there and—'

'Did you?' When? She hadn't told him that.

'Yes, with Logan, after we went kayaking, and ...' *The swine had taken her out for lunch. This just got worse.* Defeat was practically his. '... it was nice but it's got nothing on Dwynwen.'

'Well, obviously,' he said sarcastically, instantly regretting it because she looked taken aback. But it was so hard, losing the girl before he'd even had the guts to make a move.

'I know I'm an outsider, Rhodri, but sometimes an outsider can see things that perhaps insiders might overlook because they're so used to them.'

'Go on,' he said, feeling guilty. But she looked unsure now. Her confidence was replaced by a look of uncertainty.

'Please,' he said, melting as he noticed the freckles on her nose and cheeks from the last week of sunshine.

'You're going to think I'm crackers but when I saw the waterfall from the sea, it was like thunder. Immense and all-consuming and it went on going, no matter what. Like love itself … but the kind I've never had before. The type people talk about when you are in so deep, you might suffocate. Like you couldn't live without that person. My mum had it with my dad. Only briefly. I never understood it before. She'd tell me how it felt when she was with him. Nobody else existed when they were together. It was perfect. This place has brought me closer to the feeling. This is how Dwynwen affects people, not Glan-y-mor or housing developments.'

'Wow,' he said, gobsmacked and bewitched, before he realised with doom that she had come under Logan's spell. One date with him and she was already falling head over heels. Rhodri had spent weeks with her and the only falling had been on his behalf, flat on his face because he hadn't had the balls to act on his feelings. Any remote chance he'd had with her was now lost.

'I'd be happy with a life-long companion. Mates for life. Like swans and wolves and shingleback skinks.'

'Sorry?' Ceri said, as he realised he'd mumbled his feelings. He had to explain it now. What was the point in backtracking?

'Making a nest together, rearing young, looking after one another, finding happiness in the ordinary.' He sounded like some holey-jumpered bird-spotting binoculared naturalist. And it was her turn for a bit of gobsmacking – but he knew hers was out of disbelief that he was so lame.

She opened her mouth then shut it again, her eyes searching his, just as he recognised the bald head and bow tie of Councillor Llewellyn, who was one of the more influential members of the committee.

'Councillor!' he said. 'Rhodri Cadwalader. I wonder if I could have a minute?'

The bespectacled man pumped his hand with vigour. 'The application isn't up for a while but full marks for your efforts.'

'Great! Thanks! I trust we can count on your support?' Rhodri said, buoyed up by his remarks.

'It's a challenging issue. The environmental concerns are pressing and I'm full of admiration for you with the Village of Love ...' Then he rifled in his suit pocket and pulled out a piece of paper and presented it to Rhodri. 'But economic considerations must be taken very seriously. You have a fight on your hands.'

And then he was gone, leaving Rhodri with an A5 sheet, a flyer, it looked like, which featured a headshot of his father and the CadCon logo of a house and a hammer. It cried *Jobs for the locals! Homes for the people!* with a bullet-pointed list of the so-called benefits of the proposed estate. An artist's impression, computer-generated in the style of a watercolour painting, sold an idyllic country home with children playing in a generous sunny garden with sea views and dolphins. He looked down at himself and realised there was no way a cardboard costume could compete with this heartwarming whimsical CGI fantasy.

'What is it?' Ceri said, peering at it as Rhodri felt himself reeling. He knew now he'd been chasing something he would never catch. Not just with the woods but in life and love. What was that definition of madness people said? When you did the same thing over and over but expected a different outcome. That was him, what his brothers and even his mother had implied he was doing. He was moving towards a decision, although he was still too much in denial to admit what about.

'A death warrant,' Rhodri said grimly, 'for the woods. And Dwynwen as we know it. It's over, Ceri. It's over.'

21

There was so much nastiness going on in the world, it was easy to think that's all there was, Mel thought as she stared into her cupboards for teatime inspiration.

But the good deeds bestowed on Dwynwen were breeding more good deeds. When a bit of bunting became twisted, someone would straighten it out. If a packet of crisps was tucked in between the slats on one of the pub beer garden tables, a passer-by would dispose of it. English Dick was working on setting up an outdoor cinema at the caravan park to show weepies in the summer and Seren had delivered her first batch of love-heart forks to the cabin. Love would conquer all! She'd told Rhodri that enough times since the demo. He had forgiven everyone for getting there at five to two – eventually. But days later, he remained downcast, predicting the apocalypse or worse, the pub being converted into a Harvester once the housing estate was built.

He had also taken to nursing a pint by himself inside when everyone else was outdoors. Especially if Ceri was talking to Logan. For a while Mel hadn't been able to work out if Rhodri had been sweet on her because he was the same happy guy with everyone. They didn't talk about relationships really, their friendship was about day-to-day things and they both knew love wasn't their favourite subject, so they skirted it out of respect. But as soon as Logan went near Ceri, Mel noticed Rhodri became withdrawn or made his excuses. It wasn't news the two blokes weren't mates, they'd fallen out a few years ago over something or other. Rhodri, being Rhodri, had never bad-mouthed his former buddy so no one knew what it had been about. Mel was confused, because she'd once thought Ceri fancied Rhodri. But then what did she know? Whatever, Rhodri was in the doldrums as if they were in the depths of winter and not on the cusp of summer.

Having said that, May had got under way with forty-eight hours of solid rain which had made the hedges shoot up and the flowers explode and it was still pouring now. What she needed was a big bowl of something hearty to revive her. It looked like it'd have to be soup, seeing as that was all she had in, she thought, as the phone rang. She made her way across the lounge, on the actual floorboards rather than over her clutter, after a concerted effort every evening for a fortnight. *You're getting there, Mel*, she told herself.

'Oh hello, is this the right number for the White House?'

By the sound of the man's Birmingham twang it was from the electricity board's call centre and he'd be after a meter reading.

'Yes,' she sighed, her attention wandering to the next job of tidying: rows of stacked sketch pads lined up against the wall on the darkest side of the room, which she'd kept from her first pencil drawings in her last year at primary all the way through GCSE, A Level and uni. She'd need a very full stomach to tackle those.

'Great,' said the caller.

'Right,' she said, wondering if she had any sourdough bread left. It didn't matter if it was a bit solid, all the better for toasting and no excuses were needed for an inch of butter …

'I'd like to check the availability of the cottage for July if possible?'

'I'm sorry, could you repeat that?' Because it couldn't be true. The bookings diary was as empty as her fridge, it was.

'I'd like to book for a week in July. Do you know if it's free?'

'Are you sure you've got the right place? It's in Dwynwen and …' She stopped herself from saying 'nobody comes here for their holidays'.

'Well, my brother said so. The place near St Davids, he lives there. We're coming to visit him but want to stay somewhere quiet, you know, get away from the city. He sent me the link to the paper, the love thing. The pub looks right up my street, and my wife, she liked the sound of all the bunting. My brother says it's a good beach for the kids too. Am I right?'

Mel felt faint with shock. 'Yes. You are.'

'So are you the one who deals with reservations?'

'Yes.' It came out small and her mouth was dry, so stunned she was. She tried again and this time her voice was louder and it jolted her into life.

'Let me just get the book,' she said, as her face began to beam. 'It's in the drawer behind me. Hang on a second while I put the phone down. It's a gorgeous little cottage and Dwynwen is a wonderful place. I'm sure we can squeeze you in!'

Once Mr Norton (for that was his name) had rung off, Mel couldn't help but do a victory lap round the lounge. It was so exciting! This would cheer up Rhodri, she thought, as she jigged about on the spot, deciding whether to nip up to his to tell him or eat first.

But, what a coincidence, her front door went and she skipped to the top of the stairs, where she shouted, 'I was just about to come and see you, Rhod!'

Her grin slid off and lay dying on the top step when she saw her mother looking up at her from the hall with a hopeful smile.

'Hi, love! You busy? We've brought fish and chips if you fancy some?'

'We?' *Oh God, not Huw.* She did not want to listen to his skittles league stories on a Friday night.

'Ffion and me!' her mother said, brightly as her half-sister sloped in, connected to earphones, giving Mel daggers through her heavy henna fringe. Huw's skittles league stories were suddenly more appealing than listening to Fi's grunts. There was no time to invent alternative plans because they were on their way up – all she could do was move back to allow her visitors in as they wafted past, trailing the scent of vinegary paper. She was so hungry, she would suffer this invasion.

Mam gave her the biggest *cwtch* and deliberately looked nowhere but at eye level. Dad must've told her she'd been struggling – *that was why she was here*, Mel groaned. Fi did exactly as she had been told not to and gawped at the molehills of stuff dotted around the room. Mam gave Fi a stern look and then went to the kitchen for plates. The awkward silence was interrupted by a clatter of china, the rolling sound of the cutlery drawer and a rattle of knives and forks.

'Ketchup, Melyn?'

'In the fridge. I'll clear the table,' she said, feeling herself curdling with embarrassment as she began to pick up piles of old photographs, which she'd put there to sort through later. Fi pulled a chair out and sat on its edge as though it was contaminated.

'Want me to take your coat?' Mel asked, bracing herself for a dose of lip. But she shook her head and brought her sleeve to her mouth to chew it like a child before she realised it and crossed her arms. *What was up with her?* Usually she was chopsy. But on closer inspection, her blue eyes, which were the same shade as Mel's and Mam's, lacked their edge and the thick liner she normally used was faded, probably from crying. There had obviously been a telling-off. Fifteen years old, Mel remembered it well and she felt sorry for Fi then: hormones going off like a pin-ball machine, no longer a kid but so far from adulthood, feeling misunderstood and trapped. All when exams were looming. It was a pressure cooker, that was for sure.

Mel went to help her mum. 'Everything okay?' she asked in a low voice, picking up the hot parcel, her mouth watering at the prospect of crispy batter.

'Yes, fine,' Mam said, her greying bob kinking at the shoulder from the rain. Mel severely doubted it but she knew she'd spill, give it a minute or two. 'Any news?'

'Yes, actually, I've just had a booking for the White House in the summer. Takings have gone up slightly and I've been clearing the house. I'm okay. For once!'

'Oh, good. I am pleased,' Mam said, stopping to smile at her and rub Mel's back.

'Where's Huw?'

Mam suddenly looked weary and frail. Here it came. 'Out. For a pint to calm down. There was a set-to. Shop-lifting. My God, my own daughter. Luckily it was a local shopkeeper not a chain store otherwise she'd have been prosecuted. We had to beg. All for a pair of sunglasses for two pounds ninety-nine. Two ninety-nine, I ask you! She said it was a dare. I knew this crowd she was hanging around with were trouble.'

'Oh, Christ,' Mel said, putting an arm around her. 'That's hard on all of you.' A tiny bit of her was relieved she wasn't the source of trouble this time.

'She's told you then,' Fi said, as Mel returned to unwrap the fish and chips and dish them out between three.

'I am here, Ffion,' Mam said sharply, as she took a seat.

'Unfortunately.' Fi glared and pushed her plate away.

'Come on, guys, it's okay.' Both of them looked smaller tonight, as if they were weighed down. 'I know what it's like to be messed up, Fi.'

'You don't say.' She eye-rolled. But Mel didn't feel any anger – instead she was touched that Mam had come to her when she was in need, as if she was a grown-up and not the eternal teenager she'd always felt in her company.

'Mam is only trying to help,' she said softly, tucking into her delicious flaky cod. 'Those people, they don't sound good. Stay away from them. You've got to listen to Mam.'

'That right?' Fi crowed, giving their mother a defiant stare.

Mel didn't understand and looked from one to the other for explanation.

'In which case, Mel,' Fi said with venom, 'I'll be starting at the stinking cabin as soon as my exams finish, all right?'

'Sorry?' *What was she on about?*

Mam speared a chip then put down her fork. 'She needs a job to keep her out of trouble. I said perhaps you could help. Your father said it would be okay.'

Oh, did he? The fish turned to stone in her stomach and there was a bone scratching her throat. This was a damn cheek: to off-load Mam and Huw's responsibility onto her. She wasn't a bloody nanny, let alone a probation officer. They hadn't even asked her. And Dad, worst of all, had gone along with it.

'Water,' she said hoarsely, getting up rather too aggressively, making the table shake. Mam took the opportunity to lob more ammo her way.

'I mean you said yourself things were going well ... the season's going to start soon, you could do with a hand, couldn't you? She can help in the kitchen or spring-clean the cottages, save you a job? It'll just be for the school holidays.'

'Can't wait,' Fi spat.

How was Mel going to afford her wages? How was she going to put up with a surly and idle sister all summer? She'd frighten off the customers. Mel filled a glass and then let the tap run, leaning into the sink to watch the stream go down the plughole. That was where the cabin would be heading if she had to employ her half-sister. Nobody had thought to consult her. Nobody had thought to warn her. Her livelihood would be gone and she'd be all at sea once again. No better off than she had been nearly a decade ago. Except it would be worse because she was thirty now and would have a failed business behind her as well as an unfinished art degree and no money. Everything she'd been working towards these last few weeks, this slash and burn of her dead branches, would be for nothing. Mel heard raised voices then an almighty crash of a shattering plate. She held her breath and listened.

'See?' Fi screeched. 'I told you this would happen.'

Then footsteps, thumping down the stairs. And just before the front door slammed, her half-sister shouted, 'Not even the fucking family freak wants me around.'

22

Ceri had been to a film premiere before. She'd worn skyscraper heels, a silver-sequinned strapless dress, smoky eyeshadow and lash extensions – her own brand of course – and the pop of cameras on her dress should've carried a *flashing images* warning, she looked so sparkly standing on the red carpet. Which movie she'd gone to see she didn't recall, who gave a fig? It was about being seen mixing with footballers and soap stars. The video she'd made of her getting ready with a make-up tutorial, the chauffeur-driven limo which had taken her to Manchester and her wobbly, self-conscious 'I can't believe I'm here, guys!' had been one of her highest ever viewed vlogs on her YouTube channel. What working girl up and down the country didn't dream of having a Cinderella moment? It captured everything they aspired to – glamour, escape and recognition. But, crucially, they hadn't perceived it to be out of their reach, for Ceri was one of them, from an ordinary street in an ordinary town. What they *hadn't* seen was the elbowing going on behind the scenes by Z-list celebs to get in the right shot with the hottest people, the suspicious snorting in the ladies and the cubicle grunt of a Premier League player with his keks round his ankles. The following day, sales

244

of her range had exploded and she'd become a household name to beauty-obsessed teens and twenty-somethings. It had created its own problems, but overall she was very glad she'd had it.

That premiere, though, was nothing compared to what Ceri had just witnessed on the big screen in the sky. A free-to-view sunset of oranges and pinks, purples and blues, like God's own make-up palette, swirling and streaking and then sighing as it gave in to dusk and darkness. The colours were still dancing in the fire before her, which made sundown seem like it would last for ever. There was magic in the air – sparks were literally flying onto the sand in a dry and private hug of rocks close enough to the waterfall to feel dots of spray every now and again.

'Well, this is better than being slapped on the face with a wet fish,' Ceri said to Logan, who was looking dashingly handsome tonight across the rug from her.

'You say the nicest things,' he said, his white teeth standing out in a smile.

But she had to keep it light because she had a sense that something was going to happen tonight. It wasn't that she wasn't tempted by him – it was more because she still didn't feel as if she really knew him. She could hear Jade now, telling her to kiss him quick, but Ceri had always been more of a *hug me slow* type of person. The couple of times when she *had* let herself believe a man was into her, she'd been disappointed by the gold-digging which had emerged as soon as they'd come up for air. Yes, this was different because Logan didn't know she was a money bags, but even so, there was too much at stake to make a mistake in this village. Ceri was pretty sure he liked her: their kayaking trip and then lunch, plus chats on the doorstep when he didn't have any post for her and numerous drinks down the pub all added up to it. And it made her feel special: it had been that long since anyone seemed to have liked her for herself. She was veering towards feeling the same – they had chemistry and they made each other laugh. If she could crack him open a bit more, then perhaps that was all it would take to fall into his arms.

There was still room for doubt – he hadn't tried it on with her, not that he'd had much chance with all those eager eyes in the pub. Apart from Rhodri's, who was so worried about the village's future he'd gone a bit cold on everyone. Logan was a good distraction too – it meant she didn't have to think about what happened next in her professional life. Not once had she doubted her decision to stay; the details would work themselves out, she would make sure of it.

And having made the choice, she no longer felt as if she was hiding away from herself – Jade had sent her the photos from the shoot and she looked the part all right, with the perfect OMG look of surprise: wide eyes and shocking red lips, face tilted back and swishing hair. When Ceri had finally texted Tash to declare she was looking for a place to buy here, she'd been in the supermarket, stocking up in a show of commitment to Dwynwen. Tash had answered her straight away, asking if she was off her trolley. Yes, she was, she'd said, and she'd sent a snap of her actual trolley which was overflowing with cereal and pasta, rice and condiments in a sign of her commitment to her new life. But at least her news was out there – both Tash and Jade now knew she was settling here. What happened next with Cheap As Chic, she didn't know: she had to wait to see if she was missed. With any luck, Jade being the face of the business would mean Ceri could stay in the background and turn her hand to the paperwork. She could do that from here.

And so the weeks were going by and she was setting herself a routine of shower, breakfast on the decking, popping out to see Mel and going to work in the pub. In quiet moments behind the bar she'd look down to see her fingers tapping, waiting to pounce should inspiration or the next step on the road to happiness come along.

Logan had wandered into the pub towards the end of her shift this afternoon with an invitation to see the waterfall close-up at low tide. He'd get some beers, float them in a rock pool to chill. She told him not to bother – she'd bring some when she came down. And here they were now, lying on their elbows, their heads resting on their hands, their silhouettes mimicking each other as they spoke quietly into the night beneath the stars. With a shiver, Ceri had a sense of déjà vu – she couldn't help but think of her mother, falling in love on the sand by the sea with the man who had become her father.

'You cold?' Logan asked, his eyes shiny from the fire.

She shook her head. 'That sunset, it's still sinking in. It was incredible.'

'Wait till I show you the sunrise.'

It was impossible to catch any meaning on his face in the darkness. She had to analyse what he'd meant by what he'd said: *he was going to show her the sunrise*. Was he saying he'd knock on her first thing one day ... or they'd get up from the same bed to see it? It was tenuous, she knew, but the answer wasn't important. The fact she was trying to read his intentions revealed she wanted there to be more.

'I've been all over the world,' he said, 'and they don't come better.'

'What brought you here, Logan?' she asked, digging deeper to find out more about him.

'The surf. It's different to the Gold Coast and Jeffrey's Bay, Hawaii, Mexico ... mainly because it's so freezing in there. When I was younger, those places were where it was at, but the competition to teach was so high I came back to the UK. Cornwall was a crack for a while but I wanted somewhere quieter, somewhere permanent.'

Oh, she could understand that – she hadn't known how tired she was of crowds and cars until she got here.

'But why Dwynwen?' It was a speck on a map filled with possibilities.

'My parents lived here, retired from Surrey, and when they went, they left me the house. So it made sense to stay for a while. I didn't think it'd be fifteen years but it gets under your skin.'

There was no pause for her to give him sympathy – she felt it, though, she was in the same position, knowing how rudderless it was not to have a mum or a dad to back you up. And if he had their home, he'd have no mortgage, which explained why he'd said he was comfortably off when they were kayaking. *Two more similarities*, she thought, feeling the gap between them closing.

'Tell me about it,' she said, 'I didn't think I'd end up staying when I first rocked up. I thought it was a hole.'

She felt safe telling him this because he had experience behind him – he'd travelled and had worldlier insight. 'But now, I love it.'

'I suppose it all depends on where you are in your life. For me, I'd done my raging. I still hope one day I'll be able to get my kids out on surfboards. What about you? Where are you in life?' He shifted slightly forward and laid his hand between them. Would she look back and think that was the start of them inching towards one another? She even felt herself want to touch him ... but suddenly, *oh yuck*, she felt a wet sensation on her feet.

'Shite!' she said, pulling her legs towards her to sit up, catching the moonlit foam of the culprit wave.

'Jesus! Rookie mistake!' he laughed, shooting up to grab the beers.

'My jeans, they're soaking!' She started to laugh from the shock.

'You'd better take them off,' he said in a piss-take of his own smooth voice which tickled her because he'd made it sound deliberately suggestive. She kept on laughing as she got hold of the rug and shook the sand because another wave was coming her way.

'For God's sake, Logan, you're supposed to be a master of the sea,' she said, darting back and kicking off her trainers.

'It's your fault!' he said as she ran from the water, the cold sand squidging beneath her feet. 'Don't tell anyone the surfer got taken by surprise by the sea, will you!'

'And how is it my fault?' she said, looking back at him over her shoulder as he came after her in hot pursuit. Whether it was the San Miguel or the giddy feeling taking a grip of her, her brain misjudged the change in the surface as the sand became drier and her knee gave way. It sent her flying and she managed to twist herself so she landed on her bum and ended up flat on her back.

Within seconds, Logan had caught up and he'd thrown the bottles onto the rug before getting down onto his haunches. They were both in fits, making big honking sea-lion noises at the ludicrousness of their evening. When one started to recover, the other pealed off again, and so it went on until Ceri had aching tummy muscles.

'Stop!' she squealed, fighting for breath.

'Me?' he said, panting. 'This is all down to you!'

She opened her mouth wide to protest her innocence. 'How come?'

He went down onto his all fours so his face was above hers and in an instant, his expression smouldered. He was doing that thing she'd seen happen to other people, when they'd drink in someone's eyes and try to focus on all of their features, savouring them and full of desire. Logan was actually doing this to her. Seconds passed and in a mad brain flit she tried to work out if this was really what she wanted. At the same time, he was dropping down to his forearms so his mouth was inches from hers and she was trapped between wanting to and uncertainty, but her path between the two was slow and sticky as if she was wading through toffee pudding.

'It's all your fault,' he said softly, addressing her as Miss Rees like she was in trouble, 'because I forgot the time. You made me forget the time.'

Her body was ready for him and all she had to do was close her eyes. It was so tempting and she felt her hips rising towards his. But there was something going on in her head that didn't sit right. She didn't know what it was: it felt like a flash or a bit of static interrupting her brainwaves, the type you'd hear if you moved an aerial around on an ancient radio. But it took her out of herself and it made her break away, rolling to her side, forcing him to lift an arm. She sat up and shook herself to get the sand out of her hair.

'Everything okay?' he asked from beside her.

'Yeah,' she said, 'I'm just ...'

'Not ready?'

'Sort of.'

'I understand. There's no rush, eh?'

'No,' she said, feeling strangely vacant, now the moment of intimacy had gone. 'I think I just need an early night.'

'You?' he joked, pulling her up to standing. 'I'm the bloody postman! Come on, let's go,' he said, gathering their stuff. 'I'll walk you back.'

When they reached her door, she thanked him for being a gent. He leaned in and kissed her on the cheek and she knew she'd made the right decision to hold back. *If in doubt, do nowt,* Mum used to say and it was spot on tonight. As she said goodbye and closed the door, she felt dizzy and fizzy as if the thoughts in her head were muddled, unable to align into something meaningful. She rested on the hall wall and let her head fall back as if that would straighten the jumble. But nothing came and she was tired now and confused by feelings which were beyond her grasp. And then it didn't exactly hit her, it crept up on her. An emptiness as if it was loss. Her mother, she thought, waiting for the gut punch because there was no Angharad waiting up for her with a cup of tea. But it didn't come. Instead, it seeped up her body and she felt a warmth spreading as it came to her lips. *Rhodri.* She was missing him madly. Even though he was only across the way from her cottage. And she saw him most days. She hadn't kissed Logan because of him. But why? It had to mean ... but the thought was arrested there and then. Something darker, more troubling, was lurking and *boom*, it whacked her between the eyes. Like a lost memory which she'd forgotten she'd had but now stood there clear as day. Her heart stopped and her blood ran cold. Because when she was in a trance beneath Logan's body, when he'd almost put his mouth on hers and then said her name, she was certain he'd called her Miss Price.

23

'Hello, it's B&Q here ... we've had an online order ... reference 3BYG7 ... and I just wanted to double-check because it's quite large.'

'Okay.'

'So it's for the low odour, low VOC water-based eco masonry paint. Thirty-five litres. Three. Five. Is that right?'

'Yes.'

'Seven litres of each colour?'

'Yes.'

'Twenty-five masonry roller and brush sets as well? Five ladders, fifty disposable latex gloves and fifty disposable overalls?'

'Yes.'

'Right, good. Going to, it says here, the Village of Love in Dwynwen?'

'Yes. Thanks.'

'One last thing and forgive me for asking, only we'll get it in the neck from head office if it gets out ... but that's not a place for swingers, is it?'

❧

Mel stared fearfully through the cabin door at the columns of paint pots on the forecourt.

Everyone else was *oohing* and *aahing* over them, inspecting the ladders, trying out the foam rollers and Gwil already had one foot inside a white boiler suit. This month's surprise, she'd gathered from the excited clamour, was to return the cottages to their former colourful glory. It seemed their mysterious benefactor was sending a gift every few weeks: the bunting in March, the beer garden in April, and now this in late May, so they could prepare for the peak of the summer season.

But Mel was frozen. This all felt like a conspiracy. She was trying her hardest to sort herself out but obstacles kept getting in her way. The future of Caban Cwtch hung in the balance, she was expected to take on her shoplifting half-sister and now these tins of masonry weather-coat were challenging her. She hadn't picked up a brush in nearly ten years. It was as if someone out there was mocking her, waiting for her to fail. Maybe this was all connected. Could her father be the one behind all of this Village of Love stuff? Co-ordinating a campaign to force her to do something. Hadn't he said her life was in stalemate? And he was always trying to get her to mend bridges with Mam and get closer to Ffion. Mel had refused point-blank to discuss it with him when she'd seen him. But it was festering within. Worse, his attempts to help were not empowering her as he intended: they were overwhelming. The bombshell of Fi's summer job last week had sent her spiralling backwards to find the things which gave her comfort: her Etch A Sketch and her green troll which she'd packed in a box marked 'throw'. She needed certainties, not *what ifs*, she thought, as she screwed up her face and rubbed her forehead. The door tinkled and Rhodri came in. At least he had a smile on.

'You coming outside, Mel? Oh, what's wrong?'

'Just, you know ...' Her vision went dull and she knew she was heading for a funny turn. But she couldn't do this in front of him because he was in a bad way himself and they never talked about serious things. It was an unspoken pact – he knew her history, she knew his. She couldn't break it. Her body had other ideas, though, and she felt her legs weakening. Grabbing for a chair, she missed and Rhodri saved her fall.

'Mel, what is it?' His kind eyes were big with concern. Usually they were like a kaleidoscope of lovely twirling reflective and symmetrical browns, but today she saw only mud.

'The paints,' she whispered as she gave in and gave way, puddling into his arms.

'What about them?'

'Al,' was all she could say.

Then somehow he got it: he understood the connection. Because he was her oldest friend.

'The paints, they bring it all back.'

'They do, they do.'

He gave a little laugh and held her by her shoulders so he could see her face.

'Look at us both, the past has a lot to answer for.' She knew he was referring to his heartbreak over Ruth and how Dwynwen used to be. 'It's about time you and me looked forward, eh? Stopped wondering what was and why. And just accepted it. We can't change it. But we can change the future. By being here in the now. And if the houses get the go-ahead, which I suspect they will, then we have to accept that too. Come on, come outside and help. Gwil's gone all police forensics in that all-in-one.

He's zipped it to his chin and he's snapped on some gloves as if he's about to start looking for fingerprints. To find who's behind it.'

Mel giggled and looked into his eyes, their colour returning, the sparkle like disco balls.

'I'm wondering if it's my dad.'

'Lyn? I'd be very surprised. You haven't seen the colours yet. They're quite loud. Perhaps it's a stunt? Perhaps it's not from the same person as the last two. They've come from B&Q. It might be a way of getting some publicity, you know, helping out the village.'

'Really?'

'No,' he said, 'but that's the only theory I can come up with at the moment.'

He picked up a teaspoon from the counter and gave it to her and led her to the tins, gesturing for everyone to move back. Mel saw them all nod in agreement – bless them all, because she was still 'the artistic one' even after all these years of doing nothing artistic.

She approached the first and with her fingers trembling, she knelt down and levered the handle of her father's mother's brass spoon under the lid. *This could be a can of worms*, she thought, pausing. All right, one wriggle of them she could cope with but there were litres and litres of them and if they all got out, she might end up in a proper mess. Mel hung her head and the villagers let out a low rumble of worry. She saw the blob of her reflection in the shiny metal top, which was mostly scarlet from her birds of paradise jumpsuit: dare she believe in herself again? What if the sight of paint sent her back to the canvases of the past? What if her grip on now was too loose and she would slide into the darkness?

Rhodri joined her on his knees and murmured, 'This is for everyone.'

He was right. It wasn't about her but all the people who'd pulled together over these rescue packages. If she thought of the bigger picture, maybe she could cope. This would put some colour back in the cottages' cheeks. She looked up and saw her friends waiting. So she poured her upper body strength into the fingers on her left hand as she dug the spoon under the lid. A suck of a squelch then a hiss of air as the seal broke and out blew a puff of her most favourite smell in the world: wet paint. She shut her eyes and inhaled deeply as the scent of chemicals collided with the association in her heart. An explosion of a head-rush of a carousel went off: she was feeling what it had meant to be able to express herself and repli-cate the shades she saw, which had turned her shameful secretive sixth sense into something real and valid. Mel's insides bounced around like popcorn as she anticipated what colour she lay beneath. She couldn't remember, on a high, trying to control her glee as ... *oh!* the purple of regency and Prince and aubergine and Cadbury's and lavender ran from the lid in thick gloopy globules. It was a riot in which she could see the reds and blues mixed to make this most perfect of shades for the Purple House. She tore through the rest, discovering royal icing and snowdrops for the White House; Cookie Monster and hydrangea for the Blue House; and Granny Smith and Kermit for the Green House. Last was the paint for her own home, and she said a prayer it would meet the hue in her mind ... and it did! The thick pool of pink was all Mr Jelly, fuchsia and blancmange! They were the things of her childhood and yet now, miraculously, she felt very far from there: she was smack bang in the present and with gusto she grabbed one of the new huge hairy paintbrushes which took her even further away from the dainty sable watercolour brushes of her youth. The past was receding as she jumped to her feet and made enormous vertical strokes up and down into the air and wondered if it was within her to do a mural on the outside of the cabin …

'Okay,' she said to Gwen and Gwil, Seren and everyone. 'You guys fetch brooms and hard hairy brushes and hoses, take the ladders up and scrub the walls clean. We'll be able to start painting as soon as they're dry. This wind will help us.'

She would ring the three owners of the White, Blue and Purple Houses to explain that *yes, it was unbelievable* and *no, there was no catch*. Holiday lets all, the properties had been in their families for generations, passed on each time to locals who'd eventually left. Dr Davies, Mrs Llewellyn, Mr Jones and Mrs Lewis's son would agree to it – why wouldn't they, if it brought in guests? As for the Green House, it had been on the market forever so Mrs Evans would be thrilled it was getting an eye-catching facelift.

With that, everyone bustled off to get moving and Mel took a second to imagine how beautiful the homes would look on the hill. All five would smile down on the bay like a rainbow, just as they had before. People would come just to take photos of them.

Never mind the question of having faith in herself – she had it in bounds for the village.

24

R hodri put down the phone and face-planted the table.

Like the village idiot he was, he caught his forehead on the sharp edge of his latest dirty secret, which he was racing through. Normally he would savour the process, handling it ceremonially of an evening or on a Sunday, like today, to wind down from the demands of waste management. This time, though, he thought, rubbing his temple, he'd been working fast – to a deadline he was only now aware of. He was coming to a decision, so he readied himself for a think in the woods.

He zipped up his cycling jersey, because June wasn't yet flaming, and stalked out of the house and up the lane to find his spot, where the waterfall tipped over the edge, which always gave him perspective and strength.

The call had sealed it, he thought, his calves stretching with every step. Councillor Llewellyn from the planning committee had rung to divulge that CadCon's development was heading for approval this week. It was hopeless to keep fighting. The support from the village, the petition and countryside campaigners he'd contacted after the disastrous demo hadn't been enough. As the councillor said, emotion couldn't defeat housing targets

... demand was outstripping supply ... thousands of new homes were needed every year ... developers who could finance projects were like gold dust ...

Where did it leave him? That was the question he had to answer. He reached the crest of the lane and crunched through the undergrowth towards the stump which he'd claimed as his own from his childhood, when he'd flee the madness at Wolf's Castle, of fights over who was in charge of the TV remote or who'd found and eaten his chocolate stash.

But, *badger bollocks*, someone had beaten him to it. Ceri. Shit. He'd been avoiding her company because it was too painful to connect with her so easily when it meant nothing more than friendship. The grapevine told him she wasn't going out with Logan – she'd apparently resisted his charms so far. It was only a matter of time before she did, though. He was surprised by it: one bat of Logan's eyelashes and women normally dropped every-thing, mostly their pants. But then that was the Ceri he loved, she wasn't like other women. Even so, she was the last person Rhodri wanted to see; but a rustle of leaves gave him away and she turned and waved.

As he got closer, he saw she wasn't looking exactly over the moon. Had Logan upset her? What he'd do if he found out he had ... He stopped himself because she was her own woman, her own lovely woman.

'What's up?' he asked, wanting to stick his fingers in his ears and go *blah-blah-blah* if she started on about his rival.

'Stuff,' she said, budging up and patting the space beside her. He hesitated because to be close to her made him feel things he had no business to feel. 'What about you? You don't look ecstatic.'

'Stuff,' he echoed, sitting beside her because how many more opportunities would he get to look out to sea in the company of this beautiful lady?

'Quite nippy today,' she said, radiating heat through her jeans onto his thigh.

'Unseasonably so,' he said, clearing his throat, 'thirteen degrees according to my weather station.'

'Haven't seen much of you,' she said. 'Where've you been?'

'Work and DIY and that.' And hiding.

'Do you know something, your cheekbones have gone David Bowie. Have you not had time to eat?'

He felt his face and it did feel thinner. 'Funnily enough, I have lost my appetite a bit.'

'You need some of your mum's home cooking. What I'd give for a roast with mine, she did the best Yorkshires. Then some sponge and custard for afters followed by a nap on the couch.'

He felt for her: when he tormented himself about what would happen when his mother passed, he'd have a panic like the time he'd wandered off on the beach and he'd turned round to speak to her but all he could see were faces he didn't recognise. The lifeguard had picked him up and returned him to her, but she'd been so busy telling off Dai and Iolo for hitting each other with spades she hadn't even noticed he'd disappeared.

'You settled in then, to life here?'

'Yeah, I wish my sister would accept it, though. She's still kicking off about it. She thinks I'm acting irresponsibly, turning my back on Jade. But I've still got a hand in at work up there. I've found a café with wifi in St Davids and I go up there to do what needs to be done.'

'She'll come round. She must feel like she's lost you a bit. I'm the same when my brothers have gone back to their lives after Christmas. What you're going through, and so's she, is about adapting. It might not feel like it but we do cope eventually.' Where was this coming from? He sounded like a self-help book and he was the last person to embrace change. Then he worked it out – his subconscious had been incubating it all week. 'Just like I will.'

'With what?' Ceri said, eyeballing him suspiciously.

'This is what I've been occupied with …' Here it was, coming of its own accord. 'I'm going to Sweden.' There, he'd said it. And it felt okay. Not so terrifying now he'd actually managed to make up his mind.

'Sweden? Since when? And why?' Rhodri noted her voice sounded higher pitched than normal and was tinged with panic.

'A four-month sabbatical job swap to see what we can learn from them about waste management.' It came out sturdier than he'd anticipated – it was a sign he wanted to do it.

'Rhodri!' She looked like the Scream emoji. 'What about Dwynwen?'

'The houses are going to be built, Ceri. Economic needs trump environmental ones.' He sounded cold, he knew he did, but he didn't mean to. It was because it was a statement of fact and the truth could hurt. 'I've had a call. The council is going to give the green light this week. It really is over. God, how I hate money and what it does to people.'

Ceri leapt up and took him by the shoulders, her nose very close to his. He hoped he didn't smell of last night's curry. 'Rhodri, listen to me, we can do this. The Village of Love is part of the reason I wanted to stay here. You can't leg it now.'

'The Village of Love can go on. It doesn't have to stop. And I'm not legging it. I'm spreading my wings.'

She dropped her arms to her hips. 'But you're the leader! It was your idea!'

'It's time I left. I've done the most I can do here. This might be the best thing for me. Get me out of my comfort zone. I've been here my whole life nearly and I love it, but what'll happen if I stay here? I'll have forty new houses as neighbours. It'll kill me every time I open my door. And ...' he paused, because here was another reason he'd only just admitted to himself, 'I want to meet someone, have a family. I can't see it happening here.'

Ceri threw her hands up. 'You're talking as if you're not coming back.'

'I might not.'

Ceri's spine slumped and she sniffed. 'You've thought it through, have you?' She was less shouty now.

'Over and over.'

'But you could meet someone local ... get a promotion, run the whole waste shebang for Wales.'

He shook his head. *I can't stay when I can't have you*, but he didn't say that bit out loud although he was shouting it in his head and he was amazed she didn't hear it.

'When do you go?' she said finally, sitting back down next to him.

'The end of September.'

'Oh my God, I thought it'd be next year. That's so soon. Who will I turn to with my recycling needs now?

Like, I've got a load of clothes I brought with me which are just plain stupid, going-out things and dresses and whatnot. Which I'll never wear again. What am I going to do with those?'

He felt her head bend onto his shoulder and he let himself dream for a second of fulfilling her every recycling need. He stood up and faced her. 'There's a textile bin up the top road. It goes to charity.'

'Right,' she said, not actually interested. But she'd asked and it was something to say other than *I love you*.

'On the St Davids road, by the estate of old age pensioners' bungalows. Where the post office used to be.'

She was trying to recall it but she was frowning.

'You know,' he said, 'where Logan's house is.' He flinched saying his name and he looked for a glimmer of pleasure on Ceri's face. 'Well, not his house. His parents'. They've got a caravan on the drive. Although it's not always there as they go away for weeks at a time.' She looked interested at that – obviously she couldn't contain it. He continued out of environmental duty. 'The bin is orange. Which to my mind is very confusing because orange is the colour people associate with the bags for plastic, cans, aluminium foil, newspapers, magazines and cardboard. But there you are. Local authority bullshit for you.'

Ceri scratched her neck and held her chin, quiet now, and they listened to the breeze tickling the branches.

'I'm going to miss you,' she said quietly.

He was touched she cared enough to pretend. If only it was true – if only it was on a more romantic level.

'I don't go for a while,' he said, crouching down to touch her knee. 'We can write. It's only until January.'

'I could visit,' she said. Which was a bit unnecessary.

'It'll be winter. Cold and dark.' There, he'd give her an escape route.

She took a quivering breath and nodded. Just as a splat of something highly pungent landed on her trousers.

'*Ew*,' she said, pulling a face as if she'd never seen shit before. 'Still, it's supposed to be lucky, eh? To be hit by droppings.' She bent down for a leaf to scrape it off.

'Birds, yes, but never bat poo.'

Bat poo? Rhodri looked up and lifted a hand to his mouth.

'Wise move, that,' Ceri said, 'you don't want one of these in your gob.'

'No,' he said, breathless. 'Look!'

He pointed to a bundle of bats roosting in the crack of the tree above them.

'It's a maternity hospital ... they're pregnant and huddling together for warmth and safety ... and I hope I'm right, because they've got wide ears and pug-shaped noses ... I think they're Barbastelle bats,' he whispered.

'I saw those on *Countryfile* on my first Sunday here! They're rare, aren't they?' she said, making more *yuck* noises as she wiped off the guano.

'Shhh! They mustn't be disturbed. Extremely rare. And ... protected!' he said as they both silent eureka-ed at the same time with mouths wide and hands in the air.

'This will stop the development!' she said, tiptoeing around in a muted celebratory jig.

'I'll have to get the bat people out to check but I'm pretty certain.' He shook his head and let out a breath at the enormity of it. 'Planners have a legal obligation to consider whether bats are likely to be affected by a proposed development. Treelines have to be retained.'

Ceri punched the air in delight. 'Have you got your phone? Take a picture, quick!'

'Good idea!' he said, sneaking it out and being careful not to flash the bats in case they were startled. 'I'll send it to the council!'

Ceri's arms were suddenly around his waist and he considered he would be quite happy if he died there and then.

'This means you don't have to go!' Ceri said, squeezing him tight as she looked up at him, bright-eyed and beaming. Her eyes resembled smoky brown quartz, the gem regarded by Welsh druids centuries ago as a stone of power for its ability to fight negative energy. Just like her. And just like its chemical compound silicon dioxide, which could be both hard as a diamond but soft as a grain of sand.

'I wish it were so simple,' he said, fighting every cell telling him to stay. Because he would if he could be with Ceri. Feeling her against him was the most wonderfully awful thing: it sent his biology wild and his brain mad. He couldn't live this way. 'I've made up my mind. I have to go.'

He shrank from her embrace, making his excuses, he had to ring around to get a number for the bat people. He had to go. Not just at the end of summer but *now* because he wanted at least one piece of unbroken heart to keep safe for someone, if there was anyone out there waiting for him.

25

The closest thing Ceri had witnessed to this drama was when Mum's road had held a Union Jack street party for the Royal Wedding of William and Kate.

This version, though, was Welsh through and through with dragon flags and inflatable leeks – aside from the balloon bats, courtesy of a children's entertainer, dressed as Batman, who'd been stretching and squeaking all morning for the visiting schoolkids. Running down the lane between the pub and the cabin were trestle tables filled with streamers and napkins, jugs of squash and plastic cups, iced party ring biscuits on foil platters and clingfilmed sandwiches. Sneaking hands got slapped and little faces reprimanded because they had to wait until BBC Wales arrived. Hopefully it wouldn't end in fisticuffs as it had in Crewe when our Brian from number seventeen accused our Steve from three doors up of eating all the sausage rolls. Mum had been healthy then, throwing herself into cooking quiches and organising egg-and-spoon races. She'd loved a bit of a do, especially fancy dress: she'd gone as Princess Di, in a charity shop gown with blue eyeliner and a flicky fringe. Ceri, still a barmaid and on face-painting duty, had gone with Dave as Shrek and Princess Fiona. It was lovely how her memories were shifting away from the bad ones of Mum's crackling chest and bed pans to the happier times, as if her mind was resetting itself, as if she was being given a chance to scoop herself up and recover.

From her position by the cabin, Ceri felt her mother's presence now, flitting between the crowds gathered for this most momentous but hastily arranged event, which had been blessed with gorgeous blue skies and sunshine. There'd been a flurry of activity ever since the Barbastelle maternity roost had been uncovered. Once the villagers had calmed down on Sunday afternoon, they'd been escorted one by one by Rhodri to the woods on the condition they didn't make a sound. A bat survey on the Tuesday had led to an application for a protected species licence, which led in turn to the council putting the housing application on hold on Wednesday. CadCon was taking advice on what to do next, whether to challenge it or drop the plan, but Rhodri was sure his father would see sense and withdraw. His dad, he said, was a pragmatist, he wasn't going to throw the company's money away on useless appeals. Part of what made him successful in business was that he understood when to push forward and when to cut his losses. He also liked winners and he'd appreciate Rhodri had won the battle.

Gwen had suggested the celebration: 'We've already got the bunting, we just need a few extras.' The local paper had covered the story yesterday which the BBC had picked up and so today, Friday, the news crew was on its way.

Meanwhile, Ceri had worked behind the scenes to clean the bunting, weed the beer garden and help Mel finish painting the cottages, which shone above Dwynwen, as they should always have done. That was the closest she'd get to the cameras. When they started rolling, she'd tuck herself behind the bar because while it felt like home here now, it didn't feel like her victory completely. She still had to scatter the ashes and it was a source of shame she had avoided it so far through a raft of excuses. Only when she'd done it would she truly feel she was no longer an incomer. There was also the chance if she was filmed that someone would recognise her when it was broadcast. If she was rumbled, she would be treated differently – back to square one. Money and success would change how they saw her: she might be seen as a hoity-toity cow, subject to side-eye and whispers, a fantasist even, and definitely a liar. And Rhodri would probably never speak to her again. The sunshine in his heart had been warm enough to convince her there were people she could trust. If he discovered her deceit, she would die from the cold. His withdrawal before had been horrible: his absence had made her realise how much she felt for him. Then Rhodri's departure in September had doubled, trebled her emotions. Her supply was going to be cut off – forever, she suspected, because he wouldn't come back, his eyes would be opened – and it made her ache inside.

Clearly she was in no state to tell him how she came alive when she saw him: she didn't feel she could depend on her feelings. Hadn't she been attracted to Logan and then that had ebbed? Logan still hoped he was on the back-burner and while she didn't want to lead him on she couldn't make any promises. There was the issue of her misunderstanding about his parents: after Rhodri told her they were still alive, she'd mentioned it to Logan, had he meant they'd passed away? No, he'd said, definitely not! They went off caravan touring, that's what he'd said and his reaction made her think she was losing the plot. That had to be the same when she'd thought he'd called her by her real surname. Nothing had come of it, maybe she had imagined it after all. She used to be whip smart, for crying out loud, what was happening to her?

The best thing for her to do was to do nothing. Better to keep Rhodri as a friend and Logan at arm's length until she had got herself together. Avoid matters of the heart, look for a new venture, whether that was the cabin or something else, and throw herself into the village. Because here, nobody had any side. They were upfront and lived life to the full. Just as they were now, banging the poor BBC van, mobbing it to crawling pace as it tried to park up.

Ceri had never seen Dwynwen this full before – it was rammed not just with locals but with not-so-locals and wildlife experts in *I ♥ Bats* T-shirts, all buzzing around on what was unanimously agreed the biggest thing ever to happen here. Gwen parted the seas with her bosom and pointed the reporter and cameraman in Rhodri's direction, where he was positioning bins for recycling paper plates. Then it was off to the woods where the interview would take place, pursued by a Pied Piper entourage of people up the path.

'What if they need you, Ceri? You were with Rhodri when he saw it,' Mel said, pulling her with her.

'I don't think they'll want my bat poo anecdote, do you?' Ceri said, not wanting to be anywhere near the filming. 'Besides, Gwen wants me serving.'

'But there's no one left! They've all gone up.'

'You go. I'll wait here, I'd like to watch it first on the telly anyway.'

Later, when they'd all trooped back down, it was time for the scene-setting shots and everyone squeezed around the table to tuck in. Gwen was chuffed to bits she'd put on her pearls because they'd asked her to say a few words to camera too. And Mel almost wet herself when she was filmed working in the cabin. By the time the crew was ready to leave, the whole village, who'd virtually drunk the pub dry, agreed it had been a day they'd never forget. While the party was dismantled, Ceri took a breather outside where she saw the reporter packing up.

'Right, I think we've got everything,' the reporter, Felicity Jones, said to her, 'but if we've left anything behind, I've given Rhodri my number. I live in Cardiff but I'm from down the road so I can always come back. Any excuse to get my walking boots on round here.'

'Okay. You got what you wanted, though?' Ceri asked, now seeing beyond her smart suit how attractive the young woman was close up, with silky black hair, big brown eyes and a rosebud mouth.

'Yes, thanks.' She smiled, revealing two lovely dimples in her cheeks. She went to get into the van and then stopped, looking bashful.

'This is rather ... embarrassing. But you don't happen to know if Rhodri is ... er ... single? God, I don't normally do this,' she said, 'it's so unprofessional. But he's so nice, isn't he? Not to mention lush-looking.'

Ceri's stomach turned. This lady rambler who loved Wales was perfect for Rhodri. How she would love to spin her a yarn about his wife and kids waiting for him at home. But she couldn't do it.

'Yes. Yes, he is,' she said, hoping to conceal her

devastation at setting him up for at worst a last hurrah before Sweden.

'Single or lush-looking?' Felicity laughed. And there it was: Ceri couldn't deny it.

'Both,' she said, sighing, unable to contain it.

'Oh, right ... you and him, are you ...?'

'No. Unfortunately,' Ceri said, surprising herself again. There, she'd admitted it. When she'd thought this tangled mess would sit unknown forever in her belly, a chance encounter with a stranger had been all that was required to identify her true feelings.

'I was going to ask if you'd put a word in for me but I can't now, I s'pose!' Felicity was joking but there was a pleading in her voice for clarity.

But Ceri couldn't go matchmaking. So she gave a non-commital hum and then turned round – bumping straight into Mel, who was gawping. She'd heard everything, that was clear. What a total balls-up. It'd be round Dwynwen by morning.

'You can't tell him,' Ceri said, full of anguish.

'But what ... what if Rhodri ...' Mel stuttered.

'He won't feel the same ... please, I beg you.'

Mel wavered, unsure where her loyalties lay and Ceri felt terrible for putting her in that position.

'He's leaving. And it'd only make things awkward.'

It took an age, but to Ceri's relief, Mel finally nodded.

That, Ceri hoped, would be the end of it: it had to be.

26

'It's starting!' Mel yelled across the pub as she turned up the volume on Gwil's telly and the theme tune of BBC *Wales Today* blared out.

Immediately everyone went quiet and waited to see where their story featured in the headlines. Fair dos, it wasn't the first to be mentioned, nor the second, third or fourth ... and nervous looks were exchanged because what if it had been postponed or dropped? But hadn't Rhodri rung Felicity Evans to check it was definitely on tonight? Then at last they were billed as the 'and finally' piece – *How A Village Has Gone Batty For Love* – and a round of applause went up as a shot of the mother and baby bat unit filled the screen. That gave them a few minutes to refresh their drinks and pop to the loo before they came on.

'This is so exciting!' Mel squeaked to Ceri, who was navigating her way through beer taps and optics.

'I hope I don't look a total dick,' Rhodri said, joining Mel, who noticed Ceri's cheeks flare up when he smiled her way.

'You won't!' Mel said, elbowing him.

'I hope my ears aren't sticking out on camera. Felicity said I come across well ... very well ... but—'

Crash. Ceri dropped a glass and followed it to the floor to clear it up. Oh dear. Mel wished she hadn't overheard Ceri's confession that she fancied Rhodri. Then she could carry on oblivious and not worry. Because now she was feeling conflicted by the knowledge, unable to stop herself analysing the pair of them. It was all so silly. Yes, they were chalk and cheese but they were made for each other. Mel had been mulling it over all weekend and the more she considered it, the more she thought they were the yin to the other's yang. There was Ceri, streetwise and smart, and Rhodri, humble and kind, but they complemented one another like curry and chips. But perhaps Ceri was right: if he felt the same as she did, why would he be leaving? And where did Logan fit in because hadn't Ceri grown close to him too? This was why she wished she didn't know – her head was jumbled as if her colours were mixed in with her whites.

Suddenly, Mel realised the room was quiet. Only the newsreader's voice could be heard. She looked around and saw a figure in the doorway. She tapped Rhodri and he swung round, immediately getting to his feet. It was his father, Alun Cadwalader, as upright as a broom handle in a golf shirt and slacks.

'Dad,' he said, pausing, unsure like everyone else what he was doing here. A ripple of 'What a cheek!' and 'Talk about timing' broke out as backs stiffened and jaws clenched.

But Rhodri being Rhodri rose above the rankling which was surely running through his veins and asked if he wanted a pint.

'No, son, I'm not staying. I was passing ...'

There were a few shaking heads because it was

274

impossible to 'just pass' the pub seeing as it was at the end of the road.

'Right,' Rhodri said uneasily, shifting on his feet, glancing around to see if anyone had their pitchforks out.

'So . . . I wanted to say . . . first thing tomorrow, CadCon will withdraw its application for the housing development. The land, we'll give to the people of Dwynwen. Congratulations to you all.'

He stuck out a hand as people reacted with shock. Rhodri's Adam's apple rose and fell with emotion. And as he walked up to him with his palm outstretched, Mel saw pride and respect in his eyes. As they shook, his father pulled him in for a man hug and the pub burst into spontaneous applause.

'Enjoy the news,' he said to everyone, nodding as he left to the TV which was showing a panorama of the woods. Every head turned in unison to take it in. This was their moment.

'When a small West Wales village heard its ancient woodland was in danger of being turned into a housing estate,' Felicity Jones said to camera outside The Dragon, 'they pulled together to fight the plans. Despite a hard-fought campaign, the proposals were set to be approved last week to meet demand for new homes, much to the disappointment of the people of Dwynwen. But at the eleventh hour, a startling discovery sent the locals into a flap – and batting for near-certain victory.'

A shot of the roost panned away to show Rhodri pointing to them as Felicity nodded, which caused a loud cheer.

'Recycling officer Rhodri Cadwalader discovered a breeding site of rare and protected Barbastelle bats in the woods which has put the whole scheme in real doubt.'

'I thought we'd lost and we'd have forty homes on our doorstep, which would ruin our landscape and the trad-itional way of life here in Dwynwen,' Rhodri boomed, with not a sticky-out ear in sight. 'But these little crea-tures rearing their young here mean it's very unlikely it will go ahead. We're delighted.'

The broadcast cut to a scene of the street party and the beach and Mel saw herself in the cabin, making coffee. She covered her mouth at the sight of herself, looking happy and busy – and said a silent *thank you* to the telly Gods for not including a shot of her bottom.

It was back to Felicity now, who stood before a section of fluttering bunting. 'The discovery wasn't just good news for the woods. It also means the villagers can focus all their energy on bringing back tourists after a drop in the number of holidaymakers. Dwynwen has branded itself the Village of Love because of its connections to the patron saint of love, Saint Dwynwen.'

Well, this was a bonus, Mel thought, she hadn't known the report would include this!

'The idea came about after a series of anonymous acts of kindness which saw deliveries of bunting, beer garden fur-niture and paint to spruce up its row of seaview cottages.'

Everyone took in a breath as they saw the pink, white, blue, purple and green of the homes as smart as buttons on the hill. The phones would be ringing off the hook with bookings!

'Nobody knows who is behind the donations but if you do, then please get in touch. One thing is for certain, though, the village has gone batty for love. Felicity Jones, Dwynwen.'

And then it was over and a roar of excitement went up as Rhodri was hoisted into the air like a champion. Poor Gwen was putting a brave face on seeing as she didn't make the cut. At that moment, Mel saw her dad at the bar – he never came in here, preferring to drink a beer with his mates at the harbour. This, she knew, was his attempt to sort out this business of Fi working at the cabin. It was his version of an olive branch and while she acknowledged he'd made the effort, she was annoyed it had to be now when she was on a high.

'Hiya,' she said, trying not to show her irritation.

'Can I have your autograph?' he said, his eyes crinkling with love.

'You saw it then?' she said, feeling less spiky because she knew he never acted out of spite.

'Got in just as it was starting. I wondered if you fancied some mackerel for tea? Caught it myself today. Come to the boat, eh?'

'All right,' she said, she may as well. Now was as good a time as any to have it out. And she could ask him about the good deeds too because she still had a nagging feeling he was somehow involved.

Dad handed his drained glass to Ceri and Mel remembered her manners.

'This is my dad, Lyn. Dad, this is Ceri, the one I told you about, who wants to come in on the cabin.'

Ceri smiled and Dad nodded.

'We'll have to have a chat,' he said.

'Let's go,' Mel said, bidding farewell to all her friends. As they reached the door, she recalled something she hadn't told him. 'Hey, I forgot to say, Dad, Ceri's mam, she came from here.'

'Oh, aye?'

'Yes! Very sadly, she's passed away. A few months ago. But her name was Angharad. You don't remember her, do you?'

'Angharad, did you say?' he said, stepping out into the light and shading his eyes because the sun was still strong.

'Yes.' She got into the van and belted up, thinking he was doing the same. But she saw through the windscreen he was still by the pub, wincing, holding his chest and supporting himself with his other hand on a table. She rolled down the window. 'You okay? Is that your indigestion? I bet you haven't eaten since breakfast, either.'

He made it over and got in, his hand trembling as he started the ignition. 'I'm fine, don't fuss,' he murmured but she could still tell he was in pain. It made him look grey and matt, not his usual shiny silver. A rush of affection came to her: she was all he had by way of proper family. There was no one else but her to care for him. Softened, she would keep her temper tonight whatever justification he came up with for Fi's parachuting into the cabin.

'Stop at the cottage on the way,' she said gently as his brow remained furrowed, 'I've got some Rennie tablets in the bathroom cabinet. Okay?'

He glanced at her as if he hadn't heard what she'd said.

'For your indigestion,' she said, as she switched on the radio. 'Don't worry, Dad. I'll look after you.'

For he was the one man in her life who had never let her down.

27

From her sun lounger on the deck, Ceri could hear Mel calling her all the way up the lane.

She reluctantly put down her book – she hadn't made time for reading before, or to put it another way, in her old life she'd have turned to a screen; but with no wifi, paperbacks had become a passion.

'Coming,' she shouted, slipping her T-shirt dress over her bikini and heading inside, where she caught a glimpse in the hall mirror of her healthy colour from so many hours outdoors. While she'd always tanned quickly, it had mainly come out of a bottle in Crewe because of the days she'd spent underneath strip lighting. How ridiculous to think her best bronze in years had come from Wales.

'You aren't going to believe this,' Mel said, holding out a large old fashioned-looking brass key which ran the length of her palm. 'My dad, he's heard of your mam!'

'No!' Ceri hardly dared to breathe. Mel nodded and pulled up her strawberry-shaped red shades onto her head to spill the beans.

'She only grew up in the Green House!'

'Never!' Next door but one, right under her nose.

'And I thought you might want a look round ...'

Mel pressed the key into Ceri's hand. It was heavy and scratched, a true vintage of its kind with a Celtic spiral in the bow, a battered shank and proper thick teeth.

'Seriously?'

'The owner won't mind. She likes me to go in and give it an airing every now and again. It's a bit ... musty, I'm afraid.'

'Oh, Mel, thank you!' She'd see where Mum had lived as a kid, tread the same floor as she had and touch the same walls.

'I'd come in with you but I've got to get back.'

Ceri was fine with that – she'd rather go by herself because she didn't know how she'd react.

'The phone has been red-hot all day. The cottages are filling up, and fast, including yours from next week, sorry.' Mel's eyes shone with apology in the warm late afternoon sunshine.

'Don't be daft! It's great news! Just in time for the start of July! I'll find a room somewhere.'

'You can stay in my spare room if you like; I'll get it tidy soon,' Mel offered as if it was nothing. 'And don't say "I couldn't!" because you can!'

'You star. Just while I look for something else. What would I do without you?' Ceri said, hugging her tightly before setting her free so she could go back to the cabin.

'There's a barbecue on the beach in an hour, half five, Rhodri's just decided, he has, so see you down there, all right?'

'Will do!' Ceri said, waving Mel off and pulling her front door shut. It was only ten or so paces to the house but in that short space Ceri's jitters had gone from excitement to nerves. The paintwork shone like an apple but as she peered through the front window with cupped hands she could see a layer of dust on the glass inside, giving it a ghostly feel. Was she ready to see inside? An irrational fear took hold of her that she'd sense her mother's spirit and it would shake her, taking her back to the raw grief she'd felt when she'd first lost her. *Calm down, Ceri*, she told herself, Mum hasn't lived there for forty years. The house belonged to someone else now; the only trace she would find of Mum would be imagined.

Steeling herself, she put the key in the lock where it rattled, only adding to her trepidation, but with a hard turn and a grind, the wooden stable door opened and Ceri pushed it with her fingertips so it swung slowly inwards. The step was tiled and dirty so she squatted down and rubbed it with her dress in an instinctive act to make it gleam as her mother would've done in Crewe. As she did so, she looked in and saw a dark hallway leading to wooden stairs, a front room and a kitchen at the back. It was the same layout as the Blue House and it touched her that the life she'd been living metres away mirrored her mum's childhood.

Slowly, she went in and felt the floor give way slightly beneath her feet – the terracotta quarry tiles which ran throughout were loose and scuffed but it only made her feel grounded that she was in her mother's footsteps. There was a definite dank smell and the temperature had dropped from the heat outside to cool within, making her shiver. Garish floral wallpaper peeled at the edges, revealing bubbling plaster, but still she ran her palm across it to connect with the past. To her left was the sitting room, which had a distressed wood burner nestled in the fireplace as its centrepiece. There was neither furniture nor curtains, only naked black beams and brick walls, so the air, which danced with specks of dust in a shard of light coming through the timber sashes, echoed around her, yet still she could imagine lace in the windows and woollen throws on wingback chairs. The kitchen was heartbreaking with its cracked Belfast sink and manky cabinets but she felt it healing when she turned to see an Aga in the corner. No wonder Mum had kept hers in Junction Road.

Upstairs, she creaked around on floorboards, wondering which of the two tiny-windowed bedrooms had been her mum's. Fractures zig-zagged like crazy paving on the walls and dents suggested where bedposts had stood. The bathroom was as battered as the kitchen but it wasn't unwelcoming, more lived-in. Back down she went to discover the dim courtyard, squashed against the house and the mountain, a square of concrete overgrown with weeds. Who needed a garden when there was a beach to play on? A rotten door at the rear caught her eye and she unfastened the latch, suspecting a shed or an outside loo. But stairs ran down – she'd found a cellar. She hesitated, fearing the walls would topple onto her but curiosity willed her on.

The size of the entire floorspace of the house, it was a bricked area, thick with cobwebs, which contained planks and old tools, a wheelbarrow and a heap of junk. Ceri was a little disappointed that there had been no sign of her mother anywhere but she knew she was being whimsical: it was enough, she reminded herself, to have gone back in time. The dark made her feel uneasy but just as she was about to go, something caught her eye: a shape on a supporting wooden post running vertically in the centre of the room, pocked with holes. Moving closer, she saw it was possibly a letter and she licked her finger to rub away the dirt. A heart appeared, which had been crudely carved with something, inside of which were two initials, A and E. Immediately she knew it had been her mother's doing, an expression of love for her Emilio.

But, hang on, what was Ceri thinking? They'd met in Spain, not in Wales. Could this be somebody else her mother had loved as a schoolgirl? Her heart raced as did her mind, trying to work out what it meant. Tears came to her when she realised she would never know – it would remain a mystery because Mum's sister, Delyth, couldn't remember her shopping list, let alone the details of decades ago. She listened to her shaky breathing, trying to collect herself, confused again why Mum had brought her here. Because there were no answers, only a misleading set of contradictions, which tore the scab off her mourning. Her eyes smarting from the grime, she left the cellar's secret behind her and made her way to the bay, via a stop-off at home to pick up some beers. It would be a relief to be among her friends, she thought, kicking off her flip-flops, leaving them with the others at the edge of the beach like a local. The squidge of warm sand between her toes began to draw out the stress, as did the sight of Mel surfing with Rhodri, Seren, her husband Owen and their son Henry plus Logan.

Ceri sat by a coolbox and the smoking barbecue, a neat portable camping one labelled EcoBBQ, which had to be Rhodri's, and she cracked open a bottle. Slowly she felt herself relaxing as she watched the rhythm of the tide. All she knew, there was no other place she'd rather be on a sunny summer Thursday. Even when it caused her pain, to have this piece of heaven on her doorstep was worth it.

When Mel was done surfing, she carried her board back up the beach and flopped down beside her.

'How did it go?' she said, squeezing water from her ponytail.

'Good,' Ceri said, now she'd had the chance to digest it. 'I did feel closer to my mum in there. But it's like a museum piece. It needs so much work done on it.'

'Maybe you should take it on? Buy it?'

The thought hadn't occurred to her amid the emotion, but indeed, why not? 'I could, couldn't I?'

'I reckon the owner would pay you to take it off her hands!'

'It's definitely worth investigating. Wow, imagine if I bought my mum's old house! And Tash could come and stay and it would be full of love and laughter like it used to be. That's if she starts talking to me properly again.' Which reminded Ceri. 'Any conclusions on Fi working in the cabin?'

'I'm still thinking about it. I'm not sure it'll work between us. We have nothing in common. Dad looked so sad when we talked about it, how it was the kind thing to do. To treasure loved ones. And on a practical level he says I'll need the help with all the bookings. Perhaps I should give her a trial run,' she said reluctantly.

'The cabin could be what you have in common if you feel you're so different. It's worth a go. She might surprise you. Kindness begets kindness.'

'I asked him, Dad, if he was behind the gifts to the village ...' Mel said confessionally. 'People would think I was silly if I said I suspected him. Because it feels as if it's coming from someone who knows us, who knows what makes us tick. Not just in terms of what the village needs but us, the villagers, too. He didn't deny it. He just said, "Why do people care who's doing it? There isn't enough magic in the world."'

Ceri had thought long and hard about it too. Why did it matter where they had come from? To do something for nothing, behind a cloak of anonymity, showed the giving was pure: no moment of glory was sought, no gratitude was required. 'I'm an outsider so it's nowt to do with me really, but I think he's right,' she said, from the heart. 'Whoever is responsible obviously doesn't want any recognition. They're just doing it to make people happy.'

'And it's worked!' Mel said, a smile returning to her cheeks. She inspected the coals, which were turning white, and got up to head to the shore. 'Rhodri!' she called. 'The barbecue's ready.'

He was in the sea, resting on his board, waiting for the next wave. 'I'll be in in a sec, whack the sausages on. All of them, I'm hungry!'

Ceri's heart went from a trot to full canter when she saw him draw himself up by his arms to lie flat, paddling with his powerful hands before he jumped to a standing position and gracefully glided in, delivered to the shallow depths by an adoring sea. He was of this land and it would miss him as much as he'd miss home.

'Got it bad, eh?' Mel said, catching her reverie. They hadn't discussed Ceri's confession and she wasn't going to go there for fear it'd unleash a full blown unrequited love affair.

'No,' Ceri lied, swigging some beer, then almost choking on it when Logan came out of nowhere and collided with Rhodri and took him down. He collapsed into the water face first then came back up spluttering with rage as Logan held up his hands in apology. Ceri stood up quickly, shocked by Rhodri's anger; it had looked accidental and Logan was telling him to chill out. She looked at Mel then at Owen who was just surfing in now to see if they needed to step in if they went nose to nose but she realised nobody else was alarmed.

'This happens every now and again,' Mel said as if it was normal behaviour, concentrating instead on browning the bangers. 'It flashes up and then goes as quickly as it came.'

She looked back and it was already over: Rhodri had stabbed his board in the sand and Logan was waist-deep in the water, heading back out.

'What's up with those two?' Ceri cried, glad she had pressed pause on getting involved with Logan when he and Rhodri had this unexplained beef with each other. Logan was as lovely as ever, still reminding her now and again over parcels and pints that he would wait for her. She guessed he thought she was playing hard to get and he liked her all the more because he wasn't used to being resisted. But it was all about Rhodri: she couldn't think beyond his departure.

'They used to be big mates. I don't know what happened.' Ceri prompted her for more with accusatory eyebrows. 'Rhodri's never said. Honestly. P'raps he's jealous? Logan has had a few notches on his bedpost.'

'But lots of people have! If you don't meet anyone when you're young, you end up with more notches as you get older. It's not a sign you're, you know, easy or whatever. And why would Rhodri care?'

Mel pinched the air with her tongs as if she was trying to catch the elusive answer. 'Logan came here, what, fifteen years ago, about the time Rhodri was at uni, but he came back after and they hit it off. They were surfing buddies, always out there, inseparable, they were. One summer, about two years ago, they stopped talking. Rhodri would literally get up and march out if Logan came within five hundred yards of him. There's rumours it was over a girl but Rhodri has always said his ex Ruth ended it because she didn't want to live here. Neither of them has ever explained why. And we got fed up with asking.'

A shadow fell upon Ceri and she looked up to see Rhodri even taller and broader than ever. Droplets of water sat on his skin like jewels and he was grinning, his fury forgotten. Back to his fresh-faced self. Perhaps he would explain now, Ceri wondered. But he only said, 'Get the burgers on next, Mel. I could eat a cow.'

This place was unbelievable. Just when Ceri thought she had it sussed, Dwynwen boggled her mind.

28

'Gwen! Come quick! It's a sign!'

'Of what, love?'

'An actual sign!'

'Will you stop playing silly beggars, Gwil! I've just asked you what it's a sign of. Are you going to tell me or not?'

'Gwen. It is a sign for the village. A village sign. To let tourists know they have arrived at their destination of Dwynwen.'

'Why didn't you just say so, then?'

❧

The summer of love was in full swing.

A heatwave which showed no signs of stopping had begun a fortnight ago at the start of July, completely transforming the village into the Costa del Dwynwen. Everyone had wilted, shorts and flip-flops were uniform, although Gwil still insisted on wearing slacks. He couldn't command the respect of his clients with his knees on display.

'I can't believe this weather! In Wales!' began every conversation, conducted in accents which had not been heard here for years. The timing of the village sign couldn't have been better: tourists no longer arrived cross and weary, wondering if this was the right place. The metal post at the crest of the hill held a cast-iron square, which was the black of bakestone, quartered into four cut-out silhouetted images. There was the rolling sea, a fire-breathing dragon, a love heart and Dwynwen, in plaits, as her saintly fingers performed a blessing on all who entered. Beneath was the word *Dwynwen*, which sat atop *The Village of Love*. It was like a wand being waved so visitors relaxed happily into their holiday, knowing they'd reached their destination. There had been a fuss when the fourth act of kindness was dropped at the pub by a lorry – but no sooner had it gone up, the pilgrimages began and no one had the chance to mull it over. Still sunrises unwrapped smouldering days where the horizon wobbled and the sand was too hot for toes. The sea, as refreshing as ever, was full of visitors cooling off on bodyboards and the beach was awash with umbrellas, UV shades, camping chairs and kids eating cones of chips. As shadows stretched, people unable to get a table in the pub lit barbecues and early evening games of cricket and football commenced. At sunset, the bay was illuminated by small fires as crowds gathered to watch what became known as the western lights, like the northern ones but in pink, orange and purple. There was even the odd dolphin sighting from fishermen way out at sea but the Dwynwen Dolphin Watch blackboard had no new markings yet.

Inside Caban Cwtch, Ceri found Mel closing up, looking tired now she was open seven days. Mel switched off the fan on the counter; the swish gave way to the sploosh of waves and chatter in the beer garden. Straight away the air became thick and muggy and perspiration prickled on Ceri's back.

'I give in,' Mel said, blowing up into her fringe to cool herself. 'I've asked Fi to come in from next week on a trial basis. I can't do this on my own. There's too much to do, I'm not complaining, mind, just stating the facts.'

The acts of kindness had inspired Mel to put on extra shifts too – once a week, she opened up late for anything the community came up with, from book swaps to a repair café where people brought broken bits and pieces to be fixed for free. Barri's agricultural question time was in the diary and he was talking about donating a patch of land for a village allotment.

'Good for you,' Ceri said, 'I'd be stuffed if it was just me behind the bar.'

Business was so good, Gwen had brought in a new part-time barmaid plus a young chef who'd just qualified from catering college. He had ripped up the old menu and was creating sublime dishes of fresh fish and local meat which had earned Gwen and Gwil a load of five-star reviews on Trip Advisor and a pardon from the brewery because they'd turned things around. It was the same for Dwynwen's ratings too – Rhodri had finally sorted Facebook, Instagram and Twitter accounts for @TheVillageofLove and their mentions, likes and retweets were steadily growing.

'Can I retire yet?' Seren said, walking in barefoot, her dungarees slashed to cut-offs with a lilac bra top peeking out from underneath. Her hair, now white blonde, was piled on the top of her head like a Mr Whippy. She went to her Fork Off display cabinet to check what needed replenishing.

'There's been a run on your rings and bracelets,' Mel said, 'so I reckon you've got half a flight to New York.'

'Wonderful!' Seren beamed, giving her jewellery a shine with her ever-present polishing cloth. 'If this carries on I'll be able to finish at the pub for good. You going to watch *Casablanca* tonight?'

English Dick's outdoor Cosy Cinema Club had only started two weeks ago but was already legendary; he directed each showing as if he was Stephen Spielberg with deckchairs, bean bags, blankets and fairy lights, even selling tubs of ice cream and popcorn from an old-fashioned usherette tray.

'Can't!' Ceri said. 'I'm moving in with Mel tonight!'

Since she'd left the Blue House, Ceri had stayed in the pub while Mel got the spare room ready for her. It had taken Mel longer than she'd planned – her art supplies were stored there and the process of clearing it had seen her sink again. Living with Gwen and Gwil had been like staying with family but Ceri yearned to be up in the cottages. And it'd be great to spend time with Mel – girly chats made everything all right. It had always worked in the past with Jade and with Tash and Mum, when they'd chow down a Chinese and have a good mither.

'Ooh! Girls' night in, is it?' Seren said.

'There might be an ice-cold bottle of bubbly in my bag!' Ceri laughed. 'I thought we could have a toast to my roomie! And,' she said with a fanfare, 'because I've had my offer on the Green House accepted!'

The cabin went up in cheers. Ceri couldn't wait to have a place of her own and fill it with her things. She'd start again with traditional cosy furnishings in keeping with the period look of the building, which she'd have restored. She had decided to sell her flat in Alderley Edge to help pay for the mammoth task which she was sure would be unearthed by a surveyor.

'When will you move in?'

'Within a couple of months, I hope. Contracts are about to be exchanged on my mother's place so it'll be all systems go.' The crush of losing Junction Road was tempered now by the thought she'd be in her mother's childhood home.

'Brilliant!' Seren said. 'Have fun tonight, won't you. I've got to rush or I'll be late for Dick's flick.'

Ceri cackled and helped Mel finish off, by turning chairs onto the tables and sweeping the day's remains of crumbs. Then they locked up, walked past the heaving pub and climbed the hill, sweating cobs.

'Do you want to unpack straight away?' Mel said at the door of the Pink House.

'Nah, I've only got one bag!'

'Let's have that drink first then.'

Mel nipped in for wine glasses and Ceri held the cool bottle to her forehead.

'It's going to be a belter, the sunset, just you watch,' Mel said, settling down beside her.

Ceri didn't want to waste a drop of champagne so she crawled the cork into her hand. She poured it out as the scent of the bubbles mingled with the lane's wild jasmine and honeysuckle, which was sighing sweetly into the early evening. This moment was special because chances to reflect were fewer and further between now the season had started: everyone was rushed off their feet, chasing time, making sure people who had come here to wind down got the service and experience they expected. It was what the locals had dreamed of so no one minded.

But it meant life was intensely busy and thundered along at speed – on top of that, Ceri had her Cheap As Chic administrative duties to perform. She seemed to have got away with melting away from the spotlight so far: the OMG range had done so well Jade had become hot property and she'd signed up with a magazine for exclusive pictures of her wedding next month.

Ceri hadn't had a proper chat with Rhodri for ages. She missed him hugely and when it became too much, she'd convince herself he wouldn't match up to what she imagined him to be when she next saw him. It was good practice too, a test run for when he left in fast-approaching September. But whenever she did catch sight of him, perhaps across the bar or in the queue at Mel's, he was better in the flesh and his smile made her heart blossom. Every time, she would pray to have gone off him.

'Electric blue, Tuscan roof, pumpkin and tulip red. Then ... let me see ... heather, orchid and bedouin night. That's how the sky will go,' Mel said. 'If I'm wrong, well, tomorrow's a new day. I can try again.'

'Too right, kid,' Ceri said, offering her glass to Mel's for a toast. 'Here's to trying again.'

29

Where was Mel? She was supposed to have been here ages ago and she was in danger of missing out on Rhodri's pizza.

Tomorrow was the anniversary of Al's accident and Ceri had been keeping an eye on her in the days they'd been living together to check she was coping. Mel was keeping her chin up and showing no signs of a break-down: she'd said she was too busy to lose it now! At teatimes, Ceri had offered to go with her to Cardiff if she wanted company. But Mel insisted she had to do it alone – instead she'd asked her to run the cabin for the weekend. And she'd finally relented, out of necessity, offering Fi two days of work.

Even so, Ceri wanted to pop to the Pink House before she got too merry. She weaved past the locals and Rhodri's workmates, who had gathered around a table laid out with a variety of toppings to make their own. There were circles of juicy mozzarella, strips of fresh asparagus and melt-in-the-mouth prosciutto and bowls of succulent olives and mushrooms. Rhodri was nowhere to be seen so Ceri told Seren to save them some and made her way down the steps to the lane. When she got to the Murmur

Y Coed gate, she found him crouched over a box and he jumped out of his skin when he heard her.

'What're you doing?' she said, puzzled by his furtive behaviour.

'Oh, God, I knew this would happen,' he said, mumbling something which included the words 'fucking' and 'Logan' as he tried to hide the parcel.

'What is it?'

He blushed and stammered 'nothing'.

'Okay,' she said, giving him suspicious eyes. 'Absolutely nothing to see here at all apparently. I'm off to get Mel. Bye bye. But let me know not to bother coming back if it's a machine gun or a pop-up doll.'

'See? This is why he's done it,' he said, throwing his arms in the air. 'To humiliate me. Oh, you may as well know. I'm sure that's why Logan delivered it now. Reckoned he'd tried earlier, my arse. Far better to drop it now when I've got people over and he's not invited.'

'What are you on about? Are you some kind of dark web overlord?'

'Believe me, I'd feel better if I was ... it's ... Lego.' He hung his head and Ceri burst out laughing. As crimes went, it wasn't up there with the worst but she couldn't help herself.

'Lego?' she cried. 'As in those completely unenvironmentally friendly, non-biodegradable nuclear war-resistant plastic blocks? After all the recycling shit you gave me! That's classic, that is!'

'Yes, yes, I'm well aware I'm a hypocrite. Go on, do your best, go for it, rip me to shreds.'

He was actually serious. She toned down her horror.

'Rhodri, you don't have to be this perfect person, you

'know.' She gazed up at him with warm eyes, trying to express her feelings for this gorgeous man bear.

'They are developing greener plastic ...' he said, weakly. 'It's just when I was a kid, I did it with my dad but my brothers would smash up whatever I made ... me and Henry do it now. That was what was on my laptop that I didn't want you to see. It wasn't ... rude stuff. Just the Lego website.'

'It's cool,' she said. 'It makes no difference to me. I still think you're amazing.'

'Do you?' he said, shocked.

'Yes. If a bit geeky.' Not to mention a bit paranoid about Logan.

He nodded resignedly, his eyebrows drooping like they'd just given up on life. She wished she hadn't said that last bit.

'What I meant was ...'

'It's fine. Go and get Mel,' he said, as if he couldn't get away from her quickly enough.

As awkward went, it was pretty much a masterclass. So she did as she was told and went to find Mel, mulling over her hopeless heart. Why hadn't she realised she stood no chance with him? Yet for all their ridiculous differences – his eco-cleaning materials versus her bleach, his hatred of money and her stuffed purse, his humility against her swagger, his countryside upbringing and her townie life – he was either making her laugh or having a deep and meaningful with her. As much as it hurt her, she was beginning to think she needed him to go to Sweden to get over him.

She let herself in and called out for her. Mel had done a great job with the house – it was so tidy compared with when she'd first set foot in here. There were free pegs in the hallway, boots were paired up, a smell of fabric conditioner and the surface of the dresser was uncluttered except for a few letters.

'Mel! It's me,' she said at the foot of the stairs, waiting for her to answer. Still, there wasn't a peep. So she went up to the lounge, nothing; then back down to the bathroom, again nothing. Maybe she was having a nap? Her door was always closed; Ceri didn't go in there because she didn't want to invade Mel's personal space, so she gave it a light tap and put her ear to it to see if she could hear snoring before gently pulling the handle down to go in.

'Mel,' she whispered as it opened a crack onto utter darkness. No wonder she was in a deep sleep if the curtains were closed. 'Time to wake up.'

She pushed against the door but it refused to budge. Harder now, she placed her hand and her shoulder against the wood, wondering what on earth was in the way. A funny feeling came over her as the resistance continued and she called louder now while summoning all of her strength and barging her way in. A crash and a bang and a torrent of bags and clothes and magazines and books and ornaments slid on top of more rubbish – there wasn't a spot of carpet to be seen.

'Mel!' she shouted, squeezing through the gap of the door, fearing her friend had been crushed by the avalanche. The bed was stacked with more belongings, towering and teetering against the wall, leaving an inch of length which presumably Mel crawled into at night. Ceri had had a vision of her skull smashed in under the duvet but she wasn't in there, thank goodness. Now she knew Mel wasn't in mortal danger, Ceri's eyes adjusted to the room. It was chaos: every available area from her bedside cabinet and the window sill to her wardrobe and dressing table were littered or hanging or cowering beneath millions of bits and pieces, some of which she recognised from upstairs. So this was how she'd done it: transferring her possessions into one room, the place Mel wouldn't think visitors would look. Ceri felt awful she'd seen it – as if she'd read her diary behind her back.

Trying not to panic, she reasoned at least Mel had made the rest of the house habitable. But it was obvious that while Mel had been calm on the surface, underneath she was struggling with tomorrow's anniversary. Her fingers itched to make the room safe but she couldn't do it – Mel would see it as interference or, worse, a violation. What should she do? She found she couldn't move, though. It was like staring into Mel's head, seeing a photo album of her memories but not knowing why this particular troll with its green sticky-up hair was important or understanding the significance of the cracked piggy bank. Why keep a grubby My Little Pony? And a game of Hungry Hippos? What had the Etch A Sketch meant to her growing up?

A stack of vibrant canvases lay against the radiator and she crept in, wading slowly so she didn't stand on anything. Flicking through them, they were exception-ally bright watercolours of places she didn't recognise, cityscapes and a castle, a brewery and a street scene. Were they from her days at art college in Cardiff? Next to them was a cracked plastic tray bursting with worn-down Rimmel lipsticks minus lids, unused eyeshadows still in their cellophane, solid nail varnish and – oh! what were the chances of it! – an empty Cheap As Chic lip gloss. To think Mel had held Ceri's work in her hand and been unaware of it. Then Ceri caught sight of a curling photograph half-covered by a scary staring orange Furby on the floor. She picked it up, drawn to it. The picture was of a scene she knew so well – the rocks where her mother cuddled up to her father. Except it was of a, what, nine-year-old, ten-year-old beside a waterfall, Dwynwen's waterfall, on this very beach, beside a brown-haired and tanned man in a silver neck chain complete with a locket. It didn't make sense. What was Mel doing with him here? Was it even him? How could it be, unless …

She dropped the photo and reeled away as nausea took hold, her head screaming. Backing out of the room, closing the door, she barged into the dresser and as she turned to steady herself, she caught sight of the top letter, which was addressed to Mr Emlyn Thomas. Her mouth went dry and blood roared in her ears. She shut her eyes but she could still see the man's features – the eyes she'd never seen because his face was obscured in her mother's photo. They were her own – the same almond shape, the same chestnut. His nose was strong and the set of his broad smile like hers, too. She thought back to the pub when he'd come in the night the village was on the news … she'd met him and not realised. But Mel's dad was Lyn, wasn't he? She shook her head, not understanding what she'd seen, not accepting what her mind was concluding. *Mr Emlyn Thomas. Emlyn.* Could Emilio be a fabrication? But why? And how could he be two people, two fathers, if Mel was only a few months older than her?

Ceri's feet carried her forward in an out-of-body stumble to her room.

Feeling her legs go, she fell back onto the bed, trying to see through competing and muddled emotions. There was disbelief and astonishment and rejection of what couldn't be but anger at what possibly was.

She heard the front door go and Mel's footsteps, then her voice which crept round into Ceri's room.

'Ceri? Are you in?'

She couldn't hide – Rhodri would only tell Mel she had gone looking for her. And yet she couldn't let her see her like this. Because Ceri would crumble and it would all come out. Mel was too fragile to see this. Tomorrow was too important.

'In here,' she croaked, pulling the duvet over her, hiding her face.

'The bus was late but I've got a load of nibbles for Rhodri's and – oh, Ceri, what's up?'

'Just a headache, I came back to get you. Then I felt poorly. You go, they're waiting for you.'

'But what about tomorrow? Will you be okay if I go to Cardiff?'

'Yes. I just need to sleep,' Ceri said, desperately.

'Okay,' she said reluctantly. 'But any problems, just say, promise?'

'Yes.'

Ceri waited until Mel had gone before she allowed herself to cry. At first they were small dumbfounded sobs as the questions she needed answering weren't yet properly formed. Then the stabs in the dark began to shape themselves as she started to deal with the discovery of something challenging all the facts she'd grown up with. The mother she'd thought she'd known. The father she'd thought she'd had. And if it was true, it would mean she had grown up with deceit. It would mean her father wasn't dead in the water but here, alive and well.

Ceri counts her blessings

I t's the middle of the night, Mum, and I can't reach you.

Usually when I talk to you in my head, I can sense you listening in; see your smile or your frown, hear your words of encouragement or doses of common sense.

But you're somewhere else, far away, unreachable. I don't blame you – why would you want to face up to what you did? To see my distress and anger, hiding under the duvet, staring out into the dark, disbelieving and confused. To see my disappointment in you. Because you've let me down. Of all those horrible feelings, being disappointed in someone you loved and trusted and idolised is the worst. I haven't slept a wink, my eyes are sore from crying, my nose is blocked and there's a sickness in my stomach, which rises up and tastes sour and acidic, of dishonesty.

Why did you spin me such a fantasy? I remember feeling special that I had a dad from Spain. In the eyes of a child, it was exotic and dramatic – full of colour and swishing red and black polka-dot flamenco skirts. I grew up thinking I had that in my blood, and even as an adult I'd put all my success down to him, his entrepreneurial genes and you played that game too. You carried it on, saying I was just like him. It feels so cruel. How did you keep a straight face for so long? Did you start to believe it yourself? No wonder there were never any photos or telephone calls from his family. How did I not see the holes in your story? They never got in touch because your pregnancy before marriage was a sin in their Catholic eyes. All that shit about sardines and mermaids ... and the likeliest thing of all is that he was a let-down. Just like Tash's dad was. My God, you could pick them. And that makes me feel terrible that he was a rock for Mel, when she wasn't even blood. Were you and me such a bad option that he'd chosen her family over us?

Or ... *oh God* ... was there something worse? Maybe he's a monster and you were abused or manipulated and you ran and now I've got to keep this to myself ... just when I thought I'd found a place which was honest and good. I mean, I'm sleeping in Mel's house, for God's sake, she's refusing rent and it's looking like she's my sort of sister. It's a huge tangle. But why would you send me here? Why would you want me to find out he was a bastard? To confront him? To show him up? To correct the past? My gut can't accept that. But then how can I trust my gut anymore? And yet you were the epitome of kindness – whether that was how you brought Tash and me up to be or in the way you lived your life, doing favours for people, looking out for them, fetching shopping for Mrs Briggs up the road, all of that. And you'd always spoken so well of him, as if he was the love of your life. I just don't understand and I can feel this pressure in my head trying to make sense of it when how can I ever know the truth? Do I have to leave this village now and all my friends?

Because I can't mention this to Mel. She's a mess and how would it sound if her beloved father knocked you up then walked off, never to contact you again? I can't do that to her. The kindest thing to do is not say anything – and here I am spouting something you'd say and now I feel guilty because what if you never meant me to know but it was just your dementia reliving it all? *Oh, Mum, if you can hear me, I'm sorry.* And I'm even sorrier that I can't think of any blessings either. Because what bloody good is a sunset or a nice tea when you find out your whole life has been a lie?

30

A droopy bouquet hung from Mel's hand as life went on all around her.

Blocks of jerking turquoise and carrot from belching buses. Cars in postbox red, platinum and marine blue zipping past. Multi-coloured bursts of bicycles. Cookie dough bricks in the bridge. The sandwich-white clouds dotting the sweltering lunchtime sky. The truffled Taff flowing below. It was a giant moving painting of smears and layers, only slowing down when the humps and traffic lights commanded. At least she could still see the shades, at least it hadn't all gone black.

Cardiff was busier than she remembered: she felt under attack from people streaming around her and the sound of drilling: above too, caged in by the scaffolding as the city built itself higher. Only the mushroom castle and its animal wall of stone creatures, of seals and bears, hyenas and lions, were the same. Ten years ago today she had seen Alwyn's blood spill and pool and run on the tarmac; thank God the night-time had given her some protection from its shocking hue. The scream of approaching sirens as she'd cradled his miraculously untouched face, lolling in the crook of her arm, his body becoming gruesomely twisted and bent, lit by a neon flashing blue. She had vomited, immediately sober, and smelled fumes and iron on what had been a humid evening. Now, the bitter coffee from her train journey was swilling in her stomach. Why had she come? Why had she made cheese rolls? They were only ever destined to become sweaty in her rucksack, uneaten because she had no appetite.

How had she chatted to Dad about the glorious weather on the drive to Fishguard Harbour? It wasn't gorgeous, it was oppressive: more like a frying pan to the back of her head. Smiling at the conductor when she'd produced her ticket between Kidwelly and Pembrey had been a betrayal of her churning insides. The words in her book had swum in tears and she'd run out of tissues by Llanelli. The torturous row in her head swinging from *get off at the next stop* to *stay put* for the entirety of the journey. Until only Cardiff Central remained, the capital city where she was supposed to be staying the night. By then, the sprigs of candy-floss-pink dog rose, fluffy white meadowsweet and Fruit-Salad-wrapper honeysuckle had started to wither. By the time she had arrived at the spot, the once damp kitchen-roll sheath was dehydrated and the scrunched-up foil was hot from her palm.

Her anxiety was peaking and a rage bubbled as she wondered how she could have possibly thought a return here would give her closure. A counsellor had recommended it a long time ago – visiting the scene of a trauma extinguished the fear. *The accident wasn't current, it wasn't happening now, it wasn't your fault, you can recover.* If she could stay with it, then her panic would subside. But she was retching as she stared at the place where Alwyn's life had ebbed away. Three weeks from now marked the anniversary of his death but here was where it hurt, where

305

her brain returned in her nightmares, savaging her with explicit replays. If only she had suggested she'd pay for the evening, but he had wanted to treat her: his run to a cash machine was cut down by a car. The poor driver hadn't stood a chance as he nipped into her path without looking, dizzy with happiness after their first kiss. Melyn turned her back on the road to face the low and lazy river, releasing a howl from her heart. She gripped the wall, placing the bouquet on top, as she felt ripped open all over again. She wanted to go home, back to the safety of the beach, escape the suffocation.

'Hey, are you okay there?'

She saw hands to her right, held out to help. Kind eyes, of blue thistle, fixed on her from honeyed skin all the way over his shaved head.

'Are you all right?' He had a soft lilting voice and his broadness and height gave her shade.

'Yes ... Not really.' Her knees were buckling and she felt herself sway.

'Do you want some water? Or tea, sweet tea. There's a café by the entrance to Bute Park.' He pointed to an archway. 'It's cooler there.'

She nodded and he guided her along the pavement with a hand gentle on her back, letting her dictate the pace.

'My name's Carlos, I work at the museum.' He presented an ID badge hanging on a lanyard on his chest to reassure her he was genuine.

'I'm Melyn, I am. From West Wales.'

'I'm from Anglesey,' he said, and she immediately recognised the accent, as they reached a dappled courtyard filled with white metal chairs and tables. 'Sit down. Don't move. Okay?'

'Yes ... thanks,' she said, trying to produce her purse but he was waving her offer away. Her panic started to subside, helped by being out of the sun, in an open space below rustling trees. Washed out, she felt, and weak. But so very glad she was seated and still. She looked up to see Carlos covering the ground with long strides in flapping baggy linen oatmeal trousers, the cup tinkling on its saucer, which he placed in front of her.

'They let me jump the queue. Two sugars,' he said, before producing another sachet in case she needed more.

She took a gulp of the strong, stewed, sweet nectar and felt the stirrings of a revival. Exhaling, she gave him a little smile.

'Thank you so much. I can't thank you enough. I needed this, I did.'

'It must be the heatwave.'

'Yes,' she lied, afraid of going backwards yet again. 'You don't have to stay, I'm fine now. I'll give you the money.' But she only had notes. 'I'll get change.' The last time she'd been here and let someone pay, it had cost him his life.

Carlos held his hands up and she saw spots on his palms and feared her vision was about to go. 'I might be a failed artist but I can afford a cup of tea.'

'An artist!' Of course, dots of paint! She wasn't seeing things! 'So am I. Well, I was.'

She took another slurp and reminded him he had no obligation to remain with her. She'd finish her tea then head back to the station. There was no point trying to push herself any further when this was as good as it would get. A day out here and there would have to be enough.

'It's okay, I'll see you're good first. I don't have to be

back for, what, ten minutes,' he said, checking his watch, which was also splattered. 'Feeling better?'

'Much,' she said, more brightly than she really felt but she didn't want to keep him waiting any longer. 'You've been so kind. I feel as fresh as the grass now.'

'Fresh? It looks scorched to me.' He did a double-take to show he meant it.

The grass was lush, though – it'd take longer than a week of warmth to turn it to hay.

'It's still bright green!' she said. With bits of blue and yellow. Like his T-shirt.

'Ah, right. Stupid me, I forget. I'm colour-blind. A colour blind artist. Hilarious, eh?' He snorted and she laughed.

'I know how you feel but I see lots of colours, millions. I've got tetrachromacy.'

'Woah! I've heard of that ... it's rare, isn't it?'

'Yes. But to me, it's normal.'

'Same here, well at least now it is, most of the time. At school I felt like a freak, I always mixed up my crayons. Not a good combo when you're different anyway,' he said, pointing to his face. 'I was the only black kid in the village. My father's originally from Brazil. Met my mam in Liverpool; he was a docker, and they moved to the island when they had me.'

'Brazil!' she gasped, imagining a riot of feathers and sequins from Carnival, Havaianas and bright-beaked birds.

'I've never been! One day ... I think the colours would confuse the hell out of me! At first, I'd only paint in black and white. Then I realised I could see light and shape better than others so I felt braver about experimenting and ... *shit*,' he said as a clock chimed two. 'I've got to go.'

He went to leave but paused, checking yet again she wasn't about to flop.

'Honestly, I'll get a bite to eat now. Let me reimburse you.' She needed to. She could walk with him and pop into a shop for coins.

'It was only a few quid!'

'Please!' She knew she looked mad, that's what he'd be thinking, yet she didn't care.

He rolled his friendly eyes. 'If you insist. Come to the museum, I'm in the contemporary craft section.'

'I'll break a note and bring it up.' Resolution suddenly didn't seem so far away.

'Cool. I'll show you round if you like?'

'Okay ... I'd like that.'

He gave her a dazzling childlike grin, coaxing one from her, too. He was only being nice, but nice was lovely. And then he was off, cutting across the park, but turning every now and again to make sure she wasn't on the floor. Just before he disappeared from view, he put his thumbs up and raised his eyebrows to see if she really was recovered. She gave an emphatic response, then drained her tea and realised with delight that she had done it. She had actually conquered Cardiff, not with a flag, but by surviving. Not dying. Moving on. She had to call home to let them know she was safe. But not Dad. It had to be Mam. The one who'd carried her, not just in the womb but all the time when Mel had hero-worshipped her father, even though Mam had been there every day. Her mother picked up on the first ring.

'Melyn?' she said quickly, with concern.

'I'm fine, Mam, I'm okay.' She got up and walked away from the café.

'Do you need picking up from Fishguard because I can come in two shakes of a lamb's tail.'

'I do ... but tomorrow. I'm going to stay tonight.' She hadn't even realised she was going to say it but it felt right even so.

'Are you sure? You don't need to prove yourself, Melyn. We love you, we do.'

'Positive, Mam. I'm blinking thirty!'

'So you are! Do a bit of shopping then? Treat yourself.' Mel looked down at her black knee-length jumpsuit dotted with mustard foxes who were beginning to look rather mangy. Her lime sandals were scuffed too. 'Yes, I might. And Fi wants a new dress, she said last week at the cabin, so I could look for one for her too?'

'That would be wonderful.'

'Is she doing okay in the cabin?'

'Yes, love. I've rung and your friend, Ceri, she said she was a natural in the café, very helpful and polite. Hardworking too.'

'Really?'

'Yes! I know! Perhaps she just needed some responsibility.'

'Maybe. Well, that's great news.'

'So what will you get up to now?'

'I'm going to walk round the stadium. Visit the boutiques in the arcades. Then the museum. And I'll go back to the hotel and have room service. And a bath.' She'd made her itinerary up on the spot and it was thrilling.

'I'm so proud of you, love. Oh ... before you go, I wasn't going to say if you'd had it bad but listen to this

... Alwyn's mother telephoned about Betsi.' Al's sister, whom Mel had hidden from because of the pain. 'She's had a baby, born just after one o'clock this morning. She's called him Alwyn, Melvyn. Like you two. In a way!'

'That's beautiful, that is, like a circle. I must visit her. I've avoided her for so long.'

'Understandable, love. But you can make it up to her because she's asked if you'll be godmam. You don't have to decide yet because—'

'Yes,' she said, bursting. 'I'd be delighted.'

'There's lovely. Right, you go and enjoy yourself. I'll ring your father, tell him you're okay?'

Yes, she thought, as she put her mobile away and emerged into the sunshine where horns blew, where car radios blared, where life carried on, *yes, I am going to be okay*. With that, she reached into her pocket and as she passed a bin, she threw away her outward train ticket. She didn't need to hold on to it anymore.

31

Ceri was slumped on a damp bench overlooking St Davids Cathedral a little after 7 a.m. with just a polystyrene cup of coffee for company. She'd kicked the sheets all night so when dawn seeped through the curtains, she'd got up and got out, suffocated by secrets.

The weekend in the cabin had been a struggle but then hadn't work always been her saviour? She'd kept it together because she hadn't seen Mel, who'd got home late last night and Ceri had made sure she was in bed.

Beneath sultry August clouds as grey as the church, Ceri still lolled with sickness at her own naivety, for believing she was the daughter of a Spanish fisherman when Emlyn was a Welsh cruise-ship engineer. Talk about hook, line and sinker. It was an impossible situation. The only person who would be able to explain was Mel's father, but that would mean more pain and not just for her. It'd crush Mel's new-found happiness, too. She looked down and she'd absent-mindedly been ripping the rim of her cup. White chunks floated in her drink – if they were icebergs, she was the flaming *Titanic*. What the hell was she going to do? Stay and keep shtum or leave in the night, without telling anyone she was going? The pocket of her fleece vibrated. She ignored it, not wanting to talk to anyone. The only person she would've spoken to was her mother, if there'd been such a thing as a hotline from heaven. But it went again and this time she sighed and took out her phone. There were a load of missed calls and voicemails from unknown numbers but this was Jade. She had to pick up.

'Pricey,' she said urgently, 'the papers are after you. They've come to me for comment. You haven't spoken to anyone have you?'

'No. What story?' Her shoulders sagged lower at the weight of another worry.

'It's ridiculous, I've told them it is, but they're saying you've had a celebrity meltdown – you've changed your name and jacked it all in to be a barmaid. I mean, what the jeff is that all about?'

Ceri felt the sucker punch of another blow. She doubled over and hid her face in her free hand. She'd been rumbled – it was just a matter of time before people in Dwynwen learned the truth. Her mind raced, wondering who could have done it – but no one here knew she was really Ceri Price, the beauty blogger who'd made a pretty penny from her own make-up range. Neither Tash nor Jade would've grassed her up. It could only be that she'd been recognised by a holidaymaker. Yet nobody had come out and said it and she hadn't picked up on any whispers and pointing.

'And that's not all. They're also saying you're—'

'*Stop! Enough!*'

She knew what Jade had been about to say – it would be the icing on this huge pile of shit.

'Ceri? Are you all right?'

She began to rock on the seat in despair. 'Oh no, no, no, no.'

'Ceri? Is there something you need to tell me?' Jade's voice had developed an edge. She could hear her cogs whirring too. Ceri was going to have to come clean and take the consequences.

'It's true,' she said quietly, shutting her eyes, knowing Jade was about to go ballistic.

'True?' she yelled. 'Which bit?'

She gulped. 'All of it.'

'You what? You better start talking, lady. And fast! Because I've got photographers outside and my phone's red-hot. Once this gets out it'll be all over Twitter. OMG will go beserk.'

Ceri felt insignificant enough in the shadow of the cathedral – now the shame of having to admit she'd been living a fantasy made her shrivel even smaller.

'When I first got here, they misheard my name as Ceri Rees and thought I'd come about a job at the pub.' It sounded worse out loud. 'Somehow, because I was knackered and they were so welcoming and nice, I couldn't refuse, I agreed to do a few shifts.' Jade was responding to her gabble by chucking expletives like bombs. 'Look, I know it all sounds so …'

'Insane? Off your rocker?'

'Yes … but I began to like it here, no one knew me, there was no one after me for anything …' Ceri had slowed down, feeling the depth of her love for Dwynwen, 'and it was such a sad place but full of good people. I felt this pull to the village …'

'I'm sorry, cocker, but I don't understand. Why?'

'Because I wanted to be part of something real,' Ceri wept, as a defensiveness rose in her.

'To be part of something real? But it's all a big day-dream!'

'It isn't, Jade,' she cried with passion. 'Well, it wasn't.'

'Oh, Ceri, there's not more is there?'

'My dad ... He wasn't Emilio. And he isn't dead. He's called Emlyn, he's here and I've only just found out.'

The line crackled as Jade blew out her astonishment. 'It doesn't bloody rain, does it?'

Ceri felt the breath of hope running out beneath the load of her woes. 'I just don't know what to do. My mum lied to me. I worshipped her. I can't understand why she hid it. Denied me a father. How can I forgive her? My head's pounding, Jade, everything's closing in on me.'

There was silence apart from Jade's nails tapping in concentration.

'Right, I've got it. I'll stall everyone, say we'll be making an announcement, this evening. I'll draft a statement – you've had an OMG moment, everyone has them, you've been suffering from exhaustion brought on by your best-selling range and the death of your mum. All it is, you're human. And once it's died down, you can make your comeback, tits and teeth, sales will go through the roof. What do you reckon?'

What did she reckon? It was like listening to herself a few years ago – on the ball, driven and pretty much what Ceri would have devised once upon a time.

'Jade, you're the one with the fire in her belly now. Not me. You go ahead, do what you said. I've got to sort out the mess here with all the people who trusted me but who'll want rid of me when it comes out. I resign, Jade. The company, it's yours.'

'Don't talk soft, Pricey. Take a breath, will you. Get packing, come home and don't for God's sake get photographed.'

Ceri tugged her hood down to her nose, got up and started fast-walking to her car.

'Jade, I'm so sorry you've been dragged into this mess of mine.'

'Just come home.'

Ceri's phone beeped from another call waiting – it was an unknown number trying to get through. Her chest constricted because the search for her had started – she was a hunted woman. She shoved her phone into her pocket and felt disgusted at herself. She had been a shitty friend and boss, burying her head in the sand, thinking only of herself while Jade was running the business. What mattered now were the ones who'd let her belong no questions asked. She put her foot down all the way, needing to get back to work out how she was going to break it to them and screeched to a halt outside the Pink House, grateful Mel had already gone to the cabin. Inside, she put the kettle on and tried to formulate a plan. She'd have to go to the pub tonight, confess her sins to those lovely people, take it like a woman and run before they chased her out. It was the last place she wanted to go to but she had no other option: she'd have to return to her old life with her tail between her legs. As for confronting her father, she'd done enough damage here – even though her heart screamed for resolution, she couldn't put Mel through it. Ceri had survived this long without him, hadn't she? She'd have to get things back on an even keel with Tash, her true family.

A rap at the door made her jump. It'd be the bastard press after her. She tiptoed through the lounge and took a peek from the window, expecting to see a pack of reporters with notepads and dictaphones, ready to tear her to shreds. Instead, it was Logan in his postman uniform of red polo shirt and shorts. At least it was a friendly face. She went down the stairs and opened the door, managing a smile.

'Morning, Ceri!' he said with a lopsided grin, presenting a parcel and a screen for her to sign. 'Got something for you.'

'Thanks.'

'Any plans tonight?' he asked in his casual way, his blue eyes suggesting possibilities.

She hugged the package, deciding she may as well get him to spread the word on his rounds. 'Just the pub, if you or anyone else fancies it? Maybe ask on your shift?'

'Cool,' he said, looking pleased. 'I'll see you there, around seven, maybe?'

'Perfect,' she said, closing the door, returning upstairs and examining the brown cardboard box in her hands. She knew exactly what was inside: it was as if fate had decreed its arrival on her last day in Dwynwen. It would come in handy for when she was gone, she sighed. She went upstairs and made a brew, fearful of what would come her way when she told everyone the truth. Perhaps she'd even be gone by tonight – Mel might ask her to leave. The meaningful ceremony she'd planned for Mum's ashes wouldn't take place: it'd be scatter and go.

Maybe in the circumstances, after her mother's lies, it

was for the best. She was as bad as her, after all, wasn't she? Escapism was really just a form of dishonesty. That's why, deep down, she could never have told Rhodri how she felt about him: if there'd ever been a chance, and she was sure there never had been one, he could never have trusted her. Her dream of a new venture here, her bid to buy the Green House, was gone. The label on the parcel briefly blurred as she saw it through tears. Then she sat up, gasping as the realisation hit her. It was obvious. It'd been obvious all along. She knew who had tipped off the papers.

32

*'To Rhodri
For when you're away, so you'll never miss a sunset,
From the Village of Love'*

❧

Rhodri was just getting to the really incredible part of his story about the future trend of turning human waste into biodegradable plastic when he heard the *ting, ting, ting* of metal on glass.

'This better be good,' he said, annoyed to be cut short especially when Mel had been so interested, apart from when she kept dropping this Carlos from Cardiff into the conversation. She was absolutely besotted – and by the sounds of it, he was too, having rung her three times at the cabin today already. Rhodri was very happy for her: it would make leaving less sad if he knew she was in a good place. And it was coming sooner now that he'd decided he'd take some holiday to explore Sweden before he started his sabbatical. There was nothing left here for him to do: the forest was saved, he was back on good terms with Dad, Dwynwen was jam-packed with tourists and short of going out on a boat to tempt the dolphins back into the bay, he'd done what he could. Ceri had made it quite clear she thought he was a geek when she hadn't come back to his pizza night: that had been as much as he'd seen her alone in weeks. Logan would, inevitably, get the girl. He didn't want to be around when Ceri fell into his arms. The thought sat like a turd in constipated bowels. It would be better all round once he disappeared: he was almost looking forward to getting on the plane and worrying about offsetting his flight emissions rather than enduring this heartbreak.

'It's Ceri! She's by the bar!' Mel said, waving and smiling at her from their seat on the pub banquette. 'I haven't seen her since Friday! I mean, we only live together!'

'How come?' He couldn't help but stop and stare. But this wasn't the Ceri he knew. She hadn't returned Mel's hello – instead she was staring around seemingly everywhere but at nobody with a strange look on her face. Troubled and pained, but of course still beautiful with it. Each time he saw her now, even if it was just through the cabin window, he felt it even harder – to know he was going made these moments more precious.

'She was in bed when I got back yesterday and she was up and out before me this morning. I've been working all day, see. I'm dying to tell her about Cardiff. And Carlos. I wonder what she's got to say?'

'Thanks, everyone,' Ceri said to an unusually quiet bar. The heatwave was over and a cold wind was blowing in, keeping the tourists inside their cottages, caravans and tents. He saw her chin wobble as she drew breath and his arms ached to lift her face to his, to put them around her and tell her he'd make everything all right. What on earth could it be? Mel gave him a concerned look, she had noticed the change in her too.

'I just wanted to say a few words ... a thank you, really. For everything.'

What? This sounded as if she was going somewhere. He waited for her to crack the punchline. Any minute now, she'd stick on her smile and put on her jazz hands. But no, Ceri was still downcast and now she was searching for someone ... then she locked her eyes on Rhodri and began.

'I came here without knowing a soul ... I turned up alone, miserable and cynical. I was a stranger. But you took me in and your kindness has changed me. You taught me happiness, you made me trust again when the last few years have been so isolating. I'd come from a place which had once felt like home but became a cage. I didn't belong there anymore and I so needed to belong somewhere. You gave me that.'

The pub swelled with emotion, while Rhodri wondered why the hell she was directing this at him.

'But there's something you need to know ... and I'm deeply ashamed I haven't told you before ...'

Rhodri felt the mood shift as people swapped quizzical looks. Ceri looked up to the ceiling and swallowed.

'There's a story coming out in the papers tomorrow ... about me, who I am. And I wanted you to know beforehand ...'

The hairs on his neck stood up as she focused on him once more.

'My name, it isn't Ceri Rees ...'

His jaw flopped down.

'... It's Ceri Price. I'm not a barmaid, well I used to be, but a few years ago. I'm a businesswoman. I'm what they call a YouTuber ... I have two million subscribers, people who watch my videos about my life and my work, so I'm quite well known.'

Somebody let off a low descending whistle and Mel let out a squeak.

'I have my own line of make-up which you can buy on the High Street.'

'I've got some,' Mel whispered. 'I had no idea.'

There was a clatter – a can had fallen to the floor out of Gwen's rigid hand.

'I'm what you'd call not short of a bob or two ...' Ceri put her hand over her mouth to catch a sob. 'It was me behind the bunting and the pub garden and the paint and the sign. I was the one who sent all of the gifts to the Village of Love.'

Suddenly noise broke out as the locals digested her revelations. *Not who she said she was! She's loaded! And famous!* The older folk wanted to know what this YouTube thing was. Rhodri felt a bubble of anger in the pit of his stomach become a fireball of fury at her deceit, at all their heart-to-hearts, when she could've told him. Why hadn't she confided in him?

'I'm so sorry,' she said, louder, trying to be heard above the clamour. 'I never meant to cause any trouble. I just wanted to repay your kindness. To do good in my mother's memory.'

A few accusations of 'You had no right!' and 'Taken us for a ride' flew into the air. She had money and fame – and they were judging her on it rather than the person they knew ... Rhodri realised remorsefully, himself included.

'There's no excuse for my lies. I never said I was Ceri Rees. I was misheard and I was only going to stay a week ... but I started to love it here and I can only say I got carried away. I'll be out of here first thing, you'll never have to see me again.'

'You're only telling us because you've been found out. You're just sorry you've been caught!' shouted Barri.

'Leave off, Barri, you can see she's having a melt-down,' Seren said.

'There was a tip-off ... that I was here. I know who it was but I won't say who. There's no good in that.'

A fist went down on the bar and all eyes were on Gwil, who was turning puce. *Oh Christ*, the vein on his bald head was throbbing – he was going to blow his top.

'Right,' he yelled. 'I've had enough.'

Tears clung to Ceri's lower lashes and she nodded. 'Of course, I'll just get my things.'

'No you won't,' he said to her calmly. Then he resumed his ire. 'I couldn't care less if she's Ceri Rees or Ceri bastard Price. She's a damn fine barmaid. And look what she's done for this village too. All I care about is who grassed her up?' He flipped the bar partition and strode out. 'I want to know who's turned in one of us. Who's the Judas? Show yourself.'

He glared around the room and people, Rhodri in-cluded, began to look at others for signs of guilt. And bloody hell, he saw a look which took him right back – and instantly he knew who the double-crosser was. His outrage had found its proper target: Ceri hadn't gone out of her way to hurt anyone. He stared at Ceri for confirm-ation and she dropped her head, nodding gently.

Rhodri cleared his throat. 'Is it you, Logan?'

The pub gasped in horror as Logan denied it with raised palms and a shake of his head.

'Oh, come off it, Logan. You got a healthy sum, did

you, for letting on who she was? That's what it's about. Money. Right?'

Logan clenched his teeth.

'Because he's got form, ladies and gentlemen, and that's why we fell out.'

The crowd leaned in closer. It was as if they knew he had reached his limit – he would protect Logan no more.

'He copped off with my Ruth's friend, who came down on a visit with her, just before we split up. Her mate lost her wallet on the Friday night. Had two hundred quid in it for the weekend. We searched everywhere but it never turned up. After, Ruth asked me if it could've been Logan. I said, "Oh no! he's my buddy," I stood up for him because I couldn't believe bad types lived in Dwynwen. A few days later, I was getting a lift with him and there in the glove compartment, when I was looking for a pen, I saw it – her wallet. He'd nicked it and then shagged her the Saturday night. He said he'd found it empty on the beach. Yet he was the proud owner of a new surfboard.' Rhodri felt the disgust anew. 'The thing was, because I chose to believe he was innocent, when I said people didn't steal things in Dwynwen, it made Ruth think I was one-eyed and parochial. I loved Wales more than the truth. She finished it soon after.'

Logan had inched his way closer to the door, more or less conceding the game was up.

'Oh my God,' Gwen said. 'My sister said she'd sent me a tenner in a birthday card last year and I thought she was being a tight-arse because it had disappeared when it arrived.'

'And he owes me for a bacon sandwich from last year!

He's wicked, he is!' Mel cried. 'But I don't understand how he knew who you were, Ceri, because I should've known out of anyone, being into make-up.'

'Because I had post delivered to the cottage in my real name, work stuff and then invoices from the purchase of the gifts, plus a delivery yesterday, another act of kindness,' Ceri said. 'He wasn't friendly to me at first, but then he must've googled the name and realised ... because overnight he changed. All so he could get a sniff of the money.'

Gwil jabbed the air with his forefinger. 'Anything to say for yourself, Logan?'

'She called this place a hole,' he said, trying to get people on his side, 'like she was better than us. Turning up here, saving the poor little village from itself, all so she could be the big saviour, the big—'

'GET OUT OF MY PUB!' Gwil roared.

Logan puffed up his chest then thought better of it and dashed out like the coward he was. Applause rang out as the door crashed shut. Everyone fell on Ceri, who was apologising through her tears. Finally, she broke free and went straight to Rhodri.

'I'm so sorry, really, truly.' She meant it, he knew, and she knew he knew. And he knew she knew he didn't care who she was. But he didn't know how to say it without confusing himself any more.

'Why didn't you tell us?' he asked.

'Because I thought you'd treat me differently, like everyone did at home when I started making money. I didn't want it to be about me. And I'd lose all of you, you wonderful lot ... and this is what I had delivered yesterday, when I clocked it was Logan. It's for you ...' she said, finding her bag and pulling out a box.

'Me?' He pulled open the cardboard flaps.

'I see why you had your issues with Logan. I doubted you. I'm sorry.'

But he didn't care, he'd said his piece. He was too busy with this present.

'A webcam!' he said. 'With full HD image, wide screen option, swivel head, day-night recognition, optical zoom, stereo audio and check out the pixels! It's awesome. But why?'

'So anyone who leaves will always be able to see the sunset.'

He was about to blub like a boy, so thank goodness for Seren and Mel bouncing up.

'Do you know, I had a phone call today from someone asking if there was a Geri Spice working at the pub and I slammed it down on them thinking it was a crank caller,' Mel said. 'It must've been a reporter asking about Ceri Price! To think I could've stitched you up myself without even realising. And what about spare make-up, have you got any?'

Ceri answered with the biggest most grateful grin ever seen in Dwynwen.

'I don't know why you're looking so pleased with yourself,' Seren said, pulling all four of them into a group hug. 'You're done for now! We'll never let you escape!'

Caught up in the safety of numbers with Ceri's skin on his, Rhodri wanted to tell her how he felt, no longer caring how he would come across. As much as he tried, he couldn't hold it in anymore.

'I will love you forever,' he said, 'if you can sort out super-speed broadband for the webcam.'

33

'Jesus, it would've been easier to find Victoria Beckham's smile,' Tash said, hands on hips, at the door of the Pink House. 'Or Boris Johnson's hairbrush ... or ... or ... Donald Trump's brain. What is this place? Atlantis?'

'What the flip are you doing here?' Ceri said, agog at her sister standing before her in Dwynwen. 'How did you find me?'

'I asked Lord Lucan on the way ... he said this place was too remote even for him.' Her blue eyes were icy, ready for a fight. Ceri was immediately on the back foot at this unannounced visit. Which was probably the best way to be, seeing as Tash was bristling like a broom, ready to wipe the floor with her.

'You got here, though, eh?' It had sounded snide. Ceri was annoyed at herself for taking part in this spiky sparring contest. Tash would've been working herself up for hours on the drive. But it was impossible to stop herself sliding back into how it had always been.

'Oh, aye, eventually.' Tash crossed her arms, she wasn't finished yet.

'A *good morning, how are you, sorry I didn't ring* would've been nice,' Ceri said frostily.

'Er, pot. Kettle. Black.' Tash's booted foot was tapping ominously – she was revving up, ready to give her what for.

'Go on then,' Ceri said, presenting her chin, 'say what you have to say.' They could've been fifteen again, having a row about a missing body spray or an undeclared borrow of one another's clothes.

'I've been worried sick,' Tash seethed through her teeth. 'Jade rang me yesterday, I thought you were coming home last night. But you didn't show, you didn't even call. So I had to come and get you myself. Kev had to take the day off, unpaid, to look after the kids. And I left at five-thirty this morning thinking I could do a smash and grab and be home for the girls' bath. Fat chance of that now.'

'I didn't ask you to come!' Ceri regretted it instantly – she should've been pouring oil on troubled water, not setting light to petrol.

'Oh, I apologise.' Curdling with sarcasm, Tash was about to lob a grenade. 'Have you got something else on? Like a shower because you look like you need one.' Ceri got the full eyeing up and down of her dressing gown and messy ponytail.

Boom. The pair of them glowered at each other with bomb-blast faces. It took a minute for them to cool off, for their breathing to return to normal. They were at the bottom of a pit and they were going to have to help one another back up because this was no good. They had an awful lot to talk about, big stuff, so Ceri gave in first. She remembered the shock of arriving here when you were already spent from the mammoth journey.

'You must be gasping.' Ceri's voice was low and quiet

as she looked at her from beneath her eyelashes. 'Fancy a brew?'

'I've brought Eccles cakes,' Tash said meekly. 'The dead flaky ones you like.'

Ceri's absolute favourite treat in the world which beat Welshcakes hands down. It was the equivalent of a white flag, that. She stepped aside, calling a truce.

'Oh, come here, you,' she said, embracing her baby-blonde baby sister, whose stiff arms began to give way as the tension melted. How could they go from nought to sixty and back again in such a short time? How could they still be doing it at their age when they wouldn't dream of treating anyone else like that? Because they were family: only they could infuriate you, dig up such raw emotion then forgive you. 'I'm sorry I worried you.'

'I'm sorry too, for having a go.'

They rubbed each other's backs, Ceri feeling Tash's skinny-from-rushing-around-too-much frame, breathing in her trademark lily fabric conditioner, their heads resting on the other's shoulder before it was declared tea-time.

'So this is where you've been hiding,' Tash said from the sofa, unwrapping the pastries, when Ceri came in from the kitchen with two steaming mugs. 'That view's a bit different from Mum's, of Mrs Parkinson twitching her nets. Although it'd bring on vertigo if I saw that sea every day. You must like it to have been here so long.'

'It took a while to get used to but I wouldn't go back to my flat. Not for all the Eccles cakes in Crewe. Talking of which, pass me one.'

'Do you know, you sound a bit Welsh,' Tash laughed, doing the honours.

'Give over! You make me out to be like Cally Stevens from school. Remember when she went to Australia for a fortnight to see her cousins and she came back as if she was on *Home and Away*?' This was the banter she loved with her sister. It was as if they'd never fallen out in their lives.

'Ha! Yeah, sad cow. I hated her. She used to say horrible things about my dad. Probably all true, they were. But that wasn't the point.' Tash had a slurp and Ceri took a bite of cake. She shut her eyes blissfully, tasting plump raisins, buttery pastry and big grains of sugar.

'Is it true then ... about your dad? Jade told me.'

Ceri's moment in heaven was cut short. 'Yep,' she said through a mouthful. Amid all the excitement last night when she was forgiven, she'd managed to put this drama in a sealed box, ready to open another time.

'And the bar job?'

'Uh-huh.'

'And the surname thing? And the Village of Love?'

Ceri nodded, letting a smile come because it did sound ludicrous. Especially when Tash put it so bluntly.

'I told everyone last night, I really thought they were going to chase me out of the village. But I underestimated them – once they'd got over the shock, they were so nice. You didn't see if I was in the paper on your way down, did you?' Ceri asked.

'Strangely, I didn't fancy checking if my sister's breakdown made it into the news,' Tash said, dunking her cake into her tea. She liked to suck on hers for some revolting reason. 'Christ, you've never done things by halves. God, what was Mum thinking? Telling you he was Spanish? I used to envy that as well with mine coming from Scunthorpe. All that wasted jealousy.'

'To make me feel safe, I suppose. I wish she hadn't, I've spent my life feeling guilty because I can't do the flamenco.'

Tash laughed, and their woes seemed to diminish when they got on like this.

'Have you met him yet?'

'No. Only in passing. I think ... I think we've got a sister too.'

'You have.'

'No. We have. This is her place. She doesn't know yet. I only just found out.'

'Ruddy hell, like. What are you going to do?'

'God knows. Because I can't look her in the eye knowing what I know. But then what if this bloke doesn't want to know? I'm of a mind to say nothing. What would you do?'

Tash raised her eyebrows. 'Don't ask me. I'm not getting involved, Ceri. How can I? We, you and me, we haven't been involved since you left.'

Like that, the tone of her voice had become serious. The elephant in the room was flapping his ears.

'The reception is shit here. I've tried to ring. Plus I've been working evenings. You're never free in the day ...' It was so lame, Ceri thought, ashamed.

'I didn't realise you were running off to join the flaming circus! I thought it'd be a week tops. I got on with things, I had no idea you were going to have some sort of religious moment and jack it all in. It feels like you deserted me.' There was no malice in her words: they were plain-talking which at least meant they could heal their rift.

'I felt like you didn't want anything to do with Mum.

You couldn't wait to get shot of the house. You didn't even tell me it was sold, I heard it from Jade. And I know—'

'You said to deal with it! So I did!'

'I was about to admit that before you jumped in! Let me explain. I just felt it was the last bond we had, that's all. That you didn't need me. That you were sorted. I felt worthless.'

'Those noughts in the bank were real enough.'

'But they're not much company. That's what I found here. That's why I love it.'

'You're not staying? I thought you were joking earlier. You, with all your Instagram and Facebook stuff, always on the phone. How can you like it here when it's nineteen-bleeding-fifty?'

Ceri laughed. She'd had the same first impressions.

'People talk here, face to face. They've time for you. You go to the pub and no one's checking for likes or retweets.'

'It sounds like a retirement home to me.' Her grimace was over-egged, she wasn't being mean.

'It's the people. They're my friends. Mel, our sister, she's gorgeous. Seren, who's sparky as anything. Gwen and Gwil, the landlords, so kind. And Rhodri.'

'Oh, I get it! It's a man, is it?' Tash rubbed her hands.

'No! I'm steering clear. Mrs Unlucky In Love got conned by the surfboard instructor. I know – what a cliché.'

'What about this Rhodri? Because your eyes went all Lady Diana when you said his name.'

'They did not!' Ceri tried to protest. But Tash had always managed to call her out. 'He's just a friend, unfortunately. We're from different planets. He's into saving the earth, he's passionate about where he comes from. He's kind, grounded, solid, funny, caring, handsome.'

'He sounds bloody awful.' Tash rolled her eyes.

'Yeah, well, there's no point. He's off to Sweden. He won't come back.' As she said it, her tummy lurched because she couldn't imagine Dwynwen without him.

'Closest Ikea to here, is it? Or has he got a thing about meatballs?'

Ceri couldn't help but laugh.

'He's got a job lined up. It's a great opportunity for him. I'm going to miss him so much. He's been really good to me.'

Tash still wasn't buying it – she'd have to introduce them, so she could see how unsuited they were.

'What's he look like?'

'Six foot-odd, wide as a bus, in good shape.' *Very good shape ... oh shut up*, she told herself. 'Big brown eyes, messy hair, freckles, smiley.'

'My God, what's wrong with you? Why haven't you told him how you feel?'

'Because he's leaving!' Ceri said firmly, to stop her going any further.

'Don't they all, cock,' she tutted, referring to her deadbeat dad.

'Yeah. That's another reason why I don't want to know any more about my father. If he walked away from Mum, left her with a kid. It'll make it all worse.'

'Maybe that's why she tried to make it right, marrying my dad?'

'I feel really sad she made up the story about Emilio.

Like she thought she'd failed and she wanted me to think I'd been born out of love rather than a screw with a bastard from Wales.'

'She was only ever human, Ceri. Not super-human. Look, I've been thinking about her house and we exchange on Friday. But if you really wanted to keep it, we don't have to sell. We could rent it.'

'Would you do that?' Ceri said, so very touched by her offer.

'Yeah. Kev and me, we'll find another house. It was lovely, though. A new-build place, with a garden and a garage. Neat and tidy, no graffiti, close to a good school. But we could see it as an investment, run it between us, Kev could do repairs if and when and you could look after the accounts ...' She was thinking aloud now, trying to work it out. This was her all over – practical and hurdling emotion until it caught up with her. There was no way Ceri was going to let her down again.

'Not a chance. Sell it.'

'Yeah?'

Ceri took her keys from the coffee table and wound off the one for Junction Road, giving it to Tash to show she meant it. 'Mum's here with me now. And while I'm at it, here's the one for the car in Alderley Edge. Kev can have it as a thank you for sorting out Mum's house.'

'You can't give him your flash wagon!'

'I can. It's not me anymore. He can sell it or whatever. What do I need a nippy thing for when I spend most of my time behind a tractor? I'm happy with Mum's Fiesta.'

Tash's hand curled and uncurled round the keys as if she was checking they were real. 'Thanks, Ceri. That's really thoughtful. Kev will be made up.'

'My pleasure. Now, while you're here, shall we go and scatter Mum?'

'Haven't you done that already? And there's me been weeping thinking I'd missed it. Funny, though, she's everywhere at home. In the park where I take the kids, where she took us. The bingo hall. The pound shop. I find myself crying sometimes when I'm getting bin bags.'

Of course she cried. How could Ceri have thought she was over Mum? She had a lot of making up to do.

'Will you stay tonight with me?' Ceri wanted nothing more than to spend some time with Tash. 'We can twosies the bed.'

'As long as you don't kick me like you used to when we were little.'

Ceri giggled at the memory when they were forced to share because Mum had given up her room for a guest and she'd slept in with them. 'Cheek! It was you who took up the room!'

She licked her finger and ran it over the pastry crumbs before she got up and pulled her sister to her feet.

'Come on, let's go to the beach.'

'All right, you're on.' Tash grinned and they went downstairs for Ceri to get dressed and pick up the tea caddy and their mother's letter from her room. 'By the way,' Tash said, as Ceri held open the front door for her, 'you've got real colour in your cheeks from living here. It suits you.'

Ceri put her arm through her sister's and they started off for the bay.

'I'll have to get a carrier pigeon to let Kev know I'm staying over.'

'Oh, there's no need for that,' Ceri said, laughing, 'I'll

do some smoke signals. Or spell it out on the sand with sticks. The police helicopter will see it – it's always on the lookout for people who want rescuing from this asylum.'

34

The beach was as bare as a bed with the blanket pulled back to give it an airing.

It was low tide and the dimpled sheet of sand stretched out in all directions but the waterfall was calling out to Ceri. If anything was going to make Tash understand the draw of Dwynwen, that would be it.

Away from the few holidaymakers who were all-weather beach devotees, they walked towards the rocks to do what she'd come here for six months ago, but had put off for so long. There was no telling where the sea met the sky: they merged as one in a starchy overclouded whiteness Mum would've approved of. Ceri found a spot where the stream from the waterfall met lazy lapping waves; here, her mother could make her last journey. They parked their backsides on a shelf of barnacled black stone and leaned over to place the caddy on the sand, deciding against an elaborate ceremony. There had been too much emotion recently: Ceri was drained of energy. Tash sensed it and her chit-chat dropped away like the clifftops themselves. Having confessed her secrets last night, there was no rush. How different it could've been: had she hot-footed it out of here before anyone realised what she had done, who she really was, she would never have been able to return and wouldn't be able to stay here forever as she planned.

At least now she could do this without looking over her shoulder in fear and slip away. Because she'd decided she wouldn't put Mel or the village through any more drama. She'd be robbing a friend of her security. She could deal with having an errant father, just as Tash had. There were other, more important concerns now: what she would do next in her working life. She had enough in the bank to keep her going until she decided. In the meantime, she would give Jade Cheap As Chic, sell her flat, stay on at the pub and devote herself to the Green House. The only thing remaining was to read her mother's letter. She took the envelope out of her hoodie pocket and held it, studying the solicitor's neat handwriting: On the occasion of scattering the remains of Ms Angharad Bronwen Price.

Tash squeezed her arm and Ceri took a breath.

'I'm not sure I want to know what's inside,' she said. 'It could be anything. A poem or an explanation or—'

'A shopping list even. She wasn't right when she wrote it,' Tash agreed.

'Maybe she just brought me here to find out about my father. She couldn't bring herself to tell me. Then leave it up to me whether to find him?'

A wet nose dabbed her hand and she let the very waggy dog snuffle in her palm.

'Hello there,' she said, stroking his head, turning to his owner, who was approaching slowly with a slight limp from the shore on her left. The envelope flickered between her fingers in the breeze and she imagined herself lightening her grip until it was taken from her to fly away.

'This was her favourite part of the beach,' the man

said, resting on a boulder several feet from her, staring out to sea. His face was weathered with deep lines as if he was made from the rocks himself. Thick silver hair and gnarled hands, and when he turned to her, she saw her own eyes. He was as far away from a bastard as could be. And she wasn't recoiling from him as she'd thought she would. She felt still and calm, as if this was meant to be.

'Angharad would spend hours making a dam of sand and stones to divert the stream, hoping it would be there the next day,' he said, getting comfy. 'That was her. Determined, hard-working, full of fight, she was. Not like me, laid-back, happy to just be.'

'She said I took after you.' It had all been part of her mother's fairytale. 'She said you were Emilio.'

'It was her secret name for me because of my tan.' His wrinkles creased at the memory.

Tash finally grasped who it was. 'I'll go if you want some privacy.'

'No,' Ceri said. 'She was your mum too. You need to hear this.' And then to Emlyn, 'This is Tash, my sister. Whatever there is you have to say, she can hear it too.'

Emlyn nodded and then he let out a small guttural noise and sniffed with emotion. 'Goodness, you look like Angharad, Tash.'

He cleared his throat and continued. 'She'd say the sun only came out to kiss me. That was as close as we got before she left. She said she'd only kiss me if we were married. Her father, your grandfather, was a hard man, got the stick out.'

'She never talked about him,' Ceri said.

'He wasn't worth talking about,' he said, shaking his head and turning down the corners of his mouth.

'But we kept in touch, writing silly love letters. For ten years, although they faded off as we did our own thing. In 1986, July time, her mother died and Angharad came here, turned up blaming her father for her death, the stress of him knocking her about.'

Tash let out a '*no*' and Ceri placed her hand on her sister's thigh. This was so difficult to hear, to think Mum had grown up with a violent father.

'She came to find me. So I took her out on my boat, by here ... it was as hot as a coal fire, she'd brought her swimmers and I got into mine ... and she asked me to be hers just once.'

He picked a thread on his trousers in embarrassment and Ceri looked out to sea to give him room to recover. Her mother had been so proper, she must've been desperate to escape her grief to seek him out like that.

'I was with Melyn's mother Sian by then, she was expecting, three months gone, not by me. We were friendly, I had lost your mother, no one else compared. I wanted to get over Angharad. But then when the love of your life asks to be loved ...' His chin tremored and he wiped his face down to hide it. 'What can I say? I was weak.'

Ceri swallowed hard as she heard Tash's words again that their mother had been human. It seemed her father was too. But did she want that of her parents? She stared up at the sky and realised she wouldn't be here if they hadn't been human.

'But I don't regret it. Never. How could I?'

He made that guttural sound again, his composure falling away for a second, before he gave her a tender smile. Not hers, but his. She returned her own. 'Not now there's you, here.'

She had only ever known one parent: to hear the other, who was alive in front of her, tell her she was loved revived her soul, kick-starting something she had lost when Mum had died. The tears began to roll. He had something in his eye too, he said, probably sand. It made her laugh out of nowhere and she longed to reach out to him, but they had to tread carefully while this was all so new and fragile.

'I only ever had one photo of you. She kept it up on the mantelpiece, said it was taken in Spain.'

'No, it was here on this beach. Afterwards ... when we'd come back in to shore. One of the tourists took it. She had a Kodak, I remember, she got it with her fancy wages at the Rolls-Royce factory.'

'You know, I realised you were ... when I saw a photo of Mel and you in that same spot. It was in her room. I should never have gone in. But I was worried, it was full of junk.'

'That doesn't matter now.'

'Did you ...'

'Know about you?' he said grimly. 'No. It was only when I saw you in the pub, when Melyn had said who your mother was, she'd told me your age, your father was a Spaniard called Emilio and your eyes ... I just sensed it. It was like looking in the mirror. Minus all this,' he said, rubbing his hair. 'I didn't even know she'd died. It was all a huge shock. I still hoped ... love would conquer all, the old fool I am.'

'Why didn't she tell you? Because she loved you so much. If she had told you' – Ceri's voice cracked – 'then I'd have had a father. I'm not sure I can forgive her.'

Tash put her arm around her.

341

'She did it out of love, out of kindness. It's hard to understand why, I know.'

'Yes, it is.' She was struck by an anger, which rose in her chest and made her eyes smart.

'I had my responsibilities here. Sian was her friend. She was ashamed. And she didn't want to take me away from my promise, to raise Melyn. That was the decency of your mother. She didn't want you to suffer, that's why she told you a story about Emilio. To give you no reason to feel unwanted.'

It must've been the hardest thing she'd ever done, Ceri saw now. 'Did she ever get in touch? Did you try?'

'She didn't, I did. Only when Melyn's mam had left me. She met someone else, I couldn't blame her. Our marriage became an arrangement, there had been love of a kind but never the real thing. So I went up to Crewe, this would've been, what, fifteen years ago? I sat outside the factory until I found her. She told me it was too late. She had two kids by then, one of whom was you, I now know, and you, Tash, love. Had I realised ... well, I'd have tried harder. But I think she didn't tell me because it would've caused so much disruption. She must've thought I'd have to have chosen between you and Melyn. She didn't want to cause the hurt.'

He fiddled with the neck of his padded checked shirt and pulled out the locket Ceri had known forever and opened it to reveal her mother's headstone. It wasn't the same photo though; she looked younger than that one taken by the rocks. It was a gift to see her in a picture she'd never seen before, as if she was alive again. 'But I always had her in here. You know, every Valentine's Day, I'd drive up to show I'd move heaven and earth to be with her. I'd ring the bell, she'd never answer. But her doorstep was always scrubbed so clean, I knew she was okay. I'd post a card, hoping ...'

The cards ... they were from him. All those years he had been waiting for her.

'She kept every one. I found them in her drawer. Although the last one, she never saw that,' Tash said, just as overcome. 'She never forgot you. Why did you sign them with three kisses and nothing more?'

'It was our code, one for each word in *I love you*. Sometimes people can't be together. You learn to live with it, you do, but you still carry it here,' he said, patting his chest.

'That was why she wanted to be scattered here. Even with her dementia, she didn't get confused about that.'

'Well, that means a lot, thank you,' Emlyn said, as his dog bounded up again wet from the sea.

Ceri let him alone for a while even though she was preoccupied now with what came next.

'I don't think we can do this to Mel, you know,' she said. 'She's only just put Al behind her. What if this sends her backwards?'

Her dad considered her point with a see-saw of his head.

'It'd be like what Mum did, though,' Tash said gently. 'Keeping a secret.'

'But what if she thinks I've stolen her father? I couldn't live with it.'

'What if she thinks she's gained a sister?' Emlyn said. 'Lies backfire. I don't see we have much choice. Look, I'll go there now, wait for you. If you decide not to be a part of our lives, I will accept it. Bear in mind, your mother was afraid, you don't have to do the same.'

He got up, creaking on his hip, and waited, not putting his arms out because he was saying it was up to Ceri to decide. Instinct pushed her towards him, into his body, his solid shape which felt like a father. She wept into him and felt his tears fall onto her face as they hugged away the years of separation. After a while, they pulled apart but Ceri knew their bond would forever remain.

He went to leave but Ceri had to know if his version of Mum's life had been true.

'Wait!' she said, fumbling open the letter. It had been written on a sheet of her mother's special cream Basildon Bond she used for school notes – just because she was a single mother, she had standards. It was dated more than twenty years ago. Why? She'd thought it had been penned in the weeks leading up to her death.

'What happened in December 1996?' she said quickly.

He scrunched up his forehead to remember. 'When her father died, I believe. No bugger turned up for his funeral. I did, though, in case she was there. She wasn't.'

As he left, she read on ...

Dear Ceri

I've no idea when this will reach you. I don't want to be maudlin because there's lots of life left in me yet. But I want you to read this when I'm gone.

Today my father died. I'm not sorry, he changed the path of my life, made me frightened to follow my heart. I am what I am because of him. He'd say you couldn't polish a turd but it didn't stop me trying.

This will be a shock to you and I can only tell you I did this to protect you from my shame but your father is Emlyn Thomas, my first and only love. We grew up

*together in Dwynwen. Perhaps you will know when
you read this, perhaps I will have told you and you'll
understand how much I wanted to be with him. But it
was impossible. I couldn't take him away from his duty.*

*I so desperately wanted to protect you from shame.
Emlyn would've been torn between me and Sian. In
Emilio, all I wanted to do was to give you a hero.
Tash didn't have that luxury, please look after her.*

I'm so very sorry.

I was too afraid. Too proud.

Don't you make the same mistake.

All my love, forever,

Mum xxx

She had been trying to be kind. She had been trying to
protect her. From the shame her mother had felt. Shame,
it was such an old-fashioned notion. But if it had been
drummed into you as a child, well, it was nigh impossible
to throw off. Hadn't she drummed into Ceri how wonderful Emilio had been? And she'd done well because of
it. Now she felt ready to end the pain of the past. Ceri
picked up the caddy, holding it by the belly, and stepped
beside the stream.

'Tash, do you want to or shall I?'

'You do it. Do it for us.'

So Ceri opened the lid and as she shook and shook and
shook her mother into the air, as the ashes swirled and
fell and formed a dusty film on the water to be carried
away to sea, she understood she was setting her mother
and herself free. Over her shoulder, her father had made
it almost to the cabin. It was time to look forward with
her two sisters.

35

Mel's counter was stripped bare already and it was only mid-morning. *Ceri would have to divulge more secrets*, she giggled to herself, *if this is what it did to trade*. Papers, gone. Bacon baps, gone. It was the same for her Welshcakes too. And the phone, she felt as if she was working in a call centre. Other journalists chasing up the story, nosy crows and strangers who wanted to know if they could book a cottage. She couldn't blame the interest – it was an incredible turn-up.

'Make-up magnate Ceri Price is spending her fortune on turning her mum's run-down birthplace into a sexy seaside spot to seduce tourists,' went the intro. Mel knew it off by heart having read it herself over and over. It wasn't the whole story – the identity bit obviously hadn't had legs and she was glad because it would've stained a magical few weeks. Ceri's idea had brought so much happiness and excitement, she would be forgiven. It wasn't even the bit of interest to her – it was all the stuff about their Ceri's life as Ceri Price. It was 'the glam YouTuber who'd started her cosmetic brand in her mother's kitchen four years ago'; her sports car and penthouse flat; how she earned upwards of £10,000 a month and had signed a six-figure contract to be the face of her own lip gloss and blusher, mascara and eyeliner, some of which Mel applied in her bathroom mirror. Then there was the close-up of Ceri with a professional showbiz blow dry, her hair sleek and shiny, her contoured face done up to the nines with foundation, lashes and lippy. It just didn't marry up with the Ceri they knew, who was windswept and freckly. Although one person had twigged – she'd seen Logan at the crack this morning driving his poser van onto the beach to empty his surfing station. It was good riddance to bad rubbish. And poor Rhodri, having lost a friend in the process but keeping shtum because he believed in second chances.

A paw scratched at the door – it was Gelert coming in for a bowl of tea. And Dad, whose hip seemed to be playing him up.

'Need a coffee?' she asked, rushing to help him in as the dog looked around for dropped crumbs.

'I do. But not a nurse!' he said, before softening and kissing the top of her head.

'Did you hear about our Ceri? She's not who she said she was? And—'

'Yes, yes,' he said, seating himself. 'Seems she's done the place a favour. Everyone's talking about it down the harbour.'

'I can't get over it! Loads of interest,' she said, which reminded her to switch on the answerphone. It hadn't been used in forever. 'I'm glad you're here,' she said, 'we need to think about Ceri's offer. She's been hanging on for ages now to see if she can buy into the cabin.'

'We do, Melyn, we do,' he said, sighing. 'Or at least you do.'

'It's not up to me ... this is your place.' She looked

at him more closely now – he was wet in the eyes and serious when normally he was cheeky and bright.

'Turn the sign to closed, would you, love?'

She paused, her mind whirring. 'You're not ill, are you?' The thought alone propelled her to the door. The tourists would just have to wait.

'Noooo!' He smiled at her fondly, held her gaze for a while, full of love. 'Come and sit, will you.'

She perched next to him. He was tapping the salt and pepper pots, a pair of china Welsh ladies in stovepipe hats and shawls. The other tables had dragons, corgis and sheep. She'd wondered about getting rid of them, exchanging them for something more in theme with the new look, but they were vintage and characterful. It occurred to her she had made such progress to consider keeping them for a good reason like that rather than out of panic.

'Now listen to me, Melyn Thomas. You're my daughter. My first-born. You're special. Do you hear me?' She loved the way he went gruff because he was of the generation who found love hard to talk about.

'Dad, what's this about? You can tell me. I'm not a delicate daffodil, like you think. I'm better, I am.' As she'd said it, she believed it: Cardiff had cured her, perhaps not forever, maybe she would always be prone to hoarding, but now she would get back up if she was floored again. She'd worked late into the night bagging up her room, understanding she wasn't harming Ali's memory but making space for her future. And if she was to ever entertain a man again, somebody, say, like Carlos, then she'd have to get it nice. Seeing her father like this did alarm her, she wouldn't lie, because she wasn't sure what was coming, yet she felt older, as if there was a shift in responsibility happening between them. He'd been there for her before she was even born. She had to be there for him from now on; he was alone and, while happily so, he wouldn't always be so independent. 'It's time to support you, if that's what's up. I've sorted things with Mam and Fi's going to start officially tomorrow.'

'Don't you worry about me. It's nothing bad. I'm the most blessed man you'll ever meet.' There was no laughter on his face, which was strange, because he was always one to give a little wink if they were talking important matters. But she found she didn't need his reassurance. He put his warm palm on top of her hand. His knotted knuckles had seen so much hard work. She placed her other hand on his protectively and waited.

'Melyn, I have something astonishing to tell you. I'm still ... well, bewildered really and I've only known this for a few days. But it's a wonderful, wonderful thing, for me, for you, for both of us, I'm certain of it,' he said, not breaking eye contact, including her in his world. 'You see ... I've just found out you have a sister ... I have another daughter ...'

It took a second for Mel to understand what he meant. He had a sister? She had a daughter? Then it righted itself and she felt her eyes bulging in shock. 'Dad,' she whispered, 'what ... how ... *woah*, another sister ... another daughter, that's both of us!'

'It is,' he said, tickled. 'Quite right.'

'A sister ... it's not just Ffion and me ...'

'Yes. But it's not quite as straightforward.'

'What do you mean? How old is she?'

'Just thirty.' He gulped as he said it, knowing she'd be working out the maths.

'She's the same age as me? How is it possible?' She got it and felt a bit repulsed, pulling her hands away to challenge him, feeling sick. 'Dad, that means you … when you were with Mam. Doesn't it? You're not like that!' Her voice was rising and she fought to control it because this wasn't how their relationship was, not now, when the teenage hormones were years away. 'Where is she? In some port town halfway across the world? From one of your cruises?' It came out as an accusation and she felt sorry but she was in shock.

'No … she's here.' He said it neutrally, as if he would allow her this anger.

'Wales?' Again, she was harsh. But confusion was making her anxious.

'Dwynwen.'

She took a sharp intake of breath. This was like some horrible game of hot and cold and she felt as if she was about to get burned. 'Oh, Dad, this is just … well, it's not astonishing, it's all weird. I might know her. Does she know? I bet she's been laughing at me.'

He lifted his hands as if he was about to tell her to calm down but he put them back on the table, he was in no position to tell her how to feel.

'She hasn't. She's very fond of you. And you're very fond of her.'

She saw herself dashing around her brain to work it out. Frantic, she was, and her ribs felt tight.

'Melyn,' he said, almost sternly as if she was being told off. But she knew she wasn't – he was trying to put her out of her misery. 'It's Ceri. Your friend.'

'Ceri?' she spluttered. 'Is this a joke? Her father was Spanish, he was called Emilio!'

She rolled the word Emilio around her mouth a few times but it became Emlyn as the penny dropped. Mel saw his eyes were Ceri's eyes and how had she not seen it? How, with her gift, had she not noticed they had the same shiny shade of brown? Those flecks of Bournville which burned in the sunshine ...

'But she's from Crewe!' she cried, resisting but knowing it was pointless.

His shoulders drooped and he looked exhausted. And seeing him like this reminded her she was no longer a child. She was breathing too fast, she had to slow it down and she did it, she forced herself to do it so he could find the words to explain.

'This is all very fresh still so forgive me, but when you told me about your friend's mother being from here and her name was Angharad, I worked it out straight away.'

She cast her mind back to the pub and what she'd thought was indigestion. He'd been reacting to the discovery of Ceri instead.

'There was never another Angharad in the village. There was only ever her, I loved her very much. We ... once ... thirty years ago.'

Mel turned away. She didn't want to hear this about her father, whom she adored. It was like his halo had slipped. He was supposed to be a good man.

'But circumstances ... I never saw her again, not to talk to. I never even knew she was pregnant.'

'Oh, Dad,' she said, appalled.

'It wasn't like that, Melyn.' He had the gall to look put out by her reaction.

'It never is!' She wanted to throw the damn salt and pepper pots at him now.

'I had just started out with your mam,' he said, regaining his composure. 'I wanted you both to be safe and warm. It doesn't excuse my behaviour … I know I did a terrible thing.'

Hearing him admit it helped to calm her. And she began to consider what he had done for her: raised her as his own and she had never once felt anything but cherished by him. He'd put his commitment to Mam and her before his own feelings, mostly.

'You can't be criticised for one moment when you put duty before anything else,' she said bravely.

'It wasn't my duty,' he said, 'it was my choice.'

'But what if you'd known Angharad was having your baby? Would you have gone?' It was a horrible question but she needed to ask it, just once so she never needed to ask it again. 'Because she's your blood and I'm not.'

'Oh, Melyn.' His eyelids clamped shut in agony, his terrier eyebrows tried to offer them comfort. 'Would I have chosen her over you? It's like being asked to select what kind of torture I'd prefer. It's an impossible and meaningless notion. Angharad knew I was committed to you and Mam. She was trying to do the best thing, not telling me. And it was, otherwise I'd never have known you. You are my blood,' he said, taking her hand in his and shaking it.

'I know,' she said, feeling the waterworks coming. 'I just needed to hear it.' She had never felt not his.

'Biology isn't everything. I held you in these arms the day you were born. I've only just met your sister.'

'What about Mam, what will she say?' She feared it would rock the new foundations she'd laid with her mother.

'When you get to our age, you hear so much more terrible news, things happening to people you know. You've lost your parents. Nothing compares. It makes you embrace the good. We're past fighting now. I'll, of course, tell her today.'

Her worry subsided but then it was replaced by ire. This time at Ceri. For she had been sleeping in her home without a word – no wonder Ceri had been in hiding.

'I'm so cross with Ceri, she didn't tell me. I had a right to know I was living with my own sister.'

Dad shook his head. 'She found a photo of you and me.'

'She was in my room! She was going through my things on Friday. It feels like an intrusion.'

'No,' he said firmly, 'she was worried about you. She saw it because she cares. It was Friday, like you said. Think about it ...'

Friday. The day before she'd gone to Cardiff. Where she would never have gone had it not been for Ceri. The tension in her forehead and in her neck and in her fingers began to fade as she realised no one was guilty of anything but love.

'I need to see her,' she said, getting up, bashing into a chair as her sense of space became overwhelmed by a frantic yearning to get to the door.

'I asked her to come up and wait outside. I hope she's there. If she isn't, if she's gone, don't get upset, Melyn. People react to things differently. So now, you see, why it's not up to me. The cabin,' Dad said.

And she turned to him and understood. And she threw open the cabin, wishing on every star she'd ever seen she'd be there, this person who'd changed everything

353

– for the better. Ceri was in the lane with a woman and Mel hesitated, uncertain.

'This is Tash,' Ceri said. 'My sister.' The one from a different father who she considered not as a half sibling but equal.

Would she feel the same about Mel? Would Mel be able to do it too? It made her stop and think about how she'd kept Ffion at arm's length and how the gap between them had let in mould and decay. Cardiff had changed her: she'd come home and vowed to welcome Ffion into her heart. Would she be able to do it with Ceri? And then Mel realised she'd done that already with Ceri. So she stepped forward and allowed herself to feel the love between them. They hugged and then they began to rock and move in a circle as Mel called her 'my sister' over and over again.

'The cabin,' she said, seeing colours all around as if she was on a merry-go-round, 'let's do it. Let's do it together.'

36

Ceri wondered if it was possible to have lockjaw in her cheeks as she prepared to chuck confetti at Jade for the eleventh time. The magazine photographer hadn't been satisfied with the first ten attempts due to technical problems such as 'not enough boob', 'too much squinting' and 'the wrong kind of throwing'. Please God, it's boiling out here, Ceri thought, as the blushing bride had another touch-up from one assistant while another picked foil-shaped lipsticks and OMGs out of her cleavage. The powder brush attacked Ceri next. While she'd have preferred to go without, she'd agreed to a makeover for Jade's sake. It was the least she could do for Jade, seeing as she'd kept the business afloat and covered for her for months. It was the strangest thing to have primer and foundation, concealer and highlighter, blusher, shadow, fake eyelashes and lipstick on again, particularly a mask of it. She had been scared she wouldn't be able to breathe at first, these days she'd get by with a bit of eyeliner and bronzer. But then like a memory, it'd settled down and she'd thought of her mother, who would have been thrilled to get anywhere near a professional make-up artist.

'Big smiles, girls,' the snapper ordered as he counted

355

down to an AK-47 of flashes. He checked his shots and, finally happy, released them from the steps of the grand country pile. Temporarily blinded, the shriek of Jade's best pals threw themselves into a group hug of grabbing arms to make sure no one fell off their five-inch heels. Once they'd steadied themselves, they darted off to get back to the terrace for the waiters' trays of cocktails and some canapés. None of that fussy malarkey but beef in mini Yorkshire puddings, little bacon rolls and egg and cress on crustless white.

It was a beautiful ceremony but it had been ages ago – the confetti photograph had been recreated because it was to be the front page image and guests had been told to go away and loosen up before they tried again. They'd done the breakfast – a fry-up with black pudding followed by Eccles cakes and custard for afters – and speeches. Now everyone was waiting for the nightclub to open: this was Delamere Manor, once the home of Take That's Gary Barlow. His old recording studio had been converted complete with a dance floor. It was very swanky here – one of Cheshire's finest five-star venues boasting its own lake and garden follies. With a price tag to match, it showed how fast Jade's rise had been for the mag to shell out for it and two hundred and fifty guests in dickie bows and evening gowns. Her face was everywhere – all over social media and TV, on bus stop and train station posters and in Boots and the supermarkets. The punters loved her and rightly so because she was a girl done not just good but better than Ceri had managed.

'Should I go dark, Pricey, after the honeymoon?' Jade asked as they linked arms and went closer to the stone building for some shade. For a second Ceri was back to

Ceri behind the bar of the workingmen's club with her mate, where they'd discuss hairdos and celebrities. This time, though, it'd be the bosses whom Jade would have to consult.

'You'll look gorgeous whatever you do. You've scrubbed up well,' Ceri said, wiping her eyes. 'Like a film star from the 1950s.' Her platinum bob had been set and styled and her short veil kicked out at her bare shoulders, as if it was wowing at her oyster strapless dress which hugged her figure and pooled at her toes.

'It's Grace Kelly glamour, cocker,' she said, winking. 'That's what we're aiming for now, an escape from bad times. I tell you what, though, the corset is as tight as my Aunty Pat. She's staying at Mum and Dad's because she didn't want to shell out for the hotel room. Even though Mum and Dad are staying here! And she's only asked if I can sub her for a cab home. Despite there being a minibus.'

Ceri tutted at the money-grabbing, thanking her stars it was a distant memory now. Her bank account was as healthy as ever, mainly because ad revenue had more than recovered thanks to Jade's status. But it wouldn't be that way forever. Ceri, who'd been 'phased out' by the cosmetic company, aka dropped like a stone, was in the process of giving Jade a majority share in the company – she deserved it all but Jade had refused. Ceri was happy to see Jade had learned from her mistakes – she'd got herself an agent and she was donating a percentage of her earnings to good causes. It was called evolution – Ceri was proud of her. And she couldn't have been happier. In the fortnight since she'd found her father and a sister, she was well away in the cabin. Her first job had been to get a shiny coffee machine – and by God it was worth it for its rich espressos, milky lattes and chocolatey cappuccinos. Her dad, with all his humble ways, had become partial to a mocchacino. He'd suggested a Love Music festival for October, with bands in a beach marquee, which Ceri had jumped on, mainly to occupy her when Rhodri was gone. Then it'd be fireworks and Christmas and a spring food festival. Mel was loved up with Carlos – she'd been to see him on her days off, and this weekend, when he visited for the first time, they were going to paint a mural of a bursting red heart with arms hugging a blue surfboard and a black coffee on the cabin wall.

It was all good, apart from Rhodri going. It was sooner not later now, he was off next week. His brother Iolo had sorted out wifi at the cabin and he'd got the webcam working. The sunsets would make Rhodri feel at home. But in reality, a whole thousand and three miles would come between them – yes, she had checked how the crow flew. Gutted wasn't the word: chopped, fried and dished up to the dog was closer to it. It had been a stick of dynamite to her dreams. But there was no point crying over spilled tears. Besides, it would ruin her make-up. And she had to think of Jade. She gave her a hug just because.

'Thanks for coming,' Jade said, leaning into her, smelling divinely expensive while she readjusted her stiletto gel insoles.

'What? Are you kidding? I was always going to be here.' Even if Dave was in the grounds somewhere stalking a Crewe Alexandra footballer whose bit of stuff was buddies with Jade. 'That perfume's nice, what is it?'

'Only my new line! But don't change the subject. Having to face everyone, it must be hard.'

It was frigging awful. 'Not at all. It's nice to catch up,' she said, knocking back the last gulp of bubbles in her glass, which instantly disappeared from her hand, the staff were that good.

'Come off it!' Jade laughed.

'All right, all right. It's shite. Everyone rubber-necking to see what I look like. Why did you have to invite that cow from the office next door? She said the extra weight suited me!'

'I'd never have heard the last of it if I hadn't. Anyway I think you look stunning,' Jade said, holding out her hands like a quiz show hostess presenting Ceri as this week's special prize.

'I feel weird in this get-up,' Ceri said, looking down at her sleek Grecian-style emerald floor-length dress she'd picked out from her stash in her Alderley Edge flat this morning. 'It was the least outrageous thing I had. I've got flats on underneath,' she whispered, 'my arches have gone since I started wearing wellies. Don't let that slip, will you?'

'Well, I think you should get them talking about something else, don't you?' It was lovely to have this little moment together when so many were queuing up to speak to Jade.

'Anything.' And then she clocked her friend's mischievous eyes. 'What?'

'Marcus's cousin Mason thinks you're a bit tasty.'

Ceri groaned.

'No! Wait! He's not as handsome as our Marcus, granted, he's got the family nose, but he's lovely.'

'Jade, please do one. I'm not up for it.'

'Is this to do with that Taffy you liked? Rodney?'

'Rhodri. I've more chance of pulling Prince Harry.

No. I don't need some bloke sniffing round me because of what I used to be. Go and see your new husband.'

'He's been away for a few years, he won't have a clue who you are.'

'Don't tell me ... he's an ex-con.'

'No! A charity worker, something to do with engineering. He's been in Africa on a sanitation project.'

'Why's he come back?'

'He wants to settle down,' she said with a suggestive eyebrow.

Ceri glared. 'What's wrong with him then?'

'Nothing. Just been away. Go on, have a bit of fun, let your hair down, although you could do with giving it a brush first.'

'Oi!' Ceri cried, loving this lady like a sister. 'Look at you, now you're all famous!'

'Stupid, isn't it? I'd have been just as chuffed to get wed in the club, if truth be told. Pork pies and pickles. But you can't turn down this, can you? It'll last for a year or so, then it'll be gone. We're just enjoying ourselves. Marcus is loving it, bringing in lots of business at the car showroom. We're going to save every penny and invest it, so we've got a nicer house and a garden for when we have a family. Which reminds me, do you know if Tash has got the keys yet? She messaged her congrats when I was having my manicure.'

'Yes! Lunchtime. I'm popping in on her tomorrow on my way home. Shame she couldn't make it.'

'I know. But she's got her priorities right, hasn't she?'

Yep, she had. And Jade. How come it had taken Ceri so long – and to the brink – to get hers sorted?

'Right, I need to mingle,' Jade said, cooling herself with

a flap of her hands. Ceri got a nice close-up of her elegant white gold wedding band although the diamond of her engagement ring, upgraded since Marcus's proposal a year ago due to their financial good fortune, almost took her eye out. 'Marcus is waving me over for the cake-cutting photo. Catch you later for a boogie, all right?'

They kissed and then she was alone. Jade would be all right, had her head screwed on properly, she did. Ceri decided to go inside to inspect the lie of that land – and ended up heading straight into the path of Dave. With a pregnant woman in a tiara. Bloody hell, this baby bump was news.

'All right, Cez?' he said, his spiky gelled blond hair and honest blue eyes so familiar yet so foreign to her now. Like most of the men, his dickie bow was untied so he could get a proper gulp on his pint.

'This is my fiancée, Becky,' he said with pride. 'Becky, this is Ceri.' He had his arm around her and he looked at his pretty wife-to-be with a face as gooey as a melted marshmallow.

'Hi, Ceri, nice to meet you,' she said sweetly. 'I used to watch your videos all the time back in the day before this . . .' Becky nodded to her bump and gave it a smooth. 'Now it's all baby blogs for me.'

She seemed nice. Ceri was pleased for Dave. He'd be a good dad.

'When are you due?'

'Three months. We can't wait, can we, Dave?'

Ceri did a quick calculation. She'd have been pregnant in November. Dave had only started going out with her in October. But they looked very together. 'Aw!' she said, touched by their glow.

'Dave's already done up the nursery, haven't you, Dave? And he's not renewed his season ticket for the football. He wants to be home with me.' He nodded enthusiastically and then bent in for a peck on Ceri's cheek.

'Anyway, good to see you looking so well,' he said. 'We're off to the toilets, aren't we, Becky?'

'Yeah. I need to go all the time with this sprog on my bladder, don't I, Dave?'

Ceri gave them a massive smile – he'd got what he'd always wanted and she would never have been able to make him happy. She wouldn't have held hands on the way to the bog for all the sand in Dwynwen. As the boom of the baseline came from the direction of the nightclub, it was decision time. She was knackered – she could go for it, knowing another drink would give her a second wind, or she could head for home. The apartment still had gas, electric and wifi so she could get a takeaway, have a bath and go online to find an estate agent to put it on the market. But it was strange being there – the echoes of Ceri's old life were in the fabric of the place even though most of it was still in boxes marked 'shoes', 'bags' and 'walk-in wardrobe'.

There were hairdryers and straighteners, curlers and tit tape in her dressing room, a king size the area of Wales in her bedroom, a temporary metal rail sagging in the middle from all of her clothes, many still labelled and unworn plus a pile of post in the hall to look through. The only thing properly set up was a desk with her computer. She'd sat there with a cuppa earlier, bemused by her bookmarked sites – rival bloggers, *Vogue* and a load of dementia pages, which had made her fill up. And of course her own, and she'd clicked on it, just to see, tempted but fighting the urge to watch herself back ... of course, she had. It'd been like getting sucked into a rabbit hole, her first few videos where she was creating her own make-up, sort of natural and chatty because she'd had no audience. Then a few nervy ones as she became better known. The later vlogs were slick, properly lit and self-aware. On her last, recorded the day she'd walked out on her life, she'd looked weary, gaunt and lukewarm. She was far from tempted to go back there sober: it was a show home with no soul.

A man across the room caught her eye and he held up a glass of champagne to her. She didn't recognise him but she could tell it was that Mason because he was the only one here with a non-fake tan. Tall, sandy-haired and handsome, with a bit of a hooter but distinguished, he had a lovely warm smile. She mulled it over: it was Friday night and she wasn't dead yet; Mel was full of beans with Carlos; and Rhodri was about to go all Abba, destined to lay his love on a Swedish bird. Perhaps what Ceri needed was a man after midnight. So she nodded and they walked towards each other just as the DJ started playing 'Take A Chance On Me'.

Ceri counts her blessings

Morning, Mum, it's me. I'm in Crewe, parked up outside our house. Except it's not ours anymore. The new people moved in last week. Tash told me not to come, it'd only upset me. My heart was going like the clappers when I turned into Junction Road; I don't know what I expected to find ... maybe number thirty-three would have gone to pot, looking grotty and sad, without you there. I imagined the door would be peeling and the brass pair of threes would be dull and grimy – but I had the nicest surprise because it'd been given a lick of paint, the same cheerful red, and the numbers were gleaming from polish. The nets have gone, they've got posh shutters in the front room and the bedroom. It shows the owners are house-proud and that makes me happy because you'd approve. That's not to say it doesn't feel weird, knowing the layout of the place and the bumps in the walls, the radiator that always needs bleeding and the creak of the third stair. I thought about knocking and telling them I used to live there and could I have a look round but they'd think I was a nutter. *I'd* think I was a nutter because I'd be looking for ghosts and I'd probably cry at the new kitchen. But I didn't and that's a blessing, to accept I can let the place go.

Tash heard they were a couple with a baby, a hairdresser and an electrician. There's a car I don't recognise in front of me with one of those shades in the back passenger window plus a number on the rear advertising a salon. There's a van too, marked Spark of Genius, so Tash must be right. It's their first home so at least it'll mean something to them. Like it did to me. But I can see now it's okay to start a new chapter. It doesn't mean I've forgotten you or love you any less.

Tash taught me that, which is another blessing. Just because she didn't wear her grief like a face mask didn't mean she wasn't going through it too. Pushing forward was just her way of coping. And you're still with her. I saw it earlier when I popped in at her new house, a new build in a quiet cul-de-sac surrounded by fields, and she was buzzing with what you'd think of it. It's all mod cons, built-in appliances plumbed in, and plastered with carpets and an airing cupboard the size of a wardrobe! There's enough room in the garden for a slide and a swing, the girls have got their own bedrooms and Tash is made up because she's got an en suite with a walk-in shower and a fancy loo with a heated seat. Kev's got a garage and he's going to turn part of it over into a bar with a dart board.

She invited me to stop over, I was tempted because her guest room was very inviting and I didn't get much sleep last night after Jade's wedding. She looked beautiful, Mum, like Hollywood royalty, but she was still the same Jade. I met someone too, a nice bloke called Mason. Nothing happened, we just had a laugh on the dance floor and then swapped numbers. He was funny, works for a charity which runs engineering projects in developing countries, late thirties, no ties. We'll see what comes of it.

That's my third blessing, having been able to put Rhodri out of my mind for a bit. To see that some time soon I'll have got over him, because I fell hard and I've left it too late to tell him. He's leaving in a few days and the moment, if there ever had been one, has gone. But even though it'll kill me to say goodbye, I have to see him because whatever I wanted him to be he is my friend and a really good one. Maybe it'll all turn out to have been part of my grief – that I felt so many things when you'd died that they needed a focus and I transferred them on to him, like a phantom love. That would make sense because we're Venus and Mars: him, the middle class, uni-educated, rugby, recycling romantic, and me, the working-class lass with more cash and attitude than qualifications. Anyway, I've spent too long hooked on him. At least when he's gone, I can get on with my next blessing: a new business idea, arranging bespoke acts of kindness. No job too small, whether it's a bouquet to say thank you, to no job too large, working with companies to give something back to the community. I'll find out what makes that person or place tick and then project-manage it all. Like a consultancy of kindness. If I ever make a profit, I'll do good not just think about it; perhaps pay for benches in parks or turn blank school and hospital walls into murals or living walls of plants and flowers. The rest of the time, I'll throw myself into living – there's my sisters and my dad, the cabin, I might get a dog, go to Welsh classes even. What I'm trying to say, Mum, is I think I'm ready to count my blessings by myself from now on, that'll be my last one for today.

It's time for me to look ahead. I'll still check in on you now and again. But I won't forget you. I'll never stop thinking of you – after all, you'll only ever be a few feet away from me in the wind or on the beach or among the sardines and mermaids.

37

R hodri dried himself off with his new lightweight anti-bacterial bamboo fibre travel towel, vowing he was going to live it large in Sweden. His flight was a mere twenty-four hours away, he could almost taste the *semla* cream buns and hear the *skål* of cheers in a cool craft lager bar. There was so much to look forward to: urban gardening, bonding *fika* coffee breaks with co-workers, toothpaste-tubed mayonnaise and, in residential areas, never being more than three hundred metres from a recycling station. At weekends, he'd exercise his *Allmansrätten* right to roam by free camping and foraging for mushrooms and berries. And he'd ride buses powered by food waste fuel. It was going to be immense. He'd packed his rucksack – triple-checking his passport, documentation and krona were sealed away in the genius secret pocket – so today was his own. He was tingling from a couple of hours of surfing in the sun, which was freakily hot, as it was sometimes in September, and he was getting ready for a roast at Mum and Dad's. '*God morgan! God natt! Hej!*' he said, practising good morning, good night and hello while crouching to look for his pants.

'Are you talking to yourself? Oh my days, sorry! I didn't realise ...'

It was Ceri on the other side of his stripy windbreak, which he'd put up as a changing cubicle on the beach.

'Oh, hi!' he said, frantically cupping his privates.

'It's okay, I didn't see anything. Look, I've got my eyes covered.' She was very flustered and high-pitched for a woman of the world.

'Believe me, if you had seen something, you'd be overcome with ... hilarity,' he said, whipping his tight boxers on like lightning.

She laughed.

'So you did see!' he said. Oh, Christ, there was no denial. Still, he thought as he got up, she'd have seen goolies before. What was the point in worrying? His pubes only looked ginger in a certain light. Like this light. *Bollocks*. He'd have to filibuster his way through this. 'I'm not naked anymore, by the way.'

Ceri dropped her hands and blinked hard.

'It is a scorcher,' he said as she appeared to struggle to adjust to the brightness.

'What?'

'The sun, it's bright. Or is that sand in your eye?'

'Yes ... no,' she said, dazed, staring his chest up and down.

'Oh, I see! Have I got seaweed on me?' he asked, patting himself but feeling only a few drops of water he'd missed.

'No ... no. There's nothing wrong with you. On you.'

He ruffled his hair to get rid of any more potential drips and she looked away, looked back, then away again.

'Are you all right?' he said, as concern took him round the windbreak to her.

'Fine. Just a bit ... hot.' Of course. And probably she

wasn't as chatty because she was so tired from working at the pub and the cabin not to mention still coming to terms with her new family here. His quiet farewell drink at The Dragon last night wouldn't have helped: it had turned into a lock-in and he'd still felt delicate this morning. Perhaps the sight of his gingernut biscuits might have made her feel even queasier.

'Are you going to put some shorts on at some point?' It was as if a plane had gone overhead with an aerial banner spelling out his thoughts – she was trying to be her usual humorous self.

'In a sec! Still a bit damp.' He lifted his arms and had a good old stretch, feeling his skin tightening as the seawater evaporated, leaving behind salt crystals. He shut his eyes and groaned, lifting his face to the sun. When he opened his eyes again, she was peeking at him as if he was a madman.

'Just making the most of it before I hit twelve degrees Celcius tomorrow. The closest I'll get to this in Stockholm will be in a sauna. The travel guides say nudity is de rigueur.'

Ceri did a good impression of a fish as her mouth fell open.

'You haven't grown up with brothers or gone on rugby tours, have you?' Women, he'd never understand them. He laid out his wetsuit and towel to dry then sat down and dug his toes into the warm sand.

'How're you feeling?' he asked, as she joined him, taking off her trainers and socks and wiggling her feet.

'Okay,' she said, not sounding it. 'Good last surf?'

'Epic. As if Dwynwen knew it was my final chance for a while.'

'You all set?' She was inspecting the grains by her ankle so he couldn't see her expression.

'Yeah. Can't wait, actually.' He meant it. He'd never been readier to put an end to a chapter in his life.

'Great. You're doing the right thing, going.' But she didn't sound that enthusiastic.

'It'll be like heaven, living in a country where ninety per cent of aluminium cans are recycled and only one per cent of household waste ends up in rubbish dumps. I heard my recycling courses have been dropped – I know where I'm not wanted. But I'm leaving Dwynwen in safe hands – my dad, would you believe, is thinking about diversifying into eco-homes, Dai let it slip. So it's all good.'

'You'll have to let us know how it's going out there.' Her voice caught and he turned to examine her. Her back was rounded and her fingers were twiddling.

'You'll be sick of my daily bulletins after a week.'

'Don't think so,' she said, now drawing figure eights with her middle finger between them in the sand.

'No?'

She shook her head. He laid back on his elbows so she had some space and waited for her to elaborate.

'I'm going to miss you.' She glanced at him warily then looked out to sea.

'I'll miss you too!' he said brightly, because he didn't want her to be sad.

'No. I'm going to really miss you.' Her correction that he'd got her wrong and then the emphasis on the word 'really' made him fluster. What was she getting at? He was confused because it made it sound like she liked him, liked him. He refused to believe it. There'd been no vibes at all. This was her fear talking: he understood it. When people left, it made you consider your own circumstances. Maybe she was having doubts about staying now the holidaymakers had dropped off.

'It's just because I'm going ...' he tried.

Silence. Okaaaaay.

'And you've been through a lot.'

Nothing. Strange.

'I'm part of the furniture. But you won't notice I've gone.'

Still she kept quiet.

He couldn't read her at all; he only saw the wind throwing her hair around all over the place. *All over the place*, that was how he was feeling in this moment. What was going on in her head? And what was up with him? Because his heartbeat wasn't mellow like before. It was thudding fast and he felt his armpits prickle with heat. His stomach felt heavy but light as did his head and he became aware of the waves, amplified, crashing, closer. A pang of anger and frustration came to him because the easy air they shared had changed direction. He needed more oxygen so he sat up, which made him dizzy. His vision flickered with a brief surrealism: the horizon was shaking and the sea was a sharp green. Then it returned to normal and he saw her right leg jigging. She was thinking things and he was uneasy, unsure if he wanted to know what those things were. Because he had squared the circle and he'd taken so long to get there. It came out in a burst.

'Is it because of Logan? Grassing you up?' Even though it wasn't her fault, he guessed it would've left her feeling foolish.

'No.' She said it as if she was a bit cross, as if he should be a mind-reader.

This was ridiculous! Was she hinting again there was something else going on? He felt stupid, as if he'd failed somehow.

'The last few days, then. You're just feeling vulnerable.' His irritation gave way to compassion and he went to put his arm around her. But she swung round, her eyes glowering.

'Don't you tell me how I'm feeling!'

She was blowing hard, passionate with conviction.

'Well, why don't you tell me?' he said, pleading. 'I mean, it can't be any worse than being obsessed with Lego, can it?'

His attempt at lightening the mood provoked an exasperated groan through her gritted teeth.

'It's pointless. You won't understand,' she said, still heated.

'Oh, cheers! Thanks for the vote of confidence.' He lay back down, cursing himself for even thinking she had something meaningful to add to this conversation. Frankly, he thought, it'd be a relief when he got to Sweden – there'd be none of this 'talking in code' crap, just straightforward translation problems. He heard her sigh but refused to bite. She could keep dangling her fishing rod for all he cared.

'Look, Rhodri,' she started, only to make another noise of frustration. 'I think ... what I'm trying to say is ... I want to be a shingleback skink.'

Dear God, what was she on about now? 'You want to eat slugs?'

She slapped her thighs and cried, 'No!'

He'd had enough now. He sat back up and she turned to him and their eyes met.

'What, then?' he said, baffled. This was so stupid. They were good at communicating. It had never been easier with anyone else ever. Or so he thought.

'Remember when we talked at the demo and I said I thought it was about thunder and being all-consumed but you said it was more like being a swan or a wolf or a skink?' She was looking at him with such intensity he felt under pressure to understand.

'Yeees,' he said, inching towards a feeling that she was talking about love but desperately not wanting to go too close because he would wipe-out when he'd spent so long getting to standing.

'Finding happiness in the ordinary. I didn't get that then. But ordinary is beautiful, I see that now ... and ...' She was on the cusp and his heart was banging and he had to look away.

'... I didn't want to say this ... not with you going because you're going to have an amazing time but I have to say it ...'

He didn't want to hear it because he was losing his strength.

'Rhodri, I fell in love with Dwynwen because of you. Dwynwen is you, Rhodri.' She was searching his face for recognition, *had he got it*? Did he know what she meant?

His mind was scrambling, though – was she saying she loved him? Because that's what it sounded like. But no, no, it couldn't be. She didn't mean it. She was vulnerable. But she was wearing a face he'd never seen before, as if she'd been taken over by something powerful. He was trying not to believe it but there was an electricity between them and how easy it would be to touch her soft neck and to put his lips on hers. She was moving towards him and while they had always had a tactile relationship he realised now, when this was happening, they hadn't even brushed fingertips. He couldn't do this, not now. Even though every part of him wanted to lie with her and never let go. How he wanted to tell her he'd been fascinated by her from the minute they'd met, how he'd fallen head over cycling shoes in love with her. But it wasn't equal. It was too risky. Too quick. Not for him but for her. He'd dive in from the top board and she would be paddling: he'd plunge in deep, scare her off. He had to get out of here.

'I'm running behind,' he said when the truth was he was galloping mentally into a partnership and a forever. He raised a hand to his hair to form a physical barrier to stop this. It was killing him, though, seeing Ceri nodding, biting her top lip, pulling her hair up into one of those pony things so the tail bit curled like a seahorse on her bare back. She was so beautiful and lovely. He should explain but he would falter and take her in his arms and he would have to go away tomorrow. Or maybe he wouldn't go at all. It was too dangerous. So he stood up and dusted himself off, his feet staggering because he was so off-balance. His shorts ... where were they? There, and his towel and wettie, his board under his arm. The windbreak he didn't need, he'd only drop the poles and then he'd be done for because hesitation would be fatal. He had to leave right now. And not look back. He set off hard, pushing himself away from her, his soles scorched by the sand but on he went, getting closer to the lane.

'Rhodri!' she yelled up the beach. He ignored her and

wished he could cover his ears. Again she called. And again. He couldn't bear it – he shouldn't have but he turned to see her waving her arms like a banshee. He took a moment to check he was doing the right thing. Or that he wasn't doing the wrong thing. Fuck, he didn't know. The timing of this made him spin out and he wanted to scream, '*Why now?* When I'm just in my pants?'

'Dolphins!' she shouted, now jumping up and down, pointing out to sea. No. It couldn't be … they hadn't been here for years. He ran his eyes across the sea, seeing only crests of waves and flashes of birds, and then – *yes!* A fin and another! Two, three more! Their bodies like half-submerged wheels, arcing a crescent over and over, shining in the sunshine. He couldn't move, he was so transfixed. They'd come back. It was a miracle. The Dwynwen dolphins had come home. It was a sign … And then his heart began to ask to stay, begging him to run to her. But his head was firm with a *no*, hissing the moment had passed: he had to dance to his own tune, not Ceri's. He fought for his breath, his mind battling two options, because it was now or never. His decision was the hardest of his life. And he took the first step into his future.

Four and a bit months later

Epilogue

St Dwynwen's Day Eve

Ceri had only picked them up ten minutes ago but already she felt a right gooseberry.

Mel and Carlos were so inseparable they'd insisted on going in the back of the Fiesta together – their continuous stream of giggles and titters ever since was making Ceri feel like she was chauffeuring the Chuckle Brothers.

The three of them were on their way to Llanddwyn Island, a half-hour drive from Carlos's parents' house, where Mel had stayed three days for the official 'meeting mum and dad' visit. And judging by the long goodbye, she'd been a hit. Ceri had offered to bring the lovebirds home because she was on Anglesey to pay her respects to St Dwynwen for turning her life around. It wasn't going to be a drawn-out thing: she'd driven up yesterday afternoon, stayed in a pub and would be home again within twenty-four hours. It had to be a quick turnaround because tomorrow, Friday, was St Dwynwen's Day – and Mel's thirty-first. The village was fully booked for the Weekend of Love extravaganza, a brainwave she'd had in the autumn to make the most of the Welsh version of Valentine's.

It would kick off with a lovers' breakfast of heart-shaped poached eggs and fizz at Caban Cwtch before Ceri unveiled an exhibition of lovespoons which Seren had just finished ahead of jetting off to New York with Owen for Henry's international chess competition. Later on, the local choir and orchestra were putting on a concert of love songs at the rugby club – with a surprise rendition of 'Happy Birthday' for Mel. Friday night's headline act was dress-up-as-a-duet karaoke at The Dragon – Gwen and Gwil were still squabbling over whether to go as Sonny and Cher, which was his choice, or hers, John Travolta and Olivia Newton-John. On Saturday, Barri was leading 'In the Footsteps of Saint Dwynwen' walking tours, English Dick was to stage an afternoon of romantic poetry at the caravan park and then it was back to the rugby club for the gala ball. Sunday would start with a 10 a.m. hangover-busting sea swim followed by bacon butties on the beach. Then the pub was hosting a three-course lunch of the finest regional produce and the finale was Gwil's afternoon quiz on the world's greatest couples. Right on cue, there was yet more whispering from behind.

'You two!' Ceri snorted, eyeballing them in the rear-view mirror. 'Are you going to come up for air at some point?'

It was a typically sisterly thing to say and Ceri had delivered it with relish. This sort of teasing came so naturally to the two of them it was as if they'd grown up side by side.

'We're just excited, we are!' Mel grinned, playing with her St Dwynwen-inspired plaits.

Aw, Ceri thought, bless her! She was dead happy for

Mel – gorgeous Carlos was a regular visitor to the village now. They were perfect for each other: loved up and laughing in their own crazy world of art and colour. They even had their own way of communicating: she would speak to him in Welsh and he'd answer in Portuguese, which she was learning. Carlos being five years younger than Mel seemed to work, too. She'd been stuck in her early twenties for so long and meeting him had matured her, but not too much – she'd always be younger than her years. But it was Mel's transformation that was even more amazing: she was out-adventuring Bear Grylls, spending her days off in Cardiff with Carlos, working as a consultant for Dulux paints, headhunted after she took part in a university study about tetrachromacy, and preparing for a trip to Rio for next month's Carnival. They were going to stay with his relatives and then tour Brazil for four weeks when the cabin was quiet.

Ceri would use the time to keep building her new business. Called Acts of Kindness, it was a bespoke service for those who wanted to give anything from practical help to treats and surprises for deserving people or places. And it was doing very well for a young start-up, particularly as it had had lots of coverage in the media. Ceri had learned that Jade had kept the debacle over her surname out of the papers in the summer by promising interviews, which came to fruition in the autumn. People were fascinated about why she had ditched fame for a village in Wales and it led to queries from all over the UK.

The business was a family venture: Ceri sourced the stuff and Dad, who was no longer Emlyn they were so close, drove the van, decorated with a logo of hands and hearts, created by Mel. Income mainly came from the corporate world: companies turned to her when they wanted to show their caring, sharing face by providing communities with sponsored rubbish bins, climbing frames and skate parks. Time-poor professionals who needed someone to deliver with the maximum patience and minimum brief used her for highly tailored showy gifts for husbands, wives and clients they wanted to woo. She'd also teamed up with a chain of coffee shops with a gift card that came with a free latte for the next customer.

With small acts of kindness she barely covered her costs – but they were the ones that touched her most of all: the majority asking to remain anonymous so nobody felt they owed them. A cleaner to go to a friend who'd just had a baby and a dog walker for a poorly bed-bound dad. Hot meals delivered to a broken-armed granny and slippers for worn-out nurses. Waterproofs for lollipop ladies and tables for two for dinner ladies. A surprise cake for no special reason and a comedian for the old people's home. *Help yourself* umbrellas in a newsagent, children's toys for refuges, haircuts for the homeless, a weekly shop for a food bank, chews and biscuits for an animal shelter … the requests were wide-ranging, inventive and never-ending. And the feedback she received was priceless: customers felt good about giving and those on the receiving end would pass it forward, perhaps by buying someone else's bus fare or picking up litter in the street.

It was the best feel-good job on earth and it kept her going when she felt low, which was usually Rhodri-related. For he was the missing piece in her heart. She felt it every day, as if a limb was gone, hobbling when she thought she saw him on the sand or in the woods. His home was rented out to a quiet guy who'd taken over his job, securing recycling bins for Dwynwen which made Ceri choke with emotion sometimes. When she'd pass by Murmur Y Coed she'd have irrational butterflies that *maybe, just maybe* he'd come back and he'd leap out to surprise her. But hadn't he made it clear he didn't feel the same?

Work had saved her when he'd walked away. It kept her going, smothering the pain with its daily demands. Her routine was basic – get up, work, eat, sleep. But she loved it. She still loved him too. Ceri called it her what-had-she-been-thinking confession the day before he went. If someone had said the same to her after finding a father and a sister, having been fooled by a conman ex-mate and chucking a massive career, she'd have run a mile too. They had spoken about it once – she'd said she was sorry for putting him on the spot but he'd just *ummed* and *aahed*, embarrassed. As for meeting someone else, he hadn't ever brought it up. Ceri wasn't interested in any other man – she didn't have the time. She clung on to the hope he'd come back but she was convinced it was more of a case of *if* than when.

His enthusiastic emails certainly suggested it. Over the weeks, he'd described early morning mist on the Baltic Sea while he cycled to work through modern and medieval streets; and sharing coffee and cinnamon rolls with his peers, as he soaked up the zero waste ethos. The nation's mantra of *lagom*, or just enough, was reflected in the calm and tolerant people he'd met through his Swedish classes and choir. Outdoors was everything to him: he told how parents left their babies to sleep in their prams outside cafés in the open air and of lakes and hikes, snow and ice. A few curiosities made his brain ache – ketchup on pasta, paying double the rate for bread, state-run off-licences and having to book a slot in the apartment laundry room.

But he was bowled over by the countryside and the *don't destroy, don't disturb* approach to the environment. Ceri had never had a desire to go to Sweden but all she felt was a burning yearning to be where he was and to be doing what he did – *my God*, she'd even replaced the bleach with eco cleaner. There was, however, no invite for her to visit – she couldn't ask, he'd knocked her back once. Mel was devastated it had never happened between them because she thought Rhodri was secretly in love with her – but it was wishful thinking, he'd never said it and he'd gone, hadn't he? His beaming Facebook photos of fairy-lit ice rinks, ice hotels and the Arctic Circle weren't the images of a broken man, either. Thankfully, he hadn't posted anything to do with any women – that hadn't stopped her imagining him as part of a perfect Instagram couple, with some lean blonde Swede.

Living alone in the Green House was the best of worlds: when Mel told her he'd been offered a rolling extension to his post, Ceri had been able to enthuse over it before going home to cry over Thomas, a rescue scrap of fluff christened with her father's name because she wanted to stay a Price like her mum had been. Rhodri had come home for Christmas but Ceri had gone to Tash's, who wanted to be in the new house – understandably, since it was their first one there, Ceri had thought. But it turned out to be for the entirely joyful reason that Tash needed access to her en suite for morning sickness.

Ceri was glad to have had the excuse not to see him – because if she felt his pull when she saw his face in a photograph then how would she feel if he was there giving her a hug hello? The attraction she felt to him, the love he inspired in her hadn't gone – it frightened her sometimes how deep it ran, taking her breath away if she heard someone say his name. That's why she'd told Mason the charity guy that she wasn't in the right place for their friendship. Even when her feelings for Rhodri were tucked away, they still managed to colour her experiences: like now, as she paid the toll and drove through a forested nature reserve, thinking how much he'd like it here.

'This is it then,' Ceri said, forcing her emotion back and remembering she had so many blessings to count, as she pulled into the car park, sending red squirrels scarpering. It was a cold crisp morning and they were the first here.

'Oh ... It's just us,' Mel observed.

'Better than fighting the crowds, surely?' It got very busy here this time of year, according to Ceri's guide-book.

'Yeah, I suppose ... I sort of imagined it ... differently, I did,' Mel said, her breath steaming as she slammed the door.

'How?' Ceri said.

'Dunno. Sort of more romantic.' She sounded dis-appointed.

'We'll do the well, Mel,' Carlos said, trying to cheer her, and it worked as she laughed at his unintended rhyme.

He was talking about the test lovers could take at Dwynwen's Well: if fish came to the surface, it was proof a relationship would last. Ceri remembered Rhodri tell-ing her about it in the car all those months ago. There he was again, on her shoulder, and she had to stick on her sunglasses to stop her eyes from watering in public. They set off on the sandy footpath, their shadows long as the sun was still low, whooping as they came across the dunes of the beach. But when they emerged onto the stunning sweep of gold they were silenced by the expanse of the clear and sparkling Menai Strait, Snowdonia's mountains on the horizon to the right and the hump of Llanddwyn to the left.

There was no wind, thank goodness, but they still had to march to keep warm, pointing out coves and seabirds as they went. Low tide meant the island was a causeway resembling a finger of land and they went in single file on a winding dirt pathway trodden into the rocks, all the while looking around to take in the majesty of the surroundings, where darting bunnies played on the scrub beneath a sky so vast and blue it could've been a reflection of the calm sea. Ceri hadn't expected to sense any spirituality, and it may have been the freezing weather, but she was tingling, touched by a presence of something – perhaps the eternity of hope and love and kindness?

Maybe it was because she identified with Dwynwen, who'd had her heart broken and then devoted her life to love without any more participation. For here was where pilgrims had trekked over the centuries, where lovers had come to seek the saint's blessing. At the highest spot, they saw a large stone Celtic cross, which had a plaque recording her death on 25 January in the year 465. They all scratched their heads in wonderment at the ancient land beneath their feet.

Beyond was an old white lighthouse on the tip of the peninsula and to one side, what Ceri had come to see:

the weathered ruins of the church of St Dwynwen. Her heart quickened, she took off her shades and she gave her guidebook to Mel and left them, clambering down the rocky outcrop so she could pay her respects to the Welsh patron of love. It was incomprehensible this tiny spot had been so important so long ago. Yet the stone was still standing, crumbling but defiant: the rectangle of remains was a lesson to keep the faith.

'Thank you,' she whispered, reaching out to touch the only complete section of wall left standing, its carved window framing a magnificent view of the sea. Without you, she thought, welling up, I'd have been forever lost. But you gave me a chance to find myself, my father and my family.

Then in her mind, as ever, she could hear Rhodri's voice, reading aloud the words from her guidebook. 'Llanddwyn had been so rich in Tudor times that a church was built in the sixteenth century on the site of the original convent ...' It was as if he was here beside her and she covered her face to imagine he really was. Warm arms came from behind and held her, rocking her from side to side and she wished for it to be true as she opened her eyes – and ... *no frigging way* ... she felt his cheek on hers. What the flaming hell? What was going on? He was here, her body screamed. But it couldn't be – he was in Sweden. More than one thousand and three miles away. Except, inexplicably, he wasn't. *No, no*, refusing to believe it, she ran through her senses, feeling his soft touch, smelling his natural scent, then actually seeing his hands round her chest. *He was physically here!* And he was hugging her and she was spinning around, grabbing onto his arms and his waist because she feared he'd disappear if she let go. He was real – he was flesh and bones and she was gasping and laughing and so was he, his wonderful smile as wide as his shoulders.

'What the flip are you doing here?' she said, taking him in from the top, starting with his Nordic knitted blue bobble hat, tufts of brown hair, melted chocolate eyes, bold nose and lovely big lips. And what was that on his face? Only a bushy ginger beard! 'I thought I was going mad! Rhodri! What … how come … Jesus!'

He unzipped his sub-zero puffer jacket and wiped his brow as if he was in the tropics.

'Don't worry,' he said, 'I'm not going to get down to my pants like last time. I've come home. I can't stay away. The Six Nations starts next week. I've so much to bring to recycling here. And while the webcam was brilliant, it's no substitute for the real thing.'

'What?' She was flummoxed by his rambling – she needed clarity because mingled with her joy was the wariness of self-preservation. If she assumed what she was starting to, if a bloke turned up out of nowhere without warning and had his arms round you, and it didn't turn out to be for love … it made her shudder with fear.

'Hey,' he said, seeing her expression darkening, 'I'm here because I had to know … do you still feel the same?'

He was searching her eyes for an answer but she was reeling and afraid.

'Your beard,' she said, holding her own hands to her face like an idiot. But it was the shock.

'It's like a woolly hat but for my face. A face hat.' Now he was gulping.

Oh, this was classic. This reminded her of the fumbling bumbling mess on the beach when she'd told him she loved him. Stick to the facts, she thought, avoid the feelings. Give yourself some time to get your head together.

'How did you get here?' she asked, her heartbeat thumping.

'I flew in this morning to Manchester. I got a cab.'

'A cab? All the way here? What about you carbon footprint?' This was very unlike him, she thought, wondering what would have prompted such a betrayal of his values.

'I don't care about that! I'll plant some trees or something,' he said casually as if he wasn't even bothered. It was so out of character. 'Look, listen, I was supposed to be in the car park when you got there. But we hit traffic.' Okay, she could process that, he had a rucksack by his feet. Next question.

'How did you know I would be here?'

'Mel. She told me. As an act of kindness. To surprise you.' That explained her disappointment they were the only ones in the car park! No wonder Mel was near-wetting herself on the way and she'd wanted to leave the front seat empty. Ceri looked for her and there she was . . . apparently in the middle of a row with Carlos. *Oh no, it was all going weird.*

'I don't get this,' she said, crossing her arms. Rhodri nodded and put out one hand for her then the other but still she couldn't surrender.

He scruffed up his hair and took a breath and began to explain. 'I'm here, Ceri, because that day when you told me you loved me, I was too scared to admit I felt the same. That I'd fallen for you from the day I met you . . . actually, no it wasn't that day, it was the day you came to my recycling course and you took the piss out of me, that was when I fell for you.'

Her lips twitched as she dared to hope he wouldn't stop there.

'I didn't doubt you meant it but I needed to see if it was proper and true because I'd have jumped in with both size twelves without a life jacket in my pyjamas, like the swimming life-saving badge, if you remember it?'

Ceri began to believe him now and her eyes became wet with love – and the teensiest bit of hilarity at the way he kept going off the subject.

'What if it had been a flash in the pan for you and I'd missed out on Sweden?'

Tears were rolling now and she was in danger of blowing nose bubbles. He moved closer to her and they held hands. But suddenly his eyes had shifted to the right just when the moment was coming. *Oh God, no, please don't say I've read this wrong.* That he was about to say he'd tried to feel it still but it was no good.

'I'm so sorry, Ceri ...'

She dropped her chin – hope hadn't killed her, it'd strung her up by the short and curlies.

'... there's a crisp wrapper by there and I can't just leave it.'

She looked up and, of course, he'd only wanted to pick up some rubbish! Relief swept through her and she surged with joy that this was him to a tee.

'Do you mind? We could go together, walk sideways like crabs if you like, still holding hands?'

'No,' she said, pinching herself so she didn't hoot. 'It's fine, you go.'

He was back with her in seconds and resumed his position.

'Where was I? Oh, yes, I'd wondered if time and absence

would make it fizzle out for you. But then when I didn't see you at Christmas it got even more intense for me. Mel said I should tell you how I feel. And she didn't even say if you'd moved on or not. I told her I didn't want to know because it wasn't fair on her to have to reveal sisterly things … so I'm here and I want to know if you feel the same … because … Ceri,' he said, heaving, '*caru ti.*'

Her heart exploded in her breast. 'I love you too, Rhodri, from your sticky-out ears to your cycling helmet, from your—'

'I'm sorry,' he said, interrupting, 'not to be rude, and I'm aware this is rich coming from a windbag like myself, but I can't wait any longer.'

And then he kissed her and she kissed him back and they kissed and kissed at first tenderly and then with passion until they were breathless and she was dizzy and her face was smarting from his beard. Their eyes were heavy with lust and love and amazement that this was really happening. As if St Dwynwen had planned it all along.

'Do you want to see the well?' Rhodri finally asked.

'I dunno. I suppose we should get going really …' The sun was higher and they had to think about heading back if she didn't want to drive in the dark.

'Good choice. Because that's why Mel was shouting at Carlos. She said he'd swished the water with his hand to make it look as if the fish had come up to prove he was faithful.'

'Hang on,' Ceri said, squinting at them now as they waited, holding hands, 'it looks like they've made up.' She grinned and beckoned to them, reaching for Rhodri's hand herself in case Mel was in any doubt her plan had backfired. Mel cheered her delight.

'Come on!' Ceri said to them all, elated and jumping, finally letting herself trust again. 'Let's go. It's a long journey and we've got a big weekend lined up.'

Rhodri kissed her nose and put his arm around her shoulder. 'Take me home, Ceri,' he said, his eyes shining with happiness. 'Take me home to the Village of Love.'

That village on the edge of Wales where, almost a year ago, it'd felt like the end of the world.

But as Ceri nestled into Rhodri on their way across the beach, she didn't see Dwynwen as the final stop – instead, it was the start of a new beginning.

Acknowledgements

Huge thanks – and a Welsh *diolch yn fawr* – go to everyone involved in this book.

First to the dream team, made up of my agent Lizzy Kremer and Clare Hey, publishing director at Orion. Lizzy, for her peerless vision and direction – to say I worship her is playing it down a bit. And Clare, whose gorgeous heart and sharp mind transformed my manuscript.

The wonderful Clare Bowron, who was an early reader and, once again, got it ship-shape with her incredible insight. And David Higham's Harriet Moore and Olivia Barber for the cheerleading.

At Orion, Katie Seaman, for her fantastic input, and Sally Partington, who gives the best copy edit on earth – to you both, thank you for the make-over. The wonderful Lauren Woosey and Jennifer Breslin, too. Plus Robyn Neild, whose beautiful artwork not just matched my imagination but exceeded it. And I love having my name as a smile!

I must also thank Angharad Rhys, who checked my Welsh – any mistakes are mine, all mine.

Thumbs up to the author community, particularly Milly Johnson and Lucy Diamond, for the encouragement and laughs. Same goes for the book bloggers, reviewers, Facebookers, Tweeters and Instagrammers who keep me company during the long, lonely writing hours.

Big love to my friends whose kindness made this possible – you gave me your ears and shoulders and provided childcare and food parcels, which kept me going. I couldn't have done it without you.

To the king and queen of kindness, Mum and Dad, who taught me the importance of giving a warm welcome and counting my blessings. My mother-in-law Bev and father-in-law Peter, who started this all off decades ago with their holidays in West Wales.

To Paddy, you make my heart burst with happiness.

Finally to Jamie, not just my rock but my sheep rock, who'd do anything to be bored. In the meantime, you better go to the pub to check your emails.